FRENZIED FATE

A DRAGON RIDER FANTASY ROMANCE

TALES OF THE VANIR
BOOK II

Cover Design by 100 Covers
Formatted with Atticus

Thanks to the beta readers and editors who helped make this a better book:
Cindy Ray Hale and Keele Publishing
Kaitlin Slowik
Keeya Marquez

And perpetual thanks to my alpha reader, Cynthia Davis

DEDICATION

To everyone torn between two loves ...
and willing to lay down their life to save them both.
This one's for you.
Tindera's song is *I Am Only One* by We Are the Fallen

Content Warning

This book is intended for adults only, and contains subject matter that may be difficult or disturbing for some readers.

Sensitive material includes, but is not limited to: frequent profanity, violence, graphic torture and killing of people and dragons (but not the cat; nobody messes with Thor), sexual assault (but not between the main characters), emotional abuse, socio-economic power imbalances, frequent mentions of blood, and genocide (of elves).
Frenzied Fate also contains explicit, open-door sexual content.
Reader discretion is advised.

CONTENTS

GLOSSARY

Ætt: Clan/Fhord's people

Dragon's-Length: Unit of measure; sixty feet

Draikana: Female of a mated dragon pair

Drake: Male of a mated dragon pair

Draugr: Undead

Drott: Chief/leader

Dróttning: Queen

Kastali: Castle

Konungr: King

Male's-Height: Unit of measure; six feet

Meistara: Lady

Meistari: Lord

Seiðr: Ability to predict the future

Thunder: Group of dragons

Valkyrie: Shield maiden/female warrior

Vekter: Guards/police

Viku: Unit of measure; one mile

Map

TALES OF THE VANIR
NJORDHEIM
BARRIER
TRAINING GROUNDS
NORTHERN NEST
VANATIA
SOUTHERN NEST
REVALLE
TRAINING GROUNDS

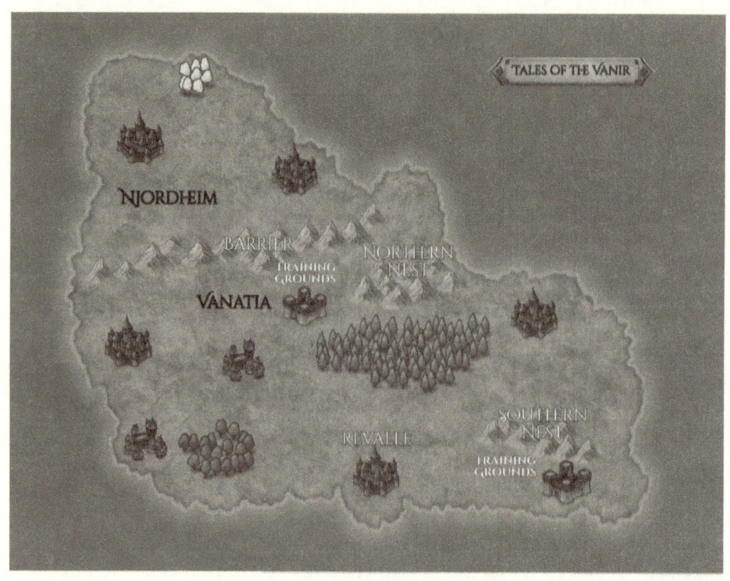

Recap

What Happened in the Last Book?

I N *Sacred Struggle*, the elf Sifa has been trapped for ten years in Vanatia, a land in which all elves are killed or imprisoned. She's working as a spy and not afraid to get her hands bloody.

Sifa uses her powerful magic—the ability to enter people's minds and create memories to manipulate them—as she tries to get access to the country's leaders, particularly the cruel queen, Dróttning Nerthus. The Dróttning controls Vanatia's dragons, and holds information Sifa needs to return home. Sifa's forged a happy life with Toffer, the troll who landed in Vanatia's northern dragon Nest at the same time as Sifa, and was tortured along with her until she found a way to break them free.

But then Bevin, the town's overseer, sends Sifa with a group of bedmates to a forbidden area: the southern dragon Nest. There, Sifa's introduced to the rebellion fighting against the

Dróttning, resolved to free the dragons from her grip. Sifa also meets Fhord, a dragon-rider with a savage living inside him and mind magic similar to Sifa's, who arouses desire and repulsion in her. He warns her to stay away from him and the Nest. Sifa's group is almost caught but they escape and return home, where Sifa hopes to never see Fhord again.

Bevin has other plans. He orders Sifa to help Fhord on a mission to free one of Bevin's spies, Thyra, from the northern Nest. Along the way, Sifa and Fhord fight their growing desire for each other but it's a losing battle. They're fated mates and can't ignore fate's draw. They succeed in their mission—freeing Thyra—but everything changes on the way home. Sifa rescues Astarot, a dragon being tortured by the Dróttning because he refuses to accept the rider selected for him. We learn that Fhord's dragon Tindera and Astarot are a mated pair; Sifa and Astarot also bond.

They find a place for Astarot to rest and heal, and Fhord leaves to take Thyra to safety. When Fhord returns, he accidentally leads the Dróttning's soldiers back with him. Sifa and Astarot are captured; Sifa is taken to the northern Nest but Astarot's injured and he can't be moved until he heals.

Fhord returns to the northern Nest, where it's revealed that he has an unusually close connection to the Dróttning, and is desperate to hide his growing feelings for Sifa. The Dróttning is determined to find Sifa—the only elf to ever escape her prison—and would try to control Fhord by torturing Tindera. The Dróttning tells Fhord she has no immediate plans to torture Sifa and Fhord decides to risk leaving the northern Nest, to go free Astarot and seek Toffer's help. He hopes the troll will be able to find unknown caverns in the Nest they can use to rescue Sifa.

But the Dróttning had lied to Fhord; she tortures Sifa while Fhord's gone and then offers Sifa to Fhord upon his return. He can't take her from the Nest, the Dróttning explains, but he can play with her while she's there. With Toffer's help, Fhord is able to free Sifa and an elf Sifa befriended in prison, Joralf. Fhord is almost caught by the Dróttning, who reveals her suspicions, now confirmed, about Fhord and Sifa.

Nevertheless, they all escape except for Tindera, who's still trapped in the Nest. Fhord plans to take Sifa and Astarot to safety and return for his dragon. He reveals his love for and commitment to Sifa. While Sifa's not ready to embrace Fhord in the same way, she can't deny her feelings for him. She leaves Toffer and the others behind, joining Fhord to find a hiding place while Astarot finishes his recovery.

CHAPTER ONE

SIFA

WE, FHORD

IS TONGUE WAKES ME.

Not the one that *consumed* me in the dead of night, dragging sensations from my body I didn't know I could experience with caresses that left me hovering on the precipice between pain and pleasure, restraint and release, anticipation and ecstasy. No, that tongue is a hint of pink barely visible between the full lips of the male snoring gently by my side. A strand of his dark, wavy hair falls across his forehead and I have to stop myself from reaching out and stroking it away, or tugging down the blanket to expose the tattoos covering his broad, firm chest.

Gods, he's beautiful. My cheeks grow hot just thinking of all the places *his* tongue explored and aroused as we pretended we're safe—pushing aside for a moment the constant threat of being found by this country's ruler, the cruel Dróttning Nerthus—before we fell into a deep sleep, the exhaustion of a long day of travel finally overtaking us.

This tongue touches me in a different way, tentative but certain, as if the dragon trailing it across my arm doesn't want to wake me but knows, deep in that place where our souls have bonded, that I'll welcome it when he does. His tongue greets me in the innocent way dragons do with their riders when they want the connection only a taste of skin can provide.

Hungry, Astarot says in the silence of my mind. As it always does, his single word relays a wealth of information. He desperately needs another meal and knows he can't risk leaving this cave without me checking first to make sure it's safe. But he slept well, his health continuing to improve.

My dragon told me before he collapsed last night that the trip to Revalle and back drained him, pushing him farther and faster than his injured body was ready to go. He should be able to fly again soon, but Fhord thinks it'll be another week or more before he can carry any weight. So we're riding Fhord's horse Sigurd and Astarot is walking with us. For now.

It didn't help that we drove both beasts hard yesterday, desperate to get as far away as we could from the dragons' Nest—the prison from which I'd escaped with Fhord's help—and the Dróttning. Fhord told me that when they're awake, he and the Dróttning can sense each other if they're a viku or so apart. That connection is tied to their conscious minds and disappears when they sleep, thank the gods. We couldn't risk stopping and giving her a chance to catch up, so we didn't. I have lots of questions for Fhord about his relationship with the Dróttning, but they'll have to wait. We need to find someplace safe first. If we can.

Twice in our race here, her warriors almost found us, forcing us to hide in caverns that barely held my enormous dragon. But the Dróttning never got close enough to follow the link between her and Fhord. We evaded the searchers and managed to reach a cave large and secluded enough to risk falling asleep. So far, it seems like the risk was worthwhile. We all needed the rest. I'll know for sure when I step outside to see if anyone waits for us.

I'm careful when I untangle from Fhord's arms and legs, hoping not to wake him yet. When he rolls to his other side and draws in a deep breath, exhaling in a loud snort, I hold back a laugh before reaching out to stroke Astarot's nose.

My dragon and I sit there for a moment, savoring the peace of the morning and the gods' gift of each other, my forehead resting lightly on his snout as my hands continue to drift over his silky feathers. I'm still astounded by the majesty of this dragon who has claimed me. His red and black feathers cover a body that reaches seventy feet or more and must weigh twenty thousand pounds, even without the weight he lost during the long months of his torture.

Hungry, Astarot reminds me as his stomach releases a grumble that really should have dragged Fhord from sleep. Gods, he must be exhausted. It finally caught up with him.

Nodding, I stand to get dressed and tug my boots on before leading Astarot toward the entrance, gesturing to him to wait while I tiptoe outside. It's nearly dawn and the morning is crisp and chill, with enough moonlight to cast a soft light over the trees around us. My breath huffs out in a whiff of smoke, hovering to remind me that we've traveled far to the north already. I don't know yet what Fhord has in mind—where he thinks we can hide from the Dróttning—but he promised we'll talk about it today. I plan to hold him to it.

Casting out my senses, which have been shockingly acute since I bonded with Astarot, I search for any movement or scent or sound that might reveal a hidden danger. The Dróttning's warriors are well-trained and certainly well-hidden, and too many can shield their minds from mine, but I have to try anyway. Maybe they're tired and sloppy in these early hours of the morning, after a long night of diligence. When I find nothing, I risk a step out of the cave, sending out a prayer to the gods that nobody waits to plunge an arrow into my chest.

After a minute or so, I take another step, then slowly start to explore the area, revealing myself more and more in the hope of exposing any threat before Astarot emerges. Finally, after another fifteen minutes of searching, I decide it's safe enough.

Come, I tell my dragon.

He doesn't need to be asked twice. More quietly than should be possible for a beast of his size, Astarot strolls from the cave, his head swinging from side to side as he checks my search with his heightened senses. Grunting his agreement that this area, at least, is safe, he follows his nose toward a lake we passed just before we reached the cave. We hadn't seen any animals last night, but the morning should bring something. Astarot seems convinced it will, his steps growing faster the closer we get.

When we're a few hundred feet from the field that lies between us and the water, we both pause, searching again for any danger that might be hiding nearby. The Dróttning knows dragons well enough to realize we'd have to find someplace like this to feed Astarot. And while this part of Vanatia is rich with herds to supply its many dragons, she has no shortage of acolytes to track those animals. But again, we find nothing, pressing forward with the hope that our pursuers aren't here. Perhaps the gods are protecting us, at last.

Astarot's excitement washes over me like a warm bath as we breach the trees, revealing a large group of sheep by the water. He pauses for a moment before his eyes land on breakfast—a huge male who's lived too long to outrun a hungry dragon. And then he's off, racing faster than I'd expected, his wings flaring out to lift him up and over the herd just enough to hunt. His aim is perfect, talons trapping his prize as his beak rips out the throat, giving the sheep a quick death. He swallows him whole, his need for food so great that his body will draw whatever nutrients it can even from the fur and bones.

Another? I ask, wondering just how hungry he is this morning.

I can almost feel the smirk in his answer. *Another.* This one, though, will take a little longer. He plans to enjoy the meal, pulling it apart as he savors the meat and picks the bones. It's been too long since he's been allowed to eat the way dragons prefer. It feels good to be able to give this to him.

I plop down, letting my thoughts wander as I watch him choose his next meal. He's the reason we're hiding from the

Dróttning. Fhord and I were sent to the North by my boss, Bevin—one of the most powerful people in the South—to free a spy who'd been captured and was being held in the northern Nest. We were done, taking her back home without anyone realizing we'd been involved, when I saw Astarot.

I didn't have a choice. He was being tortured, the Dróttning's cruel means of punishing dragons who refuse to heed her commands, so I killed his trainer and freed him. I doubt he'd have survived much longer. They tracked us and sent me to prison after Fhord convinced them I'd acted alone—his ploy to escape capture and eventually rescue me.

I wouldn't change a thing, though. Even if I have to run for the rest of my life and have nightmares every night about what they did to me there, I'll never regret saving Astarot. He's a piece of me that had been missing. I'm a bit more whole because of him.

Fhord's the other piece. I have a shitload of questions—the most important one being what his relationship is with the Dróttning. They know each other well. Fhord has too many secrets, and I'm not sure if I can trust him. But I can't deny that he's filled another hole in my soul. We've only known each other a few weeks, but he's part of me already. I'm dreading the loss I'll feel if his promises turn out to be empty.

I suck in a deep breath, watching Astarot swoop to land in front of me, a large ewe dropping to the ground. I can feel his joy as he settles down to feast.

Ewww, I tell him, turning away as his beak plunges into the belly. *It's too early for that.*

Yum, he responds, a laugh in his tone. I think he likes teasing me as much as Fhord does.

Even now, though, I can sense his need for Tindera. She's stuck in the northern Nest—the Dróttning refusing to let her go after an injury that should have healed weeks ago. She's Fhord's mount and Astarot's drakaina, his bonded dragon, which means we need to go get her. We won't be complete until she's free and traveling with us. I don't know how we'll do it, but we will.

Sighing, I let my eyes drift up to the lake in front of us, a dark jewel sitting in a sea of green. The sun has risen enough to cast a few rays on its surface, hints of sapphire revealing themselves in the ripples that flow and shimmy. It looks so much like Midgard, the world I left behind when I got sucked into this one a decade ago. I've been trying since then to find a way home for me and Toffer, the troll who got dragged here with me for reasons neither of us understands. It's why I was working for Bevin—he's connected to people who might have answers to my questions, help us find our way back home.

Now, I don't know how I could possibly leave this world, even if I could find a path. If I stay, Toffer and I will both pay a steep price. We're aging much faster here than we did in our worlds, more like humans than the elf and troll we are. I'd lived hundreds of years but only looked fifteen when I got here. Now I'm in my mid-twenties. Every day I've been here has aged me like a human in Midgard. Worse, since elves are hunted in Vanatia—all except the few who've been able to hide their identities sent to large prison-camps—I'll never be completely free.

But I'll be with Astarot. And Fhord, I hope. I'm starting to believe that's more important than getting home. I don't know how I could bring myself to abandon either of them. I'd leave most of my soul behind if I did.

Astarot turns to gaze at me, his eyes solemn as he senses my thoughts. *Mine,* he reminds me. He'd lose part of his soul, too, if I ever left him. Maybe I can find some way to fix the too-fast aging and get back the long life I'd expected to enjoy before I landed in Vanatia.

Those are questions for another day. Today, Fhord and I need to travel farther north, make sure we escape the soldiers determined to drag us back to the Nest. *Are you ready?* I ask as I glance at the pile of fur and bones he left behind, nearly stripped clean. *We should take the skin with us. Once it dries, it'll be nice and warm.*

He drops his chin once, reaching out to grab a chunk of fur and shake it loose of any bones still hidden in its midst. Laughing, I jump back from the flecks of blood and gore that spray in my direction. *Warn me next time, please.*

His eyes apologize, even as his mouth curves up in what can only be a smirk. *Perhaps,* he agrees, following as I lead us back to the cave.

Fhord's awake when we return, packing up our things while a pot of cereal cooks over the fire he started. His emerald eyes catch mine and then he smiles as they rove down to the body he worshiped last night, letting them linger on my breasts and hips before tracking back up.

"I'd hoped you'd be with me when I woke up. Now I wish I hadn't packed up so quickly."

"Tonight," I promise, strolling forward to wrap my arms around his waist and pull him close. "The sun's been up for a while. We should go."

"But there are so many things we could do if we stayed here," he whispers as his tongue reaches out and caresses the ridiculously sensitive spot he's discovered, where the tips of my ears will emerge if I let him continue.

Astarot's growl rumbles through the cave. *Draikana*, he casts at me. He hasn't been able to reach her and needs to know why.

Fhord turns to catch his eye and nods. He can't hear Astarot's word, but I'm sure he grasps the demand. For a moment, Fhord's eyes flash in what looks like guilt, or perhaps remorse, but it's gone almost before I see it. Reassurance fills his gaze, his jaw flexing as he straightens to speak to my dragon.

"I don't know," Fhord tells Astarot in a firm voice. "I can feel her. She's alive and unharmed. I haven't been able to speak with her, but I'm not surprised. She knew what I planned and that she needs to stay hidden. She's probably exploring the caves, biding her time."

Astarot holds Fhord's gaze for a long time, his thoughts silent. And I have no idea why. He seems to be weighing Fhord's words, measuring their truth. Finally, he puffs out a breath, a waft of flame emerging with it. *Soon*, he tells me.

"He needs to hear from her soon, Fhord." My hands take his cheeks, drawing his attention to me. "We can't leave her behind without knowing she's okay."

Fhord steps back, frustration taking over his expression. "Do you think I don't know that?" he demands, spinning to stalk over to the fire. Kneeling to stir the cereal, he takes a deep breath, and then another. "I'm worried too. She's my dragon, for the gods' sake. But for now, our focus needs to be on getting as far away from the Nest as possible. We need you and Astarot out of the Dróttning's reach. Tindera wants that, even if it means the Dróttning's ire is focused on her. She's strong. She can protect herself until I can go back to get her."

"We, Fhord. We'll go back to get her." Astarot harumphs his agreement, neck high as he glares down at us.

When Fhord turns to look at me, his eyes are tortured, brows pulled together so tightly, there's no space between them. But his voice is sharp, no uncertainty in his clipped words. "No, Sifa, not *we*. Me. You can't go back to the Nest, ever. You've escaped the Dróttning twice. She won't let it happen again. When—not if, but when—you're captured, she'll either kill you or send you to the elven camps that day. That hour. I can't let that happen again. I won't."

My spine stiffens of its own accord as my fingers clench into fists. I am not the female Fhord seems to want, willing to stay behind while he throws himself into the fire.

"And what about you?" I snarl, taking a step toward him. "What about the risks you'll be taking if you go back to the Nest alone?"

"Don't worry about me, rabbit. The Dróttning won't hurt me. She wouldn't dare."

Shaking my head, a chill rolling through me as memories of their rapport in her rooms fill my thoughts, I halve the distance between us. "Why, Fhord? What is it between you two? Why were you lounging in her space like you belonged there? Why did she give me to you, a meal on a platter?"

Fhord's eyes grow hard as he stands, his back straight and shoulders stiff. He barely breathes as we stare at each other for long seconds. He's unnaturally still, as if he's holding back some part of himself. Finally, he spits out his response. "There are things you don't understand. That you'll never understand."

Fuck. That. I will not be kept in the dark about something as important as this. "Then tell me, Fhord. If we're going to do this," I say as my arm gestures between Fhord and myself, "you need to be honest with me. Especially about things like the Dróttning, and what you mean to her."

My heart beats a dozen times while Fhord watches me, his chest rising and falling in breaths that slowly grow steadier. Finally, his body relaxes as the steel leaves his eyes. "I know," he says. "Not now, though. Let's get somewhere safe first. I just need to know you're not going to do something reckless, put your life at risk again. I need you to let me go back for Tindera, alone."

"You don't get to decide that," I murmur, walking toward him to rest a hand on his chest. "I decide what risks I'll take." I spin to point at Astarot. "Especially when we're talking about my dragon's drakaina. Astarot and I will be joining you. He'll be fully healed in a day or two, and we'll go together."

"Fuck, you are stubborn," he barks with a laugh full of exasperation. Still, he can't hold back the smile that seems determined to emerge. Taking the hand still resting on his chest, he raises it to kiss the palm. "We don't have to decide now. Today, we're traveling farther north. I think we all agree on that, right?"

Astarot stares at him for a few seconds before snorting out his assent. Fhord's responding nod is full of respect.

"There's a place we could hide in the south but I don't think we would make it. It's too far for Astarot to fly, and the Dróttning will expect us to return to Revalle. Her searches will be focused there. I think we'll have a better chance if we go through the northern barrier, convince the monarch, Harald, to let us stay a week or two."

Fhord pauses, shadows filling his eyes. His jaw's tight, a twitching muscle the only movement. "I don't trust Harald and he doesn't trust me," he says at last. "There's bad blood between us. But he hates the Dróttning more than me and would celebrate her defeat. I think I can convince him to help us. It'll give Astarot a chance to rest, make sure he's fully healed and as strong as he can be before we even consider going back to the Nest. Then we'll decide together what we need to do to free Tindera." His voice is soft, pleading.

"Do you think he'll let us stay? I've always heard it's dangerous to enter Harald's lands."

"It's risky. He's unpredictable but practical. I know, though, that we won't be able to find a safe place to hide in the Dróttning's lands while Astarot's healing. He'll need another week, maybe more, before he'll be able to fly far enough with two riders to reach the only true refuge I know. I think we need to try to hide in Harald's lands." He's silent for another few seconds, watching me. "And if we convinced him to fight with us, it could change everything. Harald's been biding his time to attack. My break from the Dróttning might be what he needs to join our battle."

"And when it's time, we'll go back to the Nest together?"

Fhord narrows his eyes and I can tell he hasn't given in. He just wants to delay this conversation, hoping we'll change our minds. "We'll decide once we get someplace safe."

"We can talk more later, but my answer will be the same. I'm not some fragile flower you can stick in a vase and preen over. If we're going to be together, I'll be by your side, even when it's dangerous. You need to learn to trust me. We need to learn to trust each other."

"I trust you, rabbit," he breathes, his hand reaching up to stroke a thumb across my cheek. "It's her I don't trust. And I don't want her to be able to hurt you ever again."

"I get it, Fhord. I don't want you to take risks either. But I won't sit on a shelf. This won't work if that's where you try to put me."

I can see the struggle in Fhord's eyes, their green depths shifting from a piercing jade to a soft garnet. But even when he nods, leaning in to brush my lips with his, I know I haven't won. He's giving in for now, but I can tell already this is a fight our fledgling relationship may not survive.

SIFA

NOWHERE TO HIDE

I FORGAVE HIM QUICKLY. After a long day of travel, he laid our blankets on the ground and drew me down with him. And he had me. He apologized with his tongue and his hands and then a dick that seems to be forever drawn to the spot inside me that wrings out my pleasure in pounding waves. If he'd asked, I would have promised him anything. Thank the gods he didn't. We passed out, exhausted, as soon as we curled around each other.

"You're sure we can't stay here another day?" I ask as he's pulling our bedrolls apart to pack them. "Astarot could use a day of rest." I smirk, letting my eyes track down to the perfect ass kneeling in front of me, before lifting them back to the gaze he tosses over his shoulder. "And I could use more of ... that," I add, waving my palms in his general direction. "Just ... all of that."

He stands, his grin wide as he stalks toward me and leans forward, his lips nearly touching mine. "So fucking dangerous," he hums before giving me the quickest kiss possible and returning to packing. "Astarot needs exercise, not rest. He won't heal well without it. And you may not realize this yet, but dragons are lazy beasts. If we let him, he'd stay here for weeks."

Goats, Astarot rumbles into my thoughts.

We haven't yet reached the field Tindera wants him to experience and he's anxious. I think it will help him feel connected to her despite the distance—and the fact that they've never had the chance to fully bond. One or the other of them has been trapped by the Dróttning since they discovered each other. He doesn't deny, though, that he'd be perfectly happy to lounge here for days if we had enough food for him.

"Astarot agrees," I murmur to Fhord as I gather the breakfast dishes to wash them quickly before we leave. "He needs another meal, preferably the goats Tindera told him he'd find in this area."

"We should go to the nearby herd this morning. We'll be lucky to reach the field with the goats by the late afternoon. Might have to wait until tomorrow."

"And then what? How long until we reach the North and try to find a way through the barrier?"

"I know how to get through. Don't worry." He pauses, looking toward the cave's opening as if he can see the distance between here and there. "Two days, maybe three if we have to change our route to evade someone."

"You know how to get through?" I shake my head, searching inside for the female I was a month ago, before the Nest. I should have asked this question as soon as Fhord proposed going north. My brain, though, is frazzled, still bound by the stoicism that helped me survive and resist the Dróttning's torture. I'm not as bad as I was a decade ago, but I also don't have the years it took me then to recover. I need to get my shit together now.

"I can open a passage in the barrier."

"Why do you know how to do that?" I ask as I push aside the malaise and focus on today and the future.

"What do you know about the North?" Fhord responds, spinning to give me his full attention.

"Nothing. About the same as everyone else, I thought."

He takes in a deep breath, his eyes searching mine. "I've been connected to the Dróttning for a while," he says at last before falling silent again.

"Which we still need to discuss," I prompt. My eyebrows lift with the question he hasn't answered, which scares the fuck out of me, as my imagination conjures one explanation after another, none of them good.

"Which we *will* discuss, soon. It's … a lot … and I want to be settled someplace when we do."

"Settled?" My lips quirk up at the suggestion. "I don't think we'll be settling anyplace, ever. At least not while the Dróttning lives."

His responding smile doesn't reach his eyes. "Well, I want to wait until we're paused for a few days. I have a lot to tell you and you need to be able to sit with it."

"You don't want to tell me, do you?"

The question lands heavily between us, a shadow that will block the light until it's exposed. His fists grow tight against his sides, the whites of the knuckles bright in the fire's embrace. "I don't. But I will. I promise," he says at last.

Fhord's words twist in my stomach. I won't like what he has to say but he's right. We need to get to safety first. "Okay. We can wait. But know that I don't like secrets, Fhord. I need to be able to trust you."

He steps forward once, and then twice, pausing as his hands move to his thighs, rubbing up and down. "I know, rabbit. I'll earn your trust."

I give him a quick nod as I stand and move toward the horses, taking back the space between us. Whatever he's hiding is settling in my gut, a seed that will only grow until we yank it out together. I don't want to be close to him right now. "So, what does your connection with the Dróttning have to do with us getting through the barrier to the North?"

"She and Harald have communicated over the years. They're not allies—and definitely not friends—but they've needed to work together a couple of times to protect both their lands. The Dróttning usually enlisted me when Harald asked her to send an emissary to him."

"You've been to the North? More than once?"

"Three times in the last two hundred years. Enough to know the way."

"Is there a hidden door or something?"

"It won't be quite that easy. We'll travel toward the passage-way, but without Harald's invitation, we'll need to force our way through. Chances are we'll be met by his soldiers on the other side when we do."

"Why go there, then? Why not just hide somewhere in Vanatia?"

"There's nowhere to hide, rabbit." His gaze lifts toward Astarot, eyebrows wrinkling as he sighs. "While Astarot is with us, and he will always be with us," he adds in a firm voice as he turns back to me, "we are exposed. The only true shelter I know is too far away and we won't be able to get there safely. Setting aside the fact that he's an enormous beast, who'd be impossible to hide for the next week, the Dróttning is connected to every dragon in this land. It's weaker with Astarot because he rejected her rule, but it's still there. If we stay any place more than a couple of days, she'll feel us. And she'll come."

"Can we trust Harald?"

Fhord's quiet for a long time, his head tipped back as he studies the cavern above us. "I don't know," he says at last. "He has many reasons to dislike me. But he despises the Dróttning. If I can convince him I've betrayed her, I believe he'll be an ally." He drops his chin, eyes as dark as the surrounding forest. "That is my hope."

"And if he doesn't believe you?"

Fhord's sneer is immediate. "He will believe me."

I'm not sure if he's trying to convince me or himself.

"If he'll have us, are we leaving Vanatia forever?"

"That's what I need to talk to Harald about. If he's willing to give us his support, we could hide there and maybe even push back on the Dróttning. Change some things."

I can't help the smile that lifts my lips. "Are we going to lead a rebellion, Fhord?"

"So, so dangerous," he breathes, returning my smile—the first one to reach his eyes since I asked him about the North. "First, we'll get there and convince Harald to help us. We should be able to free Tindera without him, but we'd have a better chance with him. Let's see whether he even lets us get close enough to him to ask and decide from there."

My chin dips. "All right, let's go find the northern monarch."

Traveling is ruthless today. The weather and scenery are beautiful with cool temperatures but enough sun to set the forest sparkling and warm our skin. If we could take our time and enjoy the waterfalls we pass—cyan rivers plunging into pools of foaming cobalt—it might be pleasant. Maybe.

Instead, we're racing through dense forests, over rocks and under trees, when we're not scrambling to find someplace to hide the massive beast traveling with us. The Dróttning's had enough time to gather her forces and they're everywhere. Fhord's convinced she's casting her thoughts wide to hear all the messages fed to her. It requires tremendous energy, but she should be able to sustain it for a day or so. While she's spread herself out this way, we won't be able to kill anyone quickly enough to prevent their report from reaching her.

Three times before noon, we're forced to find and then push through heavy underbrush as Astarot scrabbles on his belly to shove his way behind us, barely concealing his bulk. As he chokes down the grumbles he shares only in my thoughts, determined to conceal even the timbre of his voice, we painstakingly cover him with branches.

Ants, he proclaims as we huddle next to him the third time. He's pissed and I get it. He's a gods-damned dragon and they do not hide. They control the skies and the lands. And Astarot isn't just any dragon. As his health returns, so does his vigor.

He's one of the largest beasts in this land, born to lead and dominate. He'd need to be, to deserve his place at Tindera's side. *Yours*, he interjects as he reads my thoughts. Yet, he's forced to cower from lesser beings—the spineless humans who bow to the Dróttning. Through our bond, I feel his frustration.

When we finally decide we can safely start moving again, he erupts, tossing off the underbrush as he shakes his hide. Spinning his massive head toward me, he grunts then drops a single word in my mind. *Fly*. He doesn't want to cower on the ground any longer, smothering his very essence.

"Not yet." Fhord suggested I talk out loud to Astarot because we can't risk the Dróttning overhearing us, if she's listening for Astarot. Casting my will toward my dragon's, I fill it with the restraint we need until we can leave Vanatia. "There are too many and we can't risk them seeing you and chasing us to the barrier. We can stay hidden only if we travel by ground."

Patting Sigurd's neck, I tack on, "Besides, we can't leave Sigurd behind. Fhord would miss his favorite horse."

I can feel Astarot's struggle. He's free after being bound his entire life and while we're destined to be together, we're still two different beings, both with fierce wills. As he comes into his strength—a deep well, amplified by our connection and untapped for too many years—he *needs* to exploit it to be the dragon he was born to be.

And I understand, for the first time, that for our bond to work, I can never exert my will over him. Even if I might be able to force him to comply, I can't let myself do that. He needs to trust me and he won't if I try to control him the way the Dróttning does the rest of the dragons.

He fought too hard, suffered too much, to be anyone's drudge.

For now, though, he's realized I'm right and need to win this battle between us. As our minds volley back and forth, the alpha within him struggling to take control as I push at him, pleading for his restraint, we cross the first bridge in our bond. *Soon*, he rumbles, voicing what I already know. I'll lead us now, but not every time.

"I get it," I assure him, reaching out to stroke his snout. "I'm not your master. You sacrificed too much of yourself, suffered too much, so you could reject the Dróttning's rule. I don't want to take her place. I won't try. We'll work together to defeat her and I'll abide by your demands as often as you abide by mine."

Astarot blinks his eyes as he watches me. My dragon's still struggling to hold his dominant side in check, resist the urge to cast himself into the sky. But Astarot's prevailed over that instinct for now.

"I went through the same thing with Tindera," Fhord offers from behind me when Astarot pushes through the trees and roams down the path we'd been taking before we felt the presence of the Dróttning's guards. "We're their partners, not their rulers. It's a constant push and pull to find the best course. And we don't always get it right, even when we do decide together."

"Is this how it is with all dragons and their riders?"

Fhord snorts out a laugh. "No. Not even close."

Spinning, I stare at him for a minute. "What do you mean?"

"The Dróttning's power is absolute," he explains in a flat tone. "Most riders rely on that to control their dragons, mainly because bonds like we have with our beasts aren't common. I got lucky when my destined dragon was in the clutch for my Choosing." When my eyebrows wrinkle in confusion, he clarifies, "The Choosing is what happens when dragons and riders are joined. The prospective riders wait as eggs hatch and then they decide which dragon will be theirs."

My thoughts return to Midgard and the growing connection between the gods and dragons, as dragons began to take riders after centuries of living apart. What he's describing sounds a bit like the process there, although I hadn't actually witnessed any bonding ceremony. "How is it supposed to work?"

"Without the Dróttning's intervention, the dragons would age unbound. Only when their paths crossed with their destined rider would the bond arise. Now, though, the Dróttning forces a bond at the dragon's birth, or when they're very young, with a rider she's approved of in advance."

"And you happened to be offered when Tindera hatched?"

"We got lucky. It almost never happens. Our bond is among the strongest in Vanatia because of it."

"How did Astarot avoid that?"

Fhord lifts his eyes and smiles at Astarot for a moment, before turning back to me. "He didn't. His first rider died years ago."

Pig, Astarot hisses, his disdain for the nobleman who claimed him whispering through me.

Holding his eyes for a moment, I let my sympathy roll between us. "I'm sorry you suffered so long at his hand," I breathe.

Strong, he replies. He isn't sorry. His experience strengthened his resolve to never be connected to an unworthy rider, helped him hold out for me.

"Astarot wasn't a fan of his first rider."

"I don't blame him." Fhord's voice is kind as he watches my beautiful red beast. "Egil was a cruel man in every way. I didn't see how he interacted with Astarot—for whatever reason, our paths never crossed before we found your dragon a few weeks ago—but I knew Egil well. The Dróttning favored him."

"How did he die?"

Fhord's laugh erupts in a huff. "Do you want to tell her?" he asks Astarot.

I can feel my dragon's amusement as he shares a memory with me—an ugly man, eyes glaring an evil that draws out a tremble deep in my soul, toppling over as his dark heart gives out while he's crouched down, trying to shit in a wooded area similar to this one. Astarot and his rider are alone, and Astarot's relief, followed by joy, at his rider's demise echoes through me.

"He died trying to take a crap?" My voice is as light as theirs.

"Such a fitting end," Fhord responds. Astarot disappeared for a while afterwards and he got in trouble when he returned, but eventually, he shared what happened and led the Dróttning's people to his body.

Free, Astarot breathes, his memories of those weeks infusing me with his joy. He'd never felt so alive—at least until he found and bonded with me. When that meager link with a male wholly unworthy of him snuffed out—ending for a time the Dróttning's control over him too—he swore he would never be *forced* to bind.

"How old were you when you bonded with Tindera?"

"Not even a hundred yet. We've been together a long time."

"What would have happened if Tindera hadn't been offered when you were ready?"

"We would be with others," Fhord answers simply. My gut grows hard, a rock replacing all of the flesh, as if I can physically feel Fhord's disdain for the thought. Spinning, his eyes land on the path we'd been following before we were forced to hide. "Enough talk. We need to get going."

The afternoon isn't as bad as the morning. We're forced to hide only twice and are far enough into the mountains to find caves easily both times. When we decide to stop, we choose a deep cavern that will let us sleep far enough away from the opening to set traps that will warn us if someone enters. We both need the rest.

Fhord's got something else in mind first. As soon as we finish dinner and clean up, he reaches for my hand, pulling me to my feet. And then he starts to strip me, his fingers light as he takes his time.

When he lifts my arms and tugs my shirt over my head, my skin dimples, but not from the cold. His intense glare, consuming me with his eyes, sparks a flame I feel in every part of me, starting at my core and expanding to that spot between my thighs that belongs to him. I rub them together, the friction a burn I need, as his fingers reach down to push my pants over my hips, down my legs, and off my feet.

We stand together for long minutes—me naked and him fully dressed—as he explores my body with his eyes, then his hands, and finally his lips. I've never felt more exposed with a male, but I want nothing more than to show him even more. To reveal all the pieces and parts of myself I've kept hidden these many years.

As if he's reading my mind, Fhord drops to one knee, swings a leg over his shoulder, and drags his tongue across my core. Lazily, like he's enjoying his favorite dessert, he licks the sides and through my center, sucking and nibbling as he goes. My body trembles, and I'm about to start begging him to give me more when he starts to really get serious.

Concentrating on my clit, devouring it like he's never tasted anything better, he sticks one finger inside me before taking it out and following with two. And then he's finger fucking me, and I almost can't stand straight.

"Don't move, rabbit," he snarls as his free hand clasps my hip. "I'm not done yet."

A shiver ripples through me at his command. Alpha Fhord pisses me off anywhere else, but in the bedroom, I want nothing else. My body craves his control. "You're gonna have to hold me up then," I pant, my voice low. "I don't know if I can stand much longer."

He stops for a moment, gazing at me with eyes that smolder, green like the nearby forest. "Always, rabbit. I will always hold you up." Looking above us, he smirks and grasps my ribcage, tossing my other leg over his shoulder as he stands. "Reach up and hold on," he commands as I lift my hands to grip the ledges just above me. And then he turns back to my aching clit, supporting me with one hand while the other drops down to finger me as he continues to suck and nibble and lick. My chest is tight, my body winding around itself, gathering for the release he's drawing from me.

"Don't come yet," Fhord demands, knowing as he always does when I'm close. "I will be inside you when you come tonight."

"Then fuck me, Fhord." I drag my hands through his hair to lift his head and capture his eyes. "I need you. Now."

He's the most magnificent man I've ever seen, and when he smiles at me like he does now—wicked and playful and full of lust—I want to bury myself in his scent and wrap myself around his dick forever. "Not yet, rabbit," he grunts before sucking again on my clit. The hand that's not deep in my pussy lifts to grab my breast, squeezing it and pinching the nipple as he wrings little screams and moans from me.

As much as I want him filling me, I almost cry when he pulls out his fingers, folds me in his arms, and drops me onto his hips. My legs circle his waist, and I gasp as my center drags against the coarse material covering his hard dick. Rocking back and forth for the friction I need, I smile up at Fhord, whose lips are curving up deliciously.

"So impatient," he says, nipping at the tip of my ear as he strides over to the bedroll.

"As you know. Which makes me wonder why you're still dressed."

He lays me down, dropping his head to suck and then bite each nipple as his fingers glaze over my clit and into my pussy for the briefest moment. When he stands, his eyes try to hold mine, but I'm too interested in the clothing he's removing—and the skin, muscles and tattoos beneath—to keep his gaze.

"Do you like what you see, rabbit?" His tone is husky as I reach down to ease some of the tension he left in my body when he stopped.

"I'd like it better if it was on top of me. And inside me."

"So demanding." Gripping his dick, he stands there until I look up again into his eyes. "You're perfect," he breathes. We watch each other for a few seconds, our hands and fingers filling the void left when our bodies separated.

"I need you, Fhord. Fuck me."

And he does. Dropping to the bedroll, he flips me on to my stomach and plunges inside. I inhale sharply, the sensation nearly dragging my orgasm out before I can stop it. And then his thumb is on my clit again as he pulls out and thrusts back in. This time, I can't hold on. The orgasm rips through me in a wave, my body trembling while I ride the euphoria that Fhord always ignites.

He's just getting started, though. As he finds his rhythm, I do too. The first orgasm fades as another starts to build slowly. I feel him everywhere, sparks of ecstasy flaming with every lunge of his hips. In no time at all, I'm nearing release. But then he pauses to spin me over again.

"I want to see you when you come for me, rabbit."

This time, Fhord's slow, gentle. As if he wants to savor the lovemaking this has become. As his hips shift and buck, his fingers trace every part of my face, starting with the ears that emerge only for him, skimming over to my eyebrows, cheekbones, and finally the bottom lip that he drags down and nips. When he kisses me, the world I thought I knew eclipses, casting Fhord into its center. Now and always. The orgasms that follow—mine preceding his by only a few beats of our hearts—feel momentous. As if something has shifted, never to be the same again.

We lay together for a long time, Fhord still inside me while I cling to the emotions I only feel in these moments together. Here and now, lying naked with him, I am whole.

And I wonder whether this is the start of something that will change my world.

Or the beginning of my end.

CHAPTER THREE

SIFA

YOU'RE ALL MINE

WHEN WE REACH IT, the sun is just peeking over the tops of the trees on the other side of the field Tindera told Astarot to find. Fhord tugs on Sigurd's reins as we pause to appreciate its splendor. It's been a long time since I've seen anything so pretty. And I've seen lots of pretty fields.

I'm not sure at first what it is that makes this patch of color so special. It holds everything fields typically do—a broad swath of grass rustling in a light breeze. Flowers dotted along the edges and in patches splattered throughout, like drops of paint sprinkled from a brush held high above. A river winding across its center, rocks and splashes dancing together under the rising sun. Trees along its perimeter, holding the invisible line that always marks a meadow.

When it hits me, I gasp, not quite sure what to make of it.

The colors here—every single one—are somehow *more* than normal. The greens are deeper and impossibly vibrant, as if the gods splintered emeralds and cast them on the ground to shimmer for passing eyes. The petals, leaves and even the stalks of the hundreds of blooms are all lavish and sensuous. They seem anxious to lend themselves to a lover to carry home. The river's crisp, cool rivulets gurgle a welcome, inviting those who come close enough to wallow in its valleys.

"What is this place?" I turn to find Fhord watching me, one side of his lips cocking up as his eyes sparkle.

"It's stunning, isn't it?"

"I haven't seen a place like this for many, many years." Memories of the lands of my youth erupt in my thoughts. This valley doesn't share the hues of the worlds I grew up in, but it does share their majesty. Only Asgard is so rich and lush, and I'd always believed nothing could live up to that glorious place.

"It is almost beyond compare. One other area in Vanatia rivals it. I'm told there are none quite this remarkable in the North."

"How?"

"The water," Fhord responds as his jaw juts toward the river. "This is really why Tindera urged us to come, but she couldn't say and risk the Dróttning hearing her words. She speaks of the goats—which she insists are unlike any others around—but she wants him to drink. And heal."

"The water will ... heal him?"

"It will. Wait until you feel it." He winks and reaches behind him to draw his shirt over his head before nudging Sigurd into a trot. Pulling me closer, he smiles. "Let's go take a bath."

Within a few seconds of reaching the river's edge, he's naked and wading in, muscles in his ass rippling as he drops in deeper.

I can't move. I watch through water so clear it seems like glass as he fists himself and pumps a dick that shouldn't be nearly that hard in a stream as cold as this must be. Reading my mind he smiles and looks down. "Get in. You'll see."

He doesn't have to ask again. Dropping from Sigurd, I strip, folding my clothes into a pile on a nearby rock, and follow him. My skin comes alive as I do.

"Fuck me," I breathe, the sensations almost too much at first.

"Right?" His laugh is a gentle breeze on a warm summer night, ghosting over me.

Dropping, I submerge myself, soaking up every tingle and spark the water is triggering. When the same feelings erupt inside—as if my flesh absorbed the fluid and diffused it through my system—I take a deep breath. While still immersed, the oxygen that seems to flow from the water into my lungs fills me with even more ... life. I can't think of a better word to describe the energy and vigor that infuses me.

I lay there for a long time, inhaling water, pondering how I knew I could do this safely. It reminds me of the lake in the Nest that we swam through to escape. We breathed in that water too. But this is different. There, the water felt alive, like it wanted to protect us. I sense nothing like that here. This water simply is, its life-giving properties part of its inanimate being.

After a few minutes, Fhord joins me, twining our fingers together as we lay motionless and watch the ripples roll over us. When he leaves, standing to reach for soap and wash himself, I stay. I don't know if I'll ever experience anything like this again, and I don't want it to end.

Finally, perhaps an hour or more after I dropped into the river, I rise and find the soap Fhord left for me. Slowly scrubbing myself down, I try to extend this as long as I can. My stomach intervenes.

I realize as I look around that Fhord went to work when he got out. Astarot's thoughts drop into my mind, and I laugh. *Mine*, he explains. He offered part of his second goat to Fhord before scraping its bones. We'll be having goat steak tonight and it's already sizzling on the fire burning in the midst of our camp.

He's erecting a tent as I get dressed, smiling as his eyes lift to watch me don the clean clothes he set out for me. His lips tuck down as my shirt drops over my breasts, before mouthing, "Later."

"Later," I agree with a nod, "I'm all yours."

"You're all mine," he echoes.

His words, though, have a different meaning than mine.

"How can a place like this exist?" I ask after a moment.

"How can anything exist?" he responds with a smirk.

"That's not helpful." I stick out my tongue, wiggling it a little as he laughs.

"Like I said, later." His tongue slowly traces his lips, sending a shiver down my spine. Casting my eyes down, I wrest my thoughts back from Fhord's tongue and its many talents.

"Do you know how this place came to be?"

"Fuck no." He laughs, his eyes still sparkling like the morning grass. "Tindera and I discovered it years ago, and I suspect few others know it's here. I doubt even the Dróttning knows. She'd have established a base here if she did. We're very far north and found this only by chance."

"And will Astarot heal?"

He grunts, his snout deep in the third goat he's taken from the herd. *Healed.*

"Already?" I demand, standing as I spin to stare at him.

Grunting again, he repeats it. *Healed.*

"If he hadn't been so close to whole, it would have taken longer. It kills me that we couldn't get here after Tindera was hurt. We wouldn't have had to go to the Nest if we could have made it this far. She'd have been better by the next day. But Tindera wouldn't have survived the trip."

"How is she still trapped in the Nest? Why isn't she healed yet?"

"The Dróttning controls everything, including dragon healing. Even I don't know how—and I know most things about the Dróttning—but nobody can deny it's true. She took control of the dragons centuries ago and while she holds their leash, this country will belong to her."

"Gods, Fhord. I have so many questions about what you just told me. I know you don't want to talk about you and the Dróttning yet, but you need to tell me why you are so close to her."

Fhord's eyes hold mine for the longest time. "I will. Just give me time. What else do you want to know?"

"So much. But let's start with this. Why is the Dróttning slowing Tindera's healing?"

"That's how she controls me." His voice is flat, resigned. This pains him as much as it would me if Astarot were still trapped in the Nest. "While Tindera is under her thumb, she can use my dragon against me."

"Because of me?"

"It started before I met you. Tindera should already have healed by the time Bevin connected us. Dragons *never* take this long to heal in the Nest. The Dróttning has been losing trust in me and this is her response."

"Why is she losing trust in you?"

"I don't know." Fhord's eyes are solemn. I don't think he's lying to me. After a moment he shrugs. "I mean, she's right. She can't trust me. I don't know what I did to earn her suspicions, but I intend to find out. Not now, though. Right now, I want to enjoy this meal Astarot offered us. And then I want to take you back into that river and answer a question I've had since I met you: What will it feel like to fuck you in that water?"

His tone is husky, and the points of my ears pop out as my body heats. "Do we have to eat first?"

"Enjoy the anticipation, rabbit. I know I will."

It felt every single bit as amazing as I'd hoped it might. Maybe better. I wake the next morning wrapped up with Fhord and reliving the sensations that rocked through me as he played my body like a harp in the midst of waters that amplify every sensation. Gods, I feel good. I've never felt so *alive* and strong. I'd drag him back there now if I felt like I could ride Sigurd on the heels of the dozen or more orgasms he'd draw from me. But I don't know if I could. The water heals many things, but as my body is telling me, it can't fix the burn that comes from *lots* and *lots* of worlds-shattering sex.

"Are you thinking what I'm thinking?" My body responds like it always does to Fhord's low voice, heat fluttering through me.

"I am," I admit, tugging my arms tighter around him. "I think I'm too sore for everything that would happen there, but gods, do I wish we could."

He sighs, his breath drifting through my hair. "You're right. I hate it, but you're right."

"Especially with another day of riding ahead of me."

Fly. Astarot's thoughts are firm, unyielding. He wants to fly today.

"We can't leave Sigurd behind," I remind him as I sit up. Turning, I watch him stand and shake his massive hide, wings tucked tight into his sides.

Carry, he replies, holding my gaze.

My laugh catches me by surprise. "You can't carry a horse."

"He could." Fhord tosses off the blankets and drags himself up to walk toward the fire pit. "The horses of dragon riders are trained from an early age to be carried by dragons. We get rid of their fear so they're motionless in the talons."

"That would be too much weight, even for Astarot."

"How do you feel today, rabbit?"

"Like I could run for vikus."

"You probably could. After spending so much time in the water, we're as healthy and strong as we'll ever be. We can do things now we wouldn't be able to normally do."

"You think Astarot really could carry all of us? Even Sigurd?"

"Stretch out your wings," Fhord commands as he spins to stride toward Astarot.

Astarot harumphs in response, displeased with Fhord's tone. "He's not a dog," I remind Fhord as I follow him and grab his arm. "You can't order him around."

Now it's Fhord's turn to harumph. "Prickly bastard." He turns back to Astarot with a mocking bow. "Please extend your wings." His voice drips with sarcasm, but Astarot doesn't care. He wanted the words, and he got them.

Astarot smirks in his dragony way as he stretches, his full plumage glistening in the dappling daylight. I don't feel a hint of pain at the motion. They're better already, the wounds fully closed and healed over. He's even sprouting new feathers in the damaged areas.

Fhord nods as he inspects Astarot. "He looks good. If he thinks he can fly, we should let him. We're far enough north that the chances of seeing another dragon are slim. It would be good to get out of Vanatia."

"Okay. We'll fly today."

Astarot eats two more goats before we leave, although I have no idea where he packs them. We can't carry the water since, as Fhord explains, it will grow toxic as we put distance between it and its source, so we drink as much as we can, then pack up quickly. Within an hour, we're positioning Sigurd to be gripped by Astarot's talons before climbing aboard his massive back.

"I'm going to fly on my dragon today," I murmur, shivers running up and down my back. I'd dreamed of this on Midgard, where I might have gotten lucky and been chosen by a dragon. But I considered it impossible here. Before Astarot. Before Fhord. Turning, I gaze at this enigmatic man behind me, eyes as green as the nearby meadow staring back. Everything in my life is different—better—now.

"This first flight is unlike any that will follow," he whispers as he tugs me closer. "You'll remember it forever."

I will, I realize as Astarot lifts from the ground and hovers over Sigurd to clutch him with his talons. Fhord told me he'd be fine, but I still can't believe it when he stands still and allows himself to be lifted by the most dangerous predator in Vanatia.

When my astonishment at Sigurd's blasé attitude about being carried finally dims a bit, I take a deep breath and look up. Astarot's massive wings—a kaleidoscope of red and black feathers covering them—beat steadily as he lifts us into the sky. He's so strong. Although he's probably carrying 1,500 pounds, he doesn't seem weighed down at all. He's propelling us up toward the clouds at a speed that increases with every flap.

I've ridden dragons before but never have I felt so comfortable. My connection to Astarot—his joy at being airborne drifting through our bond—relaxes me in a way I couldn't on another beast. I sit astride him as the trees shrink into little green puffs knowing I'm safe and loved by the creature beneath me.

We fly as the sun lifts high into the sky and then starts to drop down again. Most of the time, puffy clouds float beneath us, but occasionally we get glimpses of the land below. Once, I realize we're flying over a mountain when I see its peak a few hundred feet under us, the trees at the top rustling in the powerful draft caused by Astarot's wings. I lean into Fhord and savor every minute of this unexpected trip, my thoughts drifting to home and fantasies about Fhord joining me there.

"Tell Astarot to go to that cave." Fhord's low voice pulls me out of my memories of Revalle and my evenings alone with Toffer and Thor, wondering what that time would look like if Fhord was there. I lift my eyes to find where his finger is pointing, then ask my dragon to follow his instructions. We drop slowly, my dragon's joy flitting through me as he wrings as much as he can out of our first flight together.

Too soon, we're hovering over a broad patch of dirt in front of the cave. Sigurd snickers as Astarot sets him down, shaking vigorously as if he hopes to rid himself of the feel of dragon talons. When he scatters away, I almost laugh. Trained or not, he did not enjoy that ride.

Astarot settles onto the dirt, extending his wing so Fhord and I can dismount.

More? he asks before either of us moves. He wants to take me out to play. It's been too long since he's been in the air, and he's never been free to fly the way he wants.

"Are we safe to go up again? Astarot isn't done flying yet."

"Go." Fhord's smile lifts his cheeks and crinkles his eyes. "Go south; don't try to go north. There shouldn't be anybody in the area, and I need to check some things before we can get through." He lifts his hand to brush his knuckles across my cheek. "We're in no rush. Take as long as you want." And then he's climbing down, stretching his arms above his head as he leans back and examines the sky.

Astarot's glee—there's no better word for it—is infectious. Within seconds, we're in the air again, his wings moving even faster than before. He's vibrating with his excitement, and I can't help but bounce up and down on his back. He wants to experience things he never has before.

Hold. He swings his head back to glance at me, his eyes bright and an actual smile lifting the corners of his mouth. When I nod, he tucks his wings, and we start flipping. Round and round and round we go as my stomach plunges and my mind draws up memories of being swung by my parents as a child, spinning in a meadow on a warm summer day, twisting in a lake as the water propels me in circles. The world around us blurs, and I can do nothing but cling to his feathers and laugh.

Astarot's wings snap out without warning, nearly sending me pitching forward as we level out and start flying straight. I can feel his chuckle through our bond as I settle on his neck.

"Bad dragon," I grunt but I can't hold back the giggle that emerges with my words. He enjoyed that too much.

We spend a half hour or more soaring through the sky as Astarot revels in the freedom our bond brought him. At one point, though, he stiffens. His mind is tinged with a distress I don't understand as he turns his head to glare back toward the cave. But then he huffs out a breath and relaxes, slowly pivoting to follow his gaze and return to Fhord and Sigurd.

"What is it?" I ask, rubbing his neck.

He doesn't answer, leaving me alone with his vague emotions that felt like shock at first but evolved into an odd sense of worry, fear, and a hint of anger. Wondering what shifted, I nudge him again for an explanation, but he doesn't give one, instead letting his pleasure at our first flight fill his thoughts. So I lean into him and savor the joy with him. "Thank you," I breathe as I reach forward and hug his neck. "That was magnificent."

It's only when we're flying back that I realize the land beneath us isn't what I think. The cave that Fhord's exploring sits at the base of a low mountain that at first looks oddly uniform. As we approach, though, I see that it's not just uniform. It's identical. The mountain looks exactly the same on Vanatia's side as it does on the other.

And it's not only the mountain. Everywhere I look is a perfect replica of the other side, as if a vast mirror was molded on top of the mountain and to its sides running roughly east and west. A shudder ripples up my spine as I recognize the strength of magic needed to create such a barrier. And the difficulty of getting through something like this.

"Don't touch it, Astarot," I warn as he flies directly toward the barrier. "We don't know what it does to anyone who tries to go through."

Astarot drops his chin, turning toward Fhord and dropping in that direction.

When I see Fhord's face, I realize something's wrong. The angst Astarot felt while we flew washes over me again as I watch Fhord run both hands through his hair, his brow wrinkled and lips tipping down. But then his expression changes, as if he flipped a switch. The worry in his face disappears, replaced by a grin that doesn't quite reach his eyes. He lifts his hand to wave, strolling toward the clearing Astarot chose to land.

As I crawl down from my beast, Fhord reaches toward me, but I hold back. I don't trust whatever's going on.

"What's wrong, Fhord?"

"Nothing, rabbit. Why do you think something's wrong?"

"I saw you when we were coming in. You're worried and trying to hide it."

"Rabbit," he proclaims, pulling me toward him, "I'm not hiding anything."

"I don't believe you. And I need to be able to trust you." I lean back to catch his eyes and hold them. My stomach is twisting in knots. I'm not sure what happened, but Fhord's resolve to keep it from me is much worse than any truth he might tell me.

For a moment—just a moment—Fhord looks as if he's considering the truth. I can see the question, the ambivalence, in his eyes. But then it's gone, replaced by resolve.

"If there was something you needed to worry about, I wouldn't hide it from you," he assures, drawing me in again.

This time I let him. I don't know yet what he's doing, but I'll find out. Astarot knows. He'll tell me.

And I'll make sure Fhord realizes how much damage he did when he broke my trust.

CHAPTER FOUR

FHORD

FUCKITY FUCK FUCK

F UCK.

Fuck, fuck, fuck, fuck.

Fuckity fuck fuck.

I don't know what to do.

And I always know what to do. Always.

This time, though, I'm so torn, I think I might rip in half.

I have no gods-damned idea why Astarot didn't tell her. He heard Tindera's scream too, whipping his head to glare at me as if I'd been the one to harm her. I could no more hurt my dragon than I could my rabbit. But the gods apparently have decided that one of them must always be suffering at the Dróttning's hand. The fuckers. And there's not a single thing I can do about it.

Fuck.

Fuckity fuck fuck.

Astarot's blazing eyes as he stared across the distance between us—and Sifa's response to his distress—chilled me to the bone. She came back asking questions, and I lied to her. Again. Because if she knows what I'm going to risk to try to save Tindera, she won't let me leave alone. Or she won't forgive me when I do it anyway.

I cannot—I will not—chance the Dróttning capturing Sifa again. It's even more important now because the odds of the Dróttning sensing my mating bond skyrocketed as soon as I embraced my side of the bond and made love to Sifa. It would be even worse if Sifa had accepted the bond too—which is exactly why Sifa can never fucking ever know we're mates.

The Dróttning will kill Sifa if she gets another chance. Sifa may never forgive me, but at least she'll be alive. Even if she decides to live without me, it's better than dying at my side.

Not that the Dróttning would kill me. She may torture me for a while, but I'll live. So I'll get Tindera alone.

Harald will help. He has to. Enemy of my enemy and all that. Blah, blah, blah. We just need to get to that bastard and convince him now's the time. If he agrees to send fighters with me to the Nest, we might be able to persuade Sifa that he needs her in the North. She'll let me go alone. There's no other choice.

I have to talk to Astarot, plead with him to stay silent.

Tonight, after we get through this barrier. If we can.

Squeezing Sifa one more time, I lean in to catch her scent and hold it, the lavender and rosemary filling me with a warmth I'd never felt before her. My angst seeps out of me as I embrace my mate. Reaching into her thick, dark hair, I kiss the top of her head, one of her tight curls tickling my nose.

Fuck, I love her hair. It's so alive, bouncing across her shoulders whenever she shifts with hints of auburn and mahogany. Of course, I love every single thing about this mate of mine. I don't know how I ever thought I could stay away from her.

I take a deep breath and let go, stepping back so I can look into her eyes. The shadows are still there. She knows I lied but is willing to let it go for now. Maybe she'll forget all about this by the time we get to Harald.

"The barrier's different this time," I tell her as I take her hand and lead her toward the cave. "Harald moved the entrance, and I think he's added some extra magic on his side. I should be able to get us through, but it may take a while."

"Why would he do that?"

"Harald's a prickly son-of-a-bitch. And he hates the Dróttning as much as everyone else. He changes it up sometimes to try to protect his realm."

"Can we still get through?"

"I can. I have … unique … magic. I guess it's time for you to see some of it for yourself."

"Do you hide it usually?"

"Always. The Dróttning recognizes it. What I have to do now is like a bomb that she will hear, no matter where she is in Vanatia or what else she's focused on. I can do little things without her noticing unless she's close enough to sense my presence—manipulate emotions, things like that. If there's enough magic surrounding me, it'll hide even some larger bursts of power. Breaking through the barrier, though, will require so much power, she'll hear me even in Revalle. As soon as I use it, we need to pass through, or she'll find us."

"What if it doesn't work?"

I smile at her, my lips tipping up in the slow smirk that always ... every single time ... gains the trust of the female I'm trying to persuade. "Have I ever led you astray, rabbit?"

But Sifa's already immune to my practiced charm. She knows me too well. Her bright eyes narrow. "Shameless flirt," she laughs as the back of her hand smacks my chest. "You're not going to distract me with that act. What if it doesn't work?"

"Gods, you're sexy, woman," I moan as I catch her fingers and bring them up toward me, holding her gaze while I kiss each one. "It'll work. Trust me."

She rolls her eyes, a playful scowl lifting her lips, and I can't help myself. My free hand grasps the back of her neck, my thumb caressing her jawline and lifting her chin just enough for me to capture her mouth. Groaning, I lean into this female who owns every part of me, letting her feel how much I want her. Her hands drop to my ass and pull me in closer as she rubs against the cock already straining to feel her skin.

Forcing myself to break our kiss, I lean my forehead against hers as I reach down and take her hands. "Not yet," I growl, to myself more than her, as I draw her into the cavern that should be our path to the North.

I watch Sifa's expression as we enter, waiting for the moment the magic hits her. Never before have I shared this cave with anyone save Tindera. I've wondered forever what it would feel like to come here, the magic wrapped around me as waves of pleasure consume my body. That experience will be Sifa's alone today. Just one of the "firsts" I intend to give her. I've been thinking of nothing else since we decided to come here and there's no fucking way I'll be able to concentrate on the barrier if I don't taste my little rabbit first.

It's why I didn't take her outside, despite the demands of my throbbing cock. Sifa needs to come in here, swathed in this magic, my tongue deep inside her.

Her sharp inhale and wide eyes are everything I hoped they'd be. Her cheeks flush, her fingers growing tighter in mine while the other hand stretches out on her thigh. She turns to me and sighs.

And my cock trembles. But it needs to sit the fuck back. Because this is all about Sifa. It'll get some attention when we're on the other side of the barrier. Maybe on the way back I'll let my demanding bastard join in on the fun.

"A little farther," I murmur as I squeeze Sifa's hand.

I feel her response when we're there. Our bond isn't as solid as it would be if she'd accepted it too, but it strengthened when she opened herself to me and has grown with every touch and kiss since then. The wave of desire that started to swell when we first touched the magic is reaching its edge. Now she'll feel everything I want her to feel.

I'm fucking hard just thinking about it.

Tugging her to a stop, I reach out and unbutton her blouse, my gaze never leaving hers. I don't take it off, though. I love how she looks when the fabric just barely covers her nipples, leaving a path along her stomach and between her breasts for my hungry eyes. I let my hands wrap around those breasts, caressing the soft skin and teasing the firm buds before turning to her pants.

These have to come off because Sifa needs to be unbridled when she comes for me. Pulling them down, I lift one foot and then another as I help her step out of them, then toss them aside. Now, I let my eyes wander down to the star of the show. She's barely breathing, and I can't wait to turn those shallow inhales into gusts and moans.

My fingers reach for her first, stroking her wet cunt and teasing her clit. She's so gods-damned wet for me. And we're just getting started. I need her sitting down.

Reaching inside for a hint of my magic, I thrust it toward the rocks behind us, willing them to shift and move as I form a chair curved in exactly the shape of her ass. Her eyes spin behind us, wide and unblinking, but I need her to look at me. My fingers reach for her chin to nudge it forward.

"Eyes on me, rabbit," I snarl, letting loose the reins on my savage just a bit. He needs to taste her more than I do.

Her gasp as I push her back on to the cool stone sends another twitch through my cock, but I ignore it. This is all about Sifa. A hungry smile erupts on my face and there's not a gods-damned thing I can do to stop it. I've been thinking about this for a long time.

With one more surge of my magic, Sifa's chair rises just enough to position her perfectly. I'm standing, her pussy tantalizingly close to my mouth, my hands on either side of the wall. "Ready?" I demand, my tone harsher than I thought it would be.

"I'm so fucking ready, Fhord," Sifa hums, her hands reaching forward to ease some of the tension this place and my teasing have built in her.

"None of that," I breathe as I take her hands and draw them to her sides. "I'm the only one who touches this today."

"Then touch me. I'm gonna scream if your tongue isn't inside me soon." Her words are strangled, her chest heaving with the strength of her passion.

"You'll scream," I assure her with a smile, "but that's not why."

And then I devour her. My tongue can't get enough of Sifa, her lavender and rosemary essence coating my mouth as I tease and taste her. This is not a slow buildup. She's already there, this cavern's magic thrumming through her and demanding release. My tongue laps up every bit of her nectar as I suck and nibble and lick.

"Stay put," I demand as my hands release hers, one moving straight for her cunt, two fingers reaching inside as my tongue shifts away to give them room, the other grasping for her heavy tits, tweaking one nipple after another. When I'm knuckles-deep frenzide inside her, I concentrate on her clit, sucking that perfect little bud as my fingers fuck her hard. She's writhing, and the hand fondling her breast has to stop occasionally to hold her in place.

And this is every gods-damned bit as magnificent as I hoped it would be. My cock is steel, straining against my pants, and every part of me is throbbing.

Her orgasm rips through her like a tornado, lifting her ass off the rock as her back arches fiercely, and she trembles in rolling waves. She screams, just like I promised she would, and almost slips out of my grip as I wrest every bit of pleasure out of her. I swear it lasts a minute or more and I am so fucking pleased with myself I can't hold back the laugh.

I knew she'd like it here.

"By the gods, Fhord. What did you just do to me?" Sifa throws her head back against the rock as another shiver rolls through her body.

My tongue darts out to catch the rest of her flavor as I squeeze her hips, willing my magic to shift the rock and bring her down to me. "Now we can breach the barrier," I tell her with another laugh as I start to lead her toward her discarded clothes.

"Wait." She resists, tugging me back toward her as she slaps the rock behind her. "What was this?" she asks, her eyebrow quirking adorably.

"This is the power I have to hide most of the time. We're safe here with all of the magic swirling around us, so I let it out to play a little bit ... while I played a little bit." I can't keep the smile off my face. I'm so fucking lost in this female.

"What all can you do?"

She's still standing there, barely dressed, and it takes all my strength to focus on her question.

I puff out a breath before answering. "You can convince people to do things they normally wouldn't. I can do something similar with everything. My magic isn't as deep as yours, but it's wider. I can manipulate emotions and use that to bend people to my will. Animals too—most are driven by base urges I can exploit—though again, my abilities aren't as strong as they would be if I wielded only that magic. With everything else, it's more elemental. Rocks," I explain as I reach for the hand resting on the stone and pull her again toward her pants, "and everything else are easy. I just see the change and will it."

"That would come in handy." Sifa gets dressed and lets herself be drawn along, walking at my side. "Why don't you use it more?"

"My magic has a unique signature. When I wield a lot of power, it echoes hundreds of vikus. The Dróttning can sense it, including its origin. It tells her exactly where I am, which I usually don't want her to know."

"Why were you able to manipulate the rock here?"

"That required little power. My magic would get lost amidst all the magic in the cave. Breaching the barrier, though, will require tremendous power."

"You have so much to tell me," Sifa says, her brow creasing as she watches me. "Starting with everything about this weird relationship between you and the Dróttning."

"I know, rabbit. Be patient with me. I'll tell you all you need to know."

"Not just what you think I *need*. I'm pretty sure we have different ideas about what that might be. Everything."

I dip my chin. "Everything."

"Good. So, are these super special powers why you're able to get through the barrier?"

"Super special powers?"

"That's what we'll call them from now on. Super special powers. S.S.P. for short. That way, the Dróttning's spying ears won't know what we're talking about." She's grinning, her dark eyes bright as stars.

I'm tempted to forget my promise to myself, release the cock that's still throbbing for her, and let the magic carry both of us over the edge this time.

Spinning, I plant my feet in front of hers so our noses nearly touch. "How the fuck are we supposed to get anything done when you're so gods-damned delectable?"

"Good enough to eat? Again?"

"Always. But it's not like we can stop every hour to fuck. Or for me to taste you." By the gods, though, I wish we could.

She leans up to brush her lips against mine. "You're right. Time to focus."

I nod, leading her down the cavern again as I try my damnedest to calm down my raging erection. "Call your dragon," I growl as I shift myself in my pants. "Tell him to bring Sigurd. The barrier's close, and we'll need to cross it quickly when I open it. I'm ready to get there and get you into our tent."

Sifa's silent for a moment, then turns to nod at me. "They'll be here soon." Her brow furls as she watches me. "But how? It's not like he can take Sigurd's harness."

"They're trained for this too. Astarot will herd him here. The horses all know to follow those kinds of signals from dragons."

She looks as if she has more questions, but before she can ask, we turn a corner, bringing us face-to-face with the barrier and the power concentrated in and around it. The air in the cavern is charged, crackling and popping in a way that emits no sound, every bit of the energy consumed by this wall in front of us. It's invisible, but for anyone with a hint of magic in their veins, it's impossible to miss.

Sifa's trembling—not from fear, I know as I sense the edge of her emotions, but from restraint. The barrier pulls magic from the air, and it wants our magic too. She's strong enough to withstand its grasp but the initial fight against it can be unsettling. It's why I didn't warn her what to expect. The anticipation would have done more harm than good in her first battle to resist the spells weaved in this place.

She sucks in a deep breath, exhaling slowly before taking another. Finally, she turns to me, curiosity in her eyes and on her lips. "I've never felt magic like this before. How can it exist?"

"That's a question for another day. Let's just get through it." I lift one of her hands to rest it on the barrier in front of her and hold the other. "You're going to give me strength if I need it," I tell her as I let my power fill my veins and vibrate through our connected palms. "The barrier has changed a bit since I came here last. Harald tried to reinforce it, I can tell. But it still should bow to me. Especially with your help."

"Just tell me what to do." Her back is straight, and I can feel a hint of nervousness wafting off her, but it pales next to her resolve.

"Don't resist me," I respond as I lean forward to kiss her forehead. "I'll take from you if I need it."

Turning, I place my free hand on the barrier and open myself to its power. When the song flows into my thoughts, I concentrate on it for a moment, feeling it thrum within my veins. It's an ancient melody, harsh and demanding, as it must be to bring this magic to heel. It builds within me, coursing through every part of me from the tips of my fingers to the ends of my toes.

And then I start to sing, the voice of my savage leaking through to edge every syllable and note. I need him for this because he brings the full scope of my magic with him, and I can't do this alone. Through the haze that fills my mind, I can feel Sifa's surprise as she senses my savage's presence but I let it go. She'll get to know him well enough in the weeks ahead. I can't introduce them now. She's not ready for that. He's not ready for that either. He'll destroy my little rabbit in his need to possess her if I don't control him.

Instead, I focus on this boundary between us and the North. My savage and I wield our magic, carried through the cacophonous tune like a knife. We thrust into the wall in front of us, finding its weaknesses, twisting the blade to exploit them, dragging it down to rip them open. Bit by bit, minute by minute, we bend it to our will, forcing it to open for us. Within a few minutes, I'm on the verge of hyperventilating, struggling to manipulate all that I must to hold open the places that have succumbed to my will and wrench open others.

When Sifa squeezes my hand, my power responds almost of its own accord. Reaching through our palms, it sucks in her magic like water in a parched desert. At once, I feel like I can breathe again, the spell weaved by my words gathering new vigor. As if it had been waiting for that, it heaves open the rest of the barrier, creating a passage large enough for Astarot to fit through.

"Now," I spit out between clenched teeth. "Hurry."

Astarot nips at Sigurd's ass, drawing a sharp nicker, but the horse does what his training demands. When they're safely on the other side, I pull at Sifa's hand and trudge after them, my will spilling out around us to keep the barrier at bay. Sucking in one more deep breath, I let go of the magic holding the barrier open, letting it slam shut.

And then I fall to my knees, my hands and forehead dropping to the ground as a gaping hole rips open inside me. My jaw clenches and my gut fills that empty space with a rock that threatens to consume me. I scrabble for a breath, my chest constricting as I sense Sifa drop to her knees in front of me, her hand lifting the hair from my forehead as she searches my eyes.

"She's gone," I croak, still struggling to understand the chasm inside of me. "Tindera's completely out of my reach. I feel like my heart just got ripped out."

CHAPTER FIVE

SIFA

STAY

I T TAKES FHORD NEARLY an hour to recover from the strain of opening the barrier and then losing his connection with his dragon.

Somehow, I feel it too, as if Fhord's nerves and senses have leached into me, filling my gut and mind with the emptiness that's consumed him. He can't talk. He can barely think. He is an endless gorge, nothing to stop his fall into the abyss of life without Tindera.

Astarot also grieves her loss, but it's different for him. Dragons who've never been able to consummate their bond have a more distant relationship than dragon and rider, he explains to me. Tindera disappeared from his awareness—an emptiness that feels like she died—but it won't eat at him the way it will Fhord.

He thinks Fhord won't have much time. A month or two, at best, before the loss carves away too much of his soul.

"He's wrong, Sifa." Fhord's voice is strained even as he's trying to sound strong, self-assured, after I voice Astarot's fears to him. He grunts as he drags himself from the ground, ready to start heading into Harald's territory.

"I can see how it's affecting you." I reach out to stroke his cheek, drawing his gaze to mine. "He's not wrong."

He watches me in silence for longer than I'd expected, the shadows draining all color from his face. "It's tough having no connection to Tindera," he says at last. "I've never felt such emptiness. Like half my soul is missing. I'm not sure how to deal with it."

"You haven't been separated like this before?"

His gaze drops to the floor, silence eating up the space between us. My stomach turns into a wasteland, a cavernous space that hasn't been satisfied in days, maybe weeks. I wait, my hands clenched to my sides, as I force myself to let him work through this in his own time. When he speaks, his voice is low, a whisper in a windstorm.

"In Vanatia, even if I can't communicate with her or feel her emotions, I can sense her presence. The barrier is the only thing that could cleave our link, and she always came with me when I journeyed to Harald." He pauses, his eyes looking back as if searching for her through the rock. "I've always known that riders are gutted when their dragons die, husks of the beings they once were, even before their bond. I never fully understood the chasm that opens within them. Now I do."

"I wonder if it would be like that with me and Astarot," I muse, glancing toward Astarot.

"You and Astarot are more tightly bound than you realize." His gaze follows mine. "I knew it when our powers linked. Your connection feels like one that formed years ago, not days."

"I've wondered about that. Whether our bond will differ because the fates chose us, not the Dróttning. I don't know what to compare it to, but it's hard to imagine being closer to him than I already am."

"You'll grow together with time, but it'll be more gradual than the sudden rush you both felt when the bond solidified. Tindera and I experienced the same thing, since we're destined to be together too. For others—those that have to develop an artificial bond—it can sometimes take years."

That feels right. I'm already so tightly bound to Astarot, it seems impossible for it to become more than it is now. "Will my bond be stronger in the end? Is yours with Tindera?"

"Ours is, and yours should be too. But that may be because our dragons are so powerful." Pride sneaks into his voice as his lips tip up. "We ride two of the most majestic beasts in all of Vanatia."

"We'll be back to Vanatia soon. Let's get to Harald and get this over with." I wrap my arms around him, let him feel some connection, even if it's not the one he wants.

"We will," he agrees as he folds himself into me, leaning forward to breathe in my scent. "And this is our best option," he adds, his words firmer. "If we're going to beat the Dróttning, it will be with Harald's help."

Fhord inhales again, then exhales slowly as he straightens. Giving me a quick smile of reassurance, he turns to the packs, checking the ties before we start traveling.

I don't feel reassured, though. The knowledge that Fhord's hiding something from me—some truth that he's desperate to keep to himself—fills me again. I don't know what it is, but I know it will piss me off. And may do more harm to this thing between us than he realizes.

I reach for him one more time, pulling his gaze back to mine. "You need to tell me if it gets to be too much. Promise."

Again, he's silent for longer than I'd hoped, just watching me. Finally, his chin dips. "I promise, rabbit," he says with a smile.

"I don't think you have anything to worry about," a strange voice interjects.

Fhord and I both spin to watch an even stranger man turn a nearby corner, a dozen guards flanking him. I throw back my shoulders and stand as tall as I can, placing my hands on the knives at my belt. My heart flutters in my chest before settling into a steady sprint, ready to propel me away from this unexpected threat. Astarot grumbles behind me, and I feel the heat of his ire as a flame dances in our direction. I glance at Fhord for a moment, shocked to see his casual stance, before turning back to the male.

He's tall and thin, as if the gods had a limited supply when they created him and chose to sacrifice girth to give him height. Although he looks to be Fhord's age, his deep brown eyes reveal a soul who's walked this world for centuries, if not millennia. With curly red hair and strong features, he's handsome in a haughty way, but his garish clothing conveys an irreverence that makes him appear almost clownlike. His lips, though, are firm, his features set. He's accustomed to wielding power.

"You'll have as many moments with her as you want when you return to your land," he continues in an arrogant, condescending tone. "At least until the Dróttning finds you. I'm sure she knows already that you came to me for ... something traitorous, I suspect, if the chatter I've been hearing is true. I won't take part in whatever you've planned." He pauses, his gaze finding mine. "A grave awaits you, little elf," he adds with a smile.

Now, flame ripples down my spine, a drumbeat launching in my ears as blood pounds through me. I've barely met this male, and I despise him already. Harald's not going to help us. We'll be lucky if he doesn't kill us.

I turn toward Fhord, his wide eyes focused on Harald. They narrow into angry slits as he sneers at the monarch we thought we'd need to hunt down. "Harald," he murmurs in a low tone. "I didn't expect to cross your path so soon."

"Do you think I would leave this breach unspelled? After what you did last time?" Harald sneers, wearing his hatred for Fhord in the hard lines of his face and stiff shoulders. "My magic now calls to me when anyone disturbs this barrier."

Well, we are truly fucked. The Dróttning will be waiting for us on the other side, Fhord's magic having drawn her there as he said it would. I turn toward Fhord, hoping to find some semblance of confidence in him, but there's none. He's as frustrated as me.

"I've already explained why I left the … mess … I did when I last came to your realm."

Harald's responding smile holds only malice. "And I explained that I didn't accept your excuse." He flings an arm toward Fhord, palm up, sighing deeply. "Not another word. We will not discuss that debacle. Why are you here?"

My heart beats a dozen times before Fhord answers. His voice is softer, the peremptory tone he uses with others gone. "I had hoped to discuss this in your kastali, to have the time to prove to you I speak true. But I can see this will have to do." He takes a step toward Harald, his hands lifting in the most placating gesture I've ever seen from him. "I'm ready to stand against the Dróttning. I'm here to enlist your aid in defeating our common enemy."

Harald barks out a laugh. He watches Fhord, a huge grin splitting his cheeks, as he would a grifter preparing to flip the final card and win his wallet. After a moment, the smile leaves his eyes, becoming more sinister. "You expect me to believe that?"

"I realize it isn't what you might expect. I have much to tell you. Take us to your kastali and let me explain."

"Let one of the largest beasts from the south traipse through my land, along with two of the Dróttning's most powerful vassals? You must think me a fool."

"I know you're no fool. I also know you despise the Dróttning and have spent most of your reign searching for a way to defeat her. I can give you that if you'll help me."

"And why would you turn on the Dróttning?"

"She's ruled Vanatia too long. Our land aches."

"A coup?" Harald proclaims with a single clap of his hands. "You'd like my help stealing the throne? That's beneath you, Fhord."

"I don't want the throne, and I don't give a fuck who rules after she's gone, as long as it's not one of her peons. The rebellion who pushes her out will choose a leader; there are many worthy among them. Things must change in Vanatia. I intend to help bring that change."

"How many times have you come begging on her behalf for my aid? How many ways have you shown me you belong to her?" Harald pauses, his voice dropping dangerously low. "How many of my people have you killed in her name?"

"I'm not the male I once was." Fhord's voice is firm, confident.

"What changed? You will not come to my kastali, so convince me now if you can. You haven't much time before I force the three of you back to your own lands."

"Do you know she uses our dragons to control us?"

"I know nothing of your dragons. Lest you forget, I've no such control over mine." Harald's voice is bitter, angry.

"You've never let me forget it."

"So why should I care how the Dróttning uses your beasts?"

"You asked me what changed, Harald. I'm trying to tell you." Fhord's frustration leaks into his words and Harald's back stiffens.

"Watch your tone, Fhord. You are in my lands, and I've executed people for less."

Fhord inhales deeply, his hands flexing as he watches the northern monarch. When he continues, he's taken back control of his emotions. "Tindera and I bonded more than a century ago, but it wasn't until the last two decades that I fully understood—and started to abhor—the Dróttning's control over our beasts."

"Tick tock, Fhord."

"Please, Harald. Listen."

"You have two minutes."

"Twenty-some years ago, I angered the Dróttning. She thought I should have punished a dragon and rider more harshly for a mistake. The penalty she demanded of them was far more severe than they deserved. For me, though, she reserved the truly cruel sanction. For sixty days, Tindera suffered the discipline imposed on a dragon who refuses the rider chosen for it. The Dróttning tortured her for two months because I was not cruel enough to another dragon and rider."

"This does not surprise me. You've committed such acts on her behalf."

"Never have I punished someone who didn't deserve it." I can see Fhord struggle to control his anger at Harald's accusation. After a moment, he puffs out a breath and catches Harald's gaze again. "But that doesn't matter. The fact remains that for too long, I ignored her evil. Perhaps experiencing undeserved torture through my dragon opened eyes that should have opened years ago. Perhaps I was a cruel man and have mellowed as I've aged. I have no excuse for whatever horrors I committed on her behalf. I can only change today and tomorrow."

Harald watches Fhord, his expression inscrutable. "Go on," he says at last.

Fhord's head spins, and he holds my gaze for a moment before looking back at Harald. "Sifa entered this world a decade ago. I didn't see her at the time, had no idea what she'd come to mean to me. I only knew that some ... being ... appeared in Vanatia, and the Dróttning imprisoned and tortured her until she managed to escape. I learned later that Sifa was this being. She and I are connected in a way neither of us expected."

Harald's eyes track to mine, searching. When he finds his answer, his lips tip up in a satisfied grin. "You're mates."

"No, of course not." My head spins as I look to Fhord to join me in rejecting the ridiculous idea. "Right?"

Fhord's expression tells me everything. His nostrils are flaring when I turn to him, flinty emerald eyes focused on Harald as his chest rises and falls slowly. A deep rage ripples from him, pricking my skin with its intensity. He's motionless for a few moments other than his surging ribs, as if he's waging a fierce battle inside. Then he takes a deep breath, finally reining in his galloping emotions. He inhales again, holding it for a moment, then exhales as he spins his head to gaze at me.

Now, he wears an apology in his eyes and along his shoulders, which sag in a way I've never seen before. "One of the things I haven't yet told you," he grunts as he reaches for my hand.

"You didn't know?" Harald's laugh splits the air. "How many things are you keeping from this elf, Fhord?"

"We're mates? And I'm hearing it from him?" My words come out in a hiss as I gesture somewhat wildly at Harald. Yanking my fingers from Fhord's, I take a step away from him, struggling to understand this new bit of information Harald dropped on me.

"I have so much to tell you, rabbit."

My thoughts scramble to make sense of this revelation as I stare at Fhord. I realized before I even saw his face that Fhord and I were connected. Memories vie for my focus, offering themselves to me as pieces of the puzzle to fit into place. The conflicting emotions that overwhelmed me when he dropped into my life, a repulsion paired with the most intense craving I've experienced in my long life. My fascination with his savage beauty, every sharp line in his face and his eternal eyes. The desire, the need, I've felt for him, unlike anything I've ever experienced before. The feel of his lips on mine, his hands exploring me.

The knowledge that he is part of me already, and I am whole only with him in my life.

The certainty that Fhord is my mate rolls over me, a wave coating me in its truth. I have little experience with mating bonds. I've seen them in Midgard, but never here because virtually no elves walk free in Vanatia. But I know they exist here—Joralf and his mate found each other—so I shouldn't be surprised.

And it feels right.

I'm pissed about it, though.

Fhord steps forward, reaching again for my hand. I let him keep it this time, watching through narrowed eyes as he draws it to his lips and kisses my palm. "I'm sorry you didn't learn this from me."

"I should have." I'm relieved when my voice doesn't crack and no tears form in my eyes.

Fhord reaches out a hand to my cheek. "It's one of the things I didn't want to tell you but promised I would."

"What else are you keeping from me? What other secrets were you planning to share? Or not?"

Fhord's face falls, his lips tugging down as his eyes search mine. "There is another, rabbit. And it will anger you even more."

I watch him for a long time, pulling my hand away again as I struggle to decipher my emotions. But I can't. I'm numb and I just need to get through this. "Tell me," I say at last.

"The Dróttning knows I helped you escape," Fhord responds in a flat tone. "She's taken Tindera to punish me, lure me back to the Nest. My plan was to leave you here with Harald and return without you to free Tindera."

Astarot's head swings toward us, fire hovering between his bared teeth.

"Control your dragon," Harald spits out, backing away in long strides.

"Astarot, please," I breathe, my gaze never leaving Fhord. "Let us work this out."

Together. My dragon's thoughts are scattered, but I understand his demand.

"Tindera's his mate. Astarot won't let you go alone. We're going with you."

"You can't, Sifa. Especially not now. The Dróttning and her people could be waiting on the other side of the barrier. We'll be captured and you'll be killed." His hands grasp my cheeks as his eyes plead with mine. "You can feel this truth, deep in your bones. Whatever information she's trying to get from you, it's not important enough for her to make the same mistake. She won't just imprison you. She'll kill you this time, give Astarot to a cruel rider."

Now his gaze shifts toward Astarot, dark green eyes focused on my dragon. "Tell her," he urges. "You've suffered the Dróttning's wrath. Nobody knows better than you what she'll do. Your rider will not survive another capture. And my chances of freeing Tindera are better if I go alone." He pauses, his voice growing harsh. "You recognize the truth in my words," he grates. "Much as you want to go with me, you know as well as I do it's better for me to go alone."

I can't stop the tears that erupt in my eyes because he's right. If Harald sends us back now, he signs our death warrant. "How can you be so sure she won't kill you?"

"She and I are close. You saw it in her rooms. I know the Nest better than anyone. I won't get caught but if I do, she won't do more than punish me. Tindera and I will suffer, but she won't take my life. I swear it."

"I have the solution," Harald chimes in at the worst time, his voice too fucking cheery.

Fhord turns to Harald as he renews his plea. "Let us stay here until we can return through another exit. Help us defeat the Dróttning."

"You can't stay here, Fhord. Your pretty words haven't convinced me. I know what you're capable of, how much power you wield. I don't trust you."

"What do you propose?" Fhord's voice is tired, resigned.

"I need something from each of you. If you give me what I ask, I'll give you what you ask."

"What do you need, Harald?"

"From you, I've asked many times how the Dróttning controls the dragons. Always, you've told me you don't know. I want that information."

"I spoke the truth. She keeps that knowledge even from me. If I knew, I would have challenged her long ago."

"Then find out." Harald stalks forward, bringing himself nearly nose-to-nose with Fhord. "We will be unable to defeat her while she controls those beasts. You can't deny this."

"I've searched for years for an answer to this question. I'm no closer now than I was when I began."

I place my hand on Fhord's cheek and draw his gaze to mine. "I think Joralf knows." At the question in Fhord's eyes,

I remind him, "The elf we helped escape from prison, Jo-ralf. He has a theory. He didn't want to tell me while we were there, but maybe he can help. We could go to him."

"You won't be leaving, elf." Now Harald's spinning toward me, reaching out to lift my chin. I step back, raising my hand to push his away.

"I'm going with Fhord. He'll need me when he faces the Dróttning."

"Then you won't have my help." Harald pivots and strides back toward his soldiers. "I tire of this conversation. Go. Don't return."

Fhord reaches out to me, capturing my gaze. "What do you want of Sifa?" he asks as his eyes search mine, a silent plea. After a moment, he looks at Harald, who's paused with his back to us.

Turning, Harald watches us as another stupid grin emerges on his face. "Sifa and the dragon will stay. They'll help me tame one of my beasts."

"Impossible." Fhord's tone is scathing, full of scorn. "Your beasts can't be tamed."

"Anything is possible. I've been thinking for many years that I should enlist the aid of one of your bonded pairs. Your dragon may help convince one of mine that I can be trusted."

"Surely you've tried this before?" Now, his words are layered with skepticism.

"How would I have? The Dróttning controls all the tame dragons in these lands."

72 ROCHELLE L. WILCOX

Tame? Astarot is displeased with Harald's word choice, but I wave an arm at him behind my back.

"Have you never asked her?"

"I tried once. She laughed at me. The Dróttning has no interest in helping me gain the support of dragons who might fight against her beasts in any conflict between us. And there always will be another conflict while she and I both live."

Fhord's quiet for a moment, his eyes never leaving Harald. "Do you have any reason to believe she would succeed?"

"They are the same beasts," Harald explains, his hands planting themselves on his hips. "Your dragons can communicate with each other. They should be able to talk to mine. It could work."

I take Fhord's arm, pulling his attention back to me. "I'm going with you, Fhord. We'll free Tindera together."

"You're not coming to Vanatia with me. I will not see you killed." His tone is hard, unyielding.

"I'm not a child to be ordered about." I point at Astarot. "Besides, he won't let you go without him."

Stay. Astarot's word drops into my mind, and I spin, gods-damned tears spilling into my eyes again.

"What?" I demand.

Stay. His tone is soft, but he's just as resolved as Fhord. He agrees with Fhord that the Dróttning will kill me if we return. And that Fhord's chances of helping Tindera escape will be better if he goes without me.

"Traitor," I mumble, my eyes narrowing at him.

"He knows I'm right." Fhord lays his arm across my shoulders, shifting me toward him. "We need to consider this." I let him lift my chin, hoping he can see exactly how much I hate this. "Even if we don't like it."

"You seem pretty happy about Harald's suggestion," I remind him, digging my hand into his shirt.

"I fucking hate the idea of ever leaving your side." Fhord's eyes burn as he tugs me even closer. "I despise the fact that I'm considering abandoning you with a male I can't trust. But even this terrible choice is better than taking you back to Vanatia and the Dróttning's waiting soldiers. If we do this, I will count the minutes until you're in my arms again." Leaning forward, he purrs in my ear, "Until you are wrapped around my cock, fucking me dry, soothing the savage that only rests when I'm inside you."

My core flares because this male can turn me on even in the absolute worst moments. I push back from him, holding on to my anger a little longer, even if I realize he's already won. He and Astarot, the traitor.

"Being away from you for a week or two is the price I'll pay to save your fucking life," he adds. "Because your death would destroy me. And it would destroy your dragon." He leans forward to rest his forehead on mine, his thumbs reaching up to caress my cheeks. "Stay here. Tame a dragon. But just remember. You're fucking dangerous. If anyone can do this, you can."

"We're decided, then?" Harald's words yank us back to the cave and the dozens of soldiers watching us.

"What if she can't do it?"

"Then she can't do it." Harald shrugs. "I won't punish her for failure. I just won't help you unless you both give me what I need. That's my price."

Harald's shields are ridiculously strong, but I still *feel* duplicity in his words, a blanket covering the truth he's hiding from Fhord. He's not lying. I don't think this snake will strike me. He's not going to make it easy for me, though, and he's convinced I won't succeed.

He doesn't know shit about me, and what I'm capable of.

"And if we both do what you ask?" Fhord demands. "You'll join us in defeating the Dróttning?"

"If you both succeed—you tell me how she wields such control over her dragons," his nose pointing at Fhord, "and you gain the trust of at least one dragon in my lands," turning to me, "then my armies will support your little coup."

Fhord nods, turning back to me.

My stomach twists into a knot but Fhord's right. We need to do this. My chin dips.

I fucking hate this too.

SIFA

A FAIR FIGHT

WE DECIDED—WELL, *THEY* DECIDED—THAT I would hide far back in the cavern. If the Dróttning is waiting on the other side, Fhord's chances of talking his way out of permanent imprisonment will be better if I'm not there. I agreed, reluctantly, because we need every advantage we can get.

Fhord and I tried to convince Harald to take us to another opening between the North and South, but he refused to let Fhord into his land.

"I trust you as far as I can throw you," he'd explained.

He also was convinced Fhord would act more quickly if he faced the Dróttning now, and he wants Fhord to be quick. He has a job for me and Astarot, but he doesn't trust us much more than Fhord. Harald doesn't want us in his lands longer than necessary.

His insistence that Fhord return directly to the Dróttning reassures me in a way I hadn't expected. I believe he wants

Fhord's help and wouldn't sacrifice this chance to seek his revenge against the Dróttning. I find comfort in the fact he and Fhord both are convinced Fhord will survive the Dróttning's wrath. Even if I'm terrified about what she'll do to him. What she's already doing to Tindera.

I'm also dreading the weeks I'll be separated from Fhord. Now that I understand our connection, I can see how my emotions have been tied to his since the beginning. He landed in my world with a bang and changed everything, becoming part of me before I realized it. I need him in a way I've never needed anyone. His separation from Tindera gives me a little taste of what I'll experience when we're on opposite sides of the barrier.

"Give us a minute," Fhord mutters as the monarch gestures at Fhord to follow him toward the barrier.

"I'll wait, but you won't speak with her alone." Harald gives Fhord a lazy smile, his eyes narrowing as he watches us. "I'd be a fool to give you a chance to plot against me."

Fhord glares at Harald. "Fucking asshole," he breathes, before he turns back to me. And my heart launches into my throat.

"Don't you dare get yourself killed," I murmur, trying desperately to keep tears from forming in my eyes. "We're just getting started with this thing between us."

"This thing?" Fhord echoes with a smile. He lifts his hands to my cheeks, resting them there as his gaze holds mine, while I splay my palms across his firm chest. "This mating bond, rabbit," he rumbles into my ear. "This everlasting connection

I have to you. This indestructible love I hold for you. This unbearable need I feel for you." His lips find mine, his tongue plunging into my mouth as I let myself fall into the kiss I will always crave.

But then he breaks away abruptly, as if he's forcing himself to stop. Fhord's gaze darts to Harald and back to me, his green eyes sparkling in the dim light. "Do what Harald needs, but be careful. I don't trust him. He'll do his damnedest to trick you. He'll use you and then try to toss you aside. You're smarter than him, though. You're better than him in every gods-damned way. And you're so fucking dangerous."

Digging my hands into his shirt, I draw him closer as I kiss him one more time. "And you," I declare, "will do whatever you must in Vanatia to come back to me. I *need* you, Fhord. You are the beat in my heart. It won't find a steady rhythm again until you're by my side."

"Sweet," Harald proclaims from behind me, "but boring. Let's go, Fhord. Tick-tock."

Fhord's eyes narrow as he lifts them to stare at Harald, then soften when he looks at me again. "Be safe, rabbit," he tells me before giving me one last kiss and releasing me. I can only watch in silence as he grasps Sigurd's reins and walks him down the cavern, back toward the bitch that would take him from me if she could.

I can feel Fhord and Harald working together to open the barrier. It yields under their combined magic, Fhord's power soothing my frantic soul as it wraps around me one final time. When they let go and the barrier snuffs out our connection, I'm breathless. My lungs feel as if they collapsed in on themselves, dropping into the space left in my gut the second my bond with Fhord disappears. I can feel Astarot next to me—Harald's soldiers clustered behind him—but even my dragon can't fill the gaping hole in my soul.

My mating bond, I remind myself as I lift my eyes and look at my beast and the soldiers clustered behind him, weapons in their hands. I still can't believe I heard it from Harald instead of Fhord. He'll pay for that and so much more if he makes it back to me.

When. When he makes it back to me.

Harald's smirking when he returns, his gaze finding mine. "She hadn't quite made it to the barrier yet, but she was close. Fhord might be able to stay ahead of her if his horse is as fast as he looks."

My gut twists so hard I feel like I've been stabbed. "How will we know?"

"We won't," he responds with a shrug. "All the more reason for you to be quick about this." He pauses, watching me as if pondering whether to speak again. "The Dróttning will be able to track him," he adds after a moment. "She's always had a strong connection to her son. And him to her."

My breath catches in my throat, eyes spinning toward the cavern leading to the barrier. And then my chest caves in on itself as the world shifts on its axis.

"Her son?" I demand, my voice barely a whisper.

"You didn't know?" Harald exclaims as he claps his hands once, his voice taunting and much too happy.

I sneer as my gaze spins toward him for a moment, my words erupting before I can stop them. "Be quiet. I don't need you cackling at me right now."

His grin only grows wider, the ass.

I'm not surprised, I realize, as my mind pulls up image after image of Fhord and the Dróttning. Gods, it makes so much sense. They knew each other well and I believed Fhord when he assured me they weren't lovers. Why else would the Dróttning offer me to him as some kind of prize or reward?

I saw the truth in Harald's expression when he told me. And in the Dróttning's interactions with Fhord in her chambers when she bestowed me on him like a birthday gift. And in Fhord's fear when he first looked at me in the Dróttning's rooms. I'd believed then that he feared her finding out about us. And maybe he did. But I think he was even more afraid I'd find out what they are to each other.

Of course he's her son.

I'm gonna kill Fhord when I see him.

What else hasn't he told me?

Sucking in a deep breath, my gaze lifts to Harald's. "Why is it secret? Vanatians believe the Dróttning has no children."

"Fhord has many secrets," Harald responds, pleased with himself. "I'm sure there are others. Your mate trusts few people." His smile ticks up, a crafty look sparking in his eyes. "Perhaps you are not yet one of them."

I stare at him for a long moment, struggling to hold my tongue. But then I realize there's no reason. He wants something from Astarot and me. Nothing I say will change how he treats us. "I'm not going to like you very much, am I?"

"Rulers are not liked," he declares grandly. "We are revered. Feared. Followed. That's all I care to receive from you."

"Well, you'll get none of that from me. I'll do my part, and you do yours. Nothing more."

Harald winks, waving an arm toward the cave's entrance as he strides toward a large red stallion and mounts. "Lead the way. You and your beast will walk in front of us. I don't want either of you at my back in this cave."

I nod and stalk toward the hint of sun I see ahead of us. I'm ready to get some fresh air and try to calm the anger simmering within me at the asshole who rules this land.

When we emerge, the sun is dropping in the sky to our side, an hour or two away from setting. It gives me time to appreciate the differences between this land and Vanatia. They're barely noticeable at first, the climate and environment being nearly identical on both sides of the barrier. Like in the South, though, I recognize the more subtle changes that seem to flow from the disparate magic wielded by the lands' leaders.

It's a beautiful land, wild like the northern part of Vanatia but somehow more untamed. I wonder if it's just the chaos that comes with feral dragons, or if the magic itself lacks the restraint the Dróttning demands in the South. Probably the former, I realize, as I cast my mind out, searching for other heartbeats that should surround us. I'm shocked when I can find nothing but the rapid pitter-patters of the few soaring above us.

"Where are all the animals?" I ask Harald when I can't find anything beyond our group. "I can hear and sense some birds passing overhead but nothing else. Not even any rabbits. Definitely not any bigger creatures."

Harald watches me for a long minute, I suspect wondering whether he'll speak with me at all. Finally, his words emerge in a condescending tone, as if he's speaking to a child. "The barrier repels the living. All along its edge, the lands for at least a viku north of the barrier are devoid of creatures, large and small."

"Why aren't I repelled?"

He smirks, his lips twisting. "You are magic, elf. The barrier calls to you. As it does to me"

"And the dragons? How far away are they?"

Harald purses his lips, his eyes dancing. "A dozen vikus to the west, perhaps more, you'll find the lairs of two dragons. They typically stay several vikus apart from each other, and you'll find them by searching for the emptiness that you've recognized here. Every other animal stays away. Even my own people avoid those places because dragons are rabid creatures."

"Do you mean literally rabid? As in, diseased and uncontrolled?"

He sneers at me as if he's bothered by my questions. Again, though, he relents. "More figurative than literal, but there is a literal aspect to it. The dragons here are wild. My attempts to domesticate them have led to many deaths and no success. I gave up long ago."

"Why? What's the difference between these dragons and those in the South?"

"If I knew that," Harald replies with a bitter smile, "I'd have taken charge of the beasts. Getting me that knowledge is Fhord's task." He turns to the north, tossing, "Follow me," behind his back as he strides forward.

We don't travel far. Within an hour, Harald leads us to a small opening in the forest, a creek running along one side. It's already deep with shadows, the trees, grass, and rocks along the slope of a nearby mountain all melding into a dark gray as the colors they wear during the day fade away. In the field, shifting shades of shamrock and juniper greet us, the dapples of flowers—reds and yellows and purples—dancing in a light breeze. I catch whiffs of their fragrance, hints of lilac and freesia tickling my nose.

Trees hide most of it from any eyes that might soar overhead. We're alone and it feels safe.

"How far away is your kastali?"

"You're not going to my kastali. Whatever made you think you might be?"

"Where are we going, then?"

"*We* aren't going anywhere. This field sits at the edge of the shadow of the closest mountain with a resident dragon. You will leave us here. If you succeed, the dragon will tell you how to find my kastali. They all know to stay far away from it."

"You're just going to leave me alone? I don't know a thing about your lands."

Bastard laughs, his eyes lighting up as he glances at one of his guards, who quickly plasters a grin on his own face, forcing out a short *guffaw*. Harald's hand lifts lazily as he points at my dragon. "You are not alone."

"You know what I mean. How can I get close to a dragon if I don't have someone who knows this land to help?"

Harald's eyes roll up in an exaggerated show of frustration. "Females. Always asking for more." When his gaze drops, he glares at me, all joking gone now. "I did not offer to help you, or to expose one of my people to a dragon's wrath. You are in these lands at my pleasure. My pleasure is to let you and your dragon get to your task. Alone. I will see you at my kastali if you survive."

"You told Fhord I'd be safe." And Fhord believed him, the bastard. A knot forms in my chest as I realize Fhord has again abandoned me to the whimsy of an evil ruler, long hours on the Dróttning's rack filling my thoughts as I wonder what Harald will do to me. Fhord knows Harald. He should have realized this might happen.

"I told Fhord I wouldn't punish you if you fail. And I won't. But I never said I would help you. I already have sacrificed too many people in this quest. When you agreed to pursue a dragon for me, you offered your life." He smiles, his expression devoid of any humor. "Because my dragons are rabid, as I told you."

"Are you at least going to leave me with supplies? Food? A tent?"

Harald watches me, the corners of his lips ticking up in that shit-eating smirk I've already grown to loathe. "Tell you what," he responds after a moment. "You can fight for them."

"What?" Pompous ass. He almost makes the Dróttning's rule a little more tolerable. Almost.

"Our elves here are too genteel, too civilized, to perform for me. Entitled little prigs, that's what they are. I'd like to see what you can do."

My rising anger stalls for a moment as his words sink in. "You have elves here? In positions of power?"

"I am not so insecure as the Dróttning. My people—elves and humans alike—bow to me because I am powerful." Now he's threatening, his nostrils flaring as his jaw flexes. He wants me to fear him.

"Will I meet any?"

"If you make it to my kastali astride a dragon other than this massive beast"—with a dismissive wave at Astarot—"you may dine with any elves in attendance." His lips quirk up again before he adds with a haughty laugh, "I may even let you speak with a few."

My head cocks to the side as I watch him, measuring his intent. "You want to see what I'm capable of," I posit after a moment.

His expression shifts immediately to one of boredom, a shrug lifting his shoulders as he raises his hands, palms facing the sky. "Of course I do." He cocks his eyebrow. "I'd be an idiot to let an unknown power roam my lands. I want to see what you can do."

"One fight—against a fighter of my choosing—and you give me everything I need for a week in your lands. I'll forage beyond that for food if I must."

"You truly do think me a fool." Harald's voice is angry now, his ever-shifting moods one of the confounding pieces of this mercurial monarch.

"It's you who thinks me a fool." I gesture at myself—all five-and-a-half feet and 130 pounds of me—and then at the dozens of guards watching us, each on high alert, hands on their swords as their eyes drill into me. "You want to stop me before I can even start, pitting me against your best fighters." I've always relied on being underestimated. Maybe Harald will make the same mistake.

"What I think, little elf, is that you are much more dangerous than you'd have me believe."

Guess Harald's more perceptive than I'd hoped.

"I don't think you know enough about me to believe anything."

Harald's laugh barks out into the air around us, his soldiers all—every single one—twisting their lips in fake smiles, apparently conditioned to this response. "Exactly! Which is why you must fight those I choose. We will see what you can do."

I'm silent for a long time, measuring my options. I really shouldn't expose myself to this risk. I have no idea what his people are capable of. But I know what I can do. There aren't many fighters who can best me. And I desperately need the supplies he's dangling in front of my face. Which he knows.

"What do you propose?"

"Five fights. The prizes will be food, a tent, bed supplies, a map that shows the locations of herds for your dragon, and another that gives you the nests of the three closest beasts. In that order. I choose my warriors."

Devious bastard. "Do you expect me to face your warriors in succession? Growing more tired with each fight, while they are fresh?"

"Of course. How else can we learn your strengths?"

"No. That won't do. I'll fight three of your warriors. No more. The prizes will be enough food for a week, a tent and all the supplies I need, and a map that shows both herds and nests. And the order will be different. I want the map, then food, and last, the tent and supplies."

"I choose the warriors?"

"Yes, but you'll identify them and the order I'll face them before the fights begin. I want to see who you think can defeat me."

"Done."

Well, that was too fucking quick. He got what he wanted out of me. "Our use of magic is unrestrained. We can fight with every tool we possess."

He pauses, watching me. "Of course," he declares. "How else can I see what you are capable of?" His chin lifts as he looks at my dragon. "But we'll restrain that one. We can't have him eating any of my people."

"Astarot doesn't care for the taste of our flesh." I glance at my dragon then back at Harald. "Too bland, apparently. But okay. He won't eat anyone. Otherwise, we're free to fight in any way we can."

"Done." Harald giggles—actually fucking giggles—and claps his hands, a child peering into a circus ring for the first time. "This will be so fun," he proclaims, pointing at two of his soldiers. "You, organize the others to set up a ring and seating. Those who don't fight will watch." His eyes narrow when his gaze finds mine. "We all should see what this elf can do."

"We'll fight tomorrow," I add after a moment, wishing I'd thought of this before. "I'm tired. I want to rest." I'd also really love some time to dig into his soldiers' minds, understand what they're capable of, but I don't tell him that.

"No." Harald's tone is firm, unyielding. "I won't dally here any longer than I must. You fight tonight and then we leave you and your dragon to … pursue your quest." The last words emerge with a smile and a swing of his arms, as if he's a bard extolling an epic journey.

"Tonight, then. But choose your fighters now, as your soldiers set up."

Harald cocks his head, his eyebrows pulling together. "You're trying to change the terms," he muses. He lifts a hand to rub his thumb along his bottom lip, his eyes bright. "I'll indulge you," he agrees after a moment. Spinning, he points to three of the soldiers who flanked him in the cave: a huge male; a female about my size; and another male barely larger than me. "Njal for the map. Dani for the food. Isak for the supplies." He doesn't speak to them, but that doesn't surprise me. They're weapons to him. Nothing more.

His gaze lifts as someone positions a garish chair at the edge of the clearing, and he traipses over to plop down into it, extending his legs as his hands clasp each other behind his head. *By the gods, he's ridiculous.* I shake my head, dispelling all the questions I have about this odd male, and turn to the soldiers he's chosen. My mind reaches out, testing each in turn to figure out why he picked them. What they bring to the fight.

They're shielded, but I would have been shocked if they weren't. Only one shield—the large male I'll fight first—is powerful enough to fully withstand my probing thoughts. Easily twice my size and a foot taller than me, he looks impossibly strong. I think one of his thighs may be bigger than my waist. I let my gaze rest on him as I poke and test his defenses. Nothing. He's a brick wall, no part of his psyche visible. Harald chose him for his body and his mind.

Okay. I guess I'll learn more when we fight.

The female is surprisingly open to me. I realize she wants me to know on a visceral level what she can do as I see her smirk and open, unassuming posture. She's fucking dangerous. Her mind is feeding me image after image of her victims. That's the only way to describe them. She doesn't just prevail. She dominates. Destroys. Devours. If she wins, she'll kill me without a second thought. And if Harald allows it, it'll be a painful death.

She's hoping to capture my fear. Fuck that. I smirk back and turn toward the final soldier.

His shields are weak, which is strange because his mind is strong. He's a water wielder. I glance at the lake a hundred feet away and then back at him, watching the corners of his lips rise. He blows me a kiss, not trying to hide what he's capable of. And why would he? I'm not sure what I'll be able to do against him.

Well, shit. This'll be a long night. At least the water wielder is last. I'll be gods-damned cold after he drenches me, and I'm gonna want to plop my ass down next to the fire they're already building if I win.

Not if. *When.*

When I win.

Stretching, I stalk over to Astarot, rubbing his nose as I draw him into my dilemma. *I don't think I can beat all of them.*

Powerful, he responds. About them, the bastard. He sees their strengths too, but he's not worried.

Stronger, he adds as his tongue reaches out to touch my cheek in the slightest graze.

I may not be. Stretching to scratch behind his horn, I watch Harald's soldiers as they bounce around, warming up for the physical part of the fight. I should too, but my body seems to react better when I catch it by surprise, forcing it to perform on a moment's notice. And I need to talk to my dragon.

Stronger, he repeats. This time, though, his meaning is more nuanced. None of them have a dragon and mine is powerful, in mind and body. I'm stronger because of him.

He's right. Harald thinks he's given me an impossible task, but he's never really seen the power of a true dragon-rider bond.

It'll be tough.

But maybe I can actually win.

SIFA

STRANGE MAGIC

*F*UCK ME.

Njal, the first fighter Harald sicced on me, isn't wasting a second. As soon as we stepped into the half-assed ring Harald's people put together, he attacked. Didn't even waste time with a blade. Just refused to let go of the hand I'd extended to shake before the match and yanked me toward him.

Bastard.

But I'm quick too. Before he can grab my neck I've got control of his wrist, twisting it just the right way to put pressure on the nerves that hurt the most. He smiles through the pain, using his bulk—and he's got a lot of it—to pull us down to the ground, freeing himself as we drop. We both launch ourselves back to our feet, a little farther away this time, and I take a second to appreciate his speed. He moves fast for such a big guy.

And he's not letting up. As I set my feet again, he's digging in his heels to throw himself at me, wrapping his tree trunk arms around my waist and tossing me to the ground. He leans up for a punch, giving me the split second I need to knee his groin—the sturdiest limp dick I've ever kicked—and rip myself away when he clutches at the balls that must be throbbing right now.

Gah! Harald started with him for a reason. He's gonna wear me down early.

So it's time to stop fucking around. I cast out my thoughts one more time as I watch him from across the ring, searching for any hole that might have appeared while he focused on a physical fight. Nothing. Guess I'll find out what his magic can do when he's ready.

He's trying to straighten past the trauma to his dick, so I focus on it again, throwing myself into a flip that lands just right to kick up between his legs. This kick, though, doesn't land. He's ready for me, and I finally see his magic—skimming. He's one of the few who can disappear and reappear in a different location. Usually, the distance is limited, but it doesn't matter for him. We're trapped in this ring until one of us is unconscious.

Or dead.

Harald definitely started with him for a reason.

I watch him from across the field, where he landed when he skimmed, my hands reaching for my furthest knives during this pause in our fight. This trick costs him, I can see already. And he's protective of his balls. If I can focus on them, force him to skim a few more times, he'll be mine.

Dark eyes on me, he starts to pace along the edge of the ring, massive legs pounding the ground beneath him with each step. I do the same, matching his pace as my mind continues to test his, searching for any breach in the wall he's constructed to protect it. Even with the exertion from skimming, he's too strong, and before we've exchanged positions, I give up. When I beat him, it will be with my body, not my mind. I need to knock him out or kill him.

Njal disappears again and I lift my blades, ready to defend wherever he attacks. When I feel his presence at my back, I spin then duck as I barely avoid the fist aimed for my neck—a blow that could have temporarily paralyzed me, ending this fight before it's begun.

For the next few minutes, our battle is fully physical, me with my knives and him with fists and a single blade. We're spinning and slashing, equally matched despite his bulk. While he's got strength, I'm more agile, attacking from within. Twice, he lands blows, one nearly taking out teeth and leaving me with a mouth dripping blood. But I get him too. My knives have opened tracks along his chest, arms and cheek. His spittle is red as it lands on me, slimy and hot.

I'm huffing already, the exertion digging into my energy reserves. I focus again on his weakest spot, lunging for his balls when he overcorrects from a failed blow. He skims at the last moment, keeping me from doing any real damage, although when he appears a few yards away, I can see a purple ball hanging from his ripped pants, scarlet beads dripping to the ground below. His jaw is tight, teeth grinding as he works through the pain of my blade and exhaustion from his magic.

Eyes as dark as night watch me for a moment, measuring, before he skims one last time, landing directly behind me with a knife to my throat. In his fatigue, though, he's misjudged the distance. He's six inches farther than he should be. I can feel his body stiffen as he realizes his mistake and starts to shuffle forward.

He's too late. I hike up my leg and plunge it back toward him, my heavy boot connecting with his knee. His blade scratches my throat as he stumbles, but my arm lifts just in time to stop it from digging in. He's stumbling into a kneel, trying to prevent himself from toppling over, as I spin and reverse positions. But I don't leave the space between our bodies that he did.

My arm wraps around his neck, and I hold on for dear life. Because that's what this is. A battle for my life. He can't stand on his ruined knee, so he drops us both to the ground and starts to spin. I'm on my back, his dead weight directly on top of me, before I can stop us. I realize in an instant that we're going to lay there, my arm tight across his throat while he relies on weight alone, until one of us passes out. And I'm not sure who'll go first.

My right leg circles his waist as the other pushes, trying to shift some of his bulk away. But he's got his feet planted on either side of me, holding us in place, and he's too gods-damned heavy to move. All I can do is tighten my grip and hope he fades first. I'm struggling to breathe, inhaling shallow gasps as my lungs scream for more air. My arms tighten, desperate to end this, and he somehow manages to turn into an even heavier dead weight.

I feel his shield drop as a faint creeps up on him. The wall surrounding his psyche falters, little holes appearing and then growing bigger. Spearing in before I'm too weak to take advantage of it, I find an image of his wife, frantically erecting a memory of him crushing her. He startles, a tremble rumbling through him, and pushes away, relieving some of the pressure. I shove with him, forcing him onto his belly, my arm still firmly in place.

And then he's still. I'm sucking in air, trying to fully inflate my lungs again, when Harald's slow claps start from the other side of the ring. I lift my eyes to see him striding over, his face a cloud of dismay even as his hands continue their feigned tribute. When he reaches me, he gestures to Njal, passed out beneath me.

"Impressive, elf. You've won your maps." His voice is flat, disappointed.

He'd expected Njal to take me. I wonder if that means he has less faith in the other two. Probably not. With me fatigued already, they'll be even harder to beat.

Standing, I watch as four of Harald's males come to lift Njal and drag him away. He's still unconscious but he'll live. I'm glad I didn't have to kill him.

"Oh, this'll be fun," a bitchy voice spews at my side. I spin my head to stare at my next opponent, Dani. She's smirking, a shit-eating grin on her face, sky-blue eyes thin slits as she stalks forward. She's lithe like me, her motions smooth and graceful. Two swords hang from her waist and knives are sheathed along her belt and legs. Her hair is woven into an auburn braid that drops half-way down her back.

For some reason, Mikkael pops into my thoughts. She's exactly his type, physically, but I think he'd hate her. He's always been drawn to soft women, eager to find out for themselves if the rumors of his skill and substance are true—a question I've neither pondered nor had answered.

"End this, soldier, and I'll move your quarters to the north sector as you've been requesting." Harald throws a catty grin at me and turns to stride back to his throne.

Didn't think I could dislike that male any more, but he found a way.

The second Harald's ass touches the cushion of his chair, Dani is bombarding me with graphic images of her kills. Dozens of them, blood and gore and bones and tissue and organs filling my thoughts as she relives them. While she's thrown them at me all at once, somehow dumping her memories directly into mine, my brain decides to view them one-by-one.

"So much fun," she whispers, casting her voice at me just like she did her images. "I haven't killed a skilled elf for a long time. I think I'll take my time with you." She's cold and harsh and eager.

I'm not afraid, though. That's her goal, I realize as she hovers a few yards away, watching and waiting for the nausea or flinch or shiver she must extract from most of her opponents.

Instead, I smile, a slow grin emerging as I see the gift she's unintentionally handed over. I know more about her fighting style than I ever would learn from a bit of grappling on this field.

I see her resolve settle when she realizes she won't beat me with pretty pictures. As her hands reach for her swords, I fling one of my knives, the hilt catching a wrist before it can pull the blade from its scabbard. She sucks in a breath when I hear an audible crack, but the broken bone barely phases her. She shifts to her other foot, yanking a sword and striding toward me.

I don't fight with longer blades but that doesn't mean she has an advantage. I've been fighting them for a long time, and I know how to use their weight against her, especially with one hand useless—at least until the bone gets a chance to heal.

Her sword swings toward my neck, a killing blow if it landed, but I dance out of its arc in time. As her blade finishes its stroke, I lean in and plunge a knife toward her shoulder, hoping to get a lucky strike and take out that arm too. She's quick, though, and shifts away before my knife can do more than graze her skin. Rebounding with ridiculous speed, her sword tracks back toward my neck, again barely missing me as I throw myself away, landing on my ass and scrabbling backwards before I take a second to throw myself back to my feet.

The sun is dropping behind her, glaring in my eyes as it creates a long shadow leading to my feet. I run to my left, but before I can change our positions, she's racing toward me, her sword a continuous swing of thrusts and lunges as she tries to wear me down.

For a minute or more, our blades battle, ringing through the trees and echoing off the mountains as they parry and block and slash. Twice, my feet catch on roots or rocks beneath me, barely holding myself up as Dani stalks in with every stumble and pause.

I'm gasping for breath, winded already after my battle with Njal and wondering how I'll beat Dani and then a third fighter. I really should have made sure I got Harald to agree to a little time between fights because I am spent.

But then Dani overextends as she swings for my neck, throwing her into my path as she tries to correct herself. Before she can, I plunge my knife into her gut, dragging a sharp cry from her as she drops to the ground. "Fuck." Her voice is ragged.

I follow her to the ground, straddling her hips as I jerk the blade out and place it at her throat, reaching out my other hand to wrest the sword from her grip and toss it away. We lay there motionless for long seconds.

Harald's slow-clap—barely discernible over my heaving breaths—breaks the silence. I glance up to see him striding toward me, the same annoyed look on his face as before.

He really didn't want me to beat his fighters. I realize that while he'd be happy if I found a way to reach his dragons, he doesn't think I can. He may have promised Fhord he wouldn't harm me himself, but he'd much rather I die than walk his lands. So he's hoping to get there another way.

Now I just want to beat his last fighter even more. *Bastard*.

"Good try, soldier. I guess you'll be sleeping in the barracks a while longer." His words are cold, anger simmering beneath them. He doesn't like being failed. Dani lifts herself to her feet, ignoring a wrist that's still hanging at an odd angle, and bows quickly to her monarch.

"And you"—turning to me with a smarmy smile as Dani leaves the ring—"have won food. Congratulations."

Before I can respond with the "Fuck you" that's hovering on the tip of my tongue, Harald's head spins and he starts to cackle, a true clap coming from his hands as his feet dance beneath him. He looks comfortable and confident. He chose Isak last for a reason.

I follow his gaze and watch the final fighter take Dani's place. He blows me another kiss as he extends his hands, sucking balls of water from the nearby river to juggle with them.

The males and females watching us chant their support for this fighter, his name reverberating around us. To them, he's a comrade, not just a nameless warrior. A bemused part of my brain realizes they've started stomping their feet now. I can't hold back the smile at the muffled steps that do nothing except expel energy. But perhaps that's all they need.

My thoughts spear out, testing Isak's mind, but he's too strong for me to manipulate now. He needs to wear himself down a bit if we're going to have any chance.

He doesn't waste time. Before I can palm my knives, the balls in his hands are blazing toward me, little cannons that'll probably break bones when they land. And they will land. I can see already that I won't be fast enough to evade everything he can throw at me.

I fling a blade at him, aiming for the middle of his chest, before launching myself to the left. I manage to evade two of the balls but the third slams into my hip, a red-hot ember that draws my heavy grunt as it pushes me back and to the ground. I throw myself to my feet as he pulls the knife from his shoulder, glaring at me and dropping it to extend both hands toward the river.

One missile after another erupts from the water, flying toward me at impossible speeds. The only advantage I have is the distance, which gives me a few seconds to judge the trajectory. But that's soon gone too, as Isak sends a never-ending barrage, and I'm hit again and again.

None is sharp enough to break skin but the ones that hit fuck me up. I'm sure my ribs crack with the first direct strike, buckling me in half for a moment, then I nearly collapse in pain when the next shot strikes my left ankle, twisting my foot beneath me. But even those aren't as fucked as the massive ball that bashes my right wrist—probably payback for Dani's injury—sending my favorite knife spinning to the ground, useless.

Within a minute, I'm so fucking tired, I'm ready to abandon the tent and supplies and just escape with what I've already won. Before I can fling my hands up, though, one of Isak's darts pounds into my temple, throwing me to the side, my head cracking against a rock so hard I don't know if I'll be able to stand again. I scramble with my left hand for the blade I'll need if I have any hope of surviving, trying to push myself up as Isak stalks toward me, his lips twisting into an ugly sneer as his eyes dance with the victory he's about to claim.

And I realize I'm gonna die here. Part of my brain focuses on the field that will see the end of my long life—pops of color splashed across the green grass, the scent of pine in the air that reminds me so much of Midgard, the gurgle of the creek just outside my vision, barely noticeable under the taunts of Harald's soldiers as they savor Isak's certain victory over the Vanatian dragon rider. Another part screams at the agony rippling through me, the fire in my side that feels like a blade punched into my lungs.

Most of my mind, though, belongs to Fhord and Astarot. I can almost feel my mate's hands on me, trying to take my pain away. I'm still angry at him for leaving me here, devastated that he abandoned me again, but in this moment before death, those emotions can't stand in the way of our bond. *Go to the barrier*, I tell my dragon. *Tell Fhord I understand why he left me here. We had to try. And tell him I love him. Just as I love you, my beautiful beast.*

Fight! Astarot's desperate cry drops into my thoughts. He wants to help me.

You can't, I remind him as Isak's hands fling into the air and his aqua bombs start racing toward me again—this time shaped like arrows. *You're not allowed to fight.*

SHARE! He can't incinerate Isak, but he's free to lend me his power. And it's vast, maybe enough to break through Isak's magic and bend him to my will. He wants to give me the strength I'd need to claw my way to victory, if that's even possible.

He's right. It could work. I throw myself back as a missile splits open the skin on my arm, crimson flecks of my pain showering the ground at my side, and reach out to Astarot. His relief at joining my fight washes over me, helping me find some of the strength Isak's attacks have drained out of me. And then I draw Astarot's power toward me—somehow finding another spring of magic inside myself that I didn't even realize I possessed—and spear my thoughts into Isak.

It's not immediate, and at first, I'm sure it won't work. Isak's arrows are still flinging toward me, ripping gashes into my left side and both legs. I'm struggling to stand, throwing every-thing I have into just staying alive, desperate for an opening to fling my knife at him—the only chance I have of injuring him. But buoyed by my dragon's magic, my mind is rustling through Isak's, searching for the weakness that could give me control.

When I find it, I almost laugh. Isak's shield is softening as he fights to maintain the onslaught that's keeping me on the ground, stopping me from attacking him. I push through his shield and smile as his concentration falters, his eyes growing wide and then narrowing as he realizes he's not alone and tries to push me out.

But I'm inside now, and he's not strong enough to expel me. I find Isak's image of me as his target and flip it, pushing into his mind a resolve, just for a moment, to attack himself. He does, spluttering in helpless frustration as his greatest weapon becomes his weakness, then releases his magic, dropping all the water in its place.

Before he can gather his thoughts for another attack, I fling my blade at him. It lands in the center of his chest, throwing him back with a groan. I drag myself up and hobble toward him as he comes to his senses and his hand reaches for my knife. Lunging before he can grasp it, I wrench the blade from his chest to thrust it against his neck, piercing his skin. As Isak's blood joins mine on the ground, I lift my gaze and growl at Harald.

He's pissed. He didn't think I had a single chance in Helheim of beating all his fighters. But he doesn't like me knowing that. Giving his head a barely discernible nod, he rises from his garish throne, once again bringing his palms together in a slow but grudging applause.

"A tent too. Well done, elf. Put it to good use."

I respond with a sharp dip of my chin, rising on my good leg to shove my knife back in its sheath and gather the rest of them. Fuck, I hurt. I need to collapse, but I can't let Harald see that weakness.

"I hope to see you in the kastali, where we can celebrate a true achievement. Not this little demonstration."

Gods, he's such a sore loser. "Soon," I reply, limping toward Astarot to start making room for the supplies we'll be taking with us.

Harald snaps his finger at a couple of soldiers, who scamper toward the throne to return it to whatever cart drags it around. "We go now," he snarls at nobody in particular as he turns to stalk away. But then he pauses, his steps stilling. "Oh, and Sifa," Harald calls out, his head spinning as he decides to throw one last bullet at me. "I changed my mind. Dani will join you. She'll help you tame your dragon."

"No. Fuck no. She's more injured than me. She'll just slow me down." This'll be tough enough without that little bitch following in my footsteps.

Dani doesn't voice her opinion, but her eyes spark. She doesn't like this any more than me.

"My healer works wonders. I'll even lend you his services. Can't have you dying on me, can we?" he asks with a fawning smile. It drops away when he looks at Dani, who does appear healed already. "You will go, and you might earn a spot in the north sector after all."

When his gaze returns to mine, his eyes are a chocolate agate, so hard it seems impossible to see into them. He doesn't move, just stands there with clenched teeth, tight fists and a tic bouncing in his right cheek. "I rule this land. I do not ask for permission. I command." Inhaling slowly, he relaxes his hands, lips twisting into a cocky grin. "You may not walk my lands alone. And I suspect your mate would be displeased with a male escort. Dani goes or you do not."

I turn to glare at my new companion, my eyes narrowing at her pleased grin.

Gods, this is going to be a long trip.

Chapter Eight

FHORD

The Cat's Fault

"**T**urn the fuck around. Now."

I let my savage infect my words. I do *not* need to mess with this shit today.

It's been two days since I emerged from the cavern, pushing Sigurd to his limits as we tried desperately to evade the Dróttning. My gods-damned mother. Which I couldn't tell Sifa about before I was forced to abandon her to a male I trust barely more than I trust the Dróttning. Just barely.

Sigurd and I have been racing south day and night, sleeping an hour or two at a time, as we try desperately to stay far enough away from the Dróttning to evade her pursuit. She heard my magic, just like I knew she would, but thank the gods she was too far away to get to the cave in time. We felt each other as I reached the cavern's mouth, but Sigurd managed to run fast enough to stay ahead of her. I haven't felt her presence since then, and we've hidden in time to avoid detection when one of her dragons flew overhead.

I've been lucky, but if I don't take care of this soldier I managed to ambush before he saw me, that luck's over. It may be already, if she's close enough to hear whatever message he's probably already blasted out.

I don't know this guy's name, but I recognize him. He's tall and fit, like most of the Dróttning's soldiers, with short blonde hair and dark brown eyes. But he's not as angry as most of the others. His shoulders are relaxed, and a little smirk is playing across his lips. I can only conclude he's a gods-damned idiot because if he knows my name, he also knows that if I want him dead, he is.

Maybe he thinks he can talk me into surrendering. Just like everyone else, he must know I mean something to the Dróttning. Probably thinks we're fuck-buddies. We let people believe whatever they want, so they don't figure out what we really are. Too many males—and females, since the Dróttning's known to swing both ways—want my supposed spot. They're slavering after the favor they think she gives me. They don't realize her *favor* comes at a high price. My mother's a cruel and controlling bitch, and it's hard as fuck to hide anything from her.

Which is a huge gods-damned problem since I've been working for years to push her and that weak husband of hers off the throne.

"You gonna kill me, Fhord?"

"Got no choice," I tell him. "I won't be caught. Too much at stake."

"Why's she turned on you? What'd you do?" Fucker apparently thinks we'll stand here and chat.

"None of your gods-damned business."

"Since I'm dead anyway, I may as well tell you why you shouldn't kill me."

I cock my head, searching his eyes. From what I can remember, he's not usually this forward. He's the kind that hovers near power, waiting for something that'll propel him further to the center. "Better be a good fucking reason."

"I haven't sent a message to the Dróttning about finding you. And I won't. If you're on the side I think you are, we're in this together. I can help you get where you need to be."

"And where do you think I need to be?"

"With that troll, Toffer, and the elf, Joralf. Plus some of Bevin's crew. Your Ætt are there too, from what I'm told. Oh, and the troll brought along a gods-damned cat, for some reason. Pissy little bastard, always hissing and bitching about something or another."

I'm not sure if I manage to keep the shock off my face. If the abrupt narrowing of his eyes is any clue, I don't. My connection to Bevin and my Ætt is well known. Nobody should know about Toffer and Joralf or that I'm tied to both of them now. And I have no idea how the Ætt might have ended up with them.

"Why the fuck would I want to see Bevin? Or the others, whoever they are?"

His posture relaxes. I bit at his hook. "I've wondered about you for a while," he says. "Whether you're as loyal to her as you claim. As loyal as most everyone believes. I don't think so. I think you decided a long time ago you'd play both sides. And you're hoping she's on the side that loses."

This is the Dróttning talking. Trying to trap me, like she did in her quarters, offering Sifa on a platter, me thinking I was the one winning that little game.

The Dróttning always wins. I learned that lesson a long time ago. I forgot, for a minute, while my brain and cock were so focused on my little rabbit. But she reminded me. I can't trust anything. Not the Dróttning and definitely not him.

"She'll have your head for talking like that. She'll take your skin first, and by the time she's done, you'll be begging her to take your head."

"Only if you tell her. Are you gonna tell her, Fhord?"

"I sure the fuck am. First, though, I'm gonna kill you, then I'll finish what I'm doing. After that, I'll head back up to the Nest and tell her why I killed you. She'll make sure your body's left for the birds."

"I don't know whether you're fucking with me or not, but I guess I'm dead either way if I can't convince you we're on the same side." He holds my gaze for a moment and nods before continuing. "We've been looking for you. We thought Sifa'd be with you, but I gotta assume she's somewhere safe. That troll Toffer gave us all a message to give her, so she'd know she can trust us. That he's waiting for her. I'm supposed to say, 'Home and hearth hearken.' Whatever the fuck that means."

My stomach drops. For a moment, I'm back in the caves at the Nest, watching Sifa and her troll hug and cry. She went to him first and I get it. I really do. But it still ached. He called her his "mate", and I know he doesn't mean it the way I do. But that fucking ached too. And then he told her, "Home and hearth hearken." When she turned to me with thanks for saving her from the capture *I caused*, my heart leapt into my throat.

I cough, trying to clear my head. "You met the troll?"

"Yup."

"What'd you think of him?" There's only one right answer if he really met Toffer.

"Pain in the gods-damned ass. Like a murderous little kid. We keep having to remind him he can't just kill people 'cause he feels like it. Talks like a kid too, all rhymes and nonstop rambling. But he loves that elf like a sister. And he'll be good in a fight when the time comes."

I can't hold back the laugh. I don't think I could have described him better.

"What's your name?"

"Don't remember me?"

"Some random guard from the Nest? Nope. What's your name?"

"Axel. Nice to meet you, Fhord."

He extends his hand, but I ignore it, holding his stare. No deception hides in his eyes, so I dip my chin. "I still don't trust you, but I'll go with you. I can sense the Dróttning from a viku away, at least. And she can't shield her presence from me." I don't tell him I can't shield from her, either. One of the fucked-up things about our bond. "If I think you're leading me into a trap, I'll kill you."

"No trap. I promise."

"How far do we have to go?"

"Half-day's ride. The rebellion has places like this set up across Vanatia. They put everyone in this house so they'd be close when you came south. They've got a couple people in Revalle waiting to send you there if you made it that far, but we hoped to find you first. Got everyone sympathetic with our side looking."

"There's no 'our side'. I'll give you a chance to take me to my people, but then we're on our own. We're not getting sucked into any insurgency crap right now. We've got things to do first."

He nods, a smug look on his face. "You'll see," he says before tugging on his horse's reins and leading me into the brush.

We don't find anyone else as we ride. "I made sure to get assigned to this area, near the place we're going to, so nobody else could find them," Axel explains at one point.

I grunt at him, but I'm not interested in talking. This guy's not my friend, and he's not gonna be.

Instead, my thoughts are filled with my rabbit, and Harald's sudden appearance in the cave. He told her she's my mate, because I'm a bastard who didn't trust Sifa enough to give her the truth and face the consequences together. But that's not the only thing I kept from her. I didn't give Sifa my biggest secret, that a savage lives inside me, forcing his way out sometimes. They're rare in Vanatia, a trait I share with my fucking mother, although she despises her creature, while I treasure mine. I can usually keep him in control, but it'll be rough now that he and I have accepted the mating bond. Even though Sifa hasn't yet.

He's totally obsessed with our mate. If I don't get back to her soon, he may take our skin and force us back to the North. He couldn't get through the barrier, but he'd keep us there until I gave in and agreed to go to her. I can't let that happen. If we managed to survive the shitshow Harald would throw at us, we'd never get him on our side after that.

I don't know how much Harald knows. I couldn't risk telling Sifa with him right there. If he knows and tells her, though, she may never trust me again. Not that I'd blame her. I've got too many secrets. I should have told her every gods-damned thing when I had a chance.

This is such a fucking mess.

The sun's dropping below the horizon, casting long shadows all around us, when Axel starts to slow. He whistles—clear, sharp trills that would sound natural if you didn't know what you were listening for—and gestures me to stop. And fuck if Leif doesn't appear within a few seconds.

Guess Axel really did know where to find my Ætt.

"Boss," Leif drawls as he rides toward me, his tall, lean body shifting in the saddle with each step. When he's close enough, he extends an arm for me to grasp. My breath comes easier with him by my side. "We didn't know when we'd see you again."

My chin drops in a sharp nod. "Me neither. We've got a lot to discuss. How far is it?"

Leif jerks his head toward a group of old structures a half-viku away. To anyone passing by, they'd look abandoned, but now that I'm focusing, I can see a tendril of smoke rising from the chimney. Boards cover every opening, too meticulous to be the haphazard protection given to buildings eventually abandoned.

"How long have you been here?"

"Depends who you ask. We'll tell you all about it when we get inside. It's not safe to be in the open too long."

Yanking his reins, he kicks his horse into a trot, then a gallop. Axel and I do the same, covering the distance between us and the others in a couple of minutes.

Toffer's standing in an open doorway I would have missed if he hadn't been there. He's all troll, built like a tree stump, with ruddy cheeks, a ridiculously wide nose, and a beard as long as his arms. His face falls when he sees me riding Sigurd alone, no Sifa in sight. After a moment he shakes himself—literally—and smiles. Maybe he's realized I'll have news about Sifa and that's better than nothing.

He doesn't move as I dismount, hand Sigurd's reins to Leif, and stride toward him.

"Is Sifa safe?" His voice is tense, lips tight.

I clap him on the shoulder, making sure my smile reaches my eyes. "She is. I took her to the northern monarch, Harald. The Dróttning can't reach her there. She'll help him with something while I get information he needs here."

It's basically true, even if I don't tell Toffer that Harald coerced us. And that the northern monarch is a dick. There's no need for Toffer to worry about things he can't control. I learned early that fear triggers his tongue. He'll have us all on edge if I let him. The less afraid he is for Sifa, the better for everyone.

Axel wasn't kidding about the odd mix of beings gathered here. Torsten sits next to Joralf, the elf who escaped from prison with Sifa. An elf I don't recognize—Joralf's mate, maybe—is on Joralf's other side, back stiff and eyes narrowed. Two of the bedmates who traveled with Sifa to the southern Nest where we met—Liv and Frida, I think—are at a large table with two males who worked at the tavern Bevin called home. I can't remember their names.

Oh, and the cat. He's here too, like Axel said, laying on Torsten's lap. Because of-fucking-course. The most stoic member of my Ætt, a warrior larger than anyone else in the room, glances down at the cat he's stroking and shrugs as if he's trapped.

"Where are Jorunn and Astrid?" It makes no sense that only half of my Ætt would be here. They were supposed to hide together.

"Jorunn couldn't get away quickly enough. She got trapped in Revalle and just got here. She and Astrid are ... renewing ... their bond." Leif grins as he walks in from the stables and gestures down the hall.

Torsten grumbles, his hand still caressing the ball of fur in his lap. "Their gods-damned bond don't need to be renewed," he barks. "Just tell it like it is. We can hear 'em from here."

As if to punctuate his point, a squeal erupts from the bedroom, then, "Now, JayJay. Come with me, baby." A few moans follow, muffled but impossible to miss.

I can't hold back the smile. Astrid joined my Ætt late, and she and Jorunn fell in love quickly. They're all business when they need to be, but they also find plenty of time for pleasure. And we hear a lot of it.

I'm happy for them, but my mind automatically draws up a picture of my mate and I have to take a deep breath to stop my cock from stretching out my pants. The last thing I need is this group thinking the females got me excited. There's only one female who can do that now.

Turning toward Leif, I jut my jaw at the door. "Someone taking care of Sigurd? You didn't spend much time out there."

Leif nods. "Knut sent a guy from the southern Nest. Aksell's suspicious of him, so he needs to stay away from Revalle for a while. He takes care of the horses, other shit like that, while he's hiding here."

"Food?"

Leif points toward a doorway. "You'll find meat, cheese, bread, and some other stuff in the kitchen. We already ate dinner."

My stomach's grumbling, and we can't do anything until Jorunn and Astrid come out, so I head to the kitchen and start rummaging around for a meal. And then I nearly jump out of my fucking boots as I shut a cupboard door to find Joralf standing behind it, arms crossed and eyes speculative.

"What do you want, elf?" I elbow past him toward the table and plop into a chair, starting to shovel food into my mouth.

"Why'd you lie to the troll?" His voice is calm, but I can feel his power rumbling in it. He must be good at keeping it shielded—Sifa told me he lived free in Revalle for a long time—but he's decided to unleash it now.

"About what?" I think I know what he's asking, but I haven't spent enough time with him to trust him. He needs to tell me what's on his mind.

"Harald's not as bad as the Dróttning, but he's close. You can't have left Sifa there willingly."

I exhale, holding in my temper as Joralf settles next to me. Sifa likes this elf. He helped her get through her torture. I can humor him. "How well do you know Harald?"

"Well enough. I know he's a bastard and doesn't do anything for free. If Sifa's there, he's getting something from her."

"Like I said, she's helping him with something."

"She's in danger. I don't have any idea what she's doing there, but I know it's risky. Otherwise, his people would be doing it. What's she helping him with, Fhord?"

My savage rumbles in my throat, pissed at Joralf's tone. She's our mate and our emotions are stretched thin with the barrier separating us from her. He needs to back down, stop acting like he has any right to ask about Sifa.

He doesn't even budge. His eyes narrow, but the expression on his face doesn't change. We stare at each other for a minute or more as I push back on my savage. When I break the silence, I can't keep the anger from my tone. "I know you helped Sifa when she needed it, but I don't answer to you, elf. She's mine. She's safer there than she would be here."

Torsten's voice from the other side of the door interrupts Joralf's response. "They're done, boss. Come out when you're ready."

"I'll tell everyone what you need to know." I eye my plate, wishing Joralf had stayed in the other room so I could have gotten more food down, then lift it to carry with me. They'll need to talk too, explain how the fuck they all ended up together in these shacks, and I can eat while they do.

We all settle into our spots, and I tell them enough. They know Sifa's going to try to tame one of Harald's dragons, and Toffer's excited for her while the others are hiding their fear. The troll doesn't understand the differences between northern and southern dragons, but everyone else does. They all realize it's a near-impossible task.

Almost as unlikely as what Harald demanded from me. "He needs me to figure out how the Dróttning controls the dragons here," I explain after I've told them about Sifa. Turning to Joralf, I add, "Sifa said you may be able to help." I lift a hand when he starts to talk, my gaze roaming over the others in the room. "First, though, I need to know. How did you all end up together?"

Leif laughs, settling into his chair. For just a moment, his eyes land on Frida, one eyebrow quirking some question she follows and I don't. I'm watching him, so I don't see her response, but he does. He nods, as if he's acknowledging her request, and I wait until he turns to me. He dips his chin—if

I need to know, he'll tell me whatever the fuck that was about later—then gestures toward Sifa's cat, Thor, who's still holding Torsten's lap as if it belongs to him. The little fucker looks around, assessing the rest of us, and yawns.

"It's all the cat's fault," Leif says after a moment. "Or the cat gets the credit. However you want to look at it. Toffer and Joralf went straight to Sifa's apartment when they reached Revalle…"

"I promised Sif-Sif I'd feed Thor," Toffer interjects, his tone defensive. "We had to go there."

Leif reaches out to pat Toffer's arm, and I watch the troll's shoulders relax. Leif's a good guy. He has that effect on people. And trolls. "You did good, Toff. We needed to find our friends. We're all here because of you."

Toffer blushes—such a strange look on his thick, red cheeks—and extends his arms to Thor. The cat yawns again, apparently deciding who he'll choose next, as Toffer's eyes narrow. He's probably talking to the cat—trolls can communicate with all animals—trying to woo him over. Thor finally gives in, abandoning Torsten and jumping to the troll's lap with a shallow purr.

Leif watches, a smile on his face, before turning back to me. "Astrid was there one day feeding the cat, like you asked, when Liv showed up. Nearly got herself killed when she stormed in unannounced."

"Sifa helped me," Liv chimes in. "When she disappeared, I checked at the tavern, found Mikkael, then Johan." She looks at Bevin's males as she identifies them, then back at me.

"Mikkael sent me to Sifa's apartment, said I'd find a troll who might be able to help." Liv's voice isn't defensive like Toffer's. She's comfortable in this group already.

"She found me instead," Astrid adds. "If she hadn't mentioned Sifa, she'd have been dead. As it was, she told me enough to start talking to her. We figured out quickly enough that we're on the same side."

"And that it's dangerous to be in Revalle when the Dróttning is searching for your friend," Leif adds. "She'd already sent her soldiers to question everyone who's here. We were hearing rumors from inside the guard that she planned to do more. She was convinced one of us would lead her to Sifa. We made arrangements and left overnight, quietly."

"Except me." Jorunn's voice is soft but always demands attention. It's why she leads my Ætt when I'm away. She earned that respect. "The Dróttning's soldiers found me making my way to the gate. They threw me in jail and were about to send me to the northern Nest when Mikkael and Johan got me out."

"The fuck we did." One of Bevin's males—Johan, I think—jumps into the conversation with a smirk and wink at Jorunn. He's not a big guy, a standard male's-height, and I suspect he's good at disappearing in a crowd. With short blond hair, blue eyes, and strong cheekbones, he looks like most other males in Vanatia. "We got there in time to show you the way out," he adds, "although you'd have found it without us."

Jorunn turns to him with a smile and shrug. "I wasn't planning on sticking around if I could avoid it." Her gaze bounces across the room again. "The three of us left together."

"Longest few days of my life." Astrid reaches for Jorunn's hand to tug it toward her. "I didn't want to leave without JayJay, but they convinced me we'd all be trapped here if we didn't get away when we did. And then we'd never have a shot at getting her out."

"You did exactly what you had to do," Jorunn whispers, leaning in for a kiss. "We both know it."

Astrid's hands lift to Jorunn's cheek as she gives her one more kiss. "Still a gods-damned long few days."

I can't tear my eyes away from them. I did what I had to do—I couldn't have let Sifa die—but it kills me that I brought this danger to all of them. And I'm sure as fuck gonna fix it.

"And you found your mate?" I ask, finally forcing myself to turn toward Joralf.

"Fróðr, this is Fhord. He helped free me."

Fróðr's a surprisingly beautiful elf with thick red hair and eyes like a summer lake. His features are sharp—defined jaw and cheekbones—but not overly prominent. His full lips are smiling broadly, revealing straight, white teeth.

"We are in your debt. Anything you ask is yours."

"Just your cooperfration." I let my gaze shift to Joralf. "Can you help me? Do you know what gives the Dróttning such power?"

"We suspect. Our people have been searching for this answer for many years. We haven't been able to test our theory, but we've never had a troll available to us before." He takes a moment to smile at Toffer, who beams at his praise.

"Why do you need a troll?"

"It's in the northern Nest. If we're right, the source of the Dróttning's power is also the nexus of her power. So it's time to leave. Into the snake's den we go."

I wish he was joking. He's not. If we're going to find the Dróttning's secret, we need to go back to the Nest.

Fuck. Me.

CHAPTER NINE

SIFA

TROLLS HUNGER

"I DON'T UNDERSTAND WHY your dragon can't carry my gear. We'll travel faster."

I spin in my saddle—still getting used to the persnickety mare Harald lent me when he and his soldiers left for his kastali—and glare at Dani. I woke up this morning screaming as one of the Dróttning's men carved into me, tossing one more scrap of skin onto the others as my blood wept to the floor below. She was hovering over me, her eyes wide as she shook me awake.

Fhord settles me. I don't have nightmares when he's holding me.

We got on the road quickly, and she's been nagging me about Astarot carrying her gear ever since.

"I've answered this," I tell her. "Many times. Astarot is not a drudge."

"He's got your stuff."

"And you've pointed that out. Many times. He decides what he carries, and he doesn't want your packs. He's still pissed at you." I smile at the beast lumbering in front of us. "He's pretty protective of me."

She whines—actually whines like a disappointed dog—as she nudges her stallion to catch up with me. "You need to force him. We'll go faster if Midnight is as light as Sunbeam."

Harald's horses have ridiculous names.

I can't hold back the sigh. Dani is stubborn, and I don't want to talk about this. I'm struggling to contain my frustration and hurt at Fhord bringing me here to abandon me. They're barely-contained flames that flare to life every time my still-healing wrist or ankle reminds me I'm stuck in that bastard Harald's lands because Fhord thinks he needs to protect me from his mother. I'm sure he's convinced he did the right thing, but it feels like I'm back in the Nest, crippled by despair because I realized he left me there to be tortured.

I need revenge too. I should be facing the Dróttning with him, not coddling Dani as we chase the impossible.

But Dani's not going to stop asking unless I can convince her. "I get it," I tell her in the most reasonable tone I can muster. "You don't know dragons. But trust me on this. I can't *force* him to do anything. He's with me because he wants to be. If I ask him to help me with something, he'll only do it if he wants. And thinks it's a good idea. And isn't focused on a sheep, or a deer, or a big fish."

Astarot harumphs. *Hungry.*

I shouldn't have said anything. Now that's all he'll be thinking about. He's still trying to pack on the muscle and fat he lost and eats a ridiculously large amount of food. Even for a dragon that weighs twenty tons.

"How does that work?" she asks, and I cock my eyebrow, confused at her question. "I mean, how do you work together if he only does what he wants?" She sounds genuinely curious.

"We've got a bond. It's kind of like a mating bond," I explain as Fhord's image rises in my mind, reminding me of his many secrets, "and we work together in the same way. Astarot's probably smarter than me. He's a devious strategist and he understands this world in a way I don't. If we disagree about something, we talk about it and decide. It's a partnership."

She nods, her eyes speculative. "I thought the Dróttning controls dragons in the south. That they always do what she demands."

"Well, that's true. Like Harald said, she found something a long time ago that gave her the ability to bend them to her will. Each dragon is bound to her and the rider she chose for it and has little choice but to comply. It takes tremendous strength to defy a direct command and few of the Dróttning's dragons can do it. Nobody but the Dróttning knows how she wields such control."

"Why is it different with you and Astarot? Because you're in the North, away from her influence?"

"Astarot and I are a fate-ordained pairing. He managed to defy the Dróttning, refused to be bound to the rider she'd chosen. I rescued him from the 'trainer' who was torturing him, trying to force his compliance."

Dani's eyes light up, her fingers rising to touch her throat as she watches me for a moment. "Is that why you're here?" she asks at last. "Because you defied her?"

A rueful laugh escapes before I can stop it. "I'll be killed if she catches me. Or worse. And it's not just because I defied her. I'm an elf, and elves aren't free in Vanatia. Plus, the Dróttning demands complete secrecy about dragons. The people only see what she wants. It's a death sentence just to enter the training grounds because you might see what her people do. How they abuse rebellious dragons. Or even dragons who make a mistake. Or whose riders make a mistake. I had no idea before I saw Astarot that she tortured dragons the way she does. Many serve her reluctantly and would sacrifice much to break free."

Threat. Astarot's warning thrums inside me. He senses something nearby.

"We're not alone," I tell Dani as my gaze lifts to search the valley we've just entered.

"Shit." Dani turns to look for whatever Astarot scented. "Trolls don't often come out during the day, but that's probably what it is. Hopefully not too many."

"Trolls? Plural? Do they work in groups here?"

"Yours don't?"

My mind drifts to Toffer. He's managed to control his base instincts, and I know he'd never hurt me, but he'd be dangerous if not for me. "Our trolls are solitary. They're threats but manageable because they don't join others." I glance at Astarot then back at Dani. "Isn't he a big enough threat to keep them away?"

"The northern trolls live and hunt in groups. If there are enough, they'll even attack a dragon. They're smart and always hungry. We're all food to them."

"Maybe Astarot could talk to them."

Dani barks out a laugh, spinning to stare at me like I'm an idiot. "Right. Because the trolls will definitely listen to the dragon they'd love to eat."

"They might. He could try to convince them to leave us alone."

"How the fuck would he even do that? Dance for them?"

"You don't know?"

"What?" Dani demands, her tone growing frustrated as her lips flatten into a thin line.

"Trolls can talk to dragons. All animals really." I pause, re-thinking my broad claim. "Well, I think so. The troll I know can at least. It sounds like all trolls can. They just need to be close enough—maybe a dragon's-length away from each other."

"No fucking way." She watches me for a moment, her eyes again sparking in interest. "Wait. The troll you know? You're friends with a troll?"

I can't hold back my smile as my mind pulls up Toffer's image. "He's my best friend. Other than Astarot. And a cat named Thor. And Fhord, I guess, although Fhord's my mate, so that's different." My heart actually skips a beat—it literally pauses, as if to luxuriate in my words—as I say that. I don't think I've acknowledged that bond out loud before. I still haven't really accepted it. I don't know if I trust him enough to fully embrace that kind of relationship with him. But I can't deny it's there.

"And your friend the troll can talk to dragons?"

Vexing. Astarot's grunt of affirmation prompts my giggle. Toffer's a lot, and it takes a while to get used to him. When he's nervous he talks nonstop, usually with alliteration. Astarot probably had Toffer in his head the entire time they were together.

"Astarot says 'yes'. Toffer talked to him the same way I can."

Dani shakes her head, a smile playing across her lips. "Everything in the Dróttning's realm is strange."

"Or maybe it's Harald's realm that's strange," I respond with a smirk.

She's silent, watching me longer than I expected. Finally, she dips her chin. "Maybe."

"So we're agreed? Astarot should try to get close enough to figure out what they want? Convince them to leave us alone?"

Okay by you? I assume so but best to ask.

Curious. Astarot's eager. He hasn't met many trolls and wonders if they're all like Toffer.

Can you tell yet how many there are?

Many. Astarot can't gauge a number, but he senses a lot.

Be careful. You'd feed them for a long time.

Astarot spins his head to stare at me, snout set in a thin line as his eyes narrow. He hates it when I remind him of obvious things. *Okay, okay. I just worry about you.*

Holding my eyes, Astarot snorts his disdain. Laughing, I stroke his snout. *We'll wait here.*

He's airborne in seconds, heading toward the trees on the far edge of the clearing. Minutes later, his angry bellow, tucking his wings as he spirals away from an enormous bolt, snaps me to attention. Twisting to catch Dani's eyes—both of them wide and angry—I kick at Sunbeam's sides, tugging the reins to aim her toward the trolls who tried to kill my dragon.

Stay! Astarot's command echoes through me, turning my stomach as my head fills with images of him in the forest, a bolt ripped through his guts, clinging to life. Fhord barely saved his life then. I don't know nearly enough to do that here. If he's wounded like that again, he's dead.

We can attack the trolls. Take out the archer, I suggest, struggling to control my anxiety.

Stay. This is a request, calmer. He's not hit and confident he won't be. *Talk.* He still thinks he can communicate with them, convince them to stand down.

The next ten minutes are the longest of my life. Astarot dropped to the ground when they attacked, approaching them by foot. I can feel his presence and know he's not hurt, but I need more. My pulse is racing—I can hear it pounding in my ears—and I can't unclench my teeth. The image of Astarot bleeding in the forest, surrounded by the Dróttning's soldiers, is the only thing I can see as my thoughts spear toward my dragon, searching for any news.

Finally, Astarot's voice rumbles in my mind. *Come.* He sends a warning with his beckon, but he's not afraid. Anger alone pulses through the bond. We need to be careful, but my dragon is not one tiny bit worried about whatever threat the trolls pose.

"He wants us to go there." I palm a blade and Dani's eyebrows lift. "He didn't relay much—a warning, but he's more pissed than afraid. We just need to be prepared."

She nods, pulling out her bow to notch an arrow and gesturing for me to walk in front. Nudging Sunbeam into a trot, my grip on my knife tightens as she carries me into whatever mess Astarot found.

When we crest a nearby hill, leading into another valley, I can't restrain a groan. Astarot is standing in the center of a horde of trolls—probably a hundred or more—a dozen bolts aimed at his chest. His head swings from side to side, flames erupting from his nostrils every few seconds. Occasionally, one of the bolts trembles and Astarot's snout spins, his mouth opening to flash a warning at the offending troll.

The crowd shifts and I see why he's not afraid, although I suspect he should be. A large troll is trapped in Astarot's talons. He's sitting on his ass, his legs folded beneath him and his hands resting in his lap. Like Toffer, he resembles every troll in children's stories on Midgard—a short, stocky body, bulbous features, long, thick hair and bushy eyebrows. A dark woolen cloak swathes his entire body, pooling on the ground. Although he's completely at Astarot's mercy, he appears annoyed. Nothing more.

Dani and I push our horses through the trolls, who part just enough to let us pass. They spit their disdain as we do, threatening to dine for days as soon as the beast releases their mage, and snarling their thoughts about the taste of elf and horse flesh. I snarl back. I won't be an easy kill.

"Why do you threaten my dragon?" I direct the question to the mage, although I don't sense authority rippling from him. His mind is shielded—a defense that's probably second nature to every magical being in a land in which elves are free—but I still can grasp hints of his emotions. He's waiting for his elder to join us.

"Yours this beast?" The troll's voice is cold, dismissive. "Offer yourself also?"

"We offer nothing to your clan." Dani's thrown power into her words and they echo all around us. "The dragon is ours. He came to secure our passage through this area. We will leave together."

"Leave you shan't. Supper shall you be."

I gawk at the trapped troll, wondering how he thinks he'll get out of this alive. "You're pretty confident considering Astarot's one step away from squashing you."

He shrugs his shoulders, "Short is life. Others shall feed." He looks at the archers, one by one, as if to remind me that his life is the only thing keeping them from filling Astarot with holes he wouldn't survive.

"Nobody needs to die. We simply want to pass through and we all can leave this with our lives."

"Short is life," he repeats. "Hungry they are. Eat they shall." He seems utterly blasé about his impending death.

"Dragons take," another troll roars from my side as he strides forward, stopping just in front of our horses to glare up at us. "Take from them, we shall."

"This is not one of your dragons. He's taken nothing from you."

"Dragons take," he yells, his voice sparking with anger. "Herds thin. Trolls hunger." He turns toward the gathered trolls as he says this, his words apparently intended for them, more than Dani and me.

"This dragon just entered these lands." I focus on the troll in front of me now, apparently the leader of this clan. "He's done you no harm."

"Large is dragon. Feed many trolls." He spins to gaze at the mage trapped by Astarot, who gives him a nod and a shrug, before turning back to me. "One dies; many eat."

My body starts to heat, a shiver running down my spine as the knowledge that Astarot holds little leverage over them settles within me. They will sacrifice this mage to feed the others. I know Toffer well enough to have learned that trolls place little value on life. They may be selfless with those they love, but everyone else is free game. Maybe that's a necessary part of the *need* to kill they all possess.

I'll have to come up with something else if we're going to get out of this.

"Do you hunt dragons because the herds are so thin?" I'm not sure, but I doubt this is their normal prey.

"Herds thin." The troll in front of me offers no other explanation, but I think I understand him.

"Is it because the dragons eat too many of the herd? Are you trying to control the dragons and eliminate them as competitors for the herds at the same time?"

"Herds thin; large is dragon." He repeats these words slowly while swinging one arm toward Astarot, as if he believes me too dull to fathom his meaning.

"What if I can help you control the dragons? Make them go away and stop eating your animals?"

The troll's brows pull together, forming a large caterpillar above his eyes. "Wild are dragons." He utters these words sluggishly, seemingly convinced I still need extra help to grasp what he's saying.

"My dragon isn't wild." I can't keep the exasperation from my tone. "Look, I know you need to kill. All of you." I raise my eyes and spin to look at the gathered trolls. "One dragon won't sate that demand for everyone, and merely eating isn't enough. You need to kill your prey."

"Herds thin," the troll reminds me, his eyebrows finally parting as they rise halfway up his forehead.

"I can help fix that. Harald sent me to communicate with the dragons, get them to listen to him. If they serve him, he'll feed them. They won't prey on your herds."

"Wild are dragons." Again, his response is painfully slow.

Pointing at Astarot, I dismount my horse. "Does he look wild? He and I are a team. Harald wants the dragons to heed his call as Astarot heeds mine."

Astarot snorts, his eyes slimming to burning slits. *Heed?* he demands. He doesn't like my suggestion that he *heeds* my call.

Please go along, I beg him. *They need to believe this if it's to work.*

Astarot holds my gaze, letting me feel how much he dislikes my claim. Finally, he drops his snout. *Lie*, he agrees. Because we both know it's a lie. But he's okay with it. For now.

"We seek the dragon who resides in those mountains." My blade points toward the peak we think is the dragon's nest. "Harald believes we can reach him, convince him to go to Harald's kastali with us. If we do that, he'll leave your herd alone. It can grow, the way it should."

"Dragons are many. Come will others." Turning toward the archers, he nods. They heave back their drawstrings, a dozen bolts aimed directly at Astarot's chest.

I launch myself at my dragon, drawing a few of the bolts to point toward me. "No, they won't. That's the idea. In the south, where I'm from, every single dragon serves the Dróttning. She feeds all of them. If they take from wild herds, it's rare and only with her consent. That's what Harald wants to do here."

"Wild are dragons."

Fuck. I wish he'd say something else. I refuse to be killed by a troll with a twelve-word vocabulary.

"They don't have to be. I can reach them, tame them." Astarot huffs behind me, but I ignore it. I don't need his input right now. "For hundreds of years, Harald's tried and failed. If you kill me, it'll be another hundred years or more before he'll be able to try again."

Okay, that might be an exaggeration, but the trolls don't need to know that.

The troll in front of me stands impossibly still for nearly a minute, his eyes narrowed at me as his hands—the only part of his body that's moving—play with a knife he's pulled from his belt. Every few seconds, he flings it into the air, catching the tip of its blade without fail. With the last throw, he flips it into the ground at my feet, a hair's breadth from my big toe. It takes everything in me to hold still, but I do.

"Propose what?"

"Let us go. We'll leave your herds alone and do everything we can to take this dragon from your lands."

"Trolls hunger." He needs something in exchange for the meal we're asking them to give up.

"How many beasts do you need? If she stays here as a hostage..."

"I'm not staying here!" Dani's sharp voice punctures my words.

"You will, or they won't let us go." We stare at each other for a few seconds before she nods once. She's not happy about it though.

Turning back to the troll, I capture his gaze. "Dani will stay with you. I'll go with Astarot and bring back goats, or sheep, or whatever's in that herd up there. However many you need."

Again, the troll watches me in silence. Finally, he flicks his hand. The bolts drop in unison to point at the ground. "Twelve need we," he barks. "Trolls hunger."

"Okay. Twelve. We'll get them back to you right away."

"Sunset, return you."

"No, sunset won't work. That can't be more than a couple hours away. We need more time than that. My dragon will have to make a few trips to get that many."

The troll doesn't respond with words. Instead, much faster than should have been possible, he's standing next to Midnight, yanking Dani to stand next to him. His massive hand circles her throat as another troll steps forward to force her arms behind her back and tie her wrists together, then wrap a rope around her neck, handing it to their leader.

The lead troll steps toward me, flames in his eyes as he jerks Dani's rope.

"Sunset. Or dies this one." His tone is cold, detached—a far cry from his burning eyes.

He's done debating with me.

Sunset it is, I guess.

CHAPTER TEN

SIFA

FHORD'S IMAGE

THE SUN IS LOW in the sky when Astarot and I fly away from Dani and the trolls.

It took too long for them to retrieve the ropes we'll need to have any chance of meeting the trolls' deadline. I'll need to figure out a way to tie as many sheep as I can together and then rig some kind of pulley to hang off Astarot. I have no fucking idea if it'll work. But it better. Harald will kill me if Dani dies here.

Astarot throws everything he has into speed, racing toward the herd the trolls pointed out. I'm working as hard to hold on to my lunch as I am to my dragon, my stomach twisting with every turn and shift in Astarot's flight. I haven't felt this much fear about a mission in a long time.

And I'm kind of pissed about it. This isn't me. I'm not afraid to do hard things.

But then Fhord's image drops in my mind, and I realize it's not for me I fear. Not really. If I fail—if Dani dies and Harald turns against us—he'll fail. Tindera will never break free of the Dróttning's grip. I'm still angry at him, but I can't deny I need him. I crave him. If I can't do this, I'll never feel Fhord's hands on my skin again. Taste his kiss. Savor the sensations only he can spark in me.

Ten, maybe fifteen, minutes after we left the trolls behind, we find the herd. It's massive—thank the gods—and in a valley flat and large enough for Astarot to land a hundred feet away from any sheep. He floats in gently from downwind, trying his best to not alert them to his presence. A few startle as he nears the ground, but they largely stay where they are. They must have dismissed Astarot as a threat. Dragons don't usually engage in such stealth when they attack.

I scramble from his back and pull my ropes from their ties as soon as his feet hit the ground. Within a minute, I'm racing toward the herd, the lariat tucked under an arm as I create a lasso with one end. I've never been so happy to have learned a skill I thought useless at the time. A few years herding cattle in Midgard may make the difference between life and death for Dani. And the rest of us.

I've gathered three sheep and am aiming for a fourth when I feel the presence of another dragon. Seconds later, it emerges in the air to the east, the sun shining on its plumage. It looks like most dragons in the South—a body as large as the biggest whale on Midgard, strong wings holding it aloft and propelling it forward, feathers rippling with its strokes, light glinting off copper and black plumes to resemble a fire ripping through the heavens.

For just a moment, I marvel at its beauty. The sun has reached the perfect angle, its light soft and gentle as it caresses the trees and bushes and flowers blanketing the ground in front of us. Their colors shimmer and glow in its warmth. The beast above it all hovers on the wind, wings still and strong—not a hint of sound escaping—as it glides toward us. It's trying to surprise us and must not realize it's about to attack an elf that can sense its presence.

Then I see its eyes, crimson and dripping with malice. And I understand. This dragon is livid. We've dared enter its territory. We're taking parts of its herd. It won't tolerate our presence. Especially not Astarot.

My dragon's nostrils flare as he senses the threat, his head spinning up to glare. *Stay*, he orders as he launches into the air, wings propelling him faster than I would have thought possible.

He sets a collision course, but the rogue dragon is smart. Twisting, it drops toward the ground, evading Astarot as it propels itself toward me. Astarot reacts almost immediately, spinning as if on a dime to throw himself in the attacking beast's path. Again, the beast spins and again Astarot shifts, staying between the dragon and me.

Until he's not.

At the last moment, the dragon adjusts again, looping backward to snag Astarot in its talons and toss him toward the heavens before throwing itself at the ground. And then it's running, closing the distance between us before Astarot has a chance to react. Time slows, my skin crawling as I watch the beast's talons rip into the ground, tossing dirt, rocks and debris behind it in its zeal to reach me.

My hands react before I do. I feel my power, stronger because of my bond with a dragon, vibrating through my skin. I know what to do without thinking about it. Reaching deep inside, I find the kernel of magic that has grown exponentially more potent since I crossed into this world, thrusting it toward the attacking dragon. Spreading my feet and firming my stance, I brace for the blast that will throw me backward if I'm not ready for it.

It nearly does. Struggling to stay upright, I cast my will at the beast running toward me, fighting to find some way into its psyche. I watch in horror as the dragon seems to repel the power sent its way—her way, I realize as I touch the edge of her thoughts—which flows over her in a wave. I have no fucking idea how I'll fight her off if this doesn't even slow her down.

But it's making a difference, I see as my eye catches Astarot diving toward us. Our enemy's focus is on me, her gaze so narrowed she doesn't have any idea my dragon is closing in on her. My breath hitches in my throat, a vise clamping my chest, as I watch the beasts race. The northern dragon remains oblivious to the contest, but she's winning anyway. Astarot won't reach her in time, I'm sure.

My dragon doesn't like to lose, though. And when my life is threatened, he won't. In a final burst of speed, Astarot whips through the hundred feet between him and his prey, twisting at the last second to thrust his talons forward and grasp the base of the dragon's wings. Yanking at her, Astarot pulls my pursuer off course, flinging her into the sky.

Not far enough. The copper beast, now angrier than before, rips out a screech that echoes around us as she pivots in the air and propels herself at Astarot. Fhord's description of these dragons—rabid—flickers into my mind as the drool drips down her snout. Enormous beads I can see even from this distance fall to the ground to land in splats that join her snaps and growls.

When they meet above me, bodies slamming against each other in a drumbeat that pounds through the air, I suck in my breath and hold it. Calm, I demand of my racing heart. Confident. I won't let my fears find their way to Astarot. His mind can't be muddied by my weak thoughts. He's the largest and strongest beast in Vanatia. Maybe in this land too.

He will win.

My hope splinters as I watch the copper beast. She's smaller than Astarot, but she knows how to fight dragons—something Astarot has never done. Every spin, each thrust, every feint she makes positions her to draw my dragon's blood. She knows Astarot's weak spots and exactly where to inflict the most pain. Already, my dragon's wings are pocked and dripping, while Astarot has barely made a mark on his attacker.

My heart trips through my chest, my limbs shaking so much I feel like I might collapse. I have no fucking idea what to do, and it's going to rip me in half.

Suddenly, as if he's talking to me, my mind forms an image of Fhord. "Listen to me, rabbit," he snarls, his eyes flashing.

"You can help Astarot. I haven't been able to control a dragon in Vanatia because the Dróttning's powers drown out mine. But she's not there. You're strong enough to do this, but you *must* be close to the dragon. The beast's will is steel, and it will take all you have to drag her from the fever controlling her. She needs to be nearly on top of you for it to work. Call Astarot. Make him bring his fight to the ground."

Fhord's more intense than I've ever seen him, almost sparking with his power.

Then, as quickly as he came, he's gone. I shake my head, dispelling the image. It felt real, as if some part of me connected with Fhord, even through the barrier, to find the knowledge I need to survive. I don't think it's possible. Fhord couldn't really have told me that. My mind probably forged a message I needed to hear. But I'll do it. If I don't control this dragon, we'll all die.

Opening my thoughts, I cast them frantically toward my dragon. Agony ripples through me, knives shoving into my skin, cutting through nerves and muscles and sinew everywhere. But I can't let him know how his pain affects me. Taking a deep breath, I harden my voice and throw it at him. *Bring the fight to me, Astarot.*

No! His single word blasts into my thoughts, echoing as it ricochets across my mind. He's resolved to protect me from this dragon as long as he can. *Go,* he adds, begging me to run and hide.

I won't leave you. I can help you if you come closer.

Dangerous. This word is a plea. My valiant, tortured dragon will give his life to protect mine.

Let me help you, I beg, my voice cracking. But then another emotion rises in me, eclipsing the fear that's been building since we saw the northern dragon. Fury. At this wild dragon but even more than that, at Astarot.

All I can think is typical fucking male.

I don't need you to protect me, Astarot. I need you to live. Get your dragon ass down here.

Bastard chuckles. He's dripping blood, pain pounding through every part of him, and he fucking laughs at me. *Now!* I yell. Because I am not some helpless maiden that needs to be saved. I will save him.

I can see his smile from here, feel the pride that whispers through our bond. He chose a warrior as his rider. And a warrior is what he got.

I gasp as Astarot tucks his wings, agony surging through our bond like a flame. It catches the other dragon off-guard, giving my beast a few seconds to plummet toward me and spin toward his attacker.

I cast my will as the dragon approaches and exhale, relief washing over me as I grasp all I can do. The magic seeping through my veins is unlike anything I've ever encountered. My tenuous bond with Fhord has given me his gifts as well as mine. I can absorb the essence of anything and anyone in these worlds, discern what drives it—even if those forces are nothing more than atoms spinning in an inanimate object—and manipulate them into bending to my will.

It's not the slow process my magic usually requires of me, digging into brains and learning about my subject through trial and error. His magic, which has become my magic, is immediate. Intense. I was strong before, but by the gods, Fhord and I are stronger together.

My magic, subtle though it is, adds the depth in manipulating beings that Fhord's lacks. Neither of us would have been able to control this dragon on our own. But our powers are not without limit. I know as my thoughts graze against this beast's that it would be too great a task to steal control of her feral mind and compel her to surrender to me. Maybe I could do it safely with enough time to understand the dragon—many minutes, instead of moments—but not immediately, as Fhord's magic typically works. Not without Fhord here with me.

With our powers joined, though, I should be able to mold this beast to my will in smaller matters, like forcing a retreat.

All of this cascades through my thoughts in an instant as I watch the copper dragon stall mid-flight, flapping her wings ponderously as confusion washes over her features. For a few seconds, she hovers in the air as she rages an internal battle for control of her psyche. She's wild, savage and bloodthirsty, craving Astarot's blood with a hunger that consumes her and drives every instinct. My demand that she let go of the chase—abandon this beast that would fill her belly for days—battles every urge and need thrumming through her veins.

But her thoughts aren't focused enough to withstand mine. Her fight against my command lasts twelve beats of my heart, its echo pounding through me. She surrenders with a soul-wrenching wail, tossing her head back to scream at the heavens. I push another command into her twisted brain—never attack this dragon again—and I again sense our attacker's resistance. This time, though, she yields quickly.

With one more angry shriek, spitting flames of desperation in our direction, the copper beast submits to my will. Slowly, laboriously, she turns toward the east, craving the familiarity of her nest after our heartbreaking encounter. She's beaten and confused and wants nothing more than to sleep.

I pull back my thoughts as the dragon turns into a shadow on the horizon, releasing her only when I'm sure she'll heed my command to stay away. To leave Astarot alone. I wish I could do more because I *need* to find some way to control one of these northern dragons, but right now, I don't have anything left to give. I'll learn more about the reach of our combined magic before I try again.

When the beast lets go of me too, I sway, dizzy from the fight. Dropping to the ground for a moment, I close my eyes and center myself, using Fhord as my anchor as I remember how complete I felt when his thoughts dropped into mine.

"That was amazing," I breathe, my thoughts shuffling through the intensity of the last couple of minutes. "Fhord and I are a powerful pair." And then I feel his pain. "Astarot." My gaze spins toward my injured dragon.

He looks like shit. He's extended his wings again, the agony of having them folded in on themselves too much to bear. As those beautiful fans drag on the ground—gaping holes splattered across them—echoes of his agony convulse across my back, nearly forcing me to my knees. Blood oozes out of him, dripping in heavy splats to the floor below us. The rest of his body seems okay, his attacker having focused on Astarot's weakness, but it doesn't lessen his agony.

I don't think we can do this. You can't carry sheep with those wings. I can feel my dragon's trauma.

Strong. His voice holds no tremor or hint of his pain. A rueful laugh spills from me as I catch a whiff of indignation that I might consider him too weak to do what he must. He's been through worse.

If he can fly through his pain, I sure as fuck can get through this too. *All right, big guy,* I mutter. *Let's go then.*

I steel myself as I race back to the herd. The fight took precious minutes, that we didn't have to give. I have no idea in Helheim how we're going to do this, especially with Astarot's injured wings.

My hands are trembling as I grab the rope I dropped when the dragon attacked us, checking my lasso before I turn back toward the sheep. Inhaling deeply, I struggle to control my galloping heart. We don't have time for this shit. I need to get these sheep and figure out how to get them back to the trolls.

When I've gathered the six sheep Astarot will carry the first time—two sets of three sheep tied together—I turn to find Astarot barreling toward me. *Move,* he demands. He wants me to get away from the sheep. I have no idea what he has in mind, but I also have not a single clue about how to do this. So I drop the rope and jog back to the herd, leaving our first group huddling in the clearing.

Astarot swoops in—pain trembling through our bond as he fully extends his wings—and wraps his talons around the largest sheep in each set. Flinging himself upward, he snaps the rope, breaking the necks of the other sheep as they're lifted from the ground. They hang there, literally dead weight in his claws, as he spins to aim directly toward the trolls.

I can only watch, astounded, while he flies away.

We just might make it.

Shaking my head, I gather more rope and tie another lasso, then race back toward the herd. I ignore the sun that's setting too fast behind me, focusing on preparing the next six sheep while Astarot delivers the first group. Every few minutes, Dani's face rises in my thoughts, my morbid brain conjuring an image of the trolls gutting her for their meal, but I push it away. No time for that shit.

I've just tied up the last of the sheep when I sense Astarot returning. The pain is almost too much to bear, as he moves faster than he should with his wings so damaged. I clench my chin, embracing the agony because he has no choice. He's going to do the impossible and no injury will stop him.

Again, his voice rumbles in my mind. *Move.* He doesn't want to wait for me to mount him, and I know he's right. He won't make it if he takes the time to get me; I'm not sure if he'll make it even without me. But it's our best chance.

I drop the ropes, give him a quick caress through our bond, and start running toward the trolls. I'll return on my own. It's only a few vikus, and I can't ask Astarot to come back for me.

Soon, he tells me as he dives for the sheep. I glance behind me to see him grasp the two largest sheep in this group and yank them all into the sky, again breaking the necks of the four suspended in the air. The lowest sheep barely misses me as Astarot passes overhead, slower to gain altitude this time than before. But he's strong. He'll get there. I just hope he'll be on time.

My stomach is in my throat as I run, but it's not just from exhaustion. Everything depends on Astarot's tattered wings making it to the trolls before the sun sets. He's strong, but I don't know if any dragon could do what they've demanded of him. And I can't do shit about it. I can only wait for his word, racing as fast as I can.

Finally, I sense his relief through the bond. *Safe*, he tells me.

Again, Fhord's image rises in my thoughts. This time, it's his smile, eyes crinkling as he joins me in this moment of joy. I know it's not real, but I cling to it with all I am.

Because I've come to realize in a ridiculously short amount of time that I'm empty without him.

He's part of me.

I hate it.

I still don't know if I can trust him.

But I can't deny it.

CHAPTER ELEVEN

FHORD

I DON'T ANSWER TO YOU

I CAN'T GET BACK to her.

I have no gods-damned idea what happened. How my mind got pulled into Sifa's. One minute, I'm sitting with my Ætt, talking about the supplies we'll need to travel north. The next minute my rabbit's thoughts, her surroundings, her terror, are mine. I can see the dragon attacking Astarot. Feel Sifa's helplessness.

And I know exactly what she needs to do to survive.

I barely notice Leif's wide eyes or Astrid's slack jaw as I bark out orders at my little rabbit. Her only hope is calling that huge fucking beast closer and forcing it to bend to her will. As soon as I'm done, though, she's gone. I'm back in an abandoned building in Vanatia, a long fucking way from my mate trapped in the North with a rabid dragon.

"Fuck." I can't keep the frustration, the fear, from my voice.

"What was that, boss?" Leif's worried. I would be too if I'd just watched me lose my gods-damned mind and scream at empty air.

"She's in danger. Astarot's fighting another dragon. And losing. I had a few seconds in her mind then I lost it. I don't know how to get back. To figure out whether she's safe."

"You'd know if she'd been hurt." Joralf's voice drifts to us from across the room. "If your bond is unchanged, she's alive and unharmed."

"Anything could have happened," I snarl at him. "The dragon was attacking Astarot. Maybe he's dead already."

"I suspect you'd know that as well. Intense emotions open the path between mates. If her dragon died, Sifa's grief would echo across this world. He lives."

"How do I get back to her mind? I need more than that." Or I will abandon Harald's bullshit quest now and go find Sifa. See her for my own gods-damned self.

Joralf smiles, his kind eyes watching me as I fight to control my emotions. "It's good we're going north, then. When you're closer to her, you'll have an easier time feeling her presence." He pauses, watching me for a moment. "I suspect that not many mates would be able to connect through the barrier," he adds at last. "Yours is a powerful pairing."

I suck in a deep breath, then another, forcing myself to calm down. She needs me here. I'll ruin everything if I get drawn into a half-assed rescue she doesn't need. I told her what to do, and she can sure as fuck do it. My little rabbit can take care of herself. Pausing, I search for our bond, finding it deep in my gut, the home of every magical thing about me. It's pulsing with its vigor. Sifa's alive.

"We have a strong bond," I agree at last. "Stronger than any magic that tries to stand between us." Releasing a slow exhale, I add—as much to myself as anyone else—"I guess I'll know if she needs me again."

Torsten grunts from my side. "Time to go."

He's always been a man of few words.

Within an hour, the horses are packed and we're picking our way through the nearby forest. Everyone's going except Axel and the stable boy Knut sent there to hide. Axel will maintain his façade, keeping his patrol of this area and listening to the Nest for any news that might help us. The stable boy will keep hiding. Aksell's a mean bastard, and he's got claws in both Nests. We may need someone who spent time in Aksell's household in the weeks ahead, when we're ready to move against him. If we ever get to that point.

I'm antsy. Sigurd's the best horse I could have, but he's not Tindera. I'd do almost anything to be on her back right now, racing toward the Nest. But at least we're headed in her direction. Maybe we could even get her out without Harald's help. She's not being tortured right now, but she's already suffered at the Dróttning's hands. And she'll suffer more while she's there.

I feel so fucking helpless.

We're not going to push the horses as hard as I pushed Sigurd to get here, but we'll make good time. We should reach the Nest by sunset tomorrow. That'll give us a chance to find a cave and rest before we go in again. We've been lucky so far, escaping without injury. I hope our luck holds out. I doubt it will, though. The gods have been fucking with me for a long time, and they're bound to catch up with us soon.

"There's another one up ahead," I yell at Leif as I sense someone a viku or so away—our third sentry of the day and it's not even noon yet. This'll slow us down more than we expected. but it can't be avoided. "Go west."

Leif nudges his horse to catch up with Fróðr, who's taken the lead. Turns out, Fróðr knows Vanatia well. He held a powerful job in land management in Revalle, and I still can't believe our paths never crossed. He's traveled every inch of this realm, most of it a few times. He abandoned his job when Joralf returned, joining his mate in the rebellion, but he promises he knows many in the Dróttning's service who will help if we need it.

I may not like Joralf—that fucking elf has no gods-damned right to suggest I'd put my mate at risk if I had any other choice—but he and Fróðr are strong allies. Especially if Joralf and his people really have figured out how the Dróttning controls the dragons.

We make decent progress that day, considering how often we're forced to change directions to avoid one patrol or another. Within an hour after sunset, we're trudging up to the cave we'd hoped to reach, flinging ourselves from our horses as we unpack and start to throw together a quick meal.

I'm tired, but I need to understand why Mikkael and Johan are here. Why they would have turned on Bevin. Now's as good a time as any. Plopping myself next to them by the fire after dinner, my gaze catches theirs, one by one, trying to read them.

"Liv's got good reason to fight against the Dróttning," I say when I have their full attention. "And I know where Frida stands. She's been working with Knut and other rebels embedded in the southern Nest for a long time. She's got my trust too. But Bevin sure as fuck isn't our friend. He'd like to see the Dróttning dead, but only so he can take her place. And you've been his loyal soldiers in everything." I pause, my face set in hard planes, eyes cold, making sure they know not to bullshit me. "Why should I trust you?"

"You've been the Dróttning's loyal soldier. Why should we trust you?" Mikkael's dark eyes are just as frigid as mine. His amber skin glows in the firelight, long dark hair tied back with a strap of some kind, revealing every bit of his fierce face. He's bigger than Johan, as tall as me but broader across the chest.

"You don't know shit about me," I spit out, "except that I'm in charge here. I don't have to prove anything to you. But if you're coming with us, you gods-damned well better convince me I can trust you."

Johan reaches his hand out to rest it on Mikkael's shoulder. "Don't bullshit him, Mik. He needs to know what you know."

Mikkael's quiet for a minute or more, just watching me, before he gives me a perfunctory nod. "We've been working for Bevin long enough to know what a bastard he is. He plays both sides, gathering information from wherever he can get it, but he always twists things his way. I realized when I started to look around me, really see the people working for Bevin, that Johan and Sifa were using him. They weren't fully on-board with Bevin's goals. I knew I could trust them. And then something happened about a year ago that opened my eyes."

"That would have been right after my Ætt and I landed in Revalle."

"It's not a coincidence," Johan says, his voice somber.

I spin my head to look at him. "What the fuck does that mean?"

"When you got there, Bevin took an interest in you."

"And?"

Mikkael's back straightens, his shoulders pushing back, drawing my gaze back to him. "He had me look into you. He figured he'd pissed the Dróttning off one too many times and she sent you to take his place."

"Bevin's a smart guy." Of course he suspected me.

"What'd you find?"

"I followed you for a long time. You are the most para-noid bastard I've ever tracked."

I smirk at him. "Damn straight." With the Dróttning as a mother, I have to be careful.

Mikkael smirks right back. "I caught you, though. Al-most didn't follow you that night. My girl pissed me off, so I went and tracked you while I was blowing off some steam."

"Lucky me."

"Yeah, lucky you. I wasn't the only one following you, but you gave me enough that night to convince Bevin he could trust you, even though I knew he couldn't. He pulled everyone back after that."

"What'd you see?"

"You saved Sifa from a prick who tried to get back at her after she gave Bevin some dirt on him."

"Lukan." I spew out the name, wishing he was still alive so I could kill him again, more slowly this time.

Mikkael dips his chin. "Lukan."

"And?"

"I saw it all."

Fuck. I'll never forget that night. I was a breath or two away from losing control of my savage, which hadn't happened in decades. He wanted to destroy the male who threatened Sifa. I knew then that Sifa was our mate. And that my life would be very fucking complicated if I got too close to her.

Torsten drops down next to me, shoving a cup of ale into my hand. I suck every bit of it down as my mind replays my encounter with Lukan. I realized when I came to Revalle that I'd need to keep some distance between Sifa and me. I made sure I knew what she was doing, where and when. If our paths got too close, I reinforced my barrier and used all my skill to distract her. To keep her from noticing me.

That's what brought Lukan to me. He came to the Kastali looking for money. He'd figured out that Sifa's an elf and wanted to sell her to the Dróttning. I arranged it so he would come to me instead of someone else. After I'd paid him off, I tracked him and made sure he'd never talk again. He was a slimy bastard and deserved to die for a lot of shit.

He didn't die easy or quick, but he still only suffered a small part of the pain he'd caused over the years. My savage took way too much joy in watching him bleed and squirm and beg.

And I talked too fucking much while I worked. Told him things I never tell anyone.

Lukan learned a lot about me and my allegiances before he died.

Which means Mikkael learned a lot about me. And about Bevin.

I was pissed off about what that quisling forced Sifa to do. Every fucked-up job she carried out for Bevin in her effort to find information that might lead her back home. I told Lukan every reason Bevin needed to die exactly like Lukan was dying.

Fucking sloppy. The mating bond screwed with my head that night and my savage needed to tell someone about our mate. It's a bullshit excuse, but it's the only one I've got.

"Well, the Dróttning never threw me into a hole, so I guess I can trust you."

"I've never told anyone what I heard. Never will."

"Not even Sifa?" He's supposed to be her friend. Why the fuck wouldn't he tell her that he heard her fucking mate ranting about their bond as he slowly killed someone who threatened her?

"She doesn't need this shit," Mikkael snarls before pausing, his gaze holding mine. "You lead a dangerous life, dragon rider. You're together now, and I don't think that's gonna change, but it's put a gods-damned target on her back. I wasn't gonna be the one to fuck everything up for her by throwing you in her path."

Fuck if that ain't the truth. I watch him for a long time, but I don't need to weigh his words. He's her friend, so I dip my chin. "Okay."

His lips twitch up for a second before his stoic expression returns. "Thanks."

"And him?" My chin spins to point at Johan.

"He's been working with Fróðr's people for years. They watch Bevin and his drudges nearly as much as they watch the Dróttning. Johan's given them important information. They trust him."

"All right." Reaching for Johan, I offer him my arm. He clasps it with a sharp nod before turning back toward the fire.

"Why haven't you been part of the insurrection, Fhord?" Johan's quiet voice ends the conversation in the room.

"I told Mikkael, and I'll tell you. I don't answer to you."

Johan turns toward me. His expression is guarded as he stares at me, shoulders thrown back. "We're with you no matter what. And I know I can't demand your answer. But as a friend of Sifa's, who's been quietly watching over her and protecting her secrets for a lot of years, I'm asking you. Your mate's an elf. Why haven't you been helping us, Fhord?"

"Fuck you, Johan."

"Fuck you, Fhord. Are you gonna answer me?"

"I don't answer to you," I growl, holding back the fist that itches to close that gods-damned mouth.

"Then you can answer to her," Johan growls back, eyes narrowing as he leans toward me. "But hear this, dragon rider. Mik and I have known Sifa for a long fucking time and we're here because of her. Not you. If you fuck her over ... if this is all bullshit and you *ever* expose Sifa to danger because of some asinine allegiance to the Dróttning ... we will end you. You think you're strong, but nobody's strong enough to withstand the vengeance we will rain down if you hurt her."

I smile because it soothes something deep inside of me to know these males are this committed to my rabbit. But they're still assholes so I'm sure as fuck not gonna let them know that. Standing, I shove my mug at Torsten and stalk toward the cavern's mouth.

This is why I never told my Ætt about Sifa, and why I'm not gonna try to explain myself to these males. They wouldn't understand my *need* to run from Sifa and this mating bond. None of them ride dragons. None can understand what it's like to be trapped between your dragon and your mate. Knowing that my gods-damned mother is going to make one of them suffer for my choices. Today it's Tindera, but if she captures Sifa again, it'll be my rabbit tomorrow. Maybe both. And there's not shit I can do about it while the Dróttning lives.

I stand there for a long time watching the stars, thinking about the mishmash of rebels demanding answers from me that I'll never be able to give them. Quickly, my thoughts focus on Sifa—they always do—this time reminding me how badly I fucked up with her already. She may never forgive me, and I can't blame her one little bit.

Eventually, the chatter and laughter slow down and then end as people find their blankets for the night. I stay because I don't think I can shut off my mind. And I don't want to. At least right now, I can imagine a future in which Sifa and Tindera are both mine and free of the Dróttning.

A large hand on my shoulder drags me from a memory of flying with Tindera, and I turn to look into Toffer's eyes. They're so kind. Surprisingly humane for a being born with an instinct to kill.

"Sifa's strong savior." He smiles, a lopsided grin that brings a smile to my face.

"She got caught because of me. I wasn't going to leave her there."

"Tindera's trapped today."

"She is. But we'll get her out."

"Pain pummels my pal."

His gaze holds mine for a moment and then he wraps his arms around me, pulling me close. My back straightens, and I'm too stunned for a moment to move. I have to fight the urge to push him away. Nobody except Sifa hugs me. Nobody would dare, not even my Ætt. But then I take a deep breath because he's hurting as much as me. Maybe he needs this.

Maybe I need this.

Finally, I lift my arms and hug him back. "It'll be okay, Toffer. I promise. We'll make it okay."

"Triumph together tomorrow."

A laugh bubbles out of me. A fucking laugh. Bubbles from me.

I need to get away from this troll.

I squeeze him one last time, though, before leaning back to capture his gaze. "Yes. Tomorrow we'll triumph together."

Grinning, he reaches up to pat my cheek before turning and traipsing toward his blankets. When a yawn erupts from me, I realize I might be able to rest after all. Following him in, I find my own spot and drop into sleep sooner than I would have thought possible.

"Wake up, bitches." The gnarl that drags me from sleep has me reaching for my sword before I spin toward the idiot who's decided to rob us. Or whatever the fuck he plans to do.

"I wouldn't do that, Fhord."

Flipping over, I see a stocky man outlined at the cave's entrance. "Who the fuck are you?" I demand as I stand. My sword hangs low in front of me, ready for whatever he plans.

"Don't recognize me, huh? Tindera's rider never paid much attention to the smaller dragons. But my dragon's strong enough to carry you back to the Nest."

My mind scrambles for an image of the asshole standing in our path. I can't see shit, though, with his face hidden in shadows. I don't have a single fuck of an idea who he is or why he thinks he's strong enough to threaten us. "I see one of you and twelve of us," I snarl. "How do you think you're gonna do that?"

"I don't need them," he barks with a snide laugh. "I'll tell the Dróttning where to find the rest of the traitors when I get you out of here."

"And why would I leave with you?"

"Because if you don't, my dragon will roast all of you. She's hungry. And she likes how humans ... and elves ... taste." He steps forward—just enough for the light to reveal a malicious grin on his face—and his eyes swing toward Joralf and Fróðr. They're standing along with the others, blades in hand and ready to attack.

"There's not much room for a dragon in here. I think you're talking out your ass."

"Khirta's a little bitch," he bawls. "Fucking runt the Dróttning stuck me with. But her size comes in handy sometimes. Like now. She'll fit just fine in here."

"Bring her in, then. I don't want to hurt a dragon, but we'll kill both of you if that's what we have to do."

His eyes grow distant for a moment as he talks to his beast. When a small green dragon ducks into the cavern with us, I realize we may be in trouble. We chose this cave because we thought it would be safe from just this risk. Not many dragons can fit in here. This one can.

"The Dróttning will want me alive. You can't kill them without killing me."

The rider cackles, his dragon spinning her head to watch her master spit out maniacal laughter that echoes around us. Finally, he stops, taking one step forward as he holds my gaze. "You fucked up this time, Fhord. The Dróttning wants you alive or dead. You've turned her against you at last. And I couldn't be happier that I'll get to carry your burnt body back to her."

My heartbeat falters and then quickens as his words sink in. I've always believed the Dróttning wouldn't take my life. That she'd make me suffer for turning against her, but the worst she'd do is stick me in a prison somewhere and keep me there until she'd punished me enough. Until I convinced her I could be trusted.

I've always believed that no matter what, she'd keep me alive.

If she told her soldiers to bring me in alive or dead, everything's changed.

CHAPTER TWELVE

SIFA

WATER IS LIFE

W E'RE STAYING FOR DINNER.

Not on the menu—thank the gods—but as guests. I didn't want to accept their invitation, which was more of a demand than anything else. We have to find a dragon and figure out how to get it to Harald willingly.

I need to get back to Vanatia. I don't know if I'll scream at Fhord for leaving me here or fuck him until neither of us can stand, but it'll be one or the other. Maybe both, although I have no idea in which order.

I definitely don't want to share a meal with trolls who wanted to eat my dragon an hour ago.

Dani convinced me. "Northern trolls are very peculiar about social slights," she'd explained. "Trust me, they've killed for less than turning down a dinner invitation."

Plus, Astarot desperately needs to rest and let his wings heal. So, we'll have dinner with the trolls tonight.

As soon as I nod my consent, the leader, Rockjaw, gives me a grimace that I think is supposed to be a smile. He spins to point toward a small lake a few hundred feet away, uttering, "Bathe will dragon," then strides away, the rest of the trolls scampering after him.

I'm so confused. "Does he want Astarot to bathe for dinner?"

"I think so?" Dani sounds as thrown as me. But then she turns toward the water, her eyes brightening as she gazes at the soft Azul waves. "I wonder if we could get in too?" She glances back at me with a shrug. "We'd already been traveling for a while when the Monarch felt Fhord break through the barrier. It's been many days since I've felt clean."

I look toward my dragon, who is a little bloody after his fight. *They want you to bathe.*

He responds with the blink that means yes, dropping to let me tug off my packs. We'd left them on when we went after the sheep in case we needed something, but he's eager to free his feathers. Gathering supplies to wash off, I follow him to the shore. He beats me there easily, dropping into the water with a resounding splash and his dragony grin.

By the gods, I love this beast.

River. He recognizes the sensation of bathing here. It's part of the same system that healed him in Vanatia—the liquid I breathed through that triggered every nerve in my body in a good way. And now I'm anxious to join him.

Casting my gaze around to make sure nobody's openly staring, I strip down quickly and submerge myself. I can't hold back the groan because he's right. It's the same life-giving elixir Fhord led us to in Vanatia.

My gaze finds Dani, who is shuddering as she steps into the lake. "This is amazing," I murmur. "Are there many places to find water like this here?"

She shakes her head as she fully submerges herself. "I've heard rumors but nothing more. I'm sure the Monarch knows where they are. I'm surprised there's one here, so close to your lands." She pauses, watching me with narrowed eyes. I can almost see her mind whirling. "I'm also surprised a band of trolls and a dragon make their homes here, near each other and the south. The barrier repels most life in this area."

My thoughts take me back to the Nest and the lake we swam through to escape, and then to the river that healed Astarot. They have different properties, but can it be a coincidence that dragons and trolls chose this place, even overcoming the natural repellant of the barrier to stay? What if controlling the dragons was as easy as controlling the water that sustains them?

Memories of Fhord soon take the place of the questions I can't answer as my mind replays those moments after he broke me free of the Nest, and then our time together in the river, just being close to each other. The frustration and anger I've been feeling seem to wash away—for now, at least—leaving behind an ache for him. My body tingles even without any touch, and I wonder if it's the barrier alone that's creating a chasm in my heart, or if I'll always feel like this, even when we're both in Vanatia.

Fuck, I miss him. The fates decided long ago that we should spend our lives together, and they sure as fuck knew what they were doing. Every piece of Fhord fits every piece of me, and I need that life with him more than I want to admit to myself. I just need to know making him part of my life won't drag the Dróttning into it too. Or me into hers. I won't go back to her prison. I'm not sure if I'd survive more time on the rack, losing my skin—and my sanity—slice by excruciating slice.

Healed. Astarot's thoughts drop into my mind, dragging me from the ugly place my mind had taken me. I turn to smile at him, relief filling me. Wish we could bottle this stuff.

Sheep, he adds. He's hungry and thinking about the large herd we raided.

Go. When I forced the other dragon away, I told her to leave you alone. I think she'll comply. You should be safe.

He drops his chin once before standing to saunter out of the lake, shaking like a wet dog, enormous drops of water flinging everywhere. With a strong push of his wings, he's airborne, racing toward the fields.

I drag myself out of the water soon after, throwing on some clothes before I gather our supplies to pitch a tent. Dani's still bathing, which is fine by me. I love the idea of some time alone. Just as I'm laying down, though, a troll whistles at me. "Trolls hunger," he says from a few feet away.

"Dani's not here yet," I explain as I stretch my legs in front of me. "We'll join you as soon as she gets back and dresses."

"Trolls hunger," he repeats, a bit more of a command in his tone.

I guess it's dinnertime.

Pulling myself up, my gaze follows him as he stalks to a large table that's been erected nearby, laden with food. A moment later, Dani struts toward the tent, a towel wrapped around her, with flaming eyes. I guess she got the same demand as me. At least I was dressed.

Astarot's gliding in when I reach the table, his wings extended as he lets the air carry him. He feels content, full and healthy. I wish I could go snuggle with him, but we're here. I may as well make good use of the chance to learn about the northern dragons from beings that seem to know them well.

The food's surprisingly good—mutton roasted perfectly with a sage gravy, three types of root vegetables, salads and other greens, a ridiculous amount of bread and a sticky pudding that I may obsess over for days.

And now I'm glad we stayed for dinner.

Rockjaw turns toward me when the last of our plates is empty, his gaze holding mine. He doesn't speak—these trolls are beings of few words, unlike Toffer—but he seems to want to communicate something to me. Finally, he pulls a cigarette of some sort out of a pocket and offers it to me. I shake my head, but his hand doesn't move. This seems to be as important as dinner. I nod my thanks and reach for it, letting him light it for me.

"Dragon retreats." He must have watched the dragons fight, seen the copper beast's surrender.

I hesitate to answer for a moment, but then the realization washes over me. I don't have to hide from anyone here. Harald doesn't persecute elves the way the Dróttning does. I don't have to pretend to be less than I am.

"I can manipulate other beings, to a degree," I tell him. "I was able to control her mind for a time, compel her to leave. I also told her to leave my dragon alone and I think she will. I might be able to do more if I have enough time—maybe even convince her to go with me to Harald's kastali. I'm here to try."

He takes a long drag from his cigarette, watching me in silence. At one point, he turns toward the troll Astarot had trapped and their expressions shift in what I think must be some unspoken communication. When the other troll rises and walks away, Rockjaw looks at me again. It feels like something's changed. The hostility I sensed before is gone.

"Dragon swims."

"Do you mean Astarot, or the northern dragon?"

His gaze lifts toward the distant mountain before returning to me. "Dragon swims."

My head is spinning but I think I know where he's going with this. "Are you saying that everyone is here because of the water?"

He nods, his eyes crinkling as his gaze grows sharper.

"The water is important to you? Its healing properties?"

"Water is life."

"That's true, but all water is life."

He looks toward the lake, his expression placid. Pointing, he says in a more demanding tone, "Water is life."

"The dragon needs this water? She's here for the same reason as you? Because you all need it to survive?"

He nods once. "Water is life."

"How does that help me? What do I need to do to reach this dragon? Convince her to go to Harald with us?"

Now his gaze spins toward Astarot. "Water is life. Trolls go."

I'm even more confused for a moment—struggling to understand what is so important, and how his thoughts connect—and then I get it.

"You're leaving and we should stay. Because the dragon will come here, and we can use this to try to control her?"

His eyes light up, a grin creasing his cheeks. He reaches out to pat my shoulder and stands just as the previously trapped troll returns, a large bundle of rope in his outstretched hand. He hands it to me as Rockjaw says, "Strong."

"Are you saying this rope can hold a dragon?"

Rockjaw's chin dips sharply. "Strong," he repeats.

He turns and sweeps away before I can question him further, splitting the air with a sharp whistle. The trolls respond immediately, each with their own role in cleaning up the meal they just prepared for us—some gathering the remaining food, others the dirty plates and silver, while a large group drags the tables and chairs toward waiting carts. Less than a half-hour after finishing dinner, they're tromping toward the woods, leaving Astarot, Dani, and me alone next to the lake.

"Well, that was fucking weird," Dani announces before she spins and stalks toward our tent.

I watch her for a moment and then go snuggle with my dragon, ready to finally relax together after a hard day. He's tired, his snout laying on the ground as his eyes narrow to little slits. But I don't need to talk. I just need to think. And there's no better place to do it.

The sun's peeking over the horizon when another nightmare startles me awake. It wasn't as bad as the night before—Astarot settles me too—but the memories keep finding their way into my dreams. I can hide from them during the day because I've learned how to control my mind, keep the torture from haunting me. I can't escape them at night, though.

I hadn't intended to sleep here, but I'm glad I did. I feel good. Well rested and alert. Ready for whatever the fates may have planned for me today.

That's what I thought.

Before the fates' plans appeared in the sky above us.

We're pounding the final stakes into the ground to secure the ropes the trolls left for us—that they promise are strong enough to hold a dragon—when Astarot growls, a low warning from his chest. He stands abruptly, moving closer to me as his eyes scan the sky. A chill rolls up my spine when I see a brown dragon winging our way, flames spreading out as if to light the path in front of him. He's huge. And he's pissed that Astarot is here waiting for him.

Why would a different dragon be coming here? I thought they were territorial—that only the copper dragon would be in this area.

Water. Astarot understood the troll's message last night because he now understands the significance of the water. In the Nest, in northern Vanatia, and here, water is life. He thinks it's control too. He's becoming convinced the water in the northern Nest is key to the Dróttning's control, or at least part of it.

We'll discuss that tomorrow, I tell him as I watch the large, angry dragon spiral down toward us. *For now, what are your chances of winning a fight with this dragon?*

Strong. I wish Astarot was referring to his chances but he's not. They're both strong dragons and he's not sure who would win. Especially after the copper dragon kicked his ass.

Better. He'd never fought a dragon before, he reminds me. He'll be a better fighter now than he was before. It may not be enough.

Hopefully, we don't need to find out. My thoughts are scattered and I'm not sure if I can exert my will over this beast but I'm gonna try. *We'll stay over here, let him go to the water. I'll reach out to him while he's drinking, see if I can access his thoughts.*

"You know what you're doing, right?"

Dani's frightened, her voice smaller than I've ever heard it. She didn't see the fight between the copper dragon and Astarot, but she did see Astarot's injuries. She'd be much more worried if she'd seen the copper dragon, only a few feathers lost and barely a scratch on her.

"Kind of," I whisper, waving a hand at her behind my back. I do not need her paranoia feeding my pessimism.

The brown beast swoops close, barely fifty feet from the ground and right above us. His eyes are pits of lava sitting inside a raging volcano, orange and red and black undulating together in a fevered dance. My thoughts spear out to caress his but reel back instinctively.

Chaos controls everything about this beast. Even in that glancing touch, I felt the depth of his pain and rage and violence. Sucking in a deep breath, I let those emotions dissipate, preparing myself for the insanity I'm about to delve into. I can't connect with these beasts, won't persuade them to join Harald, if I don't find a way to break through the mayhem of their minds.

Inhaling one more time, I release my thoughts again, reaching out to the dragon circling above us. Now that I know what to expect and am ready for him, I can find some order in the madness. Flashes of his life spill into my memories, giving me glimpses into the anarchy that drives northern dragons.

His first memory outside of the egg, forcing himself through the leathery shell to join a dozen siblings as they fight for the only meal available—other hatchlings. He knows nothing but pain and hunger. Instinct and need drive him as he wiggles free, barely avoiding the sharp, demanding beaks of his brothers and sisters in their drive to survive. Somehow, he prevails.

Days upon days upon days of aching as his stomach shrivels, his kin the only food his mother left for him, the shreds of meat he'd taken from them long gone. Lizards and rats and an occasional bunny keep him alive, but barely. He knows only appetite and emptiness. Nothing else matters.

Years upon years upon years of solitude, broken up only by struggles to survive when dragon paths cross. Predator and prey exist. He will destroy or be destroyed by every being he encounters. There is no middle ground. There is nobody except him.

Astarot shrieks at me, pulling my focus away from the creature's pitiful life. I shudder, the dragon's agony and anger rolling through me. Fhord was right. Harald's given me an impossible task. This dragon doesn't have a shred of sanity I can harness. I can't find a single rational thought. Nothing I can use to gain his allegiance.

Trap. Astarot saw the dragon's memories through me. He disagrees. He thinks we could help this dragon and that he could help us. But it'll only work if we can subdue him somehow, force him to stay close enough for me to wield my will over him.

Okay, I respond on an exhale. *Let's try. He needs to get close for me to have any chance at taking control. Next time he circles above us, I'll reach out to him.*

The dragon's getting more anxious now, eager to reach the lake but unwilling to risk moving toward us. Finally, though, he relents, tucking his wings to spear in our direction with a firm and unyielding glare. He wants us to know he's dangerous.

When he's a hundred feet away, I reel out my will, letting it wrap his mind and start to soothe away the animosity rolling out of him. I fill my thoughts with a melody that's calming and quiet.

For just a moment, it feels like it might work. Just for a moment. Then he rips free of my influence, baring his teeth as his tail whips him closer to me. Astarot rears up, throwing himself between the dragon and me, his teeth grasping for the beast's neck as he spins at the last moment, barely escaping.

Chase?

Let him be. We need his trust. We won't get it that way.

Astarot roars, a threat directed as much at me as the dragon. I better not fuck this up. Astarot will be all kinds of pissed at me if I do.

I smile, reaching out a hand to caress the knee that's dropped to the ground next to me. *I'll try to get this right*, I assure him.

The brown dragon turns in the air a few hundred feet away, his wings beating faster and faster as he propels himself at us. I'm sure he plans to attack Astarot, but he spins before he gets close enough for my thoughts to reach him, throwing himself into the sky as he bares his teeth and spits out a fire that chars the grass in front of us. I can feel Astarot's need to chase the dragon, but he holds himself back. For now.

The next time the dragon approaches, he's within my reach. My mind clutches on to his, abandoning the gentle approach I'd tried earlier. I controlled the copper dragon, forced her away, with a clear demand. Maybe that's the only way to control these dragons.

Land, I snap at him, raising a finger to point at a nearby field.

I can feel his anger at me, his desperate need to defy me. Now I can sense this dragon's first rational thoughts. He's never been bested by another being. Every fight, every clash of wills, every single challenge has ended with his enemy barely escaping, or him ripping their throat. Feasting on their entrails. Spewing their feathers from his blood-soaked maw. A teeny elf, not even big enough for a meal, will not be the first to defeat him.

I grit my teeth, throwing everything I have into my demand that he bend. I'm not strong enough to do this alone. But even with the barrier between us, I have Fhord's gifts. I have Astarot. And I have me. I will capture this dragon here. I will control it.

The brown dragon lands at last, as far from us as my thoughts will let him stray. He's flinging his head, howling at the vise that's gripped his mind. His emotions are deranged and disorganized, swinging from hate to anger to desperation in a matter of seconds. Most of all, though, he's more volatile and enraged than he's ever been in his life.

You will stand down, I bark at him, throwing all my power into my command. He snarls back but takes the step forward that I demand, then another. His head is still swinging erratically, as if he's trying to dislodge a rider wrapped around his snout, but he's moving toward us and the ropes we'll use to bind him when he's close enough.

Finally, perhaps five minutes after he landed, the dragon is where we need him. I'm exhausted, the demands of so much magic dragging me down, suffocating me. But I can't let him go. If I do, Dani and I are dead and Astarot's doomed.

I wrap his thoughts more tightly as we stride forward to finish this capture with its most dangerous part. We need to trap him. I hope to Helheim the trolls were right, and the ropes they left us will contain the dragon. Because we're fucked if they don't.

Grasping his psyche in mine, exhaustion nearly overtaking me, I work with Astarot and Dani to secure his neck, legs, and tail, leaving him enough room to sit but not enough to stand. He's fighting me the whole time, pushing against my will and its demand that he stay in place. Let us trap him. Twice, I almost lose it, my mind stretched too thin. But I hold on.

At last, we tie off the last rope and scamper back, putting as much space between us and our captive as we can. And I let go. My will dissipates and the dragon screeches at us, spitting out a wall of flame. Astarot leaps forward, his chest a barrier between us and the fire.

I collapse. He'll fight the ropes. Maybe he'll win. But I can't do anything about it. I'm too exhausted to care.

CHAPTER THIRTEEN

SIFA

BOB

BOB ISN'T HAPPY.

I slept long and hard last night but couldn't drag myself out of bed for a while. Instead, I lay in the tent alone, my thoughts focused on Fhord. Again. My emotions keep swinging back and forth between the anger and betrayal I feel about him leaving me here with that bastard Harald—combined with my absolute certainty that Fhord's hiding more secrets—and the desperate need I have to hold him, to feel his body next to mine. I don't know how we'll make this work if I can't trust him. But I have no idea how I'd live without him.

I finally gave up searching for answers and went out to face the day.

Where Bob greeted me with a screech.

Astarot tried to find a name in whatever part of Bob's mind my dragon could access, but he concluded our captive doesn't have one. *Alone*, he'd explained. No being ever got close enough to Bob to give him a name. We probably should have chosen a better one because Bob? We couldn't give him something a bit more dragony? Less literal?

But Dani already had settled on Bob by the time I woke up. "He's been bobbing up and down, testing the ropes, since we captured him," she'd explained.

Since Astarot couldn't offer anything else, it stuck.

That's not what Bob's pissed about. I doubt he cares what we call him. He's angry we trapped him. And who could blame him?

"I'm feeling strong enough to try again," I tell Dani over breakfast.

"The quicker you connect with him, the better. I don't know if I'll be able to rest with him nearby, just held by a few ropes. If he gets free, we'll be snacks on his way to the feast your dragon will give him."

Bob puffs out a flame, his eyes narrowing. He seems to be agreeing with Dani, although I'm not sure he grasps our language. My commands yesterday were spoken, but the magic carries a universal meaning that all beasts understand. I think his fiery outburst is just ongoing evidence of his anger.

"I don't know how I'm going to do this. He's so irrational. All anger and hunger and pain. I don't see anything I can use to reach him."

"Didn't the troll say we should use the water?"

"He did, but what does that mean? Do we keep him away, basically torturing him, until we break his will? Seems cruel."

"I guess. Torture's effective. Could be just what the dragon needs."

I stare at her for a moment, rattled by her blasé attitude about mistreating a being who's already lived a life of misery and trauma. She wouldn't be so dismissive if she'd ever been tortured. "I'd rather avoid that if I have a choice."

She shrugs, standing to head toward our tent. "Your call," she mutters over her shoulder before stalking inside and then heading toward the lake with a towel and clothes.

I turn toward Astarot, finally coming up with a semblance of a plan. *Do dragons prefer their sheep alive or dead?*

He snorts out a laugh. *Alive.* It's emasculating to offer a dead beast to a dragon—a suggestion they can't kill on their own. Only their elders choose carrion.

Alive it is, then. Let's go to the herd. You can eat and I'll get a few to bring back for Bob. I'll try to develop some pleasant feelings and emotions in him. Give him food and water while I sing a rhythm they use in Midgard to help calm angry dragons. Maybe it'll help him hate me less.

Astarot blinks one enormous eye, his silent assent, before lumbering to his feet. I duck into the tent to grab a few ropes then climb onto his back. I can't hold back the smile as he extends his broad wings. It hasn't been long since I rode my dragon for the first time and I still feel a surge of joy with every launch.

Within a minute, we're soaring toward the herd, Astarot's head swaying as he searches for the copper dragon. That beast should stay away but if she needs the water like Rockjaw suggested, she'll be back. Hopefully not today. We all need a day off.

As soon as Astarot drops me, he throws himself at an enormous sheep, swallowing it whole as he normally does with his first part of any meal. I feel his satisfaction as it slides down his throat, a smile in his eyes. He takes his time picking the next one and I can't draw my gaze away. I don't know why, but I love to watch my dragon hunt. He's quick to kill, so the sheep don't suffer more than a few seconds. The attack is feral and precise at the same time, and it feeds some base instinct in me.

When Astarot's ripped out the throat of another sheep and is settling in to pick its bones, I tie a lasso and get to work. It takes about fifteen minutes to harness three sheep, and I give Astarot a wave as I start to tug them toward our campsite and the angry dragon.

I realize as I'm walking how much I needed this time alone. My thoughts bounce around all that's happened and the things I've learned from Bob, questions dominating. *What if these dragons are the same as the southern dragons—and the Midgard dragons, for that matter—except for their brutal lives? What would love and connection feel like to a beast that's never felt either? What if fate intended these dragons to have riders too, but a cruel life denied them?*

What if this is all wishful thinking, and I'm as fucked as I feel? And not in a good way?

Astarot soars over me halfway through my walk, looking down as he passes with a satisfied gaze and a low rumble. My mind is still spinning when I make my way back to our tent, my lips tipping up when I see Dani plopped down on a blanket along the edge of the clearing in front of an enormous stump she's carving.

"What are you doing?"

"He's gonna need to drink something," she explains as she puffs out a breath to blow a piece of hair out of her eyes, her gaze never lifting from her work. "We're not letting him go to the lake, so the lake needs to come to him."

"How are we supposed to move that?"

Now her head spins, eyes narrowing at me. "Your dragon may be a lazy bastard, but he'll at least do this, won't he?"

I can't hold back the laugh as Astarot's offended *Lazy?* drops into my mind. Dani isn't making any friends.

"I'll ask him. I may be able to convince him."

"You fucking better," she grunts as her head drops again to focus on the stump.

Is now a good time to try to connect with Bob? Can you tell if he'd like a sheep or two?

Thirsty. Bob's much more focused on the water than the sheep. He came here for a reason, and while he may be a little hungry, he needs to drink more.

Dani's right. We can't move him. We won't be able to give him any water until she's done.

Move, Astarot responds. He wants Dani to give him access to the stump.

How do you plan to do that? It doesn't look like a job for a dragon's teeth or claws.

Move, Astarot repeats. Now he's a little offended that I'm questioning him.

Okay. "Dani, Astarot thinks he can do that more quickly. He wants you to move."

Her head spins, eyes wide as a slow smile emerges. "I'd like nothing more."

She stands and struts toward me, sheathing the knife before planting herself right behind me.

"He won't hurt you."

"I don't know what he's got in mind, but I don't want to be close when chips start to fly."

Astarot glares at her for a moment then takes her place. *Simple*, he tells me before puffing out a narrow, precise flame. It's long and sharp, like a poker, with a tip less than an inch across that carves into the hard wood as easily as a knife cuts through butter. Dani sucks in a breath, her surprise at Astarot's ingenuity wrapping around me, and I feel his satisfaction. I wouldn't be surprised if he started purring.

For the next ten minutes, Astarot chisels into the large stump, slowly but efficiently creating an enormous drinking bowl. With each strip and chunk he focuses on, the wood glows until a flame appears and burns long enough to wither it down to ash, which then flies away with his occasional puffs of air. When he's done, the bowl is charred on the inside, but it's smooth and surprisingly clean.

By the gods, I love my dragon.

He looks at Dani as the last bit of ash is floating away and huffs his demand for an apology. She can't speak with him, but she understands what he wants.

"All right, I agree. That was impressive."

Dropping his chin once, he turns back toward the stump, lifting it carefully and striding toward the lake. When his legs are submerged, he drops low enough to rest his snout in the water, shaking his head as a puff of smoke erupts. A few seconds later, he stands again, repositioning the stump so he can set it down without spilling any water. And then, more carefully than a beast his size should be able to move, he walks over to Bob and places a full bowl of water in front of him. *Sing*, he tells me.

Thanks for the reminder. Watching Bob, I focus on the music that helps calm dragons in Midgard, letting it consume my thoughts and then pushing it out to the dragon. I don't insert myself into his mind yet. I want him to just hear the tune and start to connect it to good things. He doesn't fight back as he drinks, letting me serenade him to my heart's content.

When he's done, he backs up enough to drop his snout to the ground. And then it's his turn to watch me. It feels like he wants me to see his anger and resolve. To know nothing's changed. But I see something else.

"He can be rational." I didn't intend to voice my thoughts, but I realized I did when Dani turned to me.

"What?"

"Bob can be rational. I didn't focus on it at the time, but he stopped complaining when Astarot went to work on the stump. He hasn't made a sound since then. When Astarot started walking toward him, he stopped fighting against the ropes and let him bring the water. He knew what Astarot was doing. Figured out this was his only way to get a drink, for now, at least. And he let Astarot get close to him."

"Did you or Astarot talk to him? Ask him to be still?"

"No. He did that on his own."

"That must be good." Dani's nodding her head, her hands on her hips as she watches Bob.

"It must be. Maybe I'll be able to get to him after all. Now's as good a time to try as any."

I walk over to the blanket Dani was sitting on and drop down, holding Bob's gaze. His eyes narrow, but he doesn't give me any other response. Taking a deep breath, I let the song play again in my head and push my thoughts out to him.

The emotions I find are the same. His thirst is sated, but he's still furious with me. His thoughts are manic, flitting from one memory to another. But hovering over everything else—driving it all—is the bitter resentment of a creature who bows to nobody yet is trapped and forced to accept the dregs we offer him.

It shows up in the hatred all dragons in this land hold toward the mothers who abandon their hatchlings to brawl amongst themselves for survival. I see it in the brutal attack by a female dragon he'd just forced to submit to his need for sex, her surprise lunge for his neck nearly taking his life. And it incites his unhinged assaults on the trolls whenever they try to steal from his herd, eat *his* sheep.

My thoughts battle with Bob's a few more minutes, but he's strong and battling wills with a dragon is fucking exhausting. "I'm not getting anywhere with him," I breathe when I yank my mind away. Dropping my head, I suck in air, as tired as I am after running for hours. "We'll try again tomorrow."

Dani just watches me in silence as I drag myself up and head toward the tent to get clothes and a towel. The water will help. And then I'm gonna eat a huge amount of mutton and pass out with my dragon.

Bob has other ideas, though. And as much as it pisses me off, it also gives me hope.

He's quiet while he watches me bathe, and afterwards, as I stuff myself with meat and bread. When I head to the tent, though, he starts to roar and growl and snarl and just generally be a dick. He doesn't stop until the sun hits the tent the next morning, and I give up and drag myself out to face the day. Then, finally, he decides he's done being the biggest asshole any dragon possibly could be.

Devious bastard.

He's smart. That means he can be rational too. I know it.

The next two days are the same. Bob calms enough to take the sheep and water we give him, but other than that, he's angry and loud and obnoxious. Every morning and evening, I try to subdue his thoughts, find order in the chaos, but nothing works. He holds on to his negative emotions like trophies—the spoils of a life filled with pain, anger, and overwhelming loneliness.

"This isn't going to work, is it?" Dani asks me on the third morning as we're sitting around the fire after breakfast.

Dani's gotten more anxious, on edge, every day. She doesn't want to be here and seems to be more worried about my possible failure than I am. And I'm fucking terrified.

"It'll work. It has to."

"When do we give up? Go to the kastali and tell the Monarch we failed?"

"We? You're not going to kill me if I decide I can't do this?"

Dani's eyes widen and then narrow, her jaw tight as her hand shifts to the blade on her belt. "What makes you think that?"

She's a lousy liar.

"Harald didn't trust me before he saw what I'm capable of. He changed his mind, sent you with me, when he realized I'm strong. An unknown threat in his lands, allied with a powerful dragon. Why else would he have sent you?"

"That doesn't mean he wants me to kill you. I could just be here as a spy." Her gaze lifts as she glances at my dragon and then back at me. "Besides, Astarot would destroy me if I even tried."

"He would. I'm guessing you've got a plan, though. Harald must have something that can immobilize dragons. Maybe even kill them. Probably one of those arrows in your packs."

I see the truth in her eyes, which widen for a moment as her gaze darts toward her quiver and back. She straightens her back, shoulders tight. "You're right about the arrows but not about me. I'm not here to kill you."

"What about Astarot? Would the arrows kill or just subdue him?"

Again, she watches me in silence, probably deciding whether or not to be honest with me. "The poison's strong," she tells me at last. "If I can strike the heart, the dragon will die. It should survive any other hit."

"You carry something that would kill Astarot in his sleep. Something you haven't mentioned before now. And you expect me to trust you?"

"I'm not here to kill you, Sifa." Her voice is firm, assured. If she's lying, she's settled into it now. It's tougher to judge.

I stare at her for a long time, testing her words in my mind. I don't know if I can believe her, but it doesn't matter. I'll watch my back no matter what. "You'll fail," I tell her at last. "Astarot and I share guard duties. We don't sleep at the same time. Not when we have an enemy in our midst."

"I'm not your enemy, Sifa."

"We'll see, Dani."

Danger! Astarot's warning drops into my thoughts as he stands, his wings snapping out. He's airborne in a few seconds, racing north to intercept a copper dot aimed straight at us.

I stare at the incoming dragon as Dani and I scramble to our feet. "Get your arrows. You'll need them."

"Shit. Shit, shit, shit." She runs to her packs, grabbing the bow and quiver as I search for the best spot for her.

"There," I yell, pointing to a tree along the side of the clearing. "It's got a thick trunk but thin foliage. You should be able to get a clear shot when she flies close enough. I'll ask Astarot to lead her past you."

Bob's on his feet now too, the wails tumbling from his snout growing more desperate and insistent. His head is swinging as he focuses on his nemesis and then back on me, demanding I release him. But the last thing I need is two dragons pissed off and determined to kill me. He needs to stay put. Let us fight this battle.

My arrows aren't poison, but I can defend Bob, hopefully give Dani a better chance at taking down the copper beast.

The dragon is barreling toward us. Even from this distance, I can see that her gaze is focused on Bob. She glances toward Astarot occasionally, but her target is the beast we captured. She can't pass up this chance to destroy the only creature in this area that could do her harm. The only challenge to her dominance in this part of Harald's lands.

I also can feel Astarot's resolve. He feels sorry for Bob. He's touched his mind, knows how much this brown beast has suffered in his life. As Astarot throws himself into the sky, I feel his intent. He won't let Bob be harmed. Not if he can prevent it.

They collide in the sky when they're barely a hundred feet from us. Astarot's ready this time. He knows how dragons fight each other, focusing his talons and beak on the sensitive and most exposed part of her body—the wings.

When the beasts bounce away from each other after their initial attack, Astarot spins and grasps the tip of one of the copper dragon's wings in his mouth. He stretches it as far as it can go and flings his talons up toward its base, digging into that easily-harmed area and holding on. They tumble toward the ground, the copper dragon unable to fly and Astarot unable to hold them both up.

My dragon spins enough to throw his attacker beneath him, cushioning his own fall. The impact, though, rips his talons free of the copper dragon's skin, breaking the contact and giving our enemy a chance to fight back. Within a few seconds, they're both on their feet, facing off with snarls and shrieks that drown out every other sound.

"I can't get a good shot!" Dani cries, her voice shrill. "Astarot's in the way."

You need to spin. Give Dani a better target. One of the arrows will take her down.

Astarot grunts his acknowledgment, shuffling to the copper dragon's side as his gaze stays locked on her. She's nearly in position for Dani's attack when she shocks all of us by leaping away from Astarot, landing on Bob's back. With a howl that rings with victory and triumph, her powerful beak clamps onto Bob's neck and wrenches it to the side.

The crack echoes all around us, Bob's snout plunging to the ground just as Dani's arrow flies, embedding itself in the copper dragon's side. She wails, flames erupting as her gaze finds Dani. Her wings flare out, but before they can pump even once, she starts to wobble.

I can only watch, my mouth hanging open, as this enormous, dangerous beast sways and then tumbles to the ground.

I really hope she's still alive.

That we didn't just destroy our two best chances at finding a dragon for Harald.

CHAPTER FOURTEEN

FHORD

I KNOW HIS DRAGON

THE OTHERS MOVE CLOSER to me, forming an arrow at my back. I don't dare take my eyes away from the asshole standing between us and our escape, but I'm sure the Ætt, at least, are ready to fight with me.

I don't recognize the asshole, but I know his dragon. Tindera took Khirta under her wing shortly after the green dragon bonded with the asshole. He's cruel. Too many riders are, but it was harder on Khirta than most because she's so small and the asshole took advantage of that. He even offered her, unwillingly, to an enormous blue dragon who'd taken on the cruelty of his rider over the century or more they'd been together. Asshole was trying to suck up to the blue dragon's rider and whored out his dragon to do it.

Fuckin' dragon almost killed her.

Tindera spent a lot of time with Khirta in the dragon's pool after that. Stood up to the blue dragon when he tried to come back for seconds.

I can see the recognition in Khirta's eyes. She heard the asshole mention Tindera and knows I'm her rider.

It kills me what he plans to make her do. If she hurts us, that guilt will weigh her down for years. Decades even.

Such an asshole.

"So your dragon's just going to burn all of us. That's your plan? And you think she'll be able to do that before I can make it over there to kill you?"

"I think we're gonna have fun trying." He watches me for a moment, his face twisting with an ugly smirk before glancing at Khirta. "Burn him first."

Her gaze spins to find mine, and I can see her conflict. Too often, dragons despise the task their riders ask them to perform, but they have no choice. The Dróttning's punishment of disobedient dragons—those who refuse a direct command from their rider—is even worse than her punishment of dragons who reject a chosen rider. Neither happens often.

Khirta's already suffered in her short life. She won't have the strength to resist.

I hold the asshole's stare as I step forward. "This is a coward's move. Fight me, one-on-one, like a dragon rider should."

He laughs, bitter cackles echoing in the cavern. "Dead men don't have opinions, Fhord. You can call me coward or pussy or fuckin' piglet. I don't care 'cause you'll be dead soon."

"You're not gonna kill me," I respond as I step forward again. He creeps back in response, moving closer to Khirta. "You and I both know the Dróttning would rather have me alive. Which means you have to subdue me. There's no fuckin' chance that'll happen."

The asshole's gaze spins toward Khirta as I take one more step forward. "Destroy them. Now." His voice is shrill, like the pig he just asked me to call him.

Khirta shrinks in on herself, her shoulders slumping as her head droops.

"Now!" the asshole shrieks, his hand lifting to point a single finger directly at me. "I want him to be a pile of ash in the next minute."

Khirta's snout lifts as I take another step forward. I'm seven or eight feet away from the asshole now, and he'll need to back up soon to avoid getting hit by any fire Khirta sends my way. She opens her mouth, an apology in her eyes, as a few flames burst from her mouth, nearly reaching me. When she doesn't follow with a firestorm, the asshole rips a strap from his belt and lashes it across her snout. She shivers and cowers as it strikes the sensitive skin there, her gaze never leaving mine.

Asshole reaches out to grasp Khirta's feathers—the ones right next to her eye, in another tender spot—and yanks her head up. "I'll hand you back to the Dróttning for punishment if you don't kill him now." His voice is cold, empty. Every bit as distant as his eyes.

Khirta shakes her head, dislodging his fingers, before starting to shuffle farther into the cave. Closer to me and the others. I feel Torsten's hand on my shoulder, a silent reminder that if I die, they're going with me.

But I don't want to die today. With a roar, I throw myself at the asshole. Maybe I'll get close enough to take him with me.

Instead, Khirta's tail whips out, circling my ankles to throw me to the ground and flick me toward my Ætt, an angry "Fuck" spilling from my lips as I slam on my back. I'm up in an instant, but before I can try again, Khirta's spitting out flames. At the asshole.

She unleashes a gods-damned sea of fire. My arm flies up to shield my eyes as the light and heat from her inferno spurts in our direction, pulling sweat from every single pore of my body. I'm backing up, pushing the Ætt and everyone else away from her, and she's just getting started.

My heart beats a dozen times or more as I watch Khirta's never-ending blaze, burning so hot I can see hints of blue in the midst of the red and orange and yellow. When she stops, I take a step forward, an intense need to go to her—to comfort her—filling me. She swings her head in warning and almost of their own volition, my feet plant where they are.

Turning back toward the asshole—now a pile of bones with scraps of flesh still clinging to them—I watch as she inhales and gushes out more flames. These are even hotter, violet melding with the indigo in places, as the other colors spin within and between them. Again, my heart beats twelve times as Khirta emits everything she can with this breath.

When she's done, after the smoke clears, the asshole is nothing but a pile of ash. Exactly what he'd expected me to be.

Khirta turns toward me and fills the cavern with a blood-wrenching wail. She hated the asshole, but he still was her rider. Even with a tenuous bond like theirs—forced into existence by the Dróttning—a rider's death always pains the dragon. Dropping to the ground, her snout landing just shy of the asshole's remains, she stills. A single tear forms in the massive golden eye I can see and cuts a path down her feathers, landing with a *plop* in the silent cavern.

I drop my sword onto the nearest bed, striding forward to kneel by her side, my arms wrapping around her neck. And there I stay, holding her as long as she's willing to be held. After an hour or more, her eyes close and her breathing settles, exhaustion and despair dragging her into sleep. Still, I stay, because sometimes Tindera feels my touch when she sleeps and I want Khirta to feel that same touch now.

Perhaps fifteen minutes later, I stand, gesture toward the others—all quietly gathering the ingredients for a meal or packing their beds—to draw them toward the back of the cave.

"She'll be starving after that, and food will help her get through the grieving process. I'll head toward that herd we saw a few vikus from here and bring her a couple of goats. Let's all eat and be ready to go when she wakes, if she's up to it."

"She's ours now?" Leif's whisper sounds hopeful. He doesn't want to abandon Khirta, despite all the problems we'll create if we take her with us.

"We can't leave her here. She wouldn't be able to protect herself. And she's small enough that the Dróttning probably would kill her for what she did to her rider. Weeding out the weak, she'd say. We owe her our lives. We'll protect hers."

I stare at each of them long enough to get their agreement. Toffer's takes less than a second and I can already tell he'll be pestering Khirta incessantly while she's with us. I wish I felt bad about subjecting her to the troll, but better Khirta than me. And I know she'd much rather be with us, even with a gabby Toffer, than with the asshole or the Dróttning. At least I think so.

When I'm done, I turn and stalk out of the cavern. The sun is barely visible over the tops of the trees, revealing crimson and cobalt birds swooping overhead, diving occasionally to claim a bug or simply savoring the joy of flight. The path in front of me grows brighter as I walk, grays giving way to fern, moss, shamrock, and a host of other shades of green. Rocks shift from a muddy brown to a mix of rust and gold.

Fuck, it feels good to be alive.

I find the goats where I expected, capturing two large males and a smaller female to take back with me. We'll give the males to Khirta and prep the female for ourselves. With a dozen people and a gods-damned cat, we can never have enough meat.

Torsten slaughters the female as soon as I get back—a hearty "Thank fuck" greeting me when I return with an extra goat—then goes to work cutting off meat for breakfast and dressing the rest to carry. The others cook and pack while I go sit with Khirta. She won't want to be alone when she wakes, and I don't want her to be. She needs to know she's ours now.

She sleeps for two more hours. Joralf and Mikkael are starting to fidget, asking if I can wake her, but I'm not interested in hearing their thoughts. We'll leave when she's rested. Khirta gave us everything, and we'll give her the sleep she needs.

When her citrine eyes open and she finds me, I smile, lifting a hand to rub her snout.

"Thank you. We owe you our lives."

She closes her eyes once in the way dragons do to acknowledge a rider's words. I can see the conflict and fear she's trying to hide. She can't talk to me, but I can answer whatever questions I think she may have. And if she's willing, Toffer can try to talk to her. I want to put her at ease first, if I can.

"Nobody here would expose you to the Dróttning," I assure her, my voice steady and calm. "We will never tell anyone what we saw today. Your secret will die with us."

Again, she blinks her eyes, watching me.

"We're traveling to the Nest, but we're not staying. We're heading north, to safety. You can't go back to the Dróttning without your rider. She'll kill you or stick you with someone worse. If there is anyone worse than that asshole. We'd like you to stay with us."

Once more, her eyes close and then open. She agrees, but she has nowhere else to go.

"We have a troll with us. He can speak with dragons, even without being bonded to them. If you have questions, he can give them to me. Would you be willing to talk to him?"

This blink of her eyes is more enthusiastic. She's anxious to tell me something.

I glance up, catching Toffer's gaze to call him over. "This is Khirta," I tell the troll when he plops down next to me.

Turning back to the dragon, I gesture toward Toffer. "Khirta, this is Toffer."

Toffer's grin could light up the whole cave. His butt is bouncing on the ground, and it's a wonder he can stay still. I place my hand on his shoulder, drawing his gaze to mine.

"You're making her more nervous. Just relax, ask her what she wants to know."

Toffer reaches out a hand to stroke the feathers on her neck, something akin to a purr rumbling from him. His eyes grow distant as he creates a connection to Khirta.

"She's asking about the water." Toffer's voice is full of confusion. "How she'll survive without it."

"I don't understand." Out of the corner of my eye, I see Joralf's head pop up from where he's sitting, chatting with Fróðr. I take a quick look at him then turn back to Toffer and Khirta. "What water?"

Now Joralf is standing, striding toward us to sit behind Toffer.

"This doesn't concern you, elf." Khirta doesn't need more people around her.

"That's where you're wrong, Fhord. This is very much my concern."

"She said it again. 'Water.'" Toffer's quiet for a moment, his brows pulled together, and then a broad grin creases his cheeks. "Oh, that water," he declares brightly.

"What water?" I need them to answer my question.

"The living water. We swam through it when we saved Sifa. Khirta says dragons need it to live."

A grin nearly as broad as Toffer's erupts on Joralf's face, his head nodding as he spins to look at Fróðr. And then he laughs, standing to stride over to his mate and tug him into his arms. "We were right."

Memories of the pool Toffer led me through when we broke Sifa out of the Nest rise in my thoughts. It's unlike anything else in Vanatia—even the river in the North that heals injuries. It feels alive in a way the other water sources don't.

"Is that it?" My gaze finds Joralf's. "The Dróttning uses that water in some way to control the dragons?" It seems too simple. Maybe it's part of her control, but it can't be the whole thing.

"We don't know exactly what she does. How it works," Joralf explains, his hand clasping Fróðr's. "But we've surmised for many years that a body of water in the Nest is the key to her power. We still have much to learn—the reason we must go to the Nest—but this is an answer we've been seeking for a long time." He turns to look at Khirta, then back at me. "How does she know?"

Toffer's eyes glaze again as he stands to scratch behind her horn, leaning his forehead to rest against her. "A big dragon hurt her," he tells us, layers of pain in his voice. "She tried to leave. To hide. But the water called to her. When she had to go back, she found the pool. And she was better." His voice drops an octave as he utters the rest. "Then the Dróttning found her. And she was worse for a while."

We pack up and leave as soon as Khirta's ready, anxious to make it to the Nest. But the closer we get, the more antsy and aggravated I get. I've betrayed the Dróttning, and my life will never be the same again. Not because of what she'll do to me if she finds me—I don't give a fuck about that—but because she'll punish Tindera, and it'll be worse for my dragon if I'm in the Nest with her. The Dróttning will torture her to punish me.

I can't let myself be caught, but the Dróttning can sense me as easily as I can her. I'm on edge as I wait for that moment. My shields are up, and I'm preparing the diversion that might let me sneak in here, but running this hot takes a shit-ton of energy. And I'll need every bit I have when we get into the Nest.

The only thing that's helping me focus is my connection with Tindera. It grows stronger with every step. I'll be able to speak with her soon. Find out what the Dróttning's been putting her through. What she plans. Whether I can do any-thing—any gods-damned thing at all—to help my dragon.

I won't tell her about Khirta. Not until I can speak the words instead of think them. I can't take any risk of the Dróttning learning I've liberated another of her beasts.

Well, Khirta liberated me, I guess. The Dróttning won't appreciate the nuance.

The bond to Sifa, which is somehow even stronger than the link between me and my dragon, helps too. I felt it even as far away as the cabin, and it's thrumming now. I sense her pres-ence, and if I concentrate hard enough, I even can gauge her moods. But I can't waste the power that requires on curiosity. There's nothing I can do for her now, so figuring out if she's happy or sad doesn't do shit. Nothing that matters.

Nothing I can let matter.

"Anything yet, boss?" Leif's on edge too. He knows what the Dróttning will do if she senses me. Like all my Ætt, he also knows she's my mother. They're some of the very few beings in this world that I trust with that knowledge. I still have no idea how Harald figured it out, but he's a devious bastard. He holds many of his enemy's secrets.

"Nothing. I don't know where else she'd be, but I can't tell yet if she's at the Nest. I fucking hope not. This'll be so much easier if I don't have to worry about hiding from her."

He dips his chin. "It'll be tough enough as it is."

"Remind me why we're bringing so many people." I spit, glancing over the motley crew.

"And a dragon," Leif reminds me.

"And a dragon." Who could forget the little green beast tagging along?

"And a cat," Leif adds with a smirk.

"And a fuckin' cat." I do *not* smirk back.

"I guess we're all sticking together for now. Where we go, they go." Leif smiles as his gaze follows mine in the way a bound dragon will smile at an unwanted rider.

"Fuck me. This can't end well."

He watches them for a moment, and I can feel his mood shift. "Or it could be exactly what we need." Now his grin is genuine for some strange reason.

"You're too gods-damned cheery. Nobody should be as happy as you are all the time."

"I've got good reason to be happy. We've been preparing for this fight for a long time. Vanatia needs it. We need it. It's finally here."

I inhale as deeply as I can, searching for some of his optimism. I've got nothing, though. "I'll be happy later. Maybe. Right now, I just need to figure out a way to free Tindera and get back to Sifa. The rest of this shit can wait."

Welcome. Tindera's voice drops in my mind, drawing out the smile I couldn't give Leif. She's as happy to be close to me as I am to her. And relieved. We've been terrified for each other, unsure whether we'd both survive to fly together again. As I sense her presence wrap around me, a knot I've been carrying in my gut unfurls and my shoulders relax. I feel lighter than I have for days.

It's risky to talk to her, but I have to chance it. We need to know everything Tindera does. *Gods, I've missed you. We need to get you the fuck away from her. I won't pass through the barrier without you again.*

Necessary. She felt it too—the hole that formed as soon as the barrier separated us, and didn't fully disappear until just now. But she realizes we had no choice.

What did she do to you?

There's only one "she" and we both know it. *Pain.* The response lands in my thoughts with a figurative shrug, not a complaint. She's mothering me, trying to take my worry. Tindera was tortured, as we'd feared. They kept that contraption on her wings for days and the scars still haven't fully healed. But then it stopped. She's not sure why.

Is the Dróttning in the Nest? That's gotta be the reason they stopped.

Gone. Tindera thinks she left a few days ago and hasn't returned. I puff out an exhale, relieved at this little bit of luck. I'll still need to be careful because she could come back anytime, but it should be easier to get into the Nest than we'd feared.

"Let the others know the Dróttning isn't in the Nest," I tell Leif. "We should get there and get out as fast as we can."

Leif nods and kicks his horse to ride up to Fróðr, who's become the unspoken leader of the stragglers we picked up. Fróðr spins to glance at me as he and Leif talk, then leans over to speak with Joralf, who does the same with Johan. Within a minute, Fróðr's kicked his horse into a trot and then a gallop, the rest of us racing along behind him.

We haven't traveled more than a viku when I sense a soldier nearby. Whistling, I scan the area, gesturing toward a grove of trees thick enough to hide us and Khirta. In unison, we spin and race in that direction, not slowing until we're deep in the woods. When I whistle again, we tug our horses to a halt, dropping into silence almost immediately.

I cast out my senses, making sure there's only one other person in the area. My heart drops when I find a second, and then a third. With the fourth and the fifth, though, my stomach clenches. I soon lose count, my thoughts touching dozens of guards as they fall into place around us. Looking up, I search for a route that would take us to safety. I can't find one.

We're trapped.

And unless I can find some way to escape with a dozen people, a dragon, and a gods-damned cat, we are well and truly fucked.

Chapter Fifteen

Sifa

A Proper Name

I NAMED THIS DRAGON before Dani had a chance to. Vulryn. A proper name for a dragon. Unlike Bob.

Astarot dragged Bob's carcass away and we tied up Vulryn so she hopefully can't kill us when she wakes up from the coma-like state she's currently in. I wish I could keep my distance until then, but I don't have a choice. The arrow didn't reach her heart—thank the gods—but it hit at the perfect angle to create a gaping wound. We need to sew her up. Her body may not be able to heal an injury this bad on its own while fighting Harald's poison.

She's barely alive when I pull at the arrow in her side, as gently as I can. I don't know if she feels pain right now, but she will. The less damage I do trying to fix this gash, the better. If we're to have any hope of reaching her, we'll need her to trust us. That won't be possible if we cause her more harm.

"You know how to heal dragons?" Dani's voice is soft, like she's afraid of talking too loudly and waking up Vulryn. The dragon isn't asleep, though. She's unconscious and hopefully will stay that way.

"This is all new to me," I mutter as I finally wrench the arrow free of the last bit of sinew, drawing a gust from the copper beast. But she doesn't stir, thankfully. The last thing I need is to cling to this psychotic dragon, trying to sew her up, while Astarot pins her down. The ropes holding her in place won't help me when I'm so close to her enormous, sharp, yellow teeth.

I miss Fhord so gods-damned much. He'd know what to do. I'm just fumbling my way through trying to save this dragon's life.

I toss the bolt down to Dani so she can add it back to her stash—hopefully without replenishing the poison. One less arrow that could kill Astarot is good by me. Then I get to work, preparing the suture Leif packed for us in case Astarot was injured, and double-checking her wound.

"What was injured?"

"I have no idea. Some people in Vanatia understand dragon physiology but not many. Most dragon riders there are lazy and privileged. They don't bother learning because there's always a doctor they can call. I've never had a chance to learn. I wasn't intended to join the rider ranks, and Astarot and I only bonded a short while ago."

"How do you know what to do?"

"Fhord told me the basics. I need to repair any internal organs then sew her up fast. Dragons are at risk of infection while their insides are exposed."

"And you think that'll work?"

I pause to look at Dani, holding her gaze. "I hope so. I'm gonna do what I can and leave the rest to the gods. Please let me be so I can concentrate."

I expect a sharp response. Instead, her eyes grow soft, and she dips her chin once. "Of course." Turning, she heads toward Bob's carcass. I have no idea why and I don't ask.

For the next fifteen minutes, I'm spread across Vulryn's side, digging the thin bone the Vanatians use for a needle through the glob of an organ Dani's arrow hit. It's the most disgusting thing I've ever done, and I've done a lot of disgusting things.

Whatever I'm sewing up has the strangest texture, like a fine, porous sponge. It shifts in my hands, making it almost impossible to hold together the parts that were split. Oh, and it emits a bright green substance that smells worse than Toffer after bean stew. Much worse. My senses refuse to adjust, so the scent is still as pungent when I finally finish as it was when I started.

Fuck me.

I lean back and take a few deep breaths before starting on Vulryn's hide. This is so much harder. The arrow sliced through her at an angle before embedding itself inside, ripping a tear as long as my arm. Vulryn's splayed out in a way that pulls the two sides apart, forcing me to yank on them as I sew. And her hide is thick and strong. It takes all my strength to push the needle through. After the first couple of stitches, I can't.

"Dani, I need you."

Her eyebrows shoot together as her head flicks up and her mouth forms a big "O". She's silent for a moment, her face slowly relaxing into a less terrified expression, before she nods. Standing, she walks toward me, eyeing the climb up a comatose dragon she'll need to take to get close enough to help.

"Up there?" she asks, her eyes begging me to say "No".

"It's not as bad as it looks."

"What if she wakes up?"

"She lost a lot of blood. I've been digging into her and she's still unconscious." I give her my sweetest smile, deciding I need to push her a bit. "I've been up here for a while. Are you afraid to join me?"

"You know dragons. Maybe you could reason with her. I can't."

I bark out a laugh. "If she comes out of this coma, or whatever it is, there'll be no reasoning with her. I'll be tossing myself as far away as I can, as quickly as I can."

"But you still think it's a good idea for two of us to be on her?"

"Probably not," I agree. "I can't do this without you, though. Just come up. If we die, at least we do it together."

She shakes her head, her gaze examining the feathers between us before shifting toward the massive teeth, nearly close enough to touch. But then she sucks in a deep breath, nods—to herself, I think—and stalks toward Vulryn's back to start clambering toward me.

"That's the long way," I point out with a smirk.

"I don't give a fuck," she responds with a matching smirk. "It's as far away from her mouth as I can get."

Within a couple of minutes, she's dragging herself next to me, her gaze darting between the still-enormous wound and Vulryn's teeth every few seconds. I snap my fingers, and she inhales deeply, focusing on me.

"Ready?" My voice is calm. She'll drag Vulryn from her coma with all the tension spewing from her.

She seems to consider it for a moment. Finally, she nods. "Yes. What do you need?"

"I can't hold her hide together and sew at the same time. I need you to pull the ends tight and keep them there while I run the suture through her."

"Can she feel this? Will it wake her up?"

"I've been at this a while and she's still down. If we can finish quickly, we should be good."

She takes one more deep breath and then steadies herself in a good position to use both her hands. We work together for more than thirty minutes as I shove the needle through Vulryn's thick hide, back and forth, back and forth. Forty-four stitches later—with no more than a finger's length left—Vulryn starts to rumble.

"Fuck, no," Dani breathes, glancing at the nearly closed gash. "You don't need me for this," she concludes, standing abruptly and slip-sliding down Vulryn's belly. As soon as her feet hit the ground, she's running toward the lake, slowing only when she can't go farther. Turning, she tosses back a quick "Sorry" before plopping her ass on the ground.

"Thanks, Dani," I mutter, waiting for the next rumble as I consider whether to tie off now or try to finish. Vulryn's still, and I'm not positive the repair will hold if I don't fully close her, so I decide to give it a try. *Astarot*, I call to my dragon. *Can you sit in front of her, try to draw her attention if she wakes up, hold her down if that doesn't work?*

He grumbles a bit in response but lumbers over, planting himself directly in front of the copper dragon. "Well, here goes nothing," I breathe as I impale her hide for the next stitch. This time, she shudders, the pain apparently finding its way into her semi-consciousness.

I'm tired and my shoulder is aching from pushing the needle through her thick skin, but now, I'm working against time. She'll be awake and pissed soon. I manage two more stitches—only two more to go—when her eyes open. And I decide I've done enough for today, thank you very much. Tugging the suture as tight as possible, I start to tie the knot that will hopefully keep my repair in place.

Before I can, though, her head is spinning, one massive and ridiculously angry eye glaring at me. A wave ripples through her, forcing me to cling to her feathers, and she twists her body upright. Now I'm hanging on for dear life because if I let go, she'll back up and broil me alive. I can only assume she hasn't done it yet because if she burns fate, she burns herself and some part of her knows that would hurt.

She wants me the fuck off her, though. She starts to shake, her body whipping from side to side even as she grunts and sneers at the pain she must be suffering. I'm barely holding on to her, oblivious to everything except the feathers thrashing around me, when Astarot's roar breaks through my focus. Vulryn pauses for a moment, her snout aiming at Astarot to emit a sharp plume of fire, and then throws everything she has into tossing me off.

I see Astarot's gaping jaw as it crashes toward me, clamping on Vulryn's neck and pinning her to the ground. Now she's wild, her entire body flinging back and forth, and I need to let go now, hope I fall right, and give Astarot space to do anything he must to force her to submit. Releasing my hands, I kick off from Vulryn's side, spinning and tucking myself to roll when I hit the ground. I'm half a dragon's-length away when I stop, far enough to be safe but close enough to see the fire in my dragon's eyes while he fights to subdue her.

Tense seconds pass as they stay locked in the same position. Eventually, Vulryn starts to slow and then still. She looks pissed. Her expression's as agitated as a dragon's can get and her red eyes glow as bright as Astarot's. But she must realize she's defeated. Finally, she stops moving completely.

My gaze searches for her wound and I almost sigh as I see that she did barely any damage to my work. A stitch or two came out, but it mostly held. Maybe I'll try again—if we can calm her down enough—or maybe I'll just let it be. She should survive. That's the most important thing.

Thank you for your help.

Astarot manages a disdainful snort while holding Vulryn's neck in his gaping maw.

Does she have a different name? Or should we call her Vulryn?

Astarot's eyes glaze over as he relaxes just a bit. He's still pinning Vulryn firmly in place, but he's not putting any pressure on it. It's a warning, not a restraint. *None*, he tells me finally. Like Bob, she's been alone, nobody to name her.

Does she know we healed her?

Angry. She knows, but she doesn't care. We attacked her. We caused her harm. That's what matters to her.

Are her thoughts any clearer than Bob's? I'm not ready to dig into her brain yet—I should rest first, since it'll be exhausting—but I'm anxious to know what we're dealing with. Whether we have any hope.

Sane. She's not as lost as Bob was.

At least it's something.

We'll let her be today. Tomorrow we'll try to reach her.

Wise, Astarot tells me. She's tired too, after what she's been through. We'll all be better off tomorrow.

Will she let you pour some of the water over her wound? It won't fully heal her, but since we're close to the lake, maybe it would retain enough magic to help.

Astarot stares at Vulryn for a long time and I wonder if they're communicating in some way. I have no gods-damned idea what she's capable of, but hopefully Astarot's figuring it out. Finally, he dips his chin, takes the makeshift bowl and strides to the lake to fill it. Within a minute, he's hovering over her, using his front claws to tip the basin and carefully soak her wound.

The copper beast huffs—a gust of relief, I'd swear to all the gods—before twisting her expression again and glaring at me with narrow eyes and a tight snout.

So I shrug and spin to head to the lake, desperate to clean off the weird gunk clinging to me and bring some relief to my aching shoulder. I'll ask Astarot later about whatever just happened between him and Vulryn. Right now, I want to float in the water that feels every bit as good as I'd hoped. It holds strong power, and I wish I could stay here, or near the river in Vanatia that Fhord found, and rejuvenate every day.

Fhord tries to push his way into my thoughts while I soak—because my vacillating emotions always seem to return to my frustrating mate—but I don't want to think about him right now. He'll be back and we'll work through our shit then. I'll figure out if I can trust him enough to ever see a future for us.

Instead, I focus on Vulryn, a bitter empathy rolling through me. I've always felt sorry for dragons in Vanatia, too many forced to accept unworthy riders. Vulryn's life is much harder, though. At least in Vanatia, dragons have each other, and sometimes riders they grow to love. Most dragons have tolerable lives, as long as they aren't forced to suffer the Dróttning's wrath. Here, they have nothing. Nobody. Hate and fear and anger. Never love.

I decide to quiz Dani a bit after dinner, hoping to find something that will help me break through to Vulryn. Because now I want to do this for my own piece of mind as well as to appease Harald. Maybe we could give these dragons better lives.

Dani and I eat in peace. She seems to be lost in thought, and I'm feeling surprisingly good. Every ache is gone and I'm more relaxed than I should be after the chaos we encountered today. I smile and bite my tongue more than once to stop myself from teasing Dani about how quickly she bailed on me when Vulryn woke up, suppressing an occasional laugh as my mind replays her response. When we sit by the fire together after dinner, I offer her my flask. As she smiles her thanks, I catch her gaze.

"I know nothing about your land," I point out, glancing beyond her at the star-topped mountains.

"As the Monarch wishes." Her expression's flat, but I'm not surprised. I've been with her long enough to know Dani's a well-trained soldier and she'll only let me see what she wants me to see.

"Maybe it would help if I had some information. Gods, I don't even know the name."

"As the Monarch wishes," she repeats, her eyebrow quirking up.

"Even the name is secret?" I demand with a scoff.

A smile tugs at her lips. "I guess I can share that with you. Njordheim."

"North home? Very original."

"We're a literal people."

"How long have Vanatia and Njordheim been separate lands?"

"That I don't know." She shrugs, her eyes fixed on the fire. "We've been enemies as long as I've lived."

"What do your histories say? That seems like it would be important. They must give a reason."

Dani's responding chortle is bitter, her gaze still focused on the flames. "We don't have 'history' books, elf. At least, not those born into my station."

"You're not taught those things?" I know the Dróttning doesn't allow it for any except her highest-ranking officials, but I assumed Harald would be different.

"*I* was not taught those things. I'm a soldier. That's what helped me climb out of the slums. I learned all I needed to follow commands and fight." She pauses for a moment, lifting her head to watch me as a hint of a smile plays at her lips. "Fhord was looking for information too, the last time he came here," she murmurs at last.

"The 'mess' Harald mentioned?"

Now her smile is genuine, the barest laugh joining it. "It was the talk of the barracks. He found a way into the Monarch's private library, some said in search of stories about Vanatia's Downfall."

"You know of the Downfall?"

This snort erupts from Dani's belly. She leans back, resting her hands at her sides. "We know all about the Dróttning's evil deeds," she declares. "Those aren't the histories the Monarch buries."

My thoughts carry me back to my trip to the Nest with Fhord and the draugr we detoured to meet. Fhord wanted me to speak with him specifically to learn about the Downfall. It can't be a coincidence. "When was this?"

"Within the last year, perhaps eight or nine months ago." Dani's blue eyes grow bright. She's enjoying telling me about this.

"And what happened?"

"The Monarch wasn't pleased," she scoffs. "Some guards found Fhord and he ripped the library in half in his zeal to escape. He's lucky he didn't end up in the dungeons. I've killed people on the Monarch's command for less than that."

I watch her for a minute or more, my thoughts bouncing between my frustrating mate and the secrecy of the rulers who control our lives. "You're one of the Monarch's elite with impressive gifts, but he denies you access to your land's own stories."

"Many in Njordheim have impressive gifts," she tells me with another shrug, her tone bland. "He tells us what we need to do our jobs. Nothing more."

I push down the frustration rising within me, a fist starting to form around my stomach and chest. She's well-trained, but there must be some way to convince her to help me. "How is your society structured?" I ask, keeping my voice measured. "Does Harald wield complete power? Or does he have councilors or anyone else to answer to?"

Now Dani's gaze finds mine. "Do you really think I would tell you that?"

"Why wouldn't you?"

"I don't know what the Monarch would want you to know. He certainly doesn't want Fhord learning anything more about his lands. So I'll tell you nothing."

"He promised I could speak with elves when I reach his kastali. He seemed fine with me getting information from them."

"Then he'll do that." Her gaze returns to the fire. "But I wouldn't be surprised if the elves he allows you to meet are as firmly bound as me. I only know that I won't be responsible for sharing knowledge he wouldn't want you to have."

Fucking Helheim. The fist in my gut is squeezing as I struggle to control my rising irritation with Dani. Asking about Harald isn't gonna work, so I'll focus on a different subject—one that's more important right now, anyway. "What can you tell me about the dragons?"

She's silent, her lips lifting for a moment before they return to the flat line she's been wearing since I started quizzing her. "A few dozen beasts live here," she offers at last, "if the estimates are true. As you've seen, they've learned to limit their own numbers so we don't have to worry too much about them. The Monarch fortified the cities well. A few dragons have tried to enter over the years, but they're always killed quickly. Most of them seem to know to stay away."

"Bob was crazy, but I think Vulryn may be better. I hope we can reach her."

"Not we. You. I won't engage with the dragon. The Monarch wouldn't want it."

"You could, though, couldn't you?" I insist, my voice rising. Maybe she needs my emotion to help release hers. "You planted images in my mind. It seemed like I was there in the moment, watching you kill. I almost felt your anger. You're powerful enough to help me get through to Vulryn."

Dani doesn't turn to me, but something seems to shift within her. Her face grows tense, lips dropping down just a bit as small lines form around her eyes. Even her breathing changes, becoming more measured, as if she's forcing herself to inhale and exhale. "The Monarch gave this task to you," she says at last. "I'm not here to help."

She's still staring into the fire, and it's bothering me. She's hiding something—from me or from herself, I'm not sure—and a little voice inside me whispers that I can't let her continue. When I reach out for the flask, I brush her arm, using the contact to capture her attention.

"What, elf?" she demands with a frustrated side-eye as I leave my hand on her skin.

"What's going on, Dani?"

"Nothing."

I hold back the growl of frustration that throbs in my chest. When I speak again, my voice is soft, persuasive. "I'm as perceptive as you. I know something about Vulryn is bothering you. Maybe it's important. Maybe we need to work through it if we're going to capture her loyalty."

Dani sits in silence for a long time, and I suspect she's not going to answer my question. I wait her out, sipping at the flask occasionally as I relax and enjoy the bright night. Finally, her gaze lifts and finds mine just for a moment before returning to the fire.

"I'm not an emotional person. I can't be, in the Monarch's army. I wouldn't be able to use my gifts if I ever let my feelings interfere with the things I must do."

"I get it." I don't elaborate because she doesn't need me to. We both know. We're alike in this, at least.

"When Vulryn started to wake, though, when I could see her anger and pain and desperation to get free, I felt that deep in my bones." Her voice is so quiet, I wonder if she's afraid to put these thoughts into words, perhaps give them life. "I've never cared at all about dragons. They lead miserable lives here, but they leave us alone and we leave them alone, for the most part. I thought they were savages, untamable."

"What do you mean, 'for the most part'"?

She spits out a bitter laugh. "The Monarch's soldiers make sure the dragons live alone and don't interact with others. Our standing orders are to kill at least one of any pairs we discover. We're told the dragons naturally are pack animals and they'd be too great a threat if we allowed them to band together."

"That's ... fucking brutal."

"The Monarch is a brutally efficient leader." She agrees, her gaze bouncing up to look at me, then back toward the fire. This delay is heavy with emotion, her hands gripping the ends of her coat as her shoulders tense. "In Njordheim, the Monarch doesn't allow us to know about the connections between dragons and riders. We don't know what could be."

"Is my relationship with Astarot the first time you've ever seen a dragon and rider work together?"

"Fhord's visited a couple of times, so most people in the kastali know it's possible. But now that I've spent time with both of you, I understand why Tindera's hidden, kept separate from Fhord, whenever they come. And I'm shocked the Monarch allowed you to stay."

Now, she lifts her gaze and stares at me. Any doubt I saw in her eyes earlier is gone. She's made a decision, and I hope to fuck it's the right one. "He must want your help with dragons desperately to let me see you," she says with the smallest twitch of her lips. "To see what it can be like to love a dragon. To be loved by a dragon."

"Why the secrecy?"

"I've been asking myself that question since Vulryn woke up. I think it's because if anybody in Njordheim is going to bond with a dragon, it better be him. He doesn't want us to know what's possible because he can't take a chance that somebody finds a way to break through. That a dragon and rider connect."

"Now you know. Does it frighten you?"

"Terribly," she tells me with a laugh that lasts only a second. Her expression's more animated now—a wistful smile and bright eyes studying me as she seems to settle fully into whatever she's going to say.

"You don't think he'll let you live when we return?" My voice is soft, comforting.

"Not unless I can convince him I don't care. Hide what I've learned. About myself."

"What have you learned?"

"I think I belong with a dragon," she tells me, a grin emerging as we watch each other. "And I want to find out if I'm right."

"Does that mean you'll help me with Vulryn?"

Again, something changes within Dani, her expression shifting with whatever emotion has pushed itself forward. Even with the stars piercing the dark, casting light all around us, and the fire reflecting in Dani's gaze, her eyes have lost their gleam. They're shadowed and haunted. She's again quiet for a long time. But then she nods, and I almost sigh as relief washes over me. The doubt is gone. She's won this battle, for now at least.

"It will be a death sentence for me if the Monarch finds out," she murmurs. "I'm sure I'll regret it. But I'm going to help you with Vulryn. And who knows, maybe she's mine."

CHAPTER SIXTEEN

SIFA

DANI'S HERS NOW

I'M LEARNING WAY MORE about Dani than I ever wanted to know. Her childhood. Her first love. Her last lay. So much more of everything, none of which belongs inside my head.

Dani had tried for nearly an hour to connect with Vulryn—who is oddly silent and still, just watching us without any reaction—but Dani's never used her gifts this way. "I plant things in people's heads," she'd explained. "I never root around in them the way you do. It's fucking invasive, and I don't even want to try."

"It's a dragon." I couldn't keep the frustration from my voice. "And a barely-sane dragon, at that. There's nothing invasive about this. This may be our best hope of doing what Harald demands."

"But I'm not supposed to be doing it," she'd complained, her hands flinging into the air as she stood and stared down at me. "The Monarch may kill me for this. What if he finds out?"

I couldn't convince her, so we're trying something different. I'm digging into Dani's mind—which she's surprisingly okay with, despite her refusal to do the same to Vulryn—and then I'll do my damnedest to connect us both with the dragon. I've never tried this before, but I failed miserably with Bob. I'm hoping Dani and I together will be strong enough to reach the copper beast.

That'll be hard enough, but the most challenging part will be making sure my shields don't fail. I'm holding them in place like a weapon because if Vulryn—or even Dani—decides to start snooping in my brain, I can't allow them in. I've suffered too much protecting my secrets to risk them now. If their thoughts venture in my direction, I'll cause them pain. Hurting them is the best way to keep Vulryn out. Dani knows, so she's promised to be careful. If she slips, she'll only do it once.

"Try to focus on whatever you know about dragons," I tell her. "It'll help me find relevant memories. And stop this stroll down memory lane. Because I do not need to see you lose your virginity. Again."

"Argh! Sorry. I'm trying, but for some reason, I can only think of the things I *don't* want you to see. It's like you've flipped the opposites switch in my mind. I can't give you anything you want." It feels like Dani's on the verge of giving up. Her heart's beating like a little bird's, frantic and ready to fly away at a moment's notice.

"Tell me about him, then. Maybe you need to get him out of your system."

"He was a lousy fuck. Gone from my system the moment he pulled out his puny pecker. That's the only thing you need to know."

"That's more than I needed to know," I mutter as Astarot's thoughts drop into my head. *Me*, he suggests. And he's probably right. "Astarot wants me to share my memories of him with you," I explain before she can respond to my complaint.

"What'll that do?" Dani's voice is trembling now, and I wonder how much longer she's willing to try this.

"You've been terrified of dragons all your life. It's gotta be tough to set that aside and enter a dragon's thoughts. Especially one that just tried to kill us. Maybe if you feel my love for Astarot and his for me, see how we bonded, you'll feel better about dragons in general."

She shrugs, her gaze fixed on Astarot. "Whatever you think."

I relax and let my mind pull up images of my time with him. Dani sucks in a deep shudder when I share my first view of Astarot, his wings trapped within the Dróttning's torture device. I let her feel the pain I sensed from Astarot before we bonded. Experience my *need* to save him. Join Fhord and me in our rescue. And then I wallow in the utter joy of freeing him, collapsing at his side after we found a safe place to rest, and waking to the realization that Astarot is mine and I'm his.

I hold on to those memories for a long time, reliving the love—his and mine—that filled my soul then and still lives in every part of me. For a moment, Astarot joins us, and she can sense his love for me too. But that feels so much more invasive than letting Dani experience my life. I push him away quickly because Astarot is mine and I can't share him in that way.

I realize when I pause for a moment that Dani's heartbeat has slowed. Her breathing is steadier. She seems calmer, ready to try again.

"Will you join me as I try to reach Vulryn?"

"Yes," she whispers, no tremble in her voice this time.

Inhaling as I steady myself, I push my mind toward Vulryn, who's as motionless as she has been all morning. Like Bob, she has no natural barrier to my invasion, and nobody here taught her to construct one. I enter easily, dragging Dani's psyche with me, and pause to try to find the sanity I know is here.

Hunger. A ravishing need for more hangs over everything Vulryn does. Like Bob, it began as she emerged from her shell, one of seven hatchlings left to try and survive. She was lucky enough to break through first, giving her a few minutes to breathe before the struggle began.

Vulryn, though, didn't attack. She stuffed the emptiness as deep within her as she could and hid from the others. Watching as they emerged and destroyed each other, she bided her time. When one other hatchling remained, tattered but alive, Vulryn leaped on him. She'd ripped out his throat before he realized he wasn't alone. And then she ate.

She's so gods-damned smart. I'm suddenly filled with an irrational hope because if we're going to connect to any dragon in this land, I want it to be her.

She has a thin grasp on her sanity, but she's more balanced than Bob, and I assume the rest of the Njordheim dragons are as bad or worse. We'd only know if we could find and trap one—a big if. Vulryn's our best hope, and we're going to make the most of this chance.

I dig into her memories, trying to find order within them. The hunger that feels like a living thing dominated her youth. The brown dragon she just killed had claimed her territory, and he kept her from the food she needed for long years. She barely survived, resorting to rabbits and even the occasional bird, although too often they weren't worth the energy it took to catch them.

Eventually, she figured out how to hunt without Bob's interference, watching one local herd until he'd gorged himself and left. In that brief window of time, Bob stayed away long enough for her to feed—but only ever long enough to take a single goat and swallow it whole. Once, she'd stayed close to the herd, hungry enough to try for seconds, but Bob returned as she took another run at her prey.

She's lucky she survived that day.

Many years passed before she felt strong enough to challenge Bob for the right to fully feed herself from the herd. Vulryn's memories linger on that fight—a source of both pain and pride. He'd nearly beaten her, forced her to continue existing on the scraps that had kept her alive until then. But she managed to capture one of his wings, damaging it enough to allow her to escape.

Bob spent days recovering from that attack. Days that Vulryn fed. And grew strong. He never drove her away from the herd again. Their paths rarely crossed.

Vulryn had never seen a dragon other than Bob in her early years, and she almost searched for him when her heat exploded within her, igniting a need even more brutal than hunger. Twice, she flew toward him, her body demanding his. Instead of giving in, though, some terrified part of her chose to injure herself both times—impaling herself on a tree once and mutilating her wing on a rock the next time. Again, she's lucky she survived.

I drag myself from her memories for a moment, forcing my tight shoulders to relax and releasing my clenched fists. I'm exhausted already, and I don't think we've accomplished anything. She feels just as distant and untouchable as she was before. I have no idea how to reach her and realize we need to stop for the day.

As I try to withdraw our minds from Vulryn's, I feel resistance I can't explain. The path behind us is murky and shifting. I'm not sure where we can go or how we can get there.

Shaking my head, I clutch my psyche more firmly, then reach for Dani. But now she's slipping away, the distance between us growing. Beside me, I feel Dani start to tremble as my view of her recedes. When I can no longer see her, my connection to her mind completely gone, she stills beside me. I know she's alive only because I can hear her heartbeat.

I focus on breathing, trying to keep myself from falling into panic, but I can't. I'm puffing and panting, my inhales erratic and growing faster with every step I take inside Vulryn's psyche, searching. My arms wrap around my stomach as I try to figure out what's gone wrong, and where I can find Dani.

My thoughts spear this way and that inside Vulryn's mind, but she's erected strong walls. I'm isolated from every part of her. I can't find any memories. No emotion. Not a single urge or need or demand.

Squeezing my eyes together more tightly, hoping to eliminate any distraction that might be pulling me away from Dani—making sure these aren't shields I created without intending to—I try again. But again, I fail. I'm alone and my only choice is to leave. The only path I can find leads out. Without Dani.

Astarot, what is happening here?

Revenge. Astarot doesn't hesitate before answering. He saw enough to understand what Vulryn did. She's every bit as smart as I suspected, but I couldn't have imagined this. While we've been examining her mind, she's been examining Dani's. She found her answer there—the ability to shield parts of her mind from others. She lured us in and attacked when I was weak.

Dani's hers now. I can't find a way to save her.

And I need to save myself first. I'll come back after I figure out what the fuck just happened. How I can fight back.

I yank my psyche, jerking it toward the only route available to me. I feel Vulryn tug back, a hesitant and uncommitted response. She must be unsure whether she can control both of us. But the more time I give her, the more aggressive she'll become. I need to get out now.

Throwing all my strength into it, I pull on my thoughts one more time, clinging as they break free and reel back into my mind. My head starts to throb, and I drop my chin for a moment, lifting my hands to clutch the back of my neck as I try to calm my breathing.

Fuck. That could not have gone worse.

When I open my eyes and look at Dani, I can't hold back the tears. At some point, she collapsed onto the mat beneath us, and she's just lying there now, as still as death but breathing. I need to trust she'll stay alive long enough for me to figure out my next step and try again.

First, though, I need to eat and sleep. I'm so gods-damned tired. I can't help her if I try again and lose myself to Vulryn's anger.

I start with the lake, dropping into it fully clothed and letting it repair some of the broken parts of me. I can't escape an anguish so deep it feels like it will never go away. It's Vulryn's eternal pain, but also a heavy guilt about what I convinced Dani to do. This is my fault. I have to fix it.

I need Fhord. I'm stronger with him, and I need the strength he'll give me.

Vulryn's wide awake, her eyes watching me, when I emerge. And Dani hasn't moved. She's still breathing. Her heart still beats. But she looks like she'll never move again.

I force myself to eat, not hungry but knowing my body requires food to recover. And then I erect a barrier above her—four sticks with a blanket between them—and collapse in the tent. I'm asleep as soon as I stop falling.

Moans wake me. They're eerie—quiet expressions of deep pain—and for a moment I can't get my bearings. When I turn to search for Dani, warn her about the strange noise, the memories roll through me, dropping into my gut like rocks. My hands clench as my spine stiffens, my body already preparing for the battle of wills I'm about to face. I must put an end to whatever Vulryn is doing to Dani.

Are you awake?

Awake. He hasn't rested yet. Even without Dani's threat, he kept watch while I slept.

Can you tell if Vulryn's thoughts are any clearer? If she'll let me take Dani back?

Anger. Nothing's changed. We trapped her and Dani tried to kill her. She wants us dead.

She created shields. Will I be strong enough to keep her out?

Maybe. He's not sure. Which terrifies me.

I have to go back in. I can't leave Dani trapped there.

Dani. He wonders if I can find Dani through her own mind, call her back that way.

I'll start with that, but if it doesn't work, I'm going back into Vulryn's. I have to get her out.

Together. He thinks he can give me the strength I need to get out.

I hope so.

Dragging myself from my mat, I gather clothes and stalk back over to the lake. It replenishes me as much as food and I'll need everything I can get from it. When I feel like I can face Vulryn again, I drag myself out, dress quickly, then find food. I eat a heartier meal today than I did yesterday. I can't risk losing myself because I run out of energy.

Finally, I'm ready to start again. Vulryn's large red eyes have followed me all morning as she watched in an unnatural silence. When I turn to hold her gaze, they fill with anger, her fire seeming eager to burn me if I get too close. Which is exactly what I plan to do.

I have no idea if she can comprehend my words, but today, I'll try talking her through what I'm doing and why. "I need to get Dani back," I tell her as I settle on the ground in front of her. "You can't have her."

An orange flame erupts from Vulryn's nostrils as she snorts at me, disdain rippling in the tone of her response and the set of her lips. She shoves against her ropes, forcing herself closer to me as she bares her teeth. They pull on her skin, digging in enough to draw blood, but she only pushes harder.

"I don't want to hurt you. I just want to understand you, offer you a way to have a better life. Like I have with my dragon."

Now she laughs, in that dragony way I've come to recognize. But this isn't a happy laugh. It's bitter. Cold.

"We don't need to do that if you don't want. I'm going into Dani's mind to call her back. If that doesn't work, I need to go back into yours. I won't let you stop me, and if you try to trap me, Astarot will kill you. We're bonded. He'll protect me at all costs. You're defenseless, and he'll win this time."

Again, she snorts, her gaze never leaving mine.

"I've gotta do this. You're going to help."

I close my eyes, trusting Astarot to keep me safe, and push my thoughts toward Dani. She still hasn't moved, laying in the exact position as she was yesterday when Vulryn captured her psyche. I push on the edges of her mind and find no resistance because she's not there.

Pausing for a moment, I search for a path toward the dragon. I don't want to take it yet, but I need to get close enough to bring Dani back. Finally, I find what looks like a string leading directly from Dani to the copper beast. I reach for it, tugging as I send my thoughts through it.

Dani, listen to me. You can come back. Vulryn can't hold you. Follow my voice. Let me lead you out of this.

For the next five minutes or more, I repeat the same message, gently urging her to return to me. Nothing happens, though. I stand alone in Dani's mind, hoping for a solution that isn't coming. I need to go find her.

Pulling again on the string, I let it draw me toward Vulryn's mind. A tremble ripples through me when I leave the calm of Dani's psyche and enter the mayhem of Vulryn's. I've never been so terrified entering any beast or person's thoughts.

I force myself to breathe normally. This is exactly what Vulryn wants. I can't give it to her. She's devious and completely sane, or she wouldn't have learned so quickly how to organize her mind and erect shields. She wouldn't have captured Dani and held on to her. But I've been doing this longer. I'm stronger than her.

The string leads deeper into Vulryn's psyche, but I can't see anything along the way. I can only follow and trust Astarot to help me find my way out again. As I wander through the labyrinth Vulryn built to hold Dani—and probably confuse me—I feed her mind images of my relationship with Astarot. Our joy at bonding. The time we spent sharing stories from our lives. The protectiveness we feel for each other. I feel the edges of Vulryn's loneliness, but she hides it well. She doesn't want me to recognize her weakness. Who can blame her?

I've lost track of time and can't let myself care. Minutes or hours might have passed, but it doesn't matter. I can only wander through the dragon's mind, forcing her to maintain shields she just learned to construct, until she grows too tired. Finally, long after I began, I sense her start to weaken. The walls grow soft, malleable. Her will seems to shift, openings emerging and then disappearing everywhere I look.

Vulryn breaks the silence first. She shrieks at me, frustration and anger warbling through her call.

Let me have Dani, and I'll leave.

No!

I'm not leaving without her. You're getting tired. You need to let her go.

No! This cry is less fierce. Her exhaustion sneaks into it.

And then I see Dani. She's laying down in the same position as her physical form. Running, pushing through walls Vulryn tries to erect in front of me, I drop down by her side, slapping her once, and then again. She needs to wake up. I don't know if I can carry her.

When her eyes open, though, I see my mistake. She shrinks into herself, wrapping her arms around her knees as she rocks back and forth, babbling. Now I'm terrified. Because Dani is completely insane. She's not going anywhere willingly.

Ripping her arms away from her legs, I drag her over my shoulder and stand, my knees almost buckling beneath me. Dani collapses, not fighting me as her dead weight hangs over me. She's at least my size, and I have no idea how far I can walk carrying her. Stumbling forward, I let my thoughts spear out to Astarot.

Lead me out.

And he does. In gentle instructions, he guides me back into Dani's psyche. Perhaps because Vulryn is exhausted, this trip goes more quickly. After a few minutes, I'm crossing the barrier between their minds. Calmness fills me, and I drop to my knees, setting Dani on the floor. Deranged eyes watch me for a moment and then she spins to her side, clutching her bent legs again as she starts to wail.

I've done all I can. Letting my thoughts reel back into my mind, I inhale deeply, forcing my breathing to slow.

And then I hear her. The same wailing. When I open my eyes, I see Dani clinging to herself, emitting a mournful cry, and I can't hold back my own sob. She turns toward me for a split second, her eyes just as insane as they were inside Vulryn's mind, and then cowers back into herself to continue keening.

CHAPTER SEVENTEEN

FHORD

WHO BETRAYED US?

WE'RE FUCKING SURROUNDED.

I can sense a hundred soldiers, maybe more, in the trees. They must have known we were coming. That's the only explanation for so many to be gathered here, waiting for us.

"Who the fuck betrayed us?" My gaze finds and holds every member of this little band of rebels, searching for the hint of guilt or righteousness somebody must be feeling right now. Ignoring my Ætt—because there's no way any of them turned on me—I focus on the males I barely know. "Answer me. Who betrayed us?"

"How do we know it wasn't you, Fhord?" Mikkael's eyes flash at me as he spits out his response. "You've been kissing the Dróttning's ass for a long gods-damned time. She's got your dragon. Maybe it was you."

I'm striding forward and slamming my fist into his face before I have time to think about it, his words and this fucked up situation igniting the savage inside me. The crunch from his nose—blood and snot flinging around us in a crimson spray—soothes something deep in my guts. But Mikkael's not the kind of guy to stand down.

His arm flies up toward me, knuckles slamming into my jaw while I'm savoring the satisfaction of finally hitting the bastard. I can't hold back my grin. I need to beat the shit out of someone, and he's exactly who I would have chosen.

Before I can destroy Mikkael, though, Johan is pushing between us. "What the fuck are you doing? We don't have time for this shit." He shoves Mikkael back, muttering something under his breath.

Sucking in a deep breath, and then another, I reach inside to the place where my savage lives. He's snapping at the restraints I keep on him, desperate to destroy Mikkael. The soldiers trapping us. Anything standing between us and Sifa. But I can't set him free unless we have no choice. Because I'm terrified that once he's out, he won't be restrained until he's found our mate. And there's no gods-damned way I'm letting that happen. Not yet.

Shoving my clenched fists into my pockets, I spin and search, my thoughts scrambling to find some path out of here. When I see it, my gaze twists toward Toffer and then back to the cave that might be our only hope.

"You," I snarl, pointing at the troll. "Can you find caverns beneath us? If there are any?"

His eyes grow wide as a grin emerges. Nodding, he drops to the ground, digging through the leaves and dirt to spread his palms as close as he can get to whatever rock lies beneath us. He's still for long seconds as my mind spears out to the Dróttning's fighters. They haven't moved yet, but they will soon. We need to get the fuck out of here.

Perhaps a minute after Toffer began searching, he starts to crawl north, deeper into the woods. He's moving closer to a large group, but for now, I let him go. Whatever he finds may be our best hope. He stops when he's traveled about thirty feet, digging his hands in deep again as his brows curl together. He's more intense than I've ever seen him.

And then another grin appears, his expression softening as he looks up at me. "Here," he says in a tone filled with satisfaction. "Sufficient space to stretch. Ramble and run to retreat."

"Is the top of the cave very dense here? I can get us through, but it'll be easiest if we start someplace that's already thin, or where the rock is mixed with some dirt."

Toffer dips his chin, dropping his hands again and then shuffling west about ten feet. "Here, entry below is easiest."

Grasping Toffer's shoulder, I squeeze lightly. "You're fucking handy to have around." His lopsided grin almost brings a smile to my face, but I shut that shit down. I can't let Mikkael think I'm over his outburst that quickly.

Spinning, I gesture everyone in as close as possible. "Dismount and be ready to go. I'm going to rip open a hole into the cavern below. We'll need to get in as fast as we can so I can close it before somebody chases us down there. When I unleash my magic, the Dróttning will know and she'll throw everything she has at us. Anyone who slows us down will be left behind. Got it?"

Each of them nods, dropping from their horses and holding on to the reins. "This'll be loud," I warn before kneeling to dig my fingers into the earth. When I've reached as far as I can go, I release my magic. For a moment, it's cathartic. I fight every day to hold in my power, which writhes in my gut like a living thing that *wants* to change our world. Letting go of the fight to restrain that magic feels like the release of a vise binding my insides.

And then I feel the pain.

I can barely hold back the scream that erupts in my chest and whips up my throat, biting my tongue at the last moment to stop myself from announcing our exact position to the hundred soldiers that surround us.

Collapsing to the ground, my arms splayed out, I try to suck in a breath, but dirt and leaves clog my airway. I sputter them out before inhaling the remnants of the muck along with enough air to satisfy, for a moment, my starved lungs.

A hundred knives have carved into wings I don't possess, digging into their most sensitive spots. It's as if they were splayed out, blades poised and ready to extract the most pain possible at the same time.

Which is probably exactly what happened to my brave, selfless dragon.

Tindera, my thoughts croak, desperate to know she still lives.

Her responding *Alive* holds none of the fearlessness, the boldness, my dragon usually wears like armor. She's being tortured. Because I'm using my gifts to try to save the Dróttning's enemies.

Fuck.

Me.

It's not my pain.

I remind myself that my body is not suffering this abuse. My wings are not being flayed of skin. My nerve endings are not on fire. This is the bond. And as much as it kills me, as much as I want to embrace and wallow in it, to feel exactly what she's feeling, I need to push it away. If I don't, we'll all die here. I'll never be able to save either of the females I love.

When I open my eyes, I can't see anything except the small hole in front of me—a passageway barely big enough for the gods-damned cat. That's the only thing that matters right now. Not the Ætt or Toffer or that bastard Mikkael. Not the traitor—whoever the fuck it is—or the elves or the others. Opening this crack in the stone enough to fit a small dragon. And then closing it again.

So that's what I do.

It's so fucking much harder this time.

Now, I have to push my magic out, my back spasming as I funnel all of my thoughts into this one thing. Open the hole. Within a few seconds after starting again, the pain doubles. I concentrate on breathing as I force myself to accept the Dróttning's plan. Tindera will be tortured every time my magic echoes through this world.

The pain is overwhelming, debilitating. Worse, though, is the knowledge that it's only an echo of her pain. That she is suffering with every push of my power. That her wings may never recover if the damage is too great.

But I do this anyway. I don't see another option.

Finally, long minutes after I started, Torsten's hand lands on my shoulder. I cringe away from him, my skin exploding every place he touches, and whip my eyes his way. "Enough?" I rasp.

"Enough." His voice is soft. They've seen this before. They know what I look like when I share Tindera's pain. "We've got Sigurd. Go. Rest. You still have to close it if you can."

Dipping my chin sharply, I try to stand, but I can't. Twisting on to my ass, I slide down the embankment I created, shoving to the side when I reach the ground to leave space for others. Dropping my head against the wall, I give up fighting the pain, letting myself experience it with Tindera. She's not being tortured right now, but she's in agony.

I'm so fucking sorry, I gasp. *So gods-damned sorry.*

Love. Her response is weak, and I wonder how much blood she's lost. Whether they'll take enough to kill her if I do try to close the gap above us. I don't think I can do it. I can't risk her being killed for my fuck-ups.

I'll fix this. I promise.

Love. She's comforting me. They're ripping apart her wings, inflicting the most pain any dragon could suffer, and she's worried about me. I don't deserve her.

I need to do more, I grunt at her. *I opened a hole, and when everyone's through, I'll close it. It's the only way to escape.*

Escape, she agrees, her tone emphatic. She knows what it means—how much she'll suffer—but it doesn't matter. She wants me to do what I must to save them.

I'm so fucking sorry. I don't know what else to say. Nothing will ever fix this.

When Torsten's hand lands on my shoulder again, I open my eyes to look around. They're all here. It's time.

Sucking in a deep breath, I tug on the magic deep inside me. But it's gods-damned stubborn. My frantic mind can't concentrate, my thoughts so fixated on Tindera's beautiful, battered wings that I can't summon my power. This has never happened before—I'm one of the most dangerous beings in this land—and I don't have a single gods-damned clue what to do about it.

"They're coming, boss." Leif's worried, and I don't blame him.

"Just hold on," I spit out, dragging my focus away from the pain still radiating all across my back. But I'm not alone anymore. My savage is awake, desperate to be set free and fight those who would hurt our dragon. Now I'm fighting that stubborn bastard too, pushing his psyche into that tight corner I trap him in.

I can't do this alone. And I don't have to, I realize as surprise ripples down my spine. I have Sifa's power too. Maybe that's what I need to break through this.

Casting my mind north, I search for my little rabbit, frantic for the calm she brings to the savage inside me. When I find her sleeping, wrapped in her dragon's arm, I exhale. Calm washes through me. I still hurt so fucking much. But it's not everything. It won't stop me from doing this thing I have to do.

Fuck, I miss you, rabbit. She can't hear me, but maybe she feels my love. Maybe she'll dream of me.

I can hear them racing our way. They're not here yet, but there are so many boots stomping across the ground toward us. It's now or never.

Bracing myself, I cast my magic again, heaving the rock and dirt back together. As if on cue, the Dróttning's torture starts again. Now Tindera's shrieking in my mind, her battered wings burning as she struggles to pull them closer to her body. She can't. Whatever holds them, extended and exposed, is stronger than my powerful dragon.

And still, my magic works. The rocks screech and moan as I drag them out, stretching the stone I had condensed as I packed it together to create our pathway. It's slower this time, the weight of Tindera's pain crushing me, but I'm doing all I can.

They arrive before I finish, a handful of soldiers throwing themselves into the cavern to stalk me. I'm so gods-damned tired, and I can't close this gap if I'm forced to fight them. My savage is tearing at my restraints, demanding that I free him.

He will end this.

He *needs* to end this.

For us. For our dragon. For our mate.

I almost do it. I'm hovering at the edge of release when an arrow slides past me and pierces the throat of the closest soldier. I can only watch, power pouring out of me, as my Ætt come to my rescue. And Toffer. Because the murderous troll sure as fuck isn't gonna pass up this opportunity. Tindera's pain smothers everything in me, dulling every sense except agony, but a sliver of ease finds its way into my consciousness. I'm so fucking relieved.

And then she's there. That's why they were waiting. The Dróttning came personally to make sure we don't get away.

I have to face the bitch, stop her from ripping this hole open again and sending her soldiers to chase down every last one of our friends. So I find the strength to climb back to the surface. My magic is battling hers now, as she rips open the hole I'm straining to close.

After a few moments, I know I'm too weak to beat her, buried in my dragon's torment. I don't want to release my savage, but I have no other choice. Gathering every ounce of magic I can, I force the hole closed. And then I free him. Energy spills through me with my savage's surge of joy. He's stronger than her. He will stop her.

This pain dances with relief, yanking my mind away from my dragon's agony. My bones shift as my body remakes itself. It's been years since I last set him free, but when it happens, it feels so familiar I find myself sighing. I savor each break and renewal of my bones. The fur that ruptures my skin, burning everything in its path. The jaw that stretches out, canines dropping into place, eager to draw blood.

My sharp vision focuses on my dam, the Dróttning, as I shove Fhord into the corner where I'm usually trapped. She's reopened a small gap, but not enough for anyone to pass through. She knows she must save her strength to face me. Fhord's a large male, but I'm an *enormous* wolf, my back standing higher than even the tallest biped in this land. I swivel my head to glance back at the others, my tongue lolling at faces revealing a mix of shock, elation, and wonder, and then I attack.

Four soldiers surround me, but they're snacks on my way to the meal my dam has gathered for me. *Bitch that she is.* The fighters come in waves of ten, fifteen, twenty, and more. I'm frolicking through them, ripping off heads, shredding throats, slashing and slurping up entrails. My teeth slice through everything in their path as I feast on their flesh, but more than that, their fear. Fhord has kept me hidden for many, many years this time. Few alive have seen me. But those who survive—if any do—will never forget me.

When I see her, I find that I want nothing more than her blood on my tongue. Her bones in my stomach.

Her death by my fangs.

She hurt our mate. And our dragon.

If she could, she would destroy all of us.

So we will destroy her. And free everyone.

I turn, clearing a path to her as I slash through the beings who would keep me from my vengeance. She stands, her gaze capturing mine whenever I look her way, a morbid smile on her face, and watches as I kill my way to her. When I'm no more than twenty feet away, she releases her magic.

It hits me in a wave I feel ruffle over and into my fur, little daggers of pain trying to cause me harm. To slow me down. To stop me from reaching her. But I'm stronger than I've ever been. She can best Fhord. She cannot best me. Not after Sifa gave herself to Fhord, strengthening us through the mating bond.

Pausing a few male's-heights away from her, I lift my snout and howl. Blood drips from my maw, my teeth coated in the flesh of her warriors, and I've never felt more alive.

"It's been a long time, wolf. Did Fhord call you to save him?"

Growling, my head swinging side to side, I step forward and bare my teeth at her. She will not speak of our male in that way.

My dam laughs at me, her hands lifting as she tries again to push me down with her pain. The snarl that rips from my chest speaks for us. Her magic ripples over my fur, its sting nothing more than an annoyance. Shaking, I snarl again and take another step forward. My muzzle can almost taste her, our teeth popping into her skin and sucking dry her veins.

When her eyes widen, a smirk twisting her features, I know she's learned our secret. Fhord will be angry, but I am proud. I want all in the land to know that Sifa is ours.

"You and that elf," she whispers, her words angry and bitter. "You wouldn't have the strength to withstand me without her. Your mate." She spits the last word as if it tastes rotten on her tongue.

And I don't hold myself back any longer. Springing toward her, I wrap my teeth around her throat. But before I can finally taste the blood that has dominated my wolfy dreams for too many years, my dam shifts. Her change is faster than mine, perhaps because more than most shifters, she personifies her other form perfectly. My canines slide across the scales of the wyrm she hides from all except me.

Lifting herself up, the Dróttning flings me away, my massive body flying thirty feet or more as I curl for the fall. I throw myself to my feet, but I can only watch as my dam's burning eyes survey the wreckage, finding any soldiers that still live. And then she kills them all. Because nobody can know that the Dróttning becomes this contemptible thing.

She's always been jealous of our glorious fur.

When she's done, her head spins toward me one last time. The anger in her eyes burns the air between us, a promise of pain. Howling, I let myself grieve for a moment for our dragon and all she will suffer at the hands of this monster who birthed us. But this is a problem we cannot solve today. We will not catch her, and we must prepare before we attack her den. Tindera will survive.

And today, our mate awaits us.

Sneering as she flicks her tongue at me and turns to slither away, I consider, for a moment, giving our skin back to Fhord. I can feel him inside, demanding that I curl back into the ball he holds deep within his bipedal form, stopping us from ever taking our skin. More than that, I can feel his fear that I will scare our mate.

I'm not afraid, though. She will love me, just as she loves him.

Turning north, I let my feet carry us to her. My joy ripples through me as I run for the first time in too many moons. Day bleeds into night, which bleeds into day again, and still I run. Nothing can slow me. I am the most powerful creature in this land.

Only when I reach the water that ripples with life do I pause, dropping into it as my mind draws up image after image of our mate. Her smile when Fhord speaks of his passion for her. Her laugh when his hands find the sensitive spots along her side. Her moans when his tongue delves deep inside her. I will give our body back—we cannot reach her without Fhord's magic—but we must be clean when we return to her. We would not disrespect our mate by presenting ourselves with the blood of our enemies caked on us or their taste in our mouth.

Hours later, we reach the cave that will carry us to our mate. I'm not ready to give up our form, but I know the northern leader's magic will keep us out. I cannot prevail over that power. And I've brought us far enough. I will sleep and Fhord will return. He'll go to her. When he does, I'll take our form again and meet our mate.

She will know me.

She will be mine, too.

Chapter Eighteen

Sifa

Not Here

IT'S BEEN A VERY long time since I've fucked anything up this badly.

Dani falls asleep within minutes of me dragging her psyche back from Vulryn's diseased mind. I huff out a sigh of relief that she's no longer howling like a pissed-off Thor and follow almost immediately. The exhaustion of mentally battling a ridiculously stubborn dragon weighs on my bones like a cavern collapsed around me. Astarot will stay awake and keep watch. I'm so thankful for my dragon.

It's dark when I wake up, but I have no idea how late it is. Only that I slept away the day, at least. Stretching on my mat, I let my thoughts replay the mess I made this morning. I'll fix this, but I have no idea how. Or when. I'm worried about Harald's response, but I'm much more worried about Dani. I need to get her back.

There's no reaching these dragons. I don't know what to do about it and have never wanted Fhord more.

When my thoughts turn to him, the oddest sensation washes over me. Letting my mind follow it, I find myself drawn to the cavern that holds the barrier. And him. He's asleep, but there's something different about him. Unease settles in my gut, stirring up a nausea I struggle to control.

Throwing on clothes and boots, I stomp out of the tent, my gaze finding Astarot's. *Fhord's on the other side of the barrier. There must be a problem, but I don't know what. I'm going to him. Watch Dani. Keep her here.*

Safe. Astarot's response is a promise and a plea. He'll keep her safe and wants my assurance I'll be careful.

Always, my majestic dragon. Always.

I toss Sunbeam's saddle on her back and gather a few things Fhord may need—I even ended up with some of his clothes in my pack—then mount her and kick her sides. I'm terrified and desperately wish I could take Astarot, but I know it's not an option. He needs to make sure nothing else goes wrong with Dani and Vulryn.

Luckily, we're not far from the barrier. We hadn't traveled a long distance when we found the trolls, perhaps eight hours walking the horses. I push Sunbeam as hard as I can today, terrified of leaving Astarot with Dani and Vulryn too long.

And I need to see Fhord.

That's the real reason, I admit to myself after a few minutes of urging Sunbeam to go faster. I miss him desperately.

We alternate between a canter and a gallop the whole way, slowing down only when we must. Less than three hours later, I'm dropping from Sunbeam at the cavern's mouth, hauling her toward the barrier. I barely notice the energy of the cave, my thoughts too focused on Fhord. I've never needed anyone this badly. The spot inside me that belongs to my mate grows larger with every step, his presence filling me with the sense that for now, at least, all's right in the world. I'll be in his arms again soon.

Still, part of my mind grasps on to my doubts, reminding me I don't trust him. I can't let myself get sucked into this relationship—this mating bond—until I know he belongs at my side. Deserves to be there. But those are fears for another day. Today, I can savor the sensations that come from my mate. Luxuriate in his arms again.

He's awake when I see him, standing with both hands on the barrier, a smile on his lips and in his eyes.

And naked. Gloriously, magnificently naked.

And of course he's hard. I'd have been disappointed if he wasn't.

For a moment, I'm speechless as I watch this male that belongs to me. Every fear within me evaporates. He was magnificent the first time I saw him, but somehow, he's even more stunning now with his firm planes and soft green eyes. A dark wave of hair rests on his forehead, and I want nothing more than to lift my hand and stroke it away. Something inside me settles when he's close, and I wonder how I could possibly have missed this connection between us. Even with all the negative emotions Fhord was throwing at me, I should have realized the first time I saw him that he's mine.

"Fuck, you're beautiful. I missed you so much, rabbit." His voice is rough, his hands pushing against the barrier.

"I missed you too." I lift my hands to place them opposite his, stepping as close as I can to him. "I'm so gods-damned glad to see you. But why are you here?"

"That's a long story and I need you in my arms, legs wrapped around me, when I tell it. Help me bring down this barrier. Then we can talk. After."

Fhord's head dips to glance at his raging erection, a grin emerging on his face. Even if I wanted to, I wouldn't be able to hold back my responding smile.

There's so much we need to talk about. Secrets and lies and too many questions bounce into my thoughts and out just as quickly. Right now, the mating bond is burning inside me, and it cares about one thing: fully fusing me to my mate. It takes a moment for me to pull my thoughts away from the feel of Fhord inside me—my body's *need* to anchor this connection between us—and concentrate on the wall standing in our way.

Finally, though, I dip my chin. "What do you want me to do?"

"Just open up to me, rabbit. I'll take what I need." He smirks, his gaze holding mine as he adds, "And then you can take every single thing you need from me."

And just like that, I am hot. Crazy hot. Need-his-hands-on-me-right-now hot. He winks—because he feels it too, echoes of his yearning finding me even through the barrier—and pushes. With my mind filled with thoughts of my sexy mate and everything he's going to do to me, I open up to him.

Fhord sucks in a deep breath, his dick jerking as his gaze tracks down to pause at my breasts before continuing to the tips of my thighs and then back up to my eyes. "So. Fucking. Dangerous," he rasps, his gaze burning into me. Somehow, he's even larger now. And I cannot wait to have him inside me. "I'll never get this open if you keep distracting me with thoughts like that," he breathes, his tongue emerging to drag across his bottom lip.

Power ripples through me as it spins in a wave, the barrier reacting with a barely-visible fold. "I'm yours," I purr, holding his gaze as I lift my hands to cup my breasts, a smile playing across my lips. "Take what you need."

The groan that emerges from Fhord is guttural, intense. The release of power that follows is unlike anything I've felt before—a hurricane of magic funneled into this wall standing between us. Far quicker than before, the barrier flickers and then bends to Fhord.

When he crosses the line between Vanatia and Njordheim to tug me into his arms, I realize I'm home again. And I can't imagine ever wanting to leave.

His kiss is fierce and hungry as his lips land on mine. Gasping as I wrap myself around him, my mouth opens and our tongues tangle, one of his hands spearing through my hair while the other grabs my hip to draw me closer. After a moment, his lips leave mine, and he explores down my neck then back up, nibbling on the ear that will only ever respond for him.

"Not here," he says as he drags himself away to hold my gaze. "Harald probably heard us, and I'll be damned if I'm going to let him interrupt what I plan to do to you." Pressing his lips against mine for one more demanding kiss, he takes my hand and leads me deeper into Njordheim. "How far is Astarot? Can you call him?"

"Are you sure it's safe for you to come here? I need your help, but I don't want to risk your life if you haven't done what Harald wants." I pause for a moment, pulling him to a stop. "Or have you?"

"I know more now than I did before, so I have an answer I can give him. We don't have everything yet, but it'll be enough if we can tame your dragon. Or have you done that already?" He's grinning now, and it's so gods-damned magnificent, I almost can't stand it.

But his question brings my failure crashing down on me, and I feel myself shrink, my shoulders drooping as my expression shifts. "Not even close," I moan as I reach out to touch his cheek.

"What happened?"

"It's a long story. Let's head to my campsite, and I'll tell you along the way."

"It's okay, rabbit. Whatever it is, we'll fix it."

"I hope so, Fhord," I mumble as I walk with him toward Sunbeam. "Because Harald will never forgive me if we can't."

I've ruined the mood, but nothing was going to happen here anyway. Fhord drags on the clothes I brought and mounts Sunbeam behind me, muttering about the bullshit name Harald gave my horse. He's still hard—I'd have been shocked if he wasn't—but his hands on my waist are gentle, not sensual. He knows we need to talk first, that this need for each other has to wait until we've fixed the problems I created.

I tell him everything as Sunbeam carries us back to Dani and Vulryn. We don't talk yet about why I found him naked on the other side of the barrier, but he assures me he'll explain once we get to Astarot.

"It involves Tindera," he explains, "and Astarot needs to hear it as much as you do."

His mood shifts as we ride deeper into Njordheim, and I wonder how long we have before his *need* for Tindera outweighs everything else.

The sun is cresting on the horizon when we get back to the camp, casting a tapestry of colors in our path. For a moment, I pause to take in the beauty of the day, the peace of an open field and crystal-clear lake, the calm of my dragon watching me with wide eyes. When my gaze lands on Dani, sees her slow breaths, I release a sigh of relief. Astarot would have told me if her heart stopped beating, but it's still a relief to see her for myself. A gust of gratitude to the gods hits me as I realize she and Vulryn both are asleep. I did *not* want to deal with an alert, angry dragon as soon as we got back.

"They're alive," Fhord rumbles in my ear as Sunbeam carries us toward them. "That's the most important thing. And I know it sounds callous, but Harald doesn't give a fuck about his people. He might appreciate getting her back like this. Having the dragon's insanity in Dani's mind would give him insight he's never gotten before."

"I guess that should make me feel better, but it doesn't. I can't leave Dani like this."

"I know, rabbit." I feel his hands move to my shoulders and give me a slight squeeze. "We'll fix this. I promise."

Anything happen while I was gone? Astarot's solemn eyes have followed us since we emerged from the forest, but he's been silent.

Tindera? He's got other things on his mind.

"Astarot's asking about Tindera. Is she okay?" Fhord sucks in a deep, shaky breath. I spin in the saddle to find his gaze. His eyes are more tortured than I've ever seen them. "What happened? Is she okay?"

He lifts his hand to stroke my cheek and drops from Sunbeam, watching Astarot as he approaches him. "You heard her cries?"

I've never heard such despair in his voice. A rock drops into my stomach as I wait for the bad news.

Pain. I can feel ripples of Tindera's agony as Astarot opens his thoughts to me.

"He didn't hear her cries—the barrier probably got in the way—but he felt her pain while it was open. What happened to her?"

"The Dróttning hurt her. She'll be okay—and it's over now—but she suffered more pain than she ever had before."

His voice is somber, an apology in every word. "Our group was surrounded, and I ripped open the ground to get access to a cave system, then closed it back up. The Dróttning punished Tindera for it."

I can feel Astarot's rage simmering through his veins. Not at Fhord or me, but at the Dróttning and her barbaric rule over Vanatia's dragons. He stands motionless for a long time, his mind thrashing as he fights a feral instinct to race back to Tindera. Finally, he calms his racing thoughts, snorting flames a half-dozen times as his breathing slows.

"You said group," I point out when Astarot nudges me to get the rest of the information. "Who was with you?"

Fhord's lips tip up just barely at the ends, a mocking smile. "The Ætt had a random mélange of people waiting for me when I went back."

"Anybody I know?"

"You know everybody. Well, nearly everybody. You met my Ætt—Leif, Torsten, Jorunn, and Astrid—plus Toffer and your cat. Thor, I think?"

"The Ætt have Toffer and Thor?" I can't hold back the smile, although I'm not sure why that makes me happy. Maybe it's because I feel so close to Fhord's Ætt through my bond with him, and I love the idea of my troll and cat getting to know them too.

"They do." Fhord reaches out to run his knuckles along my cheek, his smile mirroring mine. "They'd been joined by those bedmates Liv and Frida, Joralf and his mate Fróðr, and two of Bevin's males, Johan and Mikkael."

"How in all the worlds did that happen?"

"Pretty fucking crazy, right? I'll let them explain it to you when we see them."

"Did everyone escape?"

"I think so. I got separated and came here. There's more you should know but let's get Dani out of Vulryn first. I'll tell you the rest later." Fhord's tone is odd, almost pleading. It feels like he's leaving something big out, but maybe I've just come to expect that from him. I nod because Dani needs us more than I need to hear whatever he hasn't told me. I take his hand to drag him toward her.

We sit in front of her, Fhord's fingers still linked with mine. She hasn't moved at all. Her eyes are closed, and she seems calm.

"I have no idea what to do," I say, my gaze finding Fhord's. "It took everything I had to wrench myself free after Vulryn took Dani. I'm worried about going back in. Maybe making it worse or not being able to get out."

"We'll go in together," he assures me in a soft voice, his thumb drawing comforting circles on the back of my hand. "We're stronger than Vulryn, and I've had experience with irrational dragons before. We'll get the rest of Dani back."

"Is that what's going on? Vulryn found a way to keep part of Dani?"

"I think so." Fhord's eyebrows pull together as he glances between Dani and the copper beast, his mind whispering out in the dragon's direction. "She's so fucking smart," he mutters, the corners of his lips tipping down. "I knew it when you described what she'd done, but to touch on her thoughts ... it's staggering."

"Smarter than dragons in the south?"

"Not our dragons," he says with a glance at my beast, whose snout has risen in indignation. "But most. I think when dragons are forced to accept a lesser rider, they lose part of themselves. For a time," he adds when Astarot puffs out his objection. "It must come back when they find their destined rider."

"It must," I agree with a laugh, my gaze spinning toward Astarot, who seems appeased by Fhord's clarification.

Mate, Astarot interjects, his gaze holding mine.

"He says you're right," I tell Fhord as I turn back toward him. "Before he and I mated, he was less than he is now. Plus, northern dragons have so many more challenges than southern dragons do. They have to be smart to survive, even starting in the nest. Only one in every hatching makes it out alive."

Fhord nods and closes his eyes, reaching out again to Vulryn. "We can do this," he assures me when he opens his eyes again. "Having me this close will add the speed you can't fully capture without me joining you. We'll go in fast and work together to break through anything she throws at us." He glances at Dani and then back at the dragon. "We'll use Dani's mind as our path, follow the thread that leads us to the rest of her."

I squeeze his hand. "If you say so." I'm filled with more doubt than I've experienced in years. The jobs Bevin used to send me on seem easy and meaningless compared to this.

"Together," Fhord repeats and squeezes my hand. I feel his psyche move toward Dani's and release mine to join him there. We push ourselves in, walking hand-in-hand as we search for the path to Vulryn's mind. I can feel hints of the lunacy that seems to have captured Dani, but they're subdued, as if some survival instinct chose this coma-like sleep over the chaos of the dragon's thinking.

"Here," Fhord breathes at me, pointing toward a thread so small and effervescent, I might have missed it. He draws me in that direction, pausing at the barrier between Dani and Vulryn. "Ready?" he asks in the same low voice.

I nod and tug him across the threshold, holding my breath as I prepare myself for the madness of the other side. But it's as calm as it was when I escaped before, walls holding us in the small space we moved into.

"The walls you described." Fhord's free hand reaches out to press against one, which holds firmly in place. "Follow my lead. Ready?"

"Ready," I agree, bracing myself for whatever he plans to do.

Squeezing my hand again, his mind reaches out to mine, embracing my magic to combine with his. "Collapse," he roars, shaking everything around us, and I'm stunned I managed to keep myself from falling.

His first yell isn't quite enough, but he holds on to the command, stretching it out as the blockades begin to tremble. After long seconds, my pulse spiking as I fight to hold my thoughts open and give him everything he needs, the barricades Vulryn constructed to keep us out fall, leaving us with a thin thread running straight toward a trembling shadow of Dani in the distance.

"Run," he snarls, holding our combined magic in place as we barrel toward Dani. The mayhem of Vulryn's mind fills me. Memories of every horror she's faced—weeks of starvation, brutal attacks when she finally found food—seize my mind like an invading horde.

When we reach Dani, Fhord grasps the shadow that somehow has substance, tossing it over his shoulder before grabbing my hand again and pulling me back in the direction we'd come. Vulryn fights us with her thoughts, casting fear and desperation at us, but Fhord doesn't stop, barking out "Stop" and then "Escape" with our combined magic when I wouldn't have been able to find a way out.

I'm struggling to dredge up more magic to give Fhord, my strength wavering as he feeds from me to battle this ridiculously strong beast. "Just a little longer," he breathes, his hand squeezing mine as he funnels more of our power into fighting Vulryn.

Before we can find our way out, though, Vulryn appears in front of us, her nostrils spitting out flames. "Mine," she screams as she stalks toward us.

"Ours," Fhord responds, every bit of command layered in his voice. "Stand down."

"Mine," Vulryn repeats, this claim even angrier than the first.

"One more push," Fhord flings out, his voice sounding as depleted as I feel. "This is her last stand. We'll be free when we force her to back off."

I breathe as slowly as I can, digging to find all I have to offer. He takes everything, weaving his own strength with mine to bellow one more demand. "Stand down." His voice vibrates with power I couldn't have mustered by myself.

Vulryn collapses where she stands, anger pulsing from her wide eyes as the flames come to an abrupt stop. Fhord yanks me toward her, guiding us around the motionless beast as her gaze follows us. I can feel the bone-deep frustration she threw at me when I bested her in the field, but like then, she's paralyzed. In a few seconds, we're crossing the barrier back into Dani's psyche to drop the shadow there and escape.

My thoughts reel back like a slingshot, throwing me backwards with the impact.

And I'm so fucking tired, I don't even try to move before letting sleep suck me in.

CHAPTER NINETEEN

Sifa

We Come Together

T HE SUN IS JUST starting to peek through the leaves when I wake, a mosaic of color emerging in front of me as I watch, motionless, under my blankets. I'm not surprised I slept so long. Yesterday's journey into Vulryn's brain drained me of everything I had.

Snuggling deeper into the warmth of my makeshift bed for a few more minutes, I watch in peace as the shadows shift in our small clearing. This is a beautiful land, wild like the northern part of Vanatia but somehow more untamed. Nature calls, though, so I drag myself up, shivering in the cool breeze, and tug on some sturdier clothes.

Shuffling through the underbrush, hoping to give Fhord as much sleep as possible—he gave even more of himself than I did—I move toward the privacy I need first thing in the morning. When I'm ready to face the day, I find the creek, splash some water on my face and then stand and turn with a stretch, nearly jumping out of my skin at the hulk of a man who snuck up on me.

"Good morning," Fhord whispers as he gives me one of his sexiest smiles. My center flares when his gaze caresses me, lingering on my lips before dropping down to a chest that already is heaving under the weight of his stare. "I missed you," he says as he finally lifts his chin and leans forward for a gentle kiss, his hands wrapping around my hips to draw me closer. "I don't ever want to be away from you again."

Closing the distance between us, I lift to my toes as my lips find his, humming, "I need a better 'hello' than that." And everything in this world is right again.

Fhord's kiss is hard, demanding, as his tongue plunges into my mouth and tangles with mine. "Fuck me," he snarls before swooping me into his arms and stalking deeper into the forest.

"Not here." Pointing toward the lake, I add, "That water is just like the river in Vanatia. I want you there."

This smile is even broader. Fhord's head dips down for a luxurious meeting of our lips and tongues as he changes direction and strides to the water. "Can you wake your dragon and get him over here to shield us, in case Dani wakes up?"

"Worried she might see something she likes?" I purr with a laugh.

"I'll be damned if I'm going to share you with anyone. Because the things I'm going to do to you...."

Astarot, I call, unable to keep the pleading tone from my voice. *Can you move to the lake, between it and Dani?*

Astarot responds with a grunt but drags himself up to plop down next to the shore. He's back asleep as soon as his snout hits the ground.

Fhord laughs as he strides past him, throwing a quick "Thanks" at my exhausted dragon. And then he's dropping me to my feet to slowly—much too slowly—strip off my clothes and then his. When I try to help, he playfully smacks my hands away. "Mine," he declares with a wink.

So I let myself relax and enjoy the moment as I watch this stunning male bare himself to me. Once, I reach out to caress his chest, but he growls. "No touching until I say so," he adds with the most wicked smile I've ever seen.

Fuck. Me. I love alpha Fhord when we're both naked and I'm about to get fucked.

I'm already wet for him, my body anxious for all the sensations he can wring from it, but I hold my hands still. He wants control of this experience, and I want nothing more than to give him every single thing he wants.

Finally, Fhord takes off his underclothes and stands nude in front of me, his dick harder than I've ever seen it. He ignores it, though, every bit of his attention on my body, naked and ready for him. He sucks his thumb for a moment and then reaches out, lazily circling one nipple and then the other.

"I can't wait to taste you again, rabbit," he groans, dropping his head to suck on the nipples he was just admiring. The jolt of pleasure he drags from my breasts spears from my chest to my core, drawing even more wetness from the part of me that wants him more than anything I've wanted before.

"You don't have to wait," I remind him as my hands dig into his hair and hold him to me. "I'm yours. Always yours, Fhord."

Grinning, he stands up and then sweeps me into his arms again and closes the last few feet between us and the water, submerging both of us. The places he's touching flare to life, sensations echoing through my body as sound bounces through a cavern, flitting back and forth endlessly. I'm nearly ready to explode already, the feel of his body against mine in this place almost too much to bear.

"You're right, rabbit. This is exactly where we need to be," he says as he releases me to float on the water.

"Why aren't I dropping in?" I breathe, unsure how I'm holding myself up as he positions me, directly in front of him, my legs wide and my center his to take.

"That wouldn't be any fun, would it?" His voice is husky and so gods-damned sexy. He runs his tongue through me, sucking my clit for the briefest moment before adding, "I want the sun shining down on you as I watch you come for me. Again. And again. And again."

"Fuck me," I sigh, my gaze finding his rich green eyes as they smolder over me.

"Oh, I plan to," he laughs, a deep rumble. "Again. And again. And again."

And then he gets focused. Fhord *consumes* me as the water laps at my skin, magnifying *every single sensation* his tongue triggers. My orgasm erupts in the first minute, Fhord's satisfied laughter rumbling through me as he pauses to catch my gaze. "We're just getting started," he promises, his voice guttural.

Flipping me over, the water rushing back to create a pocket so I can breathe, he continues his assault on my senses, his tongue driving into me before he picks up my hips with one hand, giving him better access to every part of me. I feel another smile before two fingers plunge into my pussy and his lips wrap around my clit, sucking like he's never tasted anything so luscious. This orgasm is somehow even stronger, the water that caresses my breasts joining in the fun to set off the nerve endings in all my favorite places.

But Fhord's not even close to done yet. His free hand moves to one of my breasts as the water takes its place, holding me up while he tugs at and flicks my nipple, his mouth still focused on my clit as his fingers work to squeeze another orgasm out of me. Sensations pinball through me, each nerve in my body joining Fhord to give me more pleasure than I could have imagined when I started the day.

Just as I'm about to release one more time, my body demanding the wave ready to flow over me, Fhord leans back. My head swivels to catch Fhord's gaze as he places both hands on my ass and pushes me down, the water responding to his commands to bring my hips down to his. "I need to be inside you, rabbit," he snarls as he rubs the tip of his dick across my opening and then sinks into me.

"Thank fuck," I breathe as Fhord starts to pound relentlessly. I feel him in every part of my body, my inner walls vibrating with the pressure as his dick finds that spot inside me that drives me wild and sets those nerves alive too. "I'm coming,

Fhord," I yell as his pace picks up, but he slows, his thrusts growing more leisurely.

"Not yet, rabbit. We come together. And I need to be inside you a little longer before I'm ready to stop." He pulls out and flips me over, driving into me again as his fingers find my nipples and play with those tight peaks.

But then the water shifts again, creating a bed beneath us as he drops on top of me, his finger grazing across my cheek. "You're so fucking glorious, rabbit. I've missed you." His lips drop to mine, kissing me slowly and deeply as he sets that same pace with his hips, one hand caressing a breast while the other holds him up above me, his fingers speared through my hair.

"I don't ever want to be away from you again," I murmur when he breaks the kiss. "I'm only half alive when you're gone."

"I was only half alive before you, rabbit. You made me whole. You are everything I'm not, all I'll ever want, the only thing I'll ever need."

His lips drop to mine again, but this kiss is more demanding, his tongue piercing through my lips as the rest of him does the same. He's moving in and out of me at a punishing pace and I want every single bit of it. When this climax crests, a wave hovering above me before dropping down to pull me into its ecstasy, I feel Fhord coming with me. "Fuuuuuck," whispers out as his dick bulges and then releases, his thrusts growing slower as we both ride out our orgasms.

We lay there for a long time, the water covering most of us as the rush of pleasure continues to ripple through me. And then Fhord lifts himself back up on his elbow to move a lock of hair from my face and hold my gaze. "We're going to defeat the Dróttning, make all of this right, so we can live the life we deserve. Us and our dragons."

"We will," I agree, my heart expanding with his promise. "We have to."

Fhord leans down for one more kiss then stands, the water rushing away from him to clear a path to the shore. He draws me up and tugs me along, waving a hand that sucks all the moisture away, leaving both of us dry and warm. "Hungry?" he asks as we're getting dressed.

"Starving. Now that you've taken care of the rest of me, I can give a little attention to my stomach." I glance at my dragon, asleep between us and the tent. "I should check on Dani first, though, see if she's still asleep."

"Dani is not asleep," she calls from Astarot's other side, a snort warbling her words. "I don't know anybody who could sleep through the ... noises ... you two were making."

I feel the blood rushing to my cheeks, an embarrassed smile erupting as I spin toward Fhord. But he's not embarrassed at all. A cocky grin splits his cheeks as his hand drops to palm his groin. "At least she didn't see anything," he laughs as he nibbles at my ear and then drops my hand to jog in the direction of the tent.

I take a deep, calming breath and follow him around Astarot, my gaze finding Dani's as my smile grows even larger. "You look normal," I breathe. "Like nothing ever happened."

"I feel normal, more or less." She watches me approach, her gaze never leaving mine. "Thank you for getting me out—and for making sure *all* of me got out."

"You don't have to thank me." Sitting down next to her, I reach out to take her hand. "I never would have left you there. And I'm so sorry I convinced you to try."

She turns her eyes toward Vulryn, the barest smile lifting the corners of her lips as she pulls her hand from mine, resting it in her lap. "I'm not," she sighs, her voice rich with some emotion that sounds a lot like love. And then Dani looks at me and I'm sure. Her eyes are bright with adoration. "She really is mine."

I glance toward Vulryn, who's no longer asleep. She's gazing at Dani with a mix of affection and anger.

My stomach clenches, the realization of what I've done washing over me like a cold bath.

Vulryn and Dani bonded.

Dani belongs to a dragon with a tenuous grasp on her sanity. Who can never, ever be trusted.

"Oh no." I can't keep the fear from my words.

"Right? It terrified me at first. She's got a lot of issues."

Fhord sits down next to me, his gaze fixed on Dani and a question on his tongue. Before he can ask it, though, she points at him with a half-shrug. "What are you doing in Njordheim?" she asks, a laugh in her words.

"It's a long story. But Sifa needed me, so it's good I'm here. We're stronger together, and it took both of us to free you from Vulryn's mind." His gaze shifts to the copper dragon, a frown dipping his lips. "She's a fucking powerful beast."

"She is," Dani agrees, her voice soft.

"How do you know she's yours?" Fhord's tone is terse, demanding.

I can almost feel Dani's back straighten, her ire at this arrogant dragon rider spilling to the surface. "How did you know Tindera's yours? I just do. She's mine."

"Tindera's sane, born into a society in which dragons and riders bond. It's not the same thing." Fhord's softened his tone now. He's trying to be reasonable. "She trapped you in her mind, probably desperate to feel the presence of someone else. Dragons are pack animals; the ones who live here must spend their entire lives craving company. The connection you're feeling could be an echo of that."

Dani nods, her shoulders relaxing as she watches Vulryn. "I sense that in her." Turning to Fhord, her eyes haunted, she mutters the rest, as if reluctant to consider or admit it. "And I get that you know dragons and I don't. You could be right. But it doesn't matter. I'm not leaving her unless she pushes me away. I'm hers for as long as she'll have me."

Vulryn puffs out a gust of fire, her eyes burning as she stares at Dani, who turns as if called to stare back. "She says always. She doesn't know much, and there's some chaos in her mind, but she's sure of one thing. We belong together."

We sit in silence for a few minutes, just watching the beautiful, fiery dragon who's opened a door I'd feared was sealed shut. Finally, I voice the question I don't want to ask. "What now, Dani? You told me Harald would kill anyone who bonds with a northern dragon. Do you really believe that?"

"I'm sure of it." She smiles, a playfulness in her gaze I've never seen before. "I guess I'll be defecting. You're stuck with me now. Me and Vulryn."

"You can't be serious." Fhord's words simmer with anger. He sucks in a deep breath, forcing himself to calm down before he continues. "We need Harald's help. He'll never support our cause if we betray him like that. And even if that was an option, we can't take an unstable dragon with us. The situation in Vanatia already is too unpredictable."

"You don't have a choice, Vanatian." Dani's tone is as cold as the eyes she casts at Fhord. "I'm coming with you. That is, unless you're prepared to kill the two of us. Well, try to kill us." Now she stands, striding over to lean against Vulryn's nose. The dragon rubs against her for a moment and then turns blazing eyes at Fhord, snorting her anger in a gust of flame that nearly reaches us.

Reaching over, I place a hand on Fhord's arm, stilling him before he creates problems he can't fix. "Dani, we can't let Vulryn go. She tried to kill us all just a few days ago. She can't have changed that much."

"She's mine now, and I'm hers. Everything's different." Dani reaches up to scratch behind Vulryn's ears, a low purr rumbling all around us.

"She's also ridiculously smart and crafty," I point out. Dani's smile broadens at my words, her eyes growing warmer as she watches the dragon she claimed. But she missed my point. "What if she's tricking you?" I urge. "To get you to release her?"

Dani shrugs, her gaze never leaving Vulryn's. "Maybe she is. It doesn't matter. I'm going to free her. I trust her to come with me, to not do us any harm."

As if to prove her intent, Dani gives Vulryn one last scratch behind her horn, reaches out to rub her snout, and then stalks toward the closest rope as she pulls a knife from her belt. "And now's as good a time as any."

"Wait," I call, rushing forward.

Vulryn, though, does not want me near her. She lifts her snout and swivels toward me, puffing out another gust of flame. Pausing, I lift my hands toward Dani. "At least let me wake Astarot first. And let's decide what we'll do if Vulryn makes any sudden moves."

"I'll wait long enough for you to wake your dragon, but I already know what I'll do." She turns to me and then Fhord, resolve stark in her eyes. "What we'll do," she amends in a firm voice. "If Vulryn wants to go, we'll let her. We'll never hold her against her will again."

"We can do that," I assure her. "What if she attacks? We don't want to hurt her. But Astarot will fight if she tries anything."

"He can try," Dani responds with a smirk. "But she showed me what happened the first time. Vulryn's not afraid of your dragon. She's strong."

"You can't want that," Fhord snarls, standing to move to my side.

"Of course not. And it's not going to happen. We'll free Vulryn, and she'll come with us to Vanatia. She realizes it's dangerous to be in Njordheim right now. And she's curious about your dragons."

"She can't be that lucid," I plead. "Those are sane, coherent thoughts. I've shared her mind. She's not that rational."

"Don't you get it?" Dani asks, her voice low. "She's every bit as smart as you realized. You saw what she wanted you to see. But that's only part of her." Dani pauses to stride back to Vulryn's snout, standing next to her dragon as both of their gazes are fixed on me.

"Vulryn dug through my thoughts to find a way to shield her thinking and then did exactly that. She had the strength of mind to trap me and almost trap you. She's part crazy," Dani murmurs with a laugh, "but she's mostly crafty. And she is definitely rational."

I can't respond to that. I've lost, and we both realize it. "At least untie the ropes instead of cutting them. We may need them again."

Dani nods as I reach out to Astarot to wake him. She spends ten minutes removing one rope after another from Vulryn, who lays there motionless the entire time. When she's done, Vulryn stands and shakes herself, her copper feathers reflecting bursts of red and yellow. And then she extends a wing, huffing at Dani.

Dani's responding smile brightens the day. She climbs onto her dragon's back and settles in, giving us a little wave before she pats Vulryn's neck. Vulryn shakes her head once, her lips lifting in a dragony smile as she throws herself into the air and soars away.

CHAPTER TWENTY

FHORD

A TAME DRAGON

THIS CLUSTERFUCK IS NOT what I had in mind when I decided to turn to Harald for help.

I don't know how the fuck I let them talk me into this. One of Harald's most trusted soldiers and a dragon who was considered *rabid* two days ago are accompanying us in our race back to Vanatia. Where we'll all join a sundry selection of rebels and *another* dragon the Dróttning would kill us for protecting.

But she wants to kill us for a lot of reasons. It's Harald's vengeance I need to focus on now.

"I guess I don't have to beg your dragon to carry my gear anymore," Dani announces in a self-satisfied tone as she stands to throw her packed bags over her shoulder. "My dragon will take care of my stuff." She turns to find Vulryn, just emerging from the lake after a long soak, who responds with a sharp dip of her snout.

Sifa smirks at her before stiffening, spinning toward Astarot with her eyebrows drawn together. After a moment, Sifa's gaze finds mine.

"We need to leave," Sifa warns, fear in every word. "Now," she adds in a terser tone.

"What is it?" I bark out, my gaze lifting to search for whatever Astarot warned her about.

"Soldiers—a lot—a few vikus from here." Sifa's hand points to the northwest, in the direction of Harald's kastali. "They're coming this way."

"I can't be here." Dani's voice is panicked, a warble I've never heard from her in each word. "The Monarch's soldiers will recognize me. I'd have to go with them."

"We can't fly." I'm trying my damnedest to be calm and reasonable, although I know she's right. If Harald really will kill Dani for bonding with Vulryn—and I wouldn't put it past the bastard—she needs to disappear. "They'll see us and follow us back to the barrier. Let's just get going and stay ahead of them."

"No, I can't risk it." She throws a jittery look at Vulryn and then back at us. "You take Astarot and the horses with all the gear. I'll ride Vulryn but stay hidden on top, so they don't see me. They'll recognize her as a local dragon and would never think she might have a rider. If any of the soldiers knows I should be with you, just tell them we failed and I'm returning to the Monarch while you go back south."

"But why would we have both horses?" Sifa demands. "They'll think I killed you."

"Then let Midnight go." She sucks in a deep breath, looking in the direction of the approaching soldiers as if to check how much time we have left before turning to us again. "Look, chances are really good this is a different group, and they won't realize you have one more horse than you should. The Monarch *always* travels with the same soldiers, and they were going back to the kastali. You'll move faster if you take both horses." Her expression twists with frustration as she stares at us. "This'll work. Trust me," she insists after a moment.

"It's our best option," I agree. "Meet us in the cavern leading to the barrier."

Dani dips her chin once and climbs onto Vulryn, who lifts into the air to fly south seconds later. Sifa and I throw the packs together and are on the road a couple of minutes after that. Hopefully we won't cross paths with the soldiers and will be crossing the barrier within a few hours.

That's what I'm telling myself when we're caught. We'd been pushing the horses for nearly two hours—the barrier less than thirty minutes away—as Sifa relayed warnings from Astarot about how close they were getting. They mirrored each shift in direction we took, as if lured to us like a beacon. Someone powerful is guiding that group, I'd realized early in our race to the border, and we can't shake them.

The sun hangs in the sky almost directly above us, casting harsh light all around, when they finally reach us. Just as I turn to search for the source of an unexpected noise, dozens of armed soldiers erupt from the forest behind us.

"Fuck." I can't keep the anger and frustration from my outburst. "Let me handle this," I mutter before spinning to ride back to them, my hand resting on my sword. We're outnumbered, but we have a dragon. The odds are probably even that we can kill them all, although it would fuck up our chances of ever getting Harald on our side. I damn sure better not let it come to that.

"You shouldn't be here," the closest soldier yaps at us, her wide eyes focused on Astarot as she unsheathes her sword and points it at me.

"We're just traveling through, headed to Vanatia." I make sure my tone is measured, reasonable.

"The Monarch doesn't allow southern dragons here."

"He's a tame dragon. He's no threat."

"We are not *threatened*," she snarls. "As I told you, the Monarch doesn't allow southern dragons here. His decree is absolute. You are not here with his permission."

"We are," I assure her, my palms raised to the sky. "He had a task for us and gave us leave to be here." *Close enough to the truth.* "And now we're leaving."

"We'd know if he'd brought you here." The female's hold on her sword tightens as she straightens her back. Behind her, a male raises an enormous bow and positions a barbed arrow designed to take down dragons.

My heart jumps into my throat as I hold the soldier's eyes, nudging my horse to return to Sifa as she places herself between the arrow and Astarot. She reaches for my hand, drawing my attention to her as she squeezes, pulsing a hint of her power into our joined fingers.

"Why are we arguing with them?" Sifa asks in a voice that's not loud enough to be heard by the closest soldiers. "Let's just make some changes and go."

"I don't know if we can, rabbit." I don't move my gaze away from the female. She's the one who'll order the shot. "There's too many of them. It's too wide a net to hold for very long. We need to stay focused."

"Well, focus then." She pushes magic into our hands one more time and I feel her thoughts reach out to the female, ghosting across her mind in an attempt to find a way in.

Spinning toward Sifa, I give her the slightest shake of my head before turning back toward the group of soldiers, relieved when I feel her reel her powers back in.

The female's eyes narrow as she watches our brief exchange. Her gaze drops to our hands for a moment before hitching back up. "Your magic won't work against us," she warns in a low tone. Her eyebrows pull together in a deep scowl as she moves her other hand to the knife on her belt. "I think you need to come with us. Harald will want to see what we've caught." The male with the barbed arrow hauls the string even tighter at her words, his lips curling into a sneer.

"We'll go south," I growl in a tone that demands compliance, a spark of my power warming my palm as I ready it. Sifa's right. We need to try this. We can't let them take us to Harald. "You will stand down."

My spear of magic is aimed directly at the female, trusting the others will follow her command. I didn't anticipate the immediate, intense backlash. In a flash, my power is turned back at me, as if reflected by a mirror. My mind is shifted outside my body, a spirit floating overhead, and I watch as my head dips in acquiescence.

"We will stand down," I grit out, each word sand in my mouth.

"We will travel north with you," Sifa adds, her head curving in defeat.

Oh, fuck no. These soldiers have fucked with the wrong people. Pushing my mind back where it belongs, I yank on Sifa's magic through our connected hands. And I attack.

The energy pulses out of me in a massive wave crashing into the soldiers, wrapping every one of them in its power. The compulsion to comply evaporates, obliterated by my will. "Turn and leave," I grit out. And they do, spinning in unison to retreat.

Everyone except the male holding the barbed arrow. He stands there, the corners of his lips ticking up in a vicious grin, and winks at me. The bow aimed at Astarot never wavers.

"Bet you're surprised. The high and mighty dragon rider, bested by a lowly soldier in the Monarch's army?"

Dragging more of Sifa's power into me, I hold the net cast over the rest of them and add a pulse of energy aimed at him. "Stand down," I demand, my voice shaking with the magic I'm expending. "Leave with your comrades."

Fucker laughs.

And I recognize my mistake.

He's a gods-damned sieve.

I've known of the existence of two sieves in my long life—elves completely immune to all magic. The Dróttning holds them in separate prisons because they require special facilities. The magic used to bind everyone else doesn't work with these elves. So, they spend their lives in cells that only the Dróttning's most trusted guards can access. No magic involved; just strong metal and brute force.

Harald's the wiser of the two. He's put his sieve to good use, here on the border.

Exhaling, I release the magic that manipulated the rest of the soldiers, watching as they throw their shoulders back and sneer at me in anger. We need to figure out something else that won't threaten Astarot's life.

The soldier smirks at me and turns to Sifa. "He's realized your magic doesn't work on me. Nobody's does. You're coming with us, or I'll kill your dragon now."

Sifa spins, her eyes wide. "Are we going to see Harald?" she demands, her voice low.

"That's the fucking idea," I mutter. "We'll figure out something on the way."

"How long will it take to get there?"

"Two days. Enough time to come up with a plan."

She turns toward Astarot, holding his gaze as she tells him what's going on. His eyes narrow as he snorts out a puff of flame, but I see the barest nod. He'll go along. For now.

Within the first hour of travel, I realize it won't take two days to get to Harald's kastali. We're in the middle of the group, the arrow aimed directly at Astarot the entire time, and riding hard. They've got extra horses and trade out riders occasionally as a mount tires. By mid-day, they've given us fresh steeds. The pace doesn't slow at all other than a short break for food.

"When will we stop to rest?" I demand to a nearby soldier as the sun starts to drop on the horizon.

He glares at me, his eyes narrowing as he spits in my direction. "We don't stop," he finally says, one corner of his lips creasing his cheek. "Not when we escort someone the Monarch will want to see."

"We've gotta fucking stop," I snap. "I won't ride all night."

"Then we'll shoot your dragon," he responds with a shrug. "The Monarch won't have no use for it. He'll want you though. He'll be real fucking happy when we bring you in."

I turn to look at Sifa as the realization hits me, my chest caving in as bile bubbles into my throat. I can't stop this. I have three strengths—physical, mental and my savage. My physical strength is meaningless in a group this size, with an arrow pointed at Sifa's dragon. He would die if I tried anything. My mental strength doesn't matter because the sieve would shoot Astarot before I could manipulate another soldier into killing him or twist the ground enough to save us. And I can't shift quickly enough to call my savage. They'd put an arrow through us before he could attack.

I've failed in the most important thing I've ever been asked to do—protect Sifa and her dragon. And there's not a gods-damned thing I can do about it.

The sun's rays are long gone when I hear the wings above us, a steady *thwap, thwap* echoing off the mountains. The soldiers stiffen, throwing their heads back as they search for the source. Spinning, I find the sieve, frustrated as fuck to discover he's a very focused man. His arrow hasn't wavered from Astarot. Someone else apparently will raise an arrow for whatever wild dragon is about to attack.

This beast, though, must be particularly cunning. Although we can hear the wings, it doesn't appear to be approaching from high in the sky, as a dragon normally would. Every single one of us is searching, but nobody can find it. Frustration rumbles through the crowd, oaths and threats spilling out around us as the soldiers make promises to themselves about what they'll do to the beast when they find it.

The fire that erupts along the edge of the group triggers panic, as battle-hardened males and females scream and push their way into the center. I can't figure out what the fuck is going on, but I know one thing. This is the only chance we'll have to escape.

Nudging my horse closer to Sifa, I bellow at her. "Tell Astarot the soldier's aim will waver at some point. We attack him together when it does."

Sifa nods and lifts her gaze, watching her dragon for a moment before she turns back toward the arrow. Her horse is prancing as much as mine, both of them sensing the predator skimming along the edges of the throng, attacking everything in its reach. The air is thickening with dread, as soldiers and their mounts realize they are prey unable to defend themselves from an invisible threat.

The seconds slow as we compress, all the space between us disappearing as the dragon pushes everyone into the center. For a moment, my thoughts flicker to the ocean dwellers who hunt fish by herding them into tight balls, triggering a grudging respect for the dragon that might kill me tonight. Or save me.

I'm struggling to hold my reins, yanking at my horse, which keeps trying to dance away from Astarot and Sifa, when a handful of soldiers wedges between us. They shove me away from Sifa in their rush to find a place in the center of this frantic crowd. And then it happens. Another rider falls on the sieve and he drops the arrow, his gaze leaving Astarot for a moment as he reaches for another.

"Now," I howl, tugging my horse to attack if Astarot doesn't.

But I didn't need to bother. I can only watch as Sifa's dragon spins and throws himself at the sieve, his massive jaw clamping around his chest, splitting him in two. He spits out the male who threatened us and lifts his snout to roar at the gods above. And then he starts running toward the forest, his long claws impaling or crushing anyone who doesn't move out of his way quickly enough.

Sifa plunges after him and I kick frantically at my horse, following on her heels. In the chaos—with two dragons attacking their fractured group—nobody even tries to stop us.

As soon as we clear the crowd, I see them.

Vulryn and Dani came back for us. The copper dragon swoops in low, but these flames aren't just threats, like her earlier attacks. Now that we're clear, she's aiming to kill. And she does.

Seven times, Vulryn soars over the horde of soldiers, destroying everything in her path. She's vicious and thorough. Nobody survives. Nobody could.

And I can't move. Dani was a soldier in this army. She worked with these people, may have known many of them. I can't fathom why she would have killed so many, so ruthlessly.

It scares the fuck out of me. Because if she'll turn on them, she'll turn on us. I need to get Sifa away from her.

Dani's panting, tears streaming down her face, when Vulryn lands next to us, a satisfied grin on the dragon's face. I've never seen such a disconnect between dragon and rider.

"You killed them all." Sifa's voice is full of horror. "How could you have done that?"

"Fuck. You. Sifa." Dani sneers these words in a harsh whisper, still perched on Vulryn's back. I can see the blood on her hands—which grip handfuls of copper feathers that look as though they were dipped in crimson paint—but I don't think she's even noticed it. She runs her hands through her hair, dragging them down to cover her face before dropping them again to cling to her dragon.

"What the fuck was that, Dani?" I don't give a shit how she feels about me. I need her answer.

Dani turns haunted eyes toward me, opening her mouth and closing it twice before she can utter the words. When she finally responds, her grief echoes in every word. "She wouldn't stop," she mumbles, her tortured gaze dropping to stare at her jubilant dragon.

Sucking in a deep breath, Dani looks up again, finally turning back to Sifa. "We came back to see if we could help. I realized when you didn't show up that something had happened. I thought if I recognized someone, I could convince them to let you go. It was worth the chance."

She looks down at Vulryn again, her hands rubbing her thighs as her shoulders droop. Sitting up, she glances at me and then once more holds Sifa's gaze. "She hates the Monarch's soldiers. She knows I was one, but we're bonded so she's come to terms with me. Everyone else, though, is an enemy, because of what the Monarch forces us to do to the dragons who pose some threat.

"When she saw them ... realized where we were going ... she started flying low, dodging through the trees to hide herself until the last minute. I didn't know what she was doing, and she wouldn't listen to me. I wanted her to land so I could talk to them, but that's not what she wanted.

"At first, she just played with them, herding everyone together while I squealed at her, ordered her to stop. When you and Astarot broke free of the crowd, she attacked. 'They're ours,' she told me, 'and the soldiers threatened *our* dragon and riders.'"

Dani sucks in a trembling breath, her gaze darting between Sifa and me as she adds, "I couldn't do anything. I tried pulling out Vulryn's feathers, even stabbing her. Nothing worked. She wanted you safe."

Pausing again, Dani turns to stare for a moment at the empty field, then looks at us again. "More than that, she wanted them dead. And now they are."

A minute passes before Dani speaks again, her eyes growing more haunted the entire time. "And do you want to know the worst part?" Her lips lift in a grim smile, resignation to whatever she's about to say. "I love her. If I'd been able to kill her to save their lives, I wouldn't have. She's part of me. And I'm still grateful she's mine."

Fuck me.

We cannot take Dani and this dragon to Vanatia with us.

CHAPTER TWENTY-ONE

SIFA

A DRAGON LIKE THAT

"WE HAVE TO GO. Now." I've never heard Fhord so agitated.

I'm stunned senseless, my mind replaying the chaos and horror of the last fifteen minutes. Vulryn still looks like she captured a treasured prize; Dani looks too dazed to move. "We can't leave them," I declare when Fhord's words sink in.

"Well, we sure as fuck can't take them," he snarls, his voice harsh. Fhord waits a moment for my response—which I can't give him because I don't have a single idea what to do—then reaches out a hand to take my cheek and draw my gaze toward him. "Vulryn can't go with us," he argues in a softer tone. "We cannot bring a dragon like that back to Vanatia. And Dani won't abandon her, no matter what she's done. You and I need to get on Astarot and go."

"How will they survive? Harald will figure out what happened. He'll kill them."

"And Vanatia's any safer?" he demands, one arm flinging toward the barrier. "The Dróttning will hunt her down there, just as surely as Harald will hunt her down here. At least here, she's no threat to our dragons. Or us."

"She won't hurt us. I'm sure of it. And she'll have us in Vanatia. Here, she's got nothing." I place my palm on his hand, still cupping my cheek. "This is my fault. We can't abandon them."

"We can and we will." He's hissing the words out now, anger flaring in his eyes.

"I won't leave her behind." I can't keep my outrage from my voice. Sucking in a deep breath, I gather my thoughts so I can make him understand. "What if I'd left Toffer behind ten years ago? Do you know how empty my life would have been without him, before you? Or what if somebody had known I was trapped in the Nest and could have gotten me out? What if they could have saved me from everything the Dróttning did to me?"

Fhord's gaze flickers away from mine, his eyes growing guarded for a moment. But then he's mine again, staring at me with such love, it helps soften the rock that formed in my stomach when Vulryn started attacking.

"I don't think I could ever forgive someone who'd abandoned me. How would I ever forgive myself for doing that to her? I can't leave her here to die, Fhord."

"Fuck, rabbit." His thumb caresses my cheek before he turns to stare at Vulryn for a moment. His eyes soften as he looks back at me. "I'm gonna regret this," he mutters, almost to himself. "I won't stop her if she wants to come. But we need to get on our dragons now and get the fuck out of here. I want to be gone before Harald has any gods-damned idea what just happened, or that we were involved."

Nodding, I drop from my horse to walk over to Vulryn's side. Fhord stiffens in his saddle, but this dragon won't hurt me. I suspected it before, but after Dani's grim confession, I'm sure. Vulryn's been alone a long time, and she may have been all kinds of pissed at me a day ago, but when she decided to save us from Harald's soldiers, she claimed us. We're family now. She'll die to protect me as surely as Astarot would.

Dani watches me the whole time, blade in her hand. "I'm not going to hurt her," I promise as I draw close. "I just want to talk to you."

She loosens the grip on her knife but doesn't sheathe it, staring at me with blank eyes.

"We need to go back to Vanatia. Now. Harald will figure out what happened here and if he connects us to it, he won't stop until we're destroyed. We're going to ride Astarot back to the barrier, get across as soon as we can. What are you and Vulryn going to do?"

Dani blinks a few times, dropping her head as if in defeat. Twice, she shakes it, and I realize she's talking to Vulryn, probably arguing with her. And then she inhales deeply and lifts her gaze to mine.

"We're going to Vanatia," she says, her eyes pleading with me. "The Monarch will know what happened here—that the copper dragon killed all his people. I can't risk Vulryn's life by staying." She pauses for a moment, a tear slipping down her cheeks. "She promises she'll be better. She doesn't know the Dróttning's soldiers, won't react the same toward them."

"We won't leave you here," I tell her. "I wouldn't do that to you."

"Thank you, Sifa."

I give her a grim smile. It's all I can muster. "Here's what we're gonna do," I start, glancing toward Fhord, who lifts his hands, palms up, in surrender. "We're gonna let the horses go as-is. They'll go straight back to Harald's kastali, right?"

Dani nods. "They know where to go and they're trained to return quickly. They should get back safe."

"Good. We'll make it look like they tossed us and we're dead. Hopefully, Harald will believe we got caught up in what Vulryn did and we're lost too. We'll take only what we absolutely need and ride our dragons back to the barrier, high so if anybody on the ground sees the dragons, they won't realize they have riders. The night'll help hide us. We should be fine."

"When we're across the barrier," Fhord adds as he drops from Midnight, "we won't have time to rest. The Dróttning will recognize my magic. She'll know I've crossed the border back into Vanatia. Legions of soldiers will be chasing us. The reward if we're found will be un-fucking-believable." His voice lowers, every word a warning. "But it's the punishment if they don't find us that'll really motivate the bastards."

He grabs three water skins and a bag he fills with food before stalking over to Astarot, a demand in his eyes. Astarot throws a silent grumble my way but extends his leg for my bossy mate. I take one of the skins from him before he can climb up, walking over to Dani to hand it to her, then striding back to my dragon. We're in the air within five minutes, racing toward the cavern that will lead us away from here.

Astarot sets a punishing pace, but Vulryn stays close behind him. Every time I look back, I notice the smirk on the dragon's lips, the satisfied gleam in her eyes. She's still riding the high she got from killing Harald's soldiers. And Dani's still devastated, slumping on Vulryn's back, her forehead resting on blood-soaked feathers.

It's so fucking unnerving.

Twice, people appear below us, but the dragons lift into the sky, the air growing so thin I struggle to breathe. When we're far enough away, they soar down again, continuing their race toward Vanatia.

And then we're there. I ask Astarot to circle a few times to make sure nobody's hiding, but we can't see anything that might threaten us. Two or three minutes after first seeing the cave's opening, we're dropping down and throwing ourselves to the ground to run inside.

"This is gonna be fucking hard," Fhord rasps at me as his hands hit the barrier. "My magic is still depleted from controlling all the soldiers this morning. But we can't use everything. We *need* to be able to protect ourselves if the Dróttning's soldiers are nearby." He spins his head, finding Dani. "As soon as this opens, you and your dragon run through. We'll be right behind you."

She responds with a sharp dip of her chin, resting her fingers on Vulryn's snout while her eyes grow unfocused. I can't help noticing, though, that she doesn't leave it there. As soon as her gaze meets mine again, her hand drops away.

Vulryn notices too. The side-eye she gives Dani is chilling.

Watch Vulryn, I urge Astarot as I step up to the barrier and take Fhord's hand. He squeezes once—whether giving or taking reassurance, I don't know—and then he starts to sing.

Opening the barrier seems easier this time despite Fhord's prediction, perhaps because he knows the changes in the magic better now, or maybe just because we're going home. Whatever the reason, Fhord doesn't need anything from me, although immense power pulses through the cavern. He stands straight and strong, his melody filling us as it forces its way through Harald's sorcery.

I *feel* it when the first crack in the barrier appears, a vacuum that wants to suck me into Vanatia. But even without that, I'd know from Fhord's expression alone. He's tried to hide it, but he's been desolate without his connection to Tindera. I've felt the hole within him her absence created, so massive it would eat him alive if he let it. When her presence fills him, a weight lifts. He inhales and then exhales slowly. I can see his shoulders relax as he releases tension that had settled in his neck and back.

"Fuck, I missed her." The smile he gives me brings light to this dingy, dark cave.

He's not done yet, though. Turning back around, he continues his song, voice strengthening as the boundary between us and our home succumbs to his demand. Finally, perhaps five minutes after he started, he lets go of my hand and steps to the side, the other hand still grasping the barrier as if it were a physical door, instead of this invisible wall between lands.

Dani touches Vulryn's cheek, looks at me and Fhord, and then throws her shoulders back and strides through the cave, Vulryn on her heels. Astarot follows, then me, and finally Fhord.

When he steps fully into Vanatia, dropping one hand to his side as the other reaches for me, he stands motionless for a moment. "I hope we haven't fucked up bringing them here," he gripes before shaking his head, forcing a reassuring grin, and following the others, drawing me along behind him.

Dani and Vulryn are waiting twenty feet away, Dani's gaze following us as we approach and take the lead. Astarot falls into the final position, his focus on Vulryn the entire time. He doesn't trust this beast any more than we do.

Fhord walks quickly toward the entrance, and I can almost feel his *need* to put distance between us and Njordheim. He'll be nervous until we're vikus away, and for good reason. The Dróttning must have heard Fhord's magic. She knows we're back. She's gotta be even more angry now than she was when we left.

When we see our first hint of moonlight stretching into the cavern, Fhord lifts a hand and we all stop. His power shimmers across my mind as he pushes it out, searching for life nearby. His expression when he finds it sends a rock into my gut. I don't yet know what's out there, but I know it's a threat.

"A dozen soldiers and two dragons guard this entrance," he spits out, his tone sharp. "They're spread out, so the closest person is a half-viku away, but they're all within two vikus. The dragons fly, ready to attack us from the air."

"Then we attack them." Dani's voice holds grim resolve but no fear, and I wonder what she thinks we'd allow her dragon to do.

Fhord must have the same thoughts. His eyes narrow as he looks at her. "We do not harm dragons in this land." He punctuates each word with a poke of his finger in her direction. "Even dragons ridden by enemies. Their lives are more valued than ours."

Astarot joins in with an emphatic puff of flame. Although he may hold my life more important than another dragon's, he will not tolerate the brutality that dominated Vulryn's life in Njordheim.

"You'd let them harm us, or one of our beasts?" Dani's incredulous, her eyebrows shooting up her forehead as the corners of her lips plunge down.

"We'll ride our dragons. The two out there should be as reluctant to attack us as we would be to attack them."

"And if they're not? If their orders are to kill us, even if it means killing a dragon, what then?"

"Then we figure out some other way."

Dani glares at him, her lips set in a thin line. "What if we hurt them but leave them alive? Vulryn could do that. She's been fighting larger dragons all her life."

Fhord's eyes narrow again, this time with a question. He holds Dani's gaze for a moment, then turns to me, and finally Astarot. "Could you cripple another dragon without killing it?"

Astarot's responding *Yes* is slow, but it does come.

"He could," I tell Fhord. "What about the soldiers?"

He sighs, a weary sound. "We kill anyone who stands between us and the rest of Vanatia."

"Great," Dani mumbles, "because I haven't destroyed enough lives today."

"None of us wants this," I bark out, angry about what we have to do—what Astarot may have to do.

"I know. I don't have to like it."

I nod, shoving my anger down deep as I reach out to place a hand on her shoulder. "And I'm glad you don't."

Fhord strides closer to the cave's entrance, watching the sky for a moment before looking back at Astarot and Vulryn. "We'll mount here and fly as soon as your wings extend fully."

Both stretch out a leg and wait, their gazes as focused as ours. When we're settled, Vulryn runs toward the opening, Astarot close on her heels. As soon as they're free, they launch themselves into the air, soaring up as far as they can go without suffocating us. At least up here, we won't be threatened by any arrows carried on horseback.

We don't have time to savor that escape, though, because the dragons spin and race in our direction as soon as we're airborne. They're enormous and their powerful wings carry them with an efficient, driven focus. We've got a minute, if that, before they attack.

When I see what their riders carry, I suck in a deep breath, my heartbeat pounding in my ears. They hold dragon bolts, and they're pointed directly at our beasts.

The Dróttning wants us dead. All of us, including her own son and the dragon she tried desperately to curb and control.

"She'll have us all killed, the fucking bitch," Fhord mutters, almost to himself. His next words are louder, his tone firm. "Try your best to keep them alive. We don't kill other dragons unless we have no choice."

Hold, Astarot tells me, his thoughts calm. He's going to try and injure the closest dragon, a tawny beast as bright as the morning sky, before she attacks and he risks being forced to kill her.

"He wants us to hold on," I relay, gripping his feathers tightly. Fhord's arms drop from my waist as he leans over me and plants his hands next to mine, his legs squeezing my thighs.

I expect Astarot's spin, but it still takes me by surprise somehow. It isn't the playful rotation we enjoy when we soar through the sky on a carefree day. This spiral is tight and fast, twisting in unpredictable directions as Astarot tries to get close enough to the yellow female to attack without risking himself or his riders.

From the corner of my eye, I see Vulryn and Dani twisting toward a brown dragon, but I can't watch them. It takes everything I have to cling to Astarot as he fights for our lives.

When Astarot comes to an abrupt stop and shoots up, I'm shocked to discover the yellow dragon directly above us, barely twenty feet away. Astarot, throws himself upside down, nearly dislodging us as he proves that he learned his lesson when he battled Vulryn. His feet aim directly for the base of the dragon's wings, latching on to them and yanking the dragon as close to him as possible.

As soon as he has a firm hold, he rolls again, forcing the tawny beast beneath him as his hold on her wings tightens. When he senses her struggle to right herself—as ignorant of dragon fighting as he was a week ago—he stretches his beak to start digging into the most sensitive parts of her wings. She squeals her fury at Astarot.

I let my thoughts reach out to Astarot, caressing him as he goes against every instinct and attacks one of his own. *Thenra*, he tells me, his thoughts somber and full of regret. He knows this dragon and would have considered her a friend in the days before we found each other. But he also knows those days are behind us.

The lines are drawn now. The dragons in this land stand with us or they stand against us. We cannot—we will not—have mercy on any who fight for the Dróttning. While we won't needlessly take their lives, we will harm them if we must and kill them if that's what it takes to survive.

He fucking hates it, though.

Thenra's wings are peppered with injuries when she finds a way to fight back. Ripping away from Astarot—her shriek sending a shiver through my bones as his claws and beak rip through sensitive skin—she forces them together along her back, creating a rudder that digs into the surrounding air, throwing us in a different direction. Her shift is so quick, Astarot doesn't anticipate it. He loses his grip completely, shredding the base as he grapples to hold her.

As soon as she's free of us, she flings herself back in our direction, her sharp talons grasping for any part of Astarot's wings. One slices through a membrane, drawing a vicious shiver from my dragon, but his focus doesn't waver. He tucks his wings and spears toward her, throwing himself left and then right as he follows the erratic path she's using to try to escape.

When he pulls up, his wings popping out to slam us to a stop, I'm too dazed to understand why. And then I hear the collision, and the screams of Thenra and the brown dragon as they start to tumble from the sky.

My mind grows numb, Astarot's heartache echoing through me, as I realize what he and Vulryn did. He wasn't following Thenra; he was herding her. They worked together to lead our attackers into a direct path, their resolve relentless as they held the dragons' attention until it was too late.

The Dróttning's beasts slammed into each other, the strike so fast and hard, it disabled both of them. They're plummeting to the ground, and it's not clear if they'll be able to right themselves in time.

We can't let it matter. Astarot and Vulryn spin in unison, throwing all of their strength into their flight as they race south. I look back, searching for yellow and brown dots beneath us, but they're nowhere to be found. I can only hope we didn't just force Astarot to kill dragons he once called friends.

We won this battle. Those dragons won't be able to catch us.

As long as we aren't found by any others, we've survived another day.

And we're back within the Dróttning's reach.

CHAPTER TWENTY-TWO

SIFA

SHE'S WITH US

ASTAROT'S EXHAUSTED—AND SO FUCKING miserable—when we finally find a place safe enough to rest for the day.

We've flown for hours, Fhord rejecting every cave we found along the way, grunting in my ear about the Dróttning's guards and their search patterns. I can't imagine any of that will matter, though. She knows Fhord betrayed her, and that he knows where and how the guards are trained to look for us. She's savvy enough to have changed everything by now. We can't predict where her soldiers will be. And as we learned too well, we have no idea how far they'll go to kill us.

The cave Fhord reluctantly approves—probably because the sun already is inching up on the horizon—is deep enough for us to hide far inside and even holds a small pool. I go through the motions of unpacking and setting up a bed, struggling to hold back tears the entire time. I'm nearly as drained as my dragon and want nothing more than to drop into the water and lose myself there.

"Go," Fhord says as his hands land on my shoulders from behind me. "I've got this."

"I can help," I object, bothered for some reason by the idea of letting myself relax.

"I can feel your despair, rabbit. You're carrying Astarot's too, and you're going to send each other into a spiral if you don't try to let it go. For him, let this be. Soak and let your thoughts rest."

The tears I've been fighting for the last ten minutes win the battle, spilling on to my cheeks as I turn to give him a quick hug. "Thank you," I mumble before digging into my packs and heading toward the pool.

I don't know how much time has passed when Dani joins me. She doesn't say anything. Just drops down on the opposite side, rests her face in her hands, and starts crying. The tears are slow at first, little sniffles and hiccups as she seems to fight the coming hurricane. It's a losing battle. Soon, she's sobbing, deep inhalations and shuddering exhales separated by a sporadic moan.

Looking up, I catch her eyes once, wondering if I can help her. She shakes her head and looks down, so I let her be, climbing out of the pool to dress in silence and go help Fhord cook a meal.

I'm impressed she held on until we got here. What Vulryn did was fucking brutal.

Nobody speaks tonight. What could we say? As soon as we clean up, we find our beds. Fhord wraps himself around me and just holds me tight. It's everything I need right now.

When I awake, Fhord's sitting by a small fire, staring toward the cave's entrance. He's so still and solemn. I could sit and watch him for hours, if my body didn't call. As I reluctantly rise, he turns toward me, the corners of his lips tipping up into a forced smile. He's as melancholy as me.

"Hello, rabbit," he breathes, his voice soft enough to not disturb Dani. I smile in response and head deeper into the cavern. After cleaning up, I go to the fire and sit next to him, reaching for his hand.

He lifts my fingers to kiss each one, then pulls my body into his, close enough for me to lean my head on his shoulder. "Tonight will be better," he promises in a low voice. "We'll find our people, rest for a day or two."

"You know where they are?"

"There are only a few places they might be. We're close enough to check them all before the sun rises again."

"Astarot hasn't said anything, but I know he's been worried about Tindera since we got back. He can feel her pain."

Fhord's eyes shutter, his gaze lifting to the ceiling. "She hurts. I need to get her away from the Dróttning."

"We will." I glance at my dragon then back at Fhord. "He needs food." He's still snoring in the corner, but I felt his appetite before I fell asleep last night. He'll be ravenous when he wakes up.

"Vulryn must be hungry, too. I'm pretty sure we'll find a herd of goats a viku or so from here. Once we've eaten, we'll go get a few."

"Is it ready?" My stomach rumbles as the mention of food stirs my appetite.

"Should be."

He stands to dig into the packs for bowls and spoons, then scoops out breakfast for both of us. We eat in silence, then clean up and set the pan aside for Dani. Within a few minutes, we're tugging on our boots and finding ropes to go in search of goats.

"Are you going for food for the dragons?" Dani's voice is still so sad.

I turn, catching her gaze as I smile at her. "Goats, we hope. We'll bring two for Vulryn. Breakfast is in the pan, and we left a bowl and spoon for you."

"Thanks." She rolls over and throws her arm over her head. I can't offer anything comforting, so trudge out behind Fhord to find the herd.

Everyone's awake when we return, and the dragons eat quickly. Within an hour—just as the sun is setting—we're packed and ready to go.

"Like yesterday, we'll fly high. There's a lot of cloud cover tonight. If we're lucky, we can search without being seen."

We're lucky, as it turns out. We find the others sometime in the dead of the night, in the third place we look. It's a massive cave, hidden behind a patch of briars so deep and thick, it seems impossible to enter at first, especially for something the size of a dragon. But an ingenious trap door leads into the ground and then up a tunnel to the middle of the cave.

Fhord told me about the odd mix of people we'd find here—along with the dragon they rescued—so I'm not surprised to see Mikkael at the end of the passage, keeping watch. His smile when he sees us calms something inside me, and I stride into his arms for a hug I hadn't realized I needed. He's been a good friend for a long time.

But then he stiffens, a hissed, "Fuck" spearing into my ear. "What the fuck is she doing here?" he demands, stepping to the side to give himself a better view of Dani.

"You know each other?" I can't keep the shock from my voice.

"I asked what the fuck she's doing here." He stalks toward her, his large frame dwarfing hers as he pokes a finger into one of her shoulders, sending her backwards a step.

Vulryn rears up, flames barely missing Mikkael's head. His gaze jerks up to the angry dragon, then down to Dani and up again.

"I'd back the fuck up before she gets pissed," Dani snaps at him, planting both of her palms flat on his chest to shove him away.

"You keep those gods-damned hands—and every other part of you—the fuck away from me." He's not thinking straight because he takes another step closer to Dani, prompting Vulryn to blast out one more warning.

"Stop it!" Fhord barks. "I don't know what the fuck this is about, but we're not gonna do it now. Move aside, Mikkael. We're coming in."

"Not her," he howls, his finger jabbing in Dani's direction.

"She's with us. Move aside."

"Do you know what she is, Fhord? What she does to people?"

"I know. And she's still coming in."

Shock washes over Mikkael's face, his eyes widening as his brows punch toward the sky, followed quickly by betrayal. "I won't be part of anything that welcomes her," he announces as he steps toward the wall. His gaze stays on Dani as she strolls into the cavern, turning to wink at him as she passes. He spits in her direction but doesn't move.

Everyone's awake when we reach the sleeping chambers, sitting or standing near their bedrolls. I realize as I find Toffer and Thor—a sigh of relief rushing through me—that I'd been anxious about seeing them. They've been in my life for so long. I feel unsettled when we're apart.

Toffer's smile ignites one in me, and we throw ourselves at each other, laughing as we hug. He even lets Thor join in, leaning over to pick up the cat rubbing against my ankles and nuzzle into his fur as he offers him to me to pet.

"You really are getting along," I murmur, dropping my forehead into the soft fur. "I would never have believed it."

"Desolate, depressed, and desperate," he explains.

"I was gone a while," I agree. "I guess you had to get along."

"Resentful respect, really." His voice is solemn, as if he hates to admit he's grown attached to Thor.

A laugh sputters out of me, and I lift my free hand to stroke Toffer's cheek, the other still digging into soft fur. "Well, it's time. Glad something good came of my adventures."

"Many marvelous mates," Toffer responds, his gaze bouncing around the cavern at the large group he's found himself in the midst of.

Mikkael's yell from across the cavern drags my attention away. He's a dozen feet from Dani, who's leaning against Vulryn with her arms crossed and a malicious grin on her face. Mikkael seems to be barely holding himself back, his nostrils flaring as his hands clench and unclench again and again.

Fhord whispers something to the green dragon he's talking to—Khirta, I think he called her—then stalks over to them. I do the same, because we need to deal with whatever this is and get past it.

"What the fuck is this all about?" Fhord snarls at Mikkael.

"I can't believe you would bring her here," Mikkael growls at him, "after what she's done."

"Enlighten me." Fhord's tone is peremptory, a commander giving an order to a soldier.

Mikkael doesn't like that one little bit. He turns toward Fhord, his eyes narrowing. "You don't talk to me like that, Fhord. Not if you know what's best for you."

"I will talk to you any gods-damned way I please," Fhord responds, stepping into Mikkael's space and butting chests with him. "You're being a dick, and it needs to end."

"Fuck you and fuck this." Mikkael pushes past Fhord to tramp toward the tunnel leading outside.

"Good riddance," Dani declares with a wide grin, her hand reaching back to scratch behind Vulryn's horn.

"Stop teasing him, Dani." My voice is soft, but it carries through the quiet cave.

"What?" she demands, her shoulders lifting into an exaggerated shrug. "It's like Fhord said. He's being a dick."

"He's my friend," I tell her, irritation sneaking into my words. "We need him. You need to work this out with him."

"I'm not angry. That's all him."

"Just tell us what the fuck happened between you two." Fhord's still pissed, but I think he's trying to reel it back. He rakes his hands through his hair, huffing out a breath. "Let's get the fire going first—I don't think anyone's going back to sleep—and then we can all talk."

Johan stands and heads in that direction with Joralf and a male I don't recognize close on his heels. Liv and Frida linger to give me a hug but then follow the others deeper into the cavern.

And I stare at Dani as she unloads her packs from Vulryn, wondering what we did to piss off the gods or fate or whoever is screwing with our lives. Because Dani and Mikkael hating each other cannot be a coincidence. She spins and lifts an eyebrow, so I set aside those useless thoughts, sigh and point to the side of the cave opposite from Mikkael and Johan's packs. "Set your stuff over there. Then we'll join them."

Dani nods and gives Vulryn a quick scratch before stalking over to drop everything and head to the group. But Fhord lingers, pulling me into his arms as he nuzzles my hair.

"Aren't you glad we made it back to our friends?" he asks, a laugh in his tone.

"Where we'll get plenty of fighting and not a single bit of privacy?" I respond with a smile that he probably can tell is forced. I do not want to hear whatever Dani and Mikkael have to say. "What more could we want?"

His fingers lift my chin so he can hold my gaze. "As long as I'm with you, none of it matters." The kiss he gives me is soft and gentle and I lean into it.

Fhord's very good at this romance thing.

But we can't kiss forever. He steps back after a few seconds and takes my hand. Pointing toward the unknown male with a gruff, "That's Joralf's partner, Fróðr," Fhord tugs me toward the growing flame in the center of the group.

Dani's on one side of the fire by herself, everyone giving her plenty of room as they watch her with varying degrees of suspicion. I get it. They trust Mikkael, and while he may be a hothead sometimes, he's a good judge of character. If he despises Dani so thoroughly, there must be a good reason.

"I never expected to see him again," Dani says, her gaze fixed on the cave's entrance as we settle down next to her. "The Monarch has used my skills in many ways during the years I've served him. I regret some more than others."

"What can you do, Dani?" Joralf seems less wary of her than the rest of the group. He's a good elf, and I already trust his instincts.

"Do you want to tell him, Sifa?" Dani turns to me with a smile, but her eyes hold deep shadows. I realize her flippant attitude toward Mikkael was just an act. She's still devastated by what happened in Njordheim.

"When I was in the North, Harald had me fight three of his soldiers to win supplies. Dani was the second. She can plant memories in people's minds and seems to prefer visions of her kills. She's skilled and she has taken a lot of lives, many of them quite … imaginatively," I add with a rueful laugh.

"How did you come across Mikkael?" Fhord's voice is steadier than it was while Mikkael was in the cave.

"The Monarch used to send me into Vanatia, occasionally, when he needed information or to create trouble for the Dróttning. He'd sent me to Revalle to get rid of a problem and stoke some rumors. My talents make me very good at that. I can give people my own memories, but I also can change them a bit, add a memory from someone else. It lets me do things like switch out faces. If I throw my target's bloody image in a mirror after an attack, I can blame them for my actions."

"Who were you trying to blame, Dani?" Mikkael's words spear through the cavern, fury resonating in each one. I turn to look at my friend as my heart starts to pound in my chest. His words drip with acid. I've known Mikkael a long time and have never heard or seen such loathing from him.

"You," she concedes with a shrug. "You and Bevin had angered the Monarch. He sent me to take revenge."

"Are you gonna tell them everything?" Mikkael stalks over and plants himself next to the nearby wall. His shoulders are tight, back straight.

"I'm getting there." Dani looks at me with a sad smile. "I saw you while I was in Revalle. I knew I recognized you when we fought, but I didn't remember from where. I was stalking Mikkael when you came into the Inn once."

"I didn't notice you."

"I'd have been shit at my job if you had." She turns back to Mikkael, but before she does, a flicker of regret fills her eyes. "The night I made my move, Mikkael went to meet a woman. Someone he worked with, I think."

"Helga," he says, his gaze on me.

And my heart drops. "You killed Helga?" I know what Dani's going to tell me, but I have to ask anyway.

"I didn't wield the blade that killed her, but yes, I'm responsible for Helga's death."

"What did you do?"

"It was earlier than I intended, and her presence was happenstance. I'd have planted the memories in anyone's mind. It just happened to be her."

"She was my friend, Dani." I can't keep the sadness from my voice. "What did you do?"

"We've all killed enemies," Dani reminds me as her gaze finds mine, her eyes somehow more haunted than before. She shrugs, but her nonchalance is an act. Soul-deep regret ripples from her, steady waves that turn the air stale and putrid. "You know who I am. What I am. I'm sorry I killed your friend, but my talents—the things Harald forced me to do with them—are not news to you."

"Just tell us what you did, Dani." I try to keep my tone soft because I do know and can't blame her for Harald's demands. Still, I'm sure some of my angst and a rising anger found its way into my words.

"I followed them back to a room. I hadn't yet killed Bevin, but I was sure I'd get to him. Having Mikkael and the woman alone together was too good to pass up, so I moved against Mikkael a little earlier than I planned. I changed some of my memories, made it look like Mikkael killing Bevin, and showed that to Helga. She didn't respond well." Dani turns to Mikkael and smiles as she says this—a mocking grin—and the anger I felt when we were fighting fills me again. I have no idea why, but she's trying to piss off Mikkael.

"Her loyalty to Bevin was fierce." Now it's a struggle to keep a steady voice, to not let Dani's attitude get to me too. Helga's loyalty was one reason we never got too close. She was a good female, and I liked her, but I knew I couldn't trust her and that she'd always choose Bevin over me.

"She tried to kill me," Mikkael rasps, filling me with a bitter mix of grief and anger, which seeps from every pore in his body. "She nearly did. I grabbed a knife to defend myself and she spun into it while we fought. When I realized she'd moved in a way I didn't expect, I couldn't pull it away from her quickly enough. I shoved it right into something—a lung, I think—that took her fast."

"You killed Helga?" My words are clipped, confusion rippling through me. We had no idea Mikkael was involved with her death.

"I didn't fucking mean to, Sifa," Mikkael roars, lifting one shaky hand to spear it through his hair. But then he takes a deep breath, casting his gaze down before lifting it to look at me with narrowed eyes. "She attacked me because of the bullshit this bitch fed her," he growls.

"I understand, Mikkael. I was just surprised."

"How did you know Dani was involved, Mikkael?" Joralf asks. "I assume for jobs like these, she stays hidden."

"Well, I couldn't let him live after that," Dani explains, and I want to strangle her because her voice is calm, almost indifferent. I'm the only one who can feel her remorse, and I have no gods-damned idea why she seems so resolved to piss off Mikkael. "He'd just killed the person who was supposed to blame him for Bevin's death, and I knew he'd warn Bevin, make it harder to get to him. Fucked-up luck all around. The Monarch's orders always are to kill if we can't take our enemies down another way."

"I'm standing in Helga's blood," Mikkael snarls, "still holding the gods-damned knife and trying to figure out what the fuck just happened, and this cunt launches herself at me from the window. It was all I could do to keep her from driving a blade into my heart." He turns to Dani, eyes flaring. "But you fucked up."

Dani shrugs. "You were more skilled than I anticipated."

Mikkael's glare could melt ice. I've never seen such hatred in his eyes. "If only I'd killed you then."

"Well, you didn't." Dani looks back at me, her lips tipping down just a bit. "He fucked me up, though. I had to give up, get away from Vanatia. Mikkael and Bevin both survived." Her eyes darken for a moment, and she smirks. "The Monarch extracted a heavy price for that failure."

"I hope you suffered." Mikkael watches her for a moment before looking at Fhord. "I won't ride with her. If she stays, I go."

I can feel Fhord's conflict, the tightness in his chest, but there's only one answer he can give. "We can't abandon Dani or her dragon."

Mikkael's responding nod is angry. He strides toward his bedroll, Johan standing to follow him. They argue in harsh tones while Mikkael packs, but I can't catch any of the words. After a few minutes, Mikkael flings his pack over his shoulder and stalks toward the tunnel, all of us watching him in silence.

"I sure as fuck hope she's worth it," Mikkael mutters, his furious glare bouncing between Fhord and me, before spinning to walk away from us.

Chapter Twenty-Three

Fhord

Fate's Different

Of course Dani and Mikkael hate each other. Of-fucking-course.

My stomach clenches as I watch Mikkael disappear through the tunnel. I don't think he'll turn on us. Sifa trusts him, and he could have destroyed me long ago if he'd wanted. He'll probably head back to Bevin and keep watching that deceitful prick, just like he's been doing all along. But this feels prophetic. Like the gods want to rip us apart one by one because they're still playing with our gods-damned lives. The bastards.

Sifa reaches out for my hand. "I'll see if I can convince him to stay. You talk to Dani. If Mikkael's willing to come back, she'll need to give him some space, stop being such a bitch."

"I'll see what I can do." Lifting a knuckle to tap her chin, I add, "Good luck. You're gonna need it."

"I think we're both gonna need it," she sighs before tramping toward the tunnel.

Dani's sitting alone at the back of the cave, tossing little pebbles at the wall as she watches Sifa chase after Mikkael. "What do you want, Fhord?" she demands with a sidelong glance when I stride over to her.

"I've done worse things," I tell her as I plant my ass in the dirt next to hers. And I have. Much, much worse. "You've just got some shit luck, running into someone Harald had you target."

"I've been in Vanatia a lot. Made some enemies. It was bound to happen sometime." She glances at me for a moment, her eyes haunted. "I just wish it hadn't happened so soon. And that it wasn't him."

"Why'd you have to fuck with him the way you did?"

"He didn't tell you the whole story. You'd understand if he had."

"Well, what's the whole story?"

"I'm not gonna tell you either. If he wanted you to know, you'd know. I'll keep that secret for him." Her gaze turns back toward the tunnel, and she lifts a hand to start chewing at the rough edge of one of her fingernails.

"If Sifa can get him back, you need to lay off. He doesn't need that shit. We don't need that shit." I make sure to throw the authority of a commander in the Dróttning's army into my voice. Dani needs to take this seriously.

"I know." She turns to me, her eyes bright. "I am sorry, for whatever that's worth. I just had no idea what to think when I saw him. Instinct took over."

"Your instinct is to act like an absolute bitch?" I can't hold back the smirk.

"Fuck, yes. In Njordheim—and especially in the Monarch's army—that's how you survive."

"That I can believe. Harald's a dick. It's not surprising he wants the people around him behaving like dicks too." I watch her for a minute, wondering how committed she is to us now. "You and I are gonna have a talk about Harald one of these days," I tell her at last, gauging her reaction. "We've made him our enemy now. I need to learn everything I can about him."

She doesn't flinch and I suspect Dani's already starting to internalize some of Vulryn's hatred for Harald. It's tough for riders to separate their emotions from their dragons', and Dani hasn't been trained or conditioned to fight that pull.

"I'll answer your questions," she agrees, "but he's not hard to figure out. The Monarch does what's best for him. Always. He may go about it differently than the Dróttning, but the end goal is the same. It's all about power."

"How does he feel about the elven prisons? Any chance he'll join us to change that?"

She laughs. "None. Elves add to his strength in Njordheim. He uses them effectively and they're loyal to him, especially knowing what it's like in Vanatia. He won't want to risk giving the Dróttning the same advantage." She shakes her head. "He's never understood why she'd deny herself so many powerful fighters."

"The Dróttning hoards her power in other ways." That's a gods-damned understatement.

"You think Mikkael will come back?" Her eyes are on the tunnel again, like a magnet dragging her attention back to him.

"I sure the fuck wouldn't. He didn't need to be here anyway, and everyone traveling with me and Sifa is fucked. The Dróttning won't stop 'til we're found. You all should get away while you can."

She turns to me, her eyes finally losing the despair that's been sitting in them since she saw Mikkael. Her lips curve into a broad grin. "At least it won't be boring."

"Never boring."

She turns to stare at the wall again, tossing pebbles one at a time.

"Who does the little green dragon belong to?" Dani asks after a moment. Khirta's risen from her spot at the back of the cave and is walking toward Vulryn, her posture open and friendly. Vulryn hisses, eyes flashing, and Khirta stops, dropping to her belly a dozen feet away. She stays there, watching the copper beast.

"Khirta's not bonded anymore," I tell her, impressed with the little dragon. She's brave and it wouldn't be a bad thing if Vulryn connected with other dragons here.

"Anymore?"

"Her rider found us, just before I traveled back to Njordheim. He ordered her to kill us; she killed him instead."

"Shit." Dani's surprised, but she probably doesn't understand how shallow the bond between Khirta and her rider was.

"She grieved his loss, but he wasn't her destined rider. I don't know who's supposed to ride Khirta, but definitely not that bastard. When the time's right, she'll get a better match than the one the Dróttning chose for her."

"You really believe that?" The side-eye Dani throws me is full of doubt.

"What?"

"That dragons have destined riders, who they find when the time's right? Like the gods give a fuck about us?"

"Oh, I know the gods don't give one little shit about us, other than the amusement they get from watching everyone flail around and fight," I respond with a harsh laugh. "But I've seen enough to believe fate's different. That some grand plan is in play, and fate'll offer us what we need at the right time. I've found a few myths that speak of females who weave the tapestries of our lives, presenting paths that will give us happiness or fuck us up. It's up to us to choose the right one."

"And how are we doing? Are we fucking it up?" Dani's voice is teasing.

"Probably. But you never know."

"If you say so." Dani's eyes shutter. She doesn't believe me, but it doesn't matter. "The green dragon must be in a lot of shit," she adds after a few seconds.

"She's another reason it's a bad idea to travel with us. Dróttning's searching for her too."

Dani nods and sits quietly for a moment, but then her gaze lifts to find mine. "I've been wondering something," she says.

"Ask."

"Does it always hurt so much when your dragon's injured?"

"Once we bond, we feel their pain, as they feel ours. You can push it out of your mind with enough concentration, but it's not easy. A blessing and a curse." I shake my head, not sure when Dani might have felt her dragon's pain. "When was Vulryn injured?"

"While she was attacking the Monarch's soldiers." She inhales deeply, holding it for a few seconds before exhaling. She's still tossing rocks at the wall, reaching down for more whenever her hand empties. "I didn't know how to stop her, so I tried yanking out feathers and then stabbing her. I felt every wound. But how could I stop?"

"Yeah, that's fucked. I don't envy you, bonding with that dragon."

The rocks still for a moment as Dani's gaze flits over toward Vulryn and then back to the wall. "What's really fucked is that I wouldn't want any other dragon. And I don't know what that says about me."

"You must need something from each other. There's a reason the fates pulled you together."

Dani scoffs again, but she doesn't respond right away. "How does Tindera talk to you?" she asks after a moment.

"Do you mean, how are we connected?"

"No, I mean, does she talk to you like a human would? With sentences, full of emotion?"

"Dragons don't talk that way," I explain, shaking my head. "They'll speak a word, but with Tindera, it's always layered with meaning I understand. With Astarot, I have a shallow connection, through Tindera but primarily through Sifa. He can only relay the word. I don't get any of the additional meaning from him. Why?"

"That's how I thought Sifa described it. It's different with Vulryn and me."

"How is it different?"

"She talks to me in sentences, just like you would. I have access to her thoughts when she lets me, but even then, she blocks off most of her mind from mine. She mainly keeps me out and just tells me what she wants me to know."

"That's not right."

This laugh is sharp, a touch bitter. "There's a lot about Vulryn that isn't right."

"No, I mean, *all* dragons communicate the way Tindera and I do. It's part of their nature."

"It can't be, because Vulryn doesn't communicate with me that way. Must be a learned behavior in Vanatia."

"Well, fuck me." This seems important, but I can't put my finger on why. Before I can chase the thought, Dani's head pops up.

"She's back. Alone."

Dani sounds disappointed, and my gaze spins to her for a moment, my eyebrows shooting up almost of their own accord, before I turn toward the entrance. Sifa frowns as she walks in, but I think that's for my benefit. She knew what to expect from that asshole.

"That went about how you might guess," she tells us as she sits down by my side. She's talking to me, but her voice is soft, like an apology to Dani.

"What's he gonna do?" Hopefully he'll check in on Bevin. We need someone we trust watching that fucker. Mikkael's as good as anyone.

"He's not sure yet, but I think he'll go back to Revalle." She reaches for my hand, and I squeeze hers. "He's a good male," she adds as she catches Dani's eyes.

I don't look at Dani because I don't care what she thinks right now. Instead, I lean forward for the kiss I need from Sifa. It centers me. She centers me.

"He's not leaving the rebellion," I add when I finally let go of Sifa's lips. "We haven't seen the last of Mikkael."

"I'm sure you're right." Sifa glances up at the others, shaking her head. "You told me what to expect, but I'm still shocked. It's strange seeing them all here together."

"I told Dani, they all should follow Mikkael. We're the Dróttning's target. They don't need to get caught up in the shitstorm heading our way."

When Sifa turns to me, her eyes are soft. "Do you really think anyone would leave—I mean, unless we brought back their mortal enemy to join the group?"

"I'd get the fuck away from me if I could."

"So should I be following Mikkael?" Now her eyes are teasing me, a smile tipping her lips.

Fuck, she's sexy when she's playful. My cock's twitching already. "I always love a good chase," I remind her as I place a hand on the back of her neck, capturing all her attention.

"And you think you could catch me?" Her eyebrow quirks up, and it's all I can do to keep myself from throwing her over my shoulder and carrying her to the back of the cave for a quick fuck. It'd do us both good.

Instead, I dig my hands into her hair, drawing her close to me. "I will always catch you, rabbit."

Dani's scoff drags my eyes toward her. But she's not looking at my face. Her gaze is focused on my cock, which has tented my pants, and she's shaking her head and smiling. As she looks up at me and then over to Sifa, I smirk, rubbing the heel of my palm over my puffed-up prick.

I'm like a gods-damned whelp, unable to control myself around Sifa, and I don't give one little fuck. My little rabbit loves how hard she makes me.

"How the fuck do you get anything done," Dani asks in an amused voice, "with that thing distracting you every time she blinks?"

"I'm very, very talented," I tell her, but my gaze is back on my rabbit. She knows who I'm talking to.

Dani moans. "It was bad enough to hear you two while you were in the lake. I don't need to see this shit too. Can we dial it back a bit?"

Sifa holds my eyes for another moment before whispering, "Promises, promises." And then she stands and stretches, raising her arms as she twists in place, making sure my gaze follows her the entire time.

My cock grows even harder. Bastard's fucking predictable where my rabbit is concerned.

"So, so dangerous," I rasp out as I fight to keep from groping myself. "You will be the death of me, female." Dragging my gaze away from Sifa for a moment, I nod toward the fire. "You should go," I suggest to Dani.

But Sifa's not done yet. Instead, she walks over to the packs, her back to me, and bends over at the waist to start digging. I can't hold back the low groan as she slowly drops into a crouch—a position I want to see from between her legs when I'm getting ready to devour her—and my gods-damned cock starts to throb.

Still holding herself just above the ground, she turns, throws me a wink, and then stands to sashay toward the fire.

"Wicked, wicked female," I sigh as I rise to go find some privacy. 'Cause I'm not going anywhere until my cock calms the fuck down.

But gods-damn, do I love it when Sifa teases me like that.

It doesn't take long to finish with images of Sifa's tight ass and bouncing tits playing through my thoughts the entire time. When I head to the fire to join the others, I get a few smirks, but I couldn't care less.

"Guess we spent ten years trying to hide from Sifa for no reason," Astrid declares, a laugh in her voice as I stride forward. I'm watching my little rabbit, so I see her eyes flare and the corners of her lips tip down in response to Astrid's words.

I turn my head to glare at Astrid, but she somehow doesn't recognize my "shut the fuck up" face.

She just keeps digging my grave.

"I mean, that's what you said. Right, Fhord?" Astrid's gaze is spinning between Sifa and me, but she's still not done. "After we found her in the forest—when you told us she's your mate—you said that's why we were in the North for so long. You felt her when she landed in the prison, then when she escaped from the Nest, she headed south, and we went north so you could stay away from her."

It's Torsten's growl that finally gives Astrid a hint that she fucked up. She still doesn't realize how badly.

Because instead of *shutting the fuck up*, she starts tossing dirt on my dead body.

"What?" she asks, her eyebrows slamming together as she looks at Torsten and then back at me. "I just think it's funny that we stayed away from Sifa for so long only for you two to end up together. I'm happy for you. It was meant to be."

"What's she talking about, Fhord?" Sifa's words are quiet, but her tone's cold, demanding. This is another one of those secrets she knows I've been keeping from her. And it's the biggest one, that I should have revealed a long time ago.

"Not here," I rumble, reaching for Sifa's hand. She pulls it away, watching me as I stand and gesture toward the back of the cave. "Please," I add because she still hasn't moved.

Sifa looks toward Astrid, then the rest of my Ætt, and finally back at me. Dropping her chin in an angry nod, she stands and stalks into the dark. I throw one last glare at Astrid and turn to catch up with her.

"I've been trying to find the right time to tell you this," I breathe as I reach for her hand.

But Sifa doesn't want my touch right now. She flicks me away, spinning to glare at me with blazing eyes. "We've spent a lot of time together, Fhord. You haven't been trying very hard."

"This one's tough, rabbit. I didn't know if you'd understand."

She's quiet for a long time, just watching me. "Is that supposed to be an excuse?" she asks at last. "To make it okay?"

"No. Fuck, no," I spit, twisting to punch the wall next to me, because I need to experience the pain I'm about to inflict on her. I sense Sifa flinch and take a step away from me. But I can't feel a single emotion. Her shields are up—she's hiding herself from me—and it's been a long fucking time since I was so far away from her. I force myself to calm down before I turn around. She can't think I'm angry at her.

And then I face her. "I'm a gods-damned coward, rabbit." I drag my hand down my face, willing my pounding heart to slow down. "I tried everything to push you away at first. It took me too long to realize how badly I need you, and I nearly fucked it all up. Now I've got you, and I know I might not once you realize what I did." I make sure our gazes are locked before adding, "What I didn't do."

"What didn't you do?"

"I didn't free you, rabbit. I ran the fuck away instead of figuring out who you are and how I'm tied to you. I could have saved you—my mate—from everything that bitch did to you. But I didn't. I left and stayed away. Because I am just as despicable as her." My chest collapses as I finally confess my biggest secret to her. I have to remind myself to take a breath.

"You felt me when I arrived? You knew, even then, that we're connected?" Sifa's frowning, her fingers rubbing that little spot at the base of her neck that I love to lick. She tilts her head to the side, waiting for my explanation.

I drop my head, wishing I could hide from her, then look up again. I wonder if she can see the devastation in my eyes. "I had no idea who or what you were, but I knew someone had appeared in the prison, and that we were connected."

"What did you think I was?"

"I had no fucking idea. I just knew we were linked in some way. It was years before I admitted to myself that you're my mate."

"Did you know I was being tortured?"

"I did," I admit, sorrow in every word. "I felt your emotions, so I left. Got as far away from the Nest as I could while you were trapped there."

"And then when I escaped and went to Revalle, you went back to the North. To stay away from me." These are not questions. She knows the answers. She's just working through it in her mind as she realizes what a despicable, untrustworthy fuck I've been.

"I didn't want to know who you are, or how I'm bound to you."

"When did you realize I'm an elf?"

"When you escaped. I knew a female elf and a troll escaped and figured out that my connection is to you, not Toffer."

"And when did you realize I'm your mate?"

"That came a lot later—after the Dróttning sent me to Revalle, about a year ago. I'd seen you before, but something happened that drew out my savage, prompted him to claim you."

"Your savage?"

"My last secret, rabbit. Let's get through this one first."

She flinches in response to that but doesn't look away. "Why did you leave me there, when you knew we were connected in some way?"

"I didn't see another way. My relationship with the Dróttning is ... complicated ... for a lot of reasons. Mainly, she controls the dragons. She controls *my* dragon. And she uses that control to manipulate people, me more than anyone else. I knew if I let myself get close to you, Tindera would pay the price. I didn't know you then. I didn't realize how badly I'd regret staying away. How desperately I'd wish I'd done things differently."

"You knew what they did to me? The ways they hurt me?"

The pain in Sifa's eyes is ripping out my heart. I'd carve it from my chest with a blunt blade and hand it to her on a gods-damned platter if it would take away her hurt.

"I knew enough," I admit, risking a step toward her.

She shakes her head, moving away. "And now you regret it?" she scoffs, one hand shifting to the hilt of the knife she carries on her belt. "You want me to forgive you, when you could have saved me—your gods-damned mate—but decided to run away and hide instead?"

"Rabbit, I have so many regrets, and none are heavier than this. If I could take it back, I would."

Sifa's looking at me now like she has no idea who I am. Like I'm some monster she doesn't recognize.

She's right. I'm a monster.

But I'm her monster.

"I don't know what I was thinking, Fhord. How I convinced myself this could work between us." Her voice is harsh.

"It will, Sifa." My voice is just as harsh because if I know one single thing in this fucked up world, it's that she will always be the center of mine. "I'll make this right," I snarl, "no matter what it takes."

"No. You can't. I see it now." She takes two steps backward, putting even more distance between us. "She's your gods-damned mother, and you've stood by her side, done her bidding—her loyal son—for *centuries*."

Now her eyes are haunted. I can almost feel the pain she's probably reliving as her thoughts take her back to the prison and all the fucked-up shit they did to her.

"I had to stay close to have any hope of defeating her."

"How many people have you killed for her? How many have you tortured, the way they tortured me? How many lives have you destroyed because she demanded it?"

"Too many," I agree, taking a step forward as I lift a hand toward her. "But that's over now."

"It's too late." She glares at my hand like it's diseased. "Get the fuck away from me, Fhord. I don't want to talk to you right now."

But I close the distance between us, my palm rising to rest on her cheek, my lips just a few inches from hers. "Don't you get it, Sifa?" I rasp out, a hint of my rage at myself seeping into my words. "It will *never* be too late for us. I'm yours and you are mine. I will never let you go." I pause, my thumb tugging at her bottom lip. "You. Are. Mine," I repeat. Because my little rabbit sure as fuck needs to know that we belong to each other. "Today. Tomorrow. Always. Who I was before; what I did for the Dróttning—none of that bullshit matters. My life began when I saw you in Revalle. *That*'s what you need to know. That's the only thing that matters."

She sucks in a deep breath, releasing her blade as she spins and starts to walk away. She pauses after a few steps, although she doesn't look back. "Go talk to them," she tells me with a vague gesture toward the group. "I need some time alone." And then she strides deeper into the caves, her back straight and her shoulders set.

It won't do any good to chase her down. I've said what I needed to, and now I'll give her space. Turning, I stalk back to the others, plopping myself down as far from Astrid as I can get. Looking up—trying to drag my mind away from Sifa's anger—I decide we need to talk about our next steps.

"It's time to get Tindera," I say after a moment. "I know the rebellion has some priorities, but they have to wait. I need to get my dragon away from the Nest. I'm weaker while the Dróttning has her."

"Where do you think the bitch is holding her?" Leif's voice is soothing. He's trying to get rid of the tension that sits around us like a dense fog.

"Pretty sure she's in the south. We haven't been able to talk. She's not close enough, but even if she was, I can't risk the Dróttning hearing us and using the link between Tindera and me to find us. Since Tindera's too far away to be in the northern Nest, that's the only other option."

"Okay. We'll go there. Are we still traveling at night?"

I dip my chin. "The Dróttning will be throwing everything at us now. It's too easy to be found during the day." I look toward Frida, then Joralf and Fróðr. "We'll need help from your friends."

"What do you want?"

I hide my relief at Frida speaking up because she knows the southern Nest and training grounds better than most. But I can't let any of them realize I'm worried about their cooperation. They're with us, and they're gonna do whatever the fuck we tell them to do. Or they won't be with us.

"I need to confirm the Dróttning isn't in the Nest. Then someone will have to help us get in. This'll be ... fuck. Fuck!" My skin starts to crawl as I feel her presence like a scorpion creeping along my spine. I turn toward the tunnel and then back to the others. "The Dróttning's coming this way with a large contingent. I have no idea if she knows where we are, but she will soon."

"We have five minutes to pack," Torsten barks out. "Weapons, food and water skins first, then everything else.

We'll be in this cave system for three days, maybe more. Take what you need to get out the other side."

Everyone scrambles into action. Sifa, Dani, and I haven't unpacked yet, so I strap our bags onto our dragons while Dani runs after my rabbit. Then I realize I need to go now, separate myself from the others and put distance between me and the Dróttning. Maybe she won't be able to track me if she doesn't know about the cave.

I'm about to chase after Sifa myself when I see Dani and her racing back toward us. I intercept them and huff out my relief when my little rabbit lets me stop her.

"I need to get farther away from the Dróttning." I try to draw her into my arms, but she shrugs away my touch. Part of me wants to scream my anger at this entire fucked-up world, but that would make it all worse. "She can track me from a distance," I explain as I step back to give Sifa the space she wants, "but not the rest of you. I'll head deeper into the cave now. You all finish up here, then follow."

Sifa holds my gaze for a moment, then nods. "Don't do anything stupid, Fhord," she says, her eyes fierce. "I don't know where we go from here—or if there will be an 'us' after this—but it won't matter if you throw yourself away."

"There will be an 'us' after this," I snarl, leaning down to take a kiss she doesn't want to give me. "You are mine." I rumble into her lips, desperate to taste her one more time. "Every single sigh, each kiss, all your trembles belong to me. If I have to crawl in your wake until I earn your forgiveness, I will drag my belly on the fucking ground until you pull me to my feet and walk by my side." I lift a hand to cup her cheek, holding her gaze. "You. Are. Mine. You will always be mine. And I will always be yours."

Her eyes glimmer with the conflict raging inside her. I have to go lead the gods-damned Dróttning away, but Sifa needs my last secret more than I need to leave. If the Dróttning captures me—and she sure as fuck might—I can't take a chance that someone else's big mouth will tell her this too.

"There's one more thing you need to know, rabbit." My whisper's fierce and I hope it tells her how sorry I am that I hurt her.

Sifa's lips tip down as she shakes her head. "Just getting it all out now?"

"This is the last big one. I promise." She nods and I lift my other palm to her cheek. "My family has more talents than you've seen. Nobody knows this about us because the Dróttning's ashamed of her form and I've had to keep mine secret. We're the only of our kind in this world, we think."

"What are you talking about, Fhord?"

"I can't show you here. The Dróttning will hear me release my magic and it'll guide her straight to us. But when I'm far enough away, I'll change to my other form if I have to and draw her away from this group."

Sifa's eyes narrow as she realizes what I'm saying. "Your savage?" she murmurs.

"The others saw it, so they all know already. It's why I was naked when you found me at the barrier. The Dróttning caught us, and we couldn't get away without me releasing him.

He's vicious. Nobody can defeat him, not even the Dróttning unless she gets really fucking lucky."

"What are you, Fhord?"

"I'm a wolf, rabbit. An enormous, blood-thirsty wolf." Her eyes grow wide, but I can see the acceptance in them. I take one last kiss from her and then step back. "He's every bit as committed to you as I am. You're ours and you always will be. We need you to be safe," I breathe, "so we can show you how sorry we are for hurting you."

And then I let her go and turn to run into the dark cavern.

CHAPTER TWENTY-FOUR

SIFA

WORST TIMING EVER

WELL, THAT WAS THE worst timing ever.

I need a minute to process all the shit I learned from Fhord, but we do not have a minute. The Dróttning is coming, and we need to get as far away as we can, as fast as we can.

Astrid keeps throwing guilty looks my way, and I know I'll need to talk with her and the others at some point, but if there's one good thing about the approaching attack, it's taking attention away from my ill-fated mating bond with Fhord. I won't have to think about it right away. Yay.

The cavern's too small for the dragons to fly, so we're all running through the tunnels. Fróðr is casting enough light for us to see where we're going, but just barely. He's hesitant to use too much power since it looks like we'll be here for three days, probably without finding any more food along the way. He'll need all his energy to help us through.

Astarot can run much faster than me, but he's worried, hovering like a mother goose. For once, I don't mind it. His love soothes me like a healing salve. He's helping me let go of my anger at Fhord.

I still don't know if I can trust Fhord, or if there's any way to move forward knowing this. I don't want to be angry at him. We've got too many other things to worry about to let this open wound fester. Things like staying alive today.

But it's so fucking hard.

I ache inside, knowing he *felt me*, his mate, and left me to the Dróttning to be tortured. My head understands his explanation because I love Astarot as deeply as Fhord loves Tindera. It's an impossible choice, and I don't know if I would've done anything different.

My heart, though, is broken. Fhord could have prevented the *horror* Toffer and I lived through ten years ago. Instead, he ran away from me as soon as he knew I existed.

I don't know if that pain will ever heal. And I don't know how I can be with him when I feel so empty and broken inside, knowing he chose to let me suffer.

We've run for thirty minutes, maybe longer, when Jorunn slows us down. "Stop," she bellows as she lifts a closed fist. The Ætt respond immediately, apparently conditioned to Jorunn taking charge when Fhord's not around, and the rest of us fall into step behind them. "We'll kill ourselves if we keep up this pace. We'll walk and jog intermittently until we can go no farther, or Fhord comes back and tells us it's safe."

Another half hour passes as we race deeper into the cavern with no word from Fhord. And then I feel him, although he's different somehow. This Fhord is a smaller presence than the one I know. As he gets closer, I sense something powerful layered on top of him. I realize I'm about to meet his savage a moment before he rounds a corner and comes loping toward us.

I can't stop the shiver that rolls through me. He's enormous—nearly as tall as a dragon. If I were standing next to him, I probably wouldn't be able to touch his back, even on my tiptoes. Still, he's fucking beautiful, with a gray coat that shines like silver under Fróðr's light. Dark eyes find mine and even from this distance, I can see the wolf smile. It's the first time we've been face-to-face.

He doesn't slow, everyone in his way stepping aside as he bears down on me, a moth to a flame. Before he gets close enough to touch me, though, he stops abruptly, as if a string yanked him back. He sits—nothing but heavy air between us—and then drops to the ground to rest his head on his paws. A low groan rumbles out, sending a shiver down my spine, but he doesn't move.

"You're still in trouble," I mutter as I halve the distance between us. He whines, his eyes as soft as Fhord's when he asked my forgiveness, but remains still. He's controlling himself, letting me come to him if I choose. So I do. Fhord's my mate and that makes this massive beast my mate too. I won't let Fhord's failures screw up this first meeting.

His lips tip up the first time I touch him, resting my hands in the deep fur behind his ear to scratch. I can't hold back the smile as he lifts his head then reaches out his tongue to give my cheek the smallest lick. "Gross," I laugh as his saliva drips on my shoulder. He's a huge wolf, and even a little kiss is messy.

He exhales, like he's been holding his breath, and licks me one more time. Then he turns, finding Jorunn as he stands. She seems to understand him even without any speech, nodding her head as his gaze holds hers. Looking at me one more time, his eyes still a prayer for my forgiveness, he turns away and starts running toward the cave's entrance.

"He wants us to follow him," Jorunn tells us when Fhord turns a corner and disappears. "He can't shift back and let the Dróttning know how close he is, so I don't know exactly why, but we need to be alert. I suspect they found the cave, and he thinks our chances are better if we face them here and now instead of letting them trail us through the cave system."

"Fuck," Johan snarls, drawing his sword from its scabbard.

"Shut it, Johan," Jorunn growls at him. "Fhord will be the first wave, and he'll probably kill most of them before he has to face the Dróttning. We need to have his back."

"Fuck, yes, we've got his back. I'm just pissed Mikkael isn't here to join in the fun."

Leif smirks, clapping Johan on the shoulder as he strides past him. "He'll be back soon enough. Plenty of adventures for everyone." He starts jogging as he passes Khirta, who'd been taking the rear, and quickly disappears around a corner.

I throw myself after him, suddenly anxious for whatever fight Fhord plans to leave us. I'll finally have a place to release the anxious energy that started pulsating through me when

Fhord took me aside to bare his soul to me. I've been trying to smother it, but I know now what I need.

I need to kick the shit out of someone. I may not be able to reach the Dróttning today—although I plan to kill her as slowly as her body will tolerate, I hope very soon—but I can hurt the people who wield her sword. I can drain their blood and end their lives. I can destroy part of what makes her strong, and start to destroy her, bit by bit.

Now I'm running, eager to follow Fhord and find the fight before he claims too many enemies for himself. We've been traveling for an hour, but it doesn't take long to go back. The Dróttning's people must have entered the cave shortly after we escaped. Within twenty minutes, probably less, I can feel the lives racing toward us.

And I can feel the frenzy of Fhord's wolf. Our bond is nearly as strong as my bond with Fhord, and his emotions—his anger and blood-lust—wash through me as soon as I'm close enough. I think he's opened himself to me, letting me feel what he's feeling, experience what he's experiencing. The *need* I had to attack the Dróttning's soldiers is now a compulsion I'm helpless to resist.

I want to taste the blood Fhord's wolf is spilling.

When I turn the last corner and see him, I'm awestruck for a moment. He's every bit as vicious as Fhord said, ripping through the soldiers between him and the Dróttning with brutal efficiency. I can only watch as he decapitates one, swipes his razor-sharp claws to gut another, and crushes a third. He must sense my presence as strongly as I can sense his, because he pauses to spin his snout and throws a wolfy smile at me.

He even winks, the cheeky bastard.

But too many swords stand in his way. Fhord's shifting directions in an instant, throwing himself into the largest crowd as he makes a path for us. I fall in with the others—a small but lethal group—and attack.

Out of the corner of my eye, I see Toffer's ax swinging its way through the soldiers, his pack holding Thor splayed across his back. The cat watches over the troll from the rear, hissing warnings when someone gets too close. Toffer's a barbaric killer, born to do exactly what he's doing right now. He is all troll, with no sign of the gentle companion who's cooked and cared for me for a decade.

Something warm kindles inside me when I see how well he and Thor work together. After all these years.

I don't have time to gawk, though. A sword draws my eye, and I spin just in time to deflect a swing that could have been lethal. Pushing her blade away, I aim for her exposed thigh, hoping to cripple her and move on. She's too skilled for that. Her sword catches mine, and we grapple for a few seconds as we both fight for the upper hand.

I win that fight, shoving her back into another soldier, who lashes out in surprise. She's distracted for a split second, and I lunge for her stomach, a satisfying gurgle quickly smothered by her scream as my sword drives deeper into her guts. I yank it out, tossing a smirk over my shoulder as I look for my next kill.

Three soldiers follow in her path, none as skilled as her. It only takes a few seconds to cut off the sword arm of the first one, followed by a strike to the back that should kill him. The second soldier takes a bit longer but within a minute, I've gutted him, pushing his dying body into the path of my next attacker. This one smirks at me from a few feet away. He's huge and must believe I'm no match, but I surprise him when I pull a blade from my belt, flipping it directly into his eye. He goes down like a sack of potatoes.

I'm looking for my next kill in a sea of corpses when a shriek from behind me has me spinning around. Liv's eyes are wide and full of horror as she watches Johan clutch his throat, which has been split open by one of the Dróttning's soldiers. Blood seeps through his fingers as his gaze finds hers and he mumbles what looks like an apology. His eyes are so full of life, it's hard to imagine they'll ever fall to death.

But as ice freezes in my gut, ready to shatter along with my breaking heart, I accept the truth.

There's no escaping death now.

Slowly, as if time chose to extend itself before releasing Johan from this world, he drops to his knees. Now his gaze is flitting from one of us to the other, his bright eyes starting to fade. I think he wants to say a personal goodbye to each of us. When the light shutters, his eyes growing dark, Johan drops to his side. His hands fall away to leave us all with this final image of him—an enormous crimson gash separating his head from the rest of him.

I can't hold back the sob, even as the cavern seems to come back to life and another of the Dróttning's guards attacks from my side. I almost miss the sword that flies toward me, lifting mine at the last second to deflect the strike. Then I throw myself into the fight. Tears roll down my cheeks, but they throw more fuel on the anger that's burning within me now.

I'll grieve Johan's death later. Now is the time to avenge it. This male will atone for Johan's death. They all will pay the price.

Killing him doesn't staunch the fire in my gut, though. He falls too quickly, his head rolling away with the third swing of my sword. Looking up, I find a shrinking field of soldiers and realize the Dróttning called for a retreat. They're all racing toward the tunnel that will take them back into the sun.

The gods-damned Dróttning is even taking this away from me. The bitch. Now I want her blood coating my hands even more desperately.

Soon, I remind myself. I will claim my revenge soon.

Sucking in a deep breath, and then another, I try to rein in my galloping heart as I search for Fhord. But he's not here. Everyone else is standing in the sea of the bodies the Dróttning left behind. Some are injured—cuts or gashes peeking out from the blood they look to have bathed in—but none too severely.

Torsten voices my dread first. "Where the fuck is Fhord?" he demands, his voice echoing off the walls.

Leif's voice cuts through the silence that follows Torsten's question. "He was in the lead, going after the Dróttning."

"He may need us," Jorunn barks as she starts to jog, then run, toward the cavern's entrance.

"We can't leave Johan," Liv yells, a plea in each word.

"I'll carry him," Toffer offers, trudging over toward the cadaver that used to be my friend. Toffer turns to give me a sad smile, his eyes full of sorrow, before he drops to his knees to take Johan in his arms.

He knows how this will hurt me when I have time to grieve. Johan was a good friend, and it kills me that he died fighting for me and Fhord.

But now isn't the time for mourning. Fhord isn't here. He went after the Dróttning, and we need to find him. I mouth a quick "Thank you" to Toffer and then turn to jog my way through the bodies between me and Fhord. When I'm free of them, I start running after Jorunn, the others right behind me. Soon, the sharp exhales as we all push ourselves to race after Fhord bounce off the walls.

We're nearly at the entrance when we see them. And now I know why the Dróttning hates her form. She's an enormous wyrm and looks like something that emerged from Helheim. Her mottled scales are a mix of green and black. But not the green of a healthy earth, vibrant forests and lush grasses. No, this green is barf, the excrement that a diseased system will push out of its body. She is waste, and even her color attests to it.

She smells just as bad.

None of that matters, though. The only thing that matters is that she is killing my mate.

Her teeth are embedded in Fhord's throat, her enormous body crushing his wolf. She's squeezing him, as a python constricts its prey, taking his life slowly and painfully. I think Fhord's alive—a hint of movement in his chest tells me he's still breathing—but not for long. He won't survive this.

Jorunn is the first to fall on her. Her sword is slashing at everything it can reach, but the Dróttning barely notices. Any wounds her puny blade can inflict are scratches on stone, not even drawing blood. The rest of us join in, digging with our blades instead of swiping. We inflict some damage, black blood attesting to this negligible success, but none of it slows her down. Not even the dragons can help, the area of the cavern the Dróttning's chosen too small for them to squeeze in and attack.

I'm ready to roar my frustration, but then I hear him. Fhord's alive and he's finding the strength to reach out to me. My head fills with his voice. *Her eyes*, he breathes. *Climb and aim for her eyes.*

Stay with me, my love, I murmur back to him. It's the first time I've admitted, even to myself, that I love him. *You owe me some groveling.*

A weak laugh fills my thoughts, but I push him out. I don't know much about this aspect of the mating bond—how raging emotions seem to allow us to communicate mentally—but I know it's exhausting, all-consuming. Fhord doesn't have the energy to spare. He needs to concentrate on living. I'll concentrate on killing.

I throw myself at the wyrm, using her slimy scales to climb her back as I crawl toward her head. She struggles to dislodge me, throwing herself toward a wall and rolling, but she can't do much with her hold on Fhord. While she has him, still constricting so tightly I fear she'll rip him in two, she can't stop me.

Within a few minutes, I reach her neck. Now, I cling to her because her head and neck aren't wrapped around Fhord. This part of her body can move. If she tosses me away, Fhord won't have another chance. Dragging myself up, I clutch one of her massive horns, releasing one hand to unsheathe my sharpest blade. And I strike.

The squeal of pain rings through the cave, colliding with walls to fill this little space. Twice more, I drive my knife into the closest eye, clenching her horn with all that I am.

When she gives up, finally releasing Fhord, she swings herself so violently, I have to let go. She flings me toward the nearest wall—chunks of stone raining down like tears—and I can only watch as her enormous maw grasps the back of Fhord's neck. Before I can move, the wyrm is slithering toward the tunnel that will carry Fhord away from me. Faster than should have been possible, she's gone.

I leap up and race after her, desperation spilling down my spine with a cold certainty I can't escape. She has Fhord and there's nothing I can do about it. I can only hope she's changed her mind and will keep him alive.

My eyes scream at me when I emerge into a new day, and I'm forced to shield them for a moment. When I finally can look around, it takes me a few seconds to find the Dróttning and Fhord. They're both still in their other forms, Fhord trapped in her jaws as she carries him toward the Nest. The rest of the Dróttning's soldiers lay dead between us, as if she couldn't allow any witness to her evil.

He's gone, and I don't know if I'll ever be able to get him back.

CHAPTER TWENTY-FIVE

SIFA

WE HAVE TO GO

W E NEED TO BURY Johan.

He's been my friend for so many years, done so much for me, and he should be the only person I'm thinking about right now. My heart disagrees, and it's taken over. It keeps replaying the image of Fhord's wolf being carried in the jaws of the monstrosity that lives within the Dróttning. It breaks for our mate and his dragon—for all the pain and degradation they'll suffer at her hands.

I feel the guilt that comes with knowing it's my fault Johan is dead. He was only here because of me. The Dróttning chased us down, and her people killed him in her resolve to capture Fhord, my dragon, and me. I should feel more. I should be buried in my shame.

Nothing gets through my fear for Fhord, though. I'm trapped in my head, reliving everything the Dróttning did to Toffer and me, and then Joralf and me. Now, Fhord is the one on the rack. His skin is being flayed, bit by bit. His guts are being ripped out, tossed over a bar high above, and used to strangle him. His penis is being snipped off, inch by inch.

I've vomited twice—my stomach too twisted to tolerate even water—but it hasn't helped.

Nothing will help.

"Sif-Sif," Toffer mumbles as he sits next to me, Thor still swaddled on his back. "We have to go." He looks north, as if he might see the Dróttning's warriors bearing down on us, before adding, "Enemies emerge everywhere. Staying may sacrifice our sidekicks."

"You're right." I turn to give him the best smile I can muster as he stands and reaches out his hand. Taking it, I let him draw me into the hug I need. "Have they decided where we'll go?"

"We have a place," Joralf explains as he joins us, resting a hand on my shoulder to give it a small squeeze. "Fróðr found a cave system not long ago that isn't on any map. He's sure nobody else knows of its existence. We should be able to hide there for a day or two."

"And then we're going after Fhord and Tindera." I'm not asking a question. This is what we'll do.

"We'll figure that out when we get there." Joralf's voice is soft, a hint of a plea hovering in its depths.

I shake my head, letting anger flash in my eyes. "And then we're going after Fhord and Tindera," I repeat, making sure my tone mimics Fhord's when he's giving an order. "Astarot and I will go. You can join or not. We'll free them with or without you."

Joralf nods, his gaze dropping to the rock beneath us. When he looks up again, it's not at me. He knows me well enough by now to realize arguing will do no good. "We'll travel northwest," he says after a moment. "We can't wait for nightfall. It's too risky to stay here."

I find Astarot, my spirit sinking as I see the despair he's trying to hide from me. It will be so much harder to release Tindera without Fhord to help us. And my dragon knows we need to focus on Fhord for now, maybe leaving his draikana trapped even longer. Still, I can tell he's struggling to smother those emotions.

It's okay, I tell him. *I've had some time with Fhord. You've had none with Tindera. I know how desperately you need her.*

Time. His response rumbles through me. He views the world through the long lens of a dragon's life and while I used to, my accelerated aging here in Vanatia has changed that. I now see only decades ahead of me—not nearly enough time to spend with Fhord and Astarot.

We'll free them both. Or we'll die trying.

Together. The love that fills me with that word buoys my spirits more than anything. We'll fight for them together, and if it comes down to it, we'll die together.

I realize as I look around that we're packed and ready to go. A bitter laugh almost tumbles out of me. So much has happened in the last twenty-four hours. It feels strange that we can just go as if none of it matters. Leave this place behind and never return to it, just another stop along the way to whatever end the Dróttning has in store for us.

I'm so fucking tired. Astarot must be even more exhausted. But they're right. We have to leave. Joralf leads a group of horses out of a cavern I never even noticed—including Sigurd and Hilde, who the Ætt brought for us—and we mount and nudge them into a gallop.

Joralf and Fróðr set a demanding pace, pushing everyone through valleys, up hills, and even across a mountain in our race to hide from the Dróttning and her soldiers. We're constantly changing our direction to avoid people in our path or follow the trees—and the cover they give the dragons—as long as possible. Twice, I'm convinced we'll be found and captured, but the gods must be on our side for once. The threat moves away, and we continue our death-march.

It's an hour after sunset when we finally get there. Fróðr spends fifteen minutes searching for any hint it's been found. When he's confident nobody has stepped foot in this area for a very long time, he leads us, single-file, into the large cavern, then follows our path back to the nearest rocks we traveled over and hides our footprints leading here.

Thank the gods we took Joralf with us when we escaped the Nest, and that his mate can take care of all this shit. The rest of us are just barely hanging on.

We're all unpacking, finding spaces on the large floor, when Fróðr returns. "There's a pool about a quarter-mile into the cavern. Women can bathe first, then the men will go. Joralf and I will start a fire and make something we can eat.

I don't bother arguing with him. My mind is still trapped replaying Fhord's capture, with Johan's death occasionally sneaking in to reinforce my despair. I want nothing more than to lose myself in a pool and pretend Fhord will be waiting for me when I get out. The others seem to agree. As a group, we gather a few things and trudge deeper into the cavern, then strip and sink wordlessly in the water.

Liv and Frida whisper an occasional word or sentence to each other, but otherwise, we're all silent. I have no idea how long I sit motionless—my eyes closed as my head rests on the edge—but at some point, I realize Liv and I are alone. And she's crying.

I've been so lost in my own sorrow, I didn't notice hers. Johan apologized to her as he died. They'd developed a relationship I knew nothing about.

"Did you love him?" My voice is soft and gentle. I hope it tells her I'm here for her if she needs me.

"Love?" she sighs, her gaze finding mine. "Maybe. Or maybe I just hoped I would. We were just getting to know each other. I'd seen him around Bevin before but spending time together helped us realize we wanted each other."

"He was such a good man. He and Mikkael have been watching out for me for a long time, helping Toffer and others who matter to me."

"He cared for you, Sifa. Worried for you, too. I don't think he trusted Fhord. It bothered him that Fhord straddled the line between the Dróttning and the rebellion for so long, even though he knew you're mates."

"Fhord had his reasons. And I understand them. Johan would have too, eventually." I'm still angry at Fhord, but he's my mate and I get why he did what he did.

"I think Johan was starting to accept Fhord's reasons." She lifts her shoulders in a weak shrug. "I just wish he'd had more time."

"Fucking Dróttning," I mutter, unable to keep the anger from my words.

"Fucking Dróttning," Liv echoes, her tone as full of fury as mine.

"She'll pay."

"Fuck yes, she will." Liv's voice is cold, determined. "We'll start by taking Fhord and his dragon from her. If anyone's going to beat the Dróttning, it'll be him. His wolf is terrifying. She must have gotten lucky to have trapped that enormous beast."

I can't hold back the smile at my memory of Fhord's wolf. "He's vicious," I agree, "but he's so much more than that. He was gentle with me. He knew I'm angry at Fhord, and he was trying to get through to me as much as Fhord had."

"He looked completely in love with you." Liv's words finally sound lighter. Maybe we're both letting go of some of our grief.

"I think I'm already in love with him." This, more than anything, is the push I need to break out of my grief. This savage—who was anything but with me—is part of my life, and I barely got to meet him. "We need to free him and Fhord. We've done harder things. We can do this."

"Maybe not anything *harder*," Liv responds with a laugh. "But we have done hard things. And we can do this." She smiles at me, scooting over to toss an arm over my shoulder in a brief hug.

"You're right." I give her my first genuine smile of the day. "We can do this."

Dinner is better than it would have been if I'd cooked, but that's not saying much. Toffer, Thor, and I find our bedrolls as soon as we've eaten and cleaned up, laying side-by-side the way we did years ago, when the horrors of the Nest were fresh in our minds and our nightmares. I'm completely drained, but I can't sleep, the day's events rushing through my thoughts whenever I close my eyes.

"Trauma and tears today." Toffer reaches over for my hand as he turns his head to give me a sad smile.

"So much trauma; so many tears." And more tears will be on the way if Toffer's thumb keeps gently rubbing the back of my hand the way it is. It's something he did when I needed comfort in the weeks and months after escaping. These days, Toffer's rough hand in mine combined with this gentle caress always takes me back there. After a few seconds, I lose the battle with my tears, sniffling a little as they start to roll down my cheek.

"Fear for Fhord?" Toffer's voice is so soft. He knows what this is doing to me.

"I'm more afraid than I've ever been in my life, even worse than when I was in the Nest. At least then, I knew what was happening, and that you and Thor were safe. Right now, I have no idea what the Dróttning is doing to Fhord. I think he's alive—Tindera would tell Astarot if the Dróttning had killed him—but they're not checking in with each other because the Dróttning might hear them. I don't have any way to know how much he hurts."

"Strong, smart soldier."

"He is. But that's the problem, isn't it? He's spent his entire life as a soldier for the Dróttning. He's done so much evil on her behalf." I pause, struggling to keep the sob out of my voice with the next words. It's not easy. Fhord's abandonment hurts. "He left us in the Nest, you know?"

"Fhord failed his friends?"

"We didn't know him then." I realize I've fully lost this battle and give in to the tears I can't hold back. When I've shed enough for now, I squeeze Toffer's hand. "We were connected even then and he felt me when we landed in Vanatia. He might have been able to do something—get us out, or at least protect us from the worst of what the Dróttning did—but he didn't try. He went to Revalle until we escaped and moved there. Then he moved back to the North."

"Fhord failed his friends." This time it's not a question. And finally, Toffer lets go of the alliteration and just talks to me. It's a fun game for him, but often, it's a crutch when his emotions are too intense for full sentences. He hides behind the limitations of his wordplay. "We weren't friends then," he points out in a quiet voice. "Did he really fail us?"

"He should have figured out who I was. Maybe if he had, he could have freed us from the Dróttning before she hurt us so badly."

"Why would he?" Toffer looks at me, his eyebrows drawn together as his free hand scratches his cheek. He's genuinely confused.

"Because we're mates." I say this as if it should be obvious. As I speak the words, though, I realize it's not. "That doesn't matter," I add after a moment. "I know he tried to stay away from me and why. I've already decided I'm okay with that. He knew the Dróttning would find out and punish Tindera if he got close to me."

"Tindera suffers so much." His voice is even sadder now, as if he's experienced her pain. My heart squeezes with the knowledge that Fhord's kind, loving dragon is paying the price for my freedom.

"Have you been able to talk to Tindera, somehow?"

He shakes his head, his eyes dropping to our joined hands. "Khirta is her friend," he responds at last. "Dragons talk of the Dróttning's punishments."

"What do they say about her?"

"Some like the Dróttning. The mean blue dragon who hurt Khirta likes her." Toffer exhales slowly, the thumb that caresses my hand pausing for a moment before resuming its steady path.

"Fhord told me about him. It's sad some dragons are that way." Now it's my turn to comfort my troll, squeezing the fingers clinging to mine.

"He's a mean dragon," Toffer repeats. "He hurt Khirta so bad. Almost as bad as the Dróttning hurts Tindera."

"What about the other dragons? Do some wish they were free?"

"Many. The water makes them stay."

"If there were other water, would they rebel? Join us in trying to defeat the Dróttning?" I lift my gaze toward the cave's entrance, desperate to share these thoughts with Fhord. If we're going to fight back, we'll need more dragons, and this could make a difference.

"They're scared. Not many are as brave as Khirta."

"Khirta is braver than most," I agree. "We owe her much. Another dragon would have killed Fhord and the others."

"Khirta is a good friend." Toffer's smiling now, his gaze lifting to find the sleeping dragon in the corner.

"If they thought they could win, would they join us?"

He shakes his head again. "I don't know. I can ask Khirta."

"Thank you, Toffer." I feel lighter already. I always do after talking to my troll. He helps me figure out what matters and what doesn't. "I don't know what I expected Fhord to do," I say when my thoughts return to my frustrating mate. "Ten years ago, I mean."

"Such sad selections." I can feel his despair in these words, which carry the slightest wobble.

"You're right, though. Why would he try to save me, if it meant putting Tindera at risk?"

"Dragons dread the Dróttning."

"And they should. Did Astarot tell you how she tortures them? What he suffered when he was trying to resist the rider she'd chosen for him."

He nods his head, his eyes filling with tears. "Tindera too."

"Tindera's going through it now. And it kills me to know what she's suffering."

The truth of my last statement washes over me, smothering at last my anger at Fhord for not coming to our rescue ten years ago. "If Fhord had tried to save us, the Dróttning could have turned on Fhord and Tindera ten years ago," I admit to myself as I speak the words to Toffer. "There's no guarantee Fhord could have saved us. The Dróttning wanted something from me desperately. It would have been much tougher to free me than it was Thyra. And I nearly fucked that up because I went back for vengeance and got carried away."

"If he failed?"

"The Dróttning would have imprisoned them, maybe ripped Tindera away from Fhord. And she probably would have added more guards to watch us. He could have made it worse." The negative emotions are seeping away, replaced by an acceptance I cling to. I don't want to be angry at Fhord. There's already too much shit fucking with our mating bond.

"They would have suffered too." Toffer's voice is solemn. He gets it. For a being born to kill, he has so much empathy.

"They would," I agree. "And it would have been for strangers—a mate Fhord didn't realize belonged to him but wouldn't have wanted anyway because he knew it would compromise his commitment to his dragon. I would have done the same thing."

Another truth washes over me, and I take a minute to sit with it, accepting the similarities. "I did something worse," I admit to Toffer. "I hadn't even bonded with Astarot yet when I risked Fhord and Thyra's lives, maybe their freedom, to rescue Astarot. Fhord was mine by then. We knew what we would mean to each other if we let ourselves. But I still chose Astarot over him—a random dragon, for all I knew at the time. Freed him from the trainer even though it could have doomed Fhord and Thyra along with me."

"You had to free Astarot." Toffer's voice holds no doubt.

"I did, and I wouldn't change anything. But Fhord could have blamed me for choosing Astarot. He didn't. He accepted my choice because he knows what it's like to be bonded to a dragon."

Toffer smiles, lifting a hand to rest it on my cheek. "He loves you," he adds. "The wolf does too."

"They love me." A sense of home washes over me, but I realize it's not a place. It's him, and now, his wolf. They're my home. I've been fighting it, but it's time to stop and acknowledge what I already know. "They've accepted the mating bond. I guess it's time for me to do that too."

In that moment, I know as surely as I know the feel of my mate's touch that I'm resting on the edge of something important. A shift in my relationship with Fhord—my full and unreserved acceptance of him and the mating bond—will change everything. I set my mind free, telling the gods and fate and anyone else who will listen that Fhord is my mate. I embrace the bond that ties me to him.

I am his and he is mine.

The change in my relationship with Fhord is sudden and dramatic. I've realized since I first felt his presence that he was connected to me, although it took me too long to understand how. Now, it's not just a connection. It's an identity. Fhord is me and I am him. I don't just have access to his abilities or his thoughts. They are mine. And mine are his.

I know where he is without having to ask him. I feel his agony, his anger and angst, as he hangs on the rack for the first time in his life. I know which parts of his body have been skinned off, and which still cling to him. I plan with him the revenge on the male who always hated him and has embraced his torture with too much fervor.

And I know how to find him when we go into the Nest.

It won't be easy. The Dróttning has seen how much power Fhord and I can summon. She won't be humiliated again. But it's possible. I can't ask for anything else.

Toffer and I are silent after that, and sleep finally takes me.

I dream of Fhord and the life we'll live together when we're finally free of the Dróttning.

FHORD

HER CARVERS

THIS IS EVERY BIT as fucked-up as I thought it would be.

I've been in this room before—too many times—but never as the pathetic bastard hanging on the rack. Always before, I've been the one leading the torture. Usually not by my own hand. I refused to do some of the fucked-up shit she demanded so I relied on her carvers—the Dróttning's preferred term for the blood-thirsty soldiers she assigns to this room. But the Dróttning expected me to play along with everything she did to her prisoners, so I interrogated my share of traitors with the carvers' help.

Traitors like the humans and elves currently traveling with my little rabbit, who are probably trying to figure out a way to free me. It won't work. The Dróttning lost Sifa twice, and she's reinforced everything. Even my connections to Sifa and Tindera are gone, no hint of their emotions—or the pain I know my dragon is suffering—reaching me. Maybe Sifa and the others could have gotten me out before. Not now. I'm trapped here until I convince the Dróttning I won't betray her again.

It's gonna be a long fucking stay.

They haven't taken my cock yet, but I suspect I'll find out soon if Joralf's right that it grows back bigger. That'd be one good thing to come out of this bullshit—if Sifa's still alive whenever I get out of here. I'll cut the damn thing off myself if she's not. I won't need it if my rabbit's dead.

I don't know how many hours I've been hanging here when I find a reason to believe I might actually see her again. Sifa accepts our mating bond—she accepts me, in spite of all the fucked-up shit I've done—filling me with a wave of love and hope and resolve. The big, ugly male had just sliced off my left nipple, but I barely noticed it. Instead, my whole being started thrumming with energy, our combined power rippling through me for a second, despite the manacle.

She's hundreds of vikus away, but for that moment in time, I feel closer to her than I ever have before.

The torture doesn't matter. Whatever pain I may suffer here doesn't matter. My fury at the Dróttning doesn't matter. The only thing that matters is that Sifa's mine. She's embraced our bond, and it's become all it can be. Our connection is deep and abiding. We now share everything.

I can't actually talk to her. Not with the manacle the Dróttning created for my rabbit around my throat and too much distance between us. But we shouldn't need to talk. The manacle should just bind me. Sifa should be able to reach out to me and know where I am and what I think. If I can formulate an escape plan, she should know it and be able to get me out. She should even be able to speak with Tindera the way I do.

Should. If I'm right, this could change everything. I hope to fuck I'm right.

I barely notice the skin that's flayed off over the next hour or more. I'm shredded, blood pooling beneath me and strips of flesh flung across the room, but my mind isn't here. I'm in the pool with my rabbit, watching her perfect tits hover just beneath the waterline. I'm between her legs feasting on her, sucking down every bit of the honey her body gives me. I'm deep inside her, fucking her as I watch her moan my name. I'm hanging on the rack hard as a rock and I don't care. I'm gonna savor my fantasies while I can.

The familiar *click-clack* of the Dróttning's heels as she strolls down the hallway pulls my thoughts away from my rabbit—and collapses my cock. Steeling my spine and drawing up memories of the Dróttning's evil, I lift my head so she'll see hatred and anger in my eyes when she walks in. She's pissed at me now, but I'm still her son. Somewhere in that cold, decrepit heart is a spark of light she's kept alive for me all these years. She doesn't want to kill me. At least, not yet. She'll just hurt me. A lot.

"Leave us," she commands when she steps into the room. Her tone is soft, like she's making a request, but everyone knows it's no such thing. She'd sooner kill them than give another order, even if they are her favorite carvers—at least for now. She doesn't tolerate disobedience.

The Dróttning pauses a moment when they're gone and I can feel her mind ooze out, searching the area to make sure we're truly alone. She smiles, a cruel smirk, when she confirms they've all left.

"I've never seen you like this," she muses, lifting a finger to run it through the open wound on my abdomen. She doesn't lift the blood to her lips, like normal. Instead, she wipes it on a nearby towel, which she then wraps around my waist.

My mother doesn't want to see me naked.

Who'd have thought she could be squeamish about me after all these years?

"Tindera will continue to pay for your ... transgressions ... but apparently that's not enough to stop this foolishness. You'll be my prisoner too until you tell me where I'll find the elf and the escaped dragon." She looks up, tapping her long, sharp fingernail against her chin, a speculative look in her eyes.

"I'm going to leave you on the rack," she adds after a moment. "As you know, I like my ... toys ... to be flawless when I play with them." Stepping closer, she places her palm on my cheek. "But you're my son. I couldn't do that to you. That's why I'm having someone else do it. Some of them don't like you, but that's to be expected. They all know how I've favored you over the years."

She smiles again, turning toward the door for a moment. "They're enjoying this chance to teach you what it means to serve me. And they don't mind what you look like while they take your skin."

"What are you doing to Tindera?" I snarl as she spins away and starts striding toward the edge of the room, playing with one of the knives on the large table of "supplies" she keeps there. The Dróttning's people did something to the manacle after Astarot helped Sifa escape. Now it's even more effective, stopping my connection to my dragon. I don't have a single gods-damned clue what the Dróttning has been doing to her and that's fucked me up more than anything the carvers have done to me.

"You don't have to worry about that," she sighs. "I'm punishing her, like you should have, for betraying me." She turns to me, her eyes flashing. "She should have told me when you betrayed Vanatia. I've trusted you so much, given you such leeway. That's over now."

"I didn't betray Vanatia," I growl at her. "I betrayed you. Because I love Vanatia enough to fight for its freedom from you."

She stalks forward again, poking a long fingernail into one of my exposed ribs as she spits out the next words. "You forget who you are, Fhord. You forget who I am." Stepping back, she smiles again. "I am the Dróttning. I control every living thing in this land, and they all must bow to me. Especially you."

Her lips drop into the smallest frown as she continues. "Tindera forgot that. She didn't tell me what you've been doing these past weeks—how much time you've spent with that elf, where you've gone, what you've done. I had no idea you had deceived me so thoroughly." Her voice rises, her eyes flashing as she adds. "You may have been her rider, but that was only because I allowed it."

Now, anger rumbles through every word. "Tindera belongs to me. You belong to me. By the time you leave here, you will swear your fealty to me again. And you will mean it."

"What the fuck have you done to my dragon?" I growl again. Because I need a fucking answer from this bitch before I lose my gods-damned mind.

"She's not your dragon anymore. You lost that privilege. She's being trained to accept another rider—someone I can trust. When she's ready, I'll give her to Ragnar. He's loyal to me. He's earned a strong dragon."

Fucking Ragnar. I don't let the Dróttning see the effect her words have on me but *fuck*. I will destroy Ragnar if he touches my dragon. He's a cruel bastard and it's no wonder the Dróttning likes him. He rode his last dragon to death. Pushed her so gods-damned hard and fast she didn't wake up in time to fight off the wolves who attacked her in the middle of the night. Fucker had left his dragon in the forest to go fuck a bedmate who'd pissed him off and didn't even bother making sure she would be safe.

Instead of letting her sense the rock in my stomach or see the bile rising in my throat, I force myself to smile. And then I capture her gaze, let her see every bit of hatred that's built up over the centuries of serving her. I make sure she knows the price she'll pay if she harms my dragon. If I can ever get the fuck out of here.

"Do you really think your secret will die with me?" I ask in a flat voice. "That when you get rid of me, you won't have to worry about *everyone* learning what you did?" Her eyes narrow. I've got her attention. "I told my Ætt, but you already suspect that. They'll make sure everybody learns your secret if Sifa senses my death. And she *will* sense it if you kill me.

"You probably think you'll be able to stop my Ætt. Maybe you can, if you ever find them. But they're not the only ones. I won't tell you how many other people hold your secret, how many other places I've hidden it. Just know that if I die, I'm taking you down with me."

She smiles, closing the distance between us as she places her hand on my cheek again. "You can try, son," she purrs to me. Then she turns toward the door and strolls out, the blood on her feet leaving a crimson path in her wake.

Twelve days have passed since the Dróttning captured me and strung me up here. I'm sleeping more than I'm awake. But I'm well fed because as she reminds me every day, I'm still her son. Despite what her soldiers said when they tried to capture us, she's not ready to kill me yet. My *mother* is convinced I'll repent and play the part of her obedient soldier again with the right kind of encouragement.

Fuck. That.

I will never be that male again.

Every inch of my skin has been peeled off, slice by slice. I'm in a constant state of regrowth, with about half my skin pink and itchy and the other half gone, slowly regenerating. The pain is constant, but I learned long ago how to live through pain. My physical state doesn't bother me. Not much.

The thing that's killing me is that I'm utterly alone in a way I haven't been for two hundred years. The connection I had with Sifa lasted a split second, but I haven't felt her since. I think the manacle is limiting my ability to feel her, and that she still senses me as fully as I did her for that moment in time. I don't fucking know for sure, though, and that's driving me insane.

Maybe even worse, I haven't felt Tindera's presence since the Dróttning slapped this manacle on me. After the vacuum I felt in Njordheim, my mind reconnected to Tindera again for such a short time. It reminded me of how much I need her, how empty I am without her. She's been a part of me since we bonded a century ago, and I feel incomplete when I can't sense her. I'm half-alive now but not because of what these assholes are doing to my body. I'm only a shadow of the dragon rider that is the real me.

Fucking Dróttning. Every day I fantasize about how I'm going to kill her. It's keeping me alive and hopeful, almost as much as my dreams about fucking my rabbit and riding my dragon. But not in that order. I *need* to be inside my rabbit again. That's more important than anything else. My savage is shoved deep inside me, the manacle imprisoning him as much as me, but he agrees. He's living for Sifa as much as me.

I'm surprised when I hear the Dróttning stalking toward the room. She was here earlier and never comes twice in one day. I think she dislikes seeing me this way—a reminder of how badly she fucked up. She never wanted to be a *good* mom, but she wanted to not be a shit mom. She ended up being the shittiest shit of a mom any shit mom could be.

She sneers when she strides in, her normal bloodlust dampening a bit when she sees my pathetic form, gaping wounds seeping or dripping to the floor below. Twice every day, they wash away my blood, and I've grown to enjoy watching it swirl down the drain. A regular reminder that they're taking things I can afford to lose. They haven't taken anything that matters. And they won't. Bastards.

I narrow my eyes to glare at her. "You're back," I say, making sure my voice is light and playful. "I've missed you. Come to finally play a bit?"

Her glare deepens as she looks me up and down, her eyes resting on the half-grown cock sitting between my legs. I think it might be growing in bigger. At least, that's what I'm gonna tell Sifa when I see her. She can let me know if I'm right when she wraps her lips around it.

But I let go of those thoughts right away. They'll make me hard, even strapped here with my gods-damned *mother's* gaze on me, and I will not let that happen. Although maybe it would help if she thought I'm getting off on this shit. She wouldn't put it past me, and the last thing she wants is for me to enjoy my time here.

"I think you're ready to see Tindera," she tells me, her lips tipping up in the smallest smile.

My stomach drops. If she wants to take me to Tindera, my dragon is fucking miserable. She's going to show me what my decisions have done to her. What I've inflicted on her.

And that might just break me.

I return her smile anyway. Because fuck her. "Can't wait."

She nods at her guards, and they release me, stepping away as I collapse on the floor. The agony that rips from my toes to my fingertips stuns me for a moment. Every part touching the floor has erupted in flames, as if I'm laying atop a bonfire as it eats away at me. But that's not the worst thing. It's the prickles in all my extremities, which haven't had regular blood flow for close to two weeks, that suck me into a dark place.

Fuck. Me.

I lay there for a minute or more, letting the feelings filter back into my limbs, little explosions of pain following the blood that's working its way through my system. I don't think I can move yet, but at least I no longer wish I was dead. My need for vengeance is back, giving me the strength I need to muster up some saliva and spit it at the Dróttning.

"Get him up," she demands, her voice as flat as always. The cold-hearted bitch can control her emotions as well as she controls everything else in this land.

A guard kicks my flayed gut, sending a spasm through me as a hundred knives seem to impale me at once. "Give me a minute," I snarl. So he kicks me again.

I've got just enough saliva for one more gob, and I spend it on him. His foot sends me sprawling on my back this time.

Still worth it.

Pushing myself over and on to my knees, I glare at both of them before dragging my maimed body from the ground. I'm not sure at first if I'll make it—my legs are jelly beneath me as they fight to hold me up—but I'll be damned if I'm going to collapse in front of *her*. I throw whatever strength they've left me into my pathetic appendages, forcing them to do their job. They straighten and I stand to stare down at the fuckers who think they're going to break me.

Fuck. Them.

"Follow me, Fhord." The Dróttning doesn't look back to confirm I heed her command, but I'd have been shocked if she did. She'd hear the strike from her guard if I didn't turn and stumble after her. And even if I wanted to disobey, I wouldn't be able to keep myself from chasing her to wherever she's keeping my dragon.

We walk a long way, and I stumble three times, not sure if I'll make it. The first flight of stairs is tough. The second flight is nearly impossible, but I manage to keep up with the leisurely pace she sets. The manacle's restraint on my power is fucking with more than my mind. I've been through worse, and my power has always—every single time—given me the adrenaline rush I need to fight through. This time, though, I feel like a human, trapped within a limited, weak body.

Finally, deep within the Nest, I get the barest hint of Tindera's presence. She must be close for us to connect, with the manacle dampening my magic. I almost cry—literally cry, something I haven't done since I was a snot-faced kid—when I see her. The Dróttning *never* tortures dragons this way. She's tried it on a dozen different beasts over the years and every one has been the same. It breaks their spirits, turning them into useless shells of the majestic beasts they once were. Even a few days can destroy a dragon's will to live. I've been strung up for twelve days and I'm guessing Tindera's been here, exactly like this, that entire time.

Now I collapse, dropping on my ass as I hold my tortured dragon's gaze. She wants to put on a brave front—I can see her fight within herself to soften her expression—but she fails. She's more broken than I've ever seen her, and I don't know how she could recover from this.

Trainers use contraptions like this but always while the dragon is on the ground. The pain is intense but not as overwhelming as it is when a dragon is suspended in the air, like Tindera is now.

A hundred or more massive bolts pierce her golden wings, triggering every pain point in them. Each bolt is secured on one side with a lock of some kind, cinching it in place. The other side holds a chain that runs up toward the roof and latches there. The chains spread out in different directions, pulling her wings taut between each. They look to be on the verge of ripping through, even with the bolts holding them in place. Blood pools around her, an endless supply dripping down her body to her legs and then trickling from her feet.

I can't feel her pain and it fucking kills me. I need to share it with her, experience exactly what she's experiencing. Even that would be better than the absence of her. She finds a way to tell me what she wants though. And that pierces me more deeply than anything else that's happened in these last twelve days.

Death, she begs. She's given up, all her strength gone. I can't blame her. But I can't let her go.

Shaking my head, I glare at my defeated dragon. "You will live. I will free you, and we will fly again."

Her response is that single plea—*Death*—with none of the extra meaning that always comes with her word. She's so fucking tired.

"No, you won't," the Dróttning purrs as she drops down into a crouch in front of me and places her hands on my cheeks. "You and Tindera are mine forever. When you accept that and prove your loyalty again, I will let her go to her new rider. Until then, this is where she'll stay."

She smiles, patting my cheeks one more time before standing, turning her back to me, and striding away.

I fall to the cold ground beneath me, unconscious as soon as my head slams against the rock.

CHAPTER TWENTY-SEVEN

SIFA

IT'S IMPOSSIBLE

I T'S BEEN A MISERABLE twelve days and I'm not sure if I have any hope left.

We've been sneaking south through Vanatia for twelve gods-damned days. Every time we think we have a clear route, another group of the Dróttning's soldiers shows up, forcing us to divert into the mountains or toward one impossible path or another. I'm exhausted and teetering on the edge of hopelessness. The steady presence of my dragon and friends has kept me on the right side of that edge.

Them, and Fhord. In addition to the mind-numbing travel, I have lived through everything Fhord has over these past twelve days. Every slice of skin. Every puncture deep into a vital organ. Every loss of one appendage or another. It's not like my connection to Astarot. I can't experience his pain, although I desperately wish I could. I have all the emotions without any of the agony. Having been there myself, I can imagine his torment, and it kills me a little more each day.

But I still cling to it like a convict to her last hope. He lives. I will get him back. Nothing else matters.

Today was the worst of all. The Dróttning took him to see Tindera, and I felt his despair. Astarot has gotten hints of her torture but knowing exactly what she's going through has changed both of us. We were driven before. Now we're possessed, a desperation to free our mates building with each plodding step south. Twice, we've talked about abandoning all of them and flying to the Nest alone, but the rational parts of our minds won out.

It'll be so fucking hard to free them, and we won't be able to do it without a plan and a lot of help.

It's nearly sunset when we reach the compound Fróðr's leading us to. He's confident the Dróttning won't find us here and we'll be able to spend the day or two we need to connect with the rebels and plan our rescue. He's not convinced it's possible, but I don't care. Astarot and I will get them ourselves if it comes down to it.

The broken-down buildings look deserted, which I expected. Fhord described the place where he met the others while I was in Njordheim as something like this. There are little signs if you know to look for them. More footprints litter the ground than would be expected for abandoned structures. Someone tries to cover them up regularly but not often enough. A blackberry bush to the east should have abundant fruit this time of year. One of the rebels must favor blackberries.

I'm not surprised to find Troels—the man from the southern Nest who met with Knut and Frida—waiting for us inside.

His importance to the rebellion was clear from their conversation. Ulfhild surprises me. I wouldn't have expected her to involve herself in this way.

Frida walks in last, and I'm watching her when she realizes Troels is here. Her eyes grow wide before she casts them to the ground, as if trying to hide the emotion that sparked within them. His reaction, as before, is more passive. Walking over, he gives her a hug—his eyes finding Liv over her shoulder, although she's ignoring him—and then a quick kiss. Troels is playing Frida. Disgust ripples through me, even as I try to quell it. He's important in the rebellion, and I don't need to make him my enemy.

It pisses me off, though. Frida deserves better than his disdainful attention.

We don't sit down together yet. They show us our rooms—I'm grateful to see a warm bath drawn in mine—and tell us they'll have food ready in an hour. I sink into the bath and don't move, letting the heat soothe my aching muscles and tattered heart. Anxious thoughts occasionally drop into my mind, but I push them out. Now isn't the time for worry. That will come later. Right now, I need to relax my body and spirit.

I'm pretty sure I've spent the entire hour in the water when I finally force myself to get out. It was worth it, though. I'm ready to face whatever they're going to throw at me. I think.

Dinner is a simple but satisfying mutton stew with crispy bread. As soon as we eat, we're led into a massive room where three dozen or so have gathered. My group scatters about, leaning against walls or each other to hold ourselves up.

There's no furniture, Joralf explains, because if they have to leave, it needs to look unused. They'll even toss dirt and debris back into the tubs we just used. They've gotten good at making them look as neglected as the rest of this place.

The rebels have made an art out of hiding from the Dróttning. It'll be good to have them around, even if I'm forced to interact with Troels.

Fróðr takes the lead as soon as we all find spots, explaining to everyone what happened while they were traveling with Fhord, then introducing Dani, Astarot, Vulryn and Khirta. He looks at me, prompting a nod, before moving on to why we're here, and what we need from them.

"Fhord's dragon, Tindera, has been held by the Dróttning for months. She was in the Nest for an injury, but Fhord's sure the Dróttning manipulated her healing to keep her longer. She questioned Fhord's loyalty and held his dragon for leverage. As soon as she knew for certain that Fhord's allegiance had shifted, she started torturing his dragon. Now, the Dróttning has Fhord too. We're going to get both of them out."

"No, we're not." Troels doesn't need to raise his voice when he speaks. It carries through the room, silencing us all. He's still standing, and every eye turns toward him. "Fhord isn't part of this movement," he adds. "We won't risk anyone to save him."

"This isn't your decision, Troels." Joralf's flinty response has gazes spinning in his direction. He'd been in prison for a while, but they all seem to know him well enough to realize he's not quick to anger. And he's respected enough—especially after protecting their secrets for two long years—to get their attention. "I'm out and Fróðr has his mate back because of Sifa. We're going to do what we have to do to free her mate."

"I've been watching Fhord a long time," Troels declares, his tone as contentious as before. "He's always done the Dróttning's bidding. Killed and tortured too many of our people. We can't trust him and we're not gonna help him."

"We're not debating this." It's Fróðr this time and he's angry. "Whatever he was before, Fhord's committed to Sifa now. Their gods-damned dragons are even mates. We watched him shift and kill a hundred of the Dróttning's soldiers. She captured him while he was trying to protect us."

"We owe him our lives," Joralf adds. "We'll do this with or without you." He pauses, his gaze bouncing about the room as he looks at every single person gathered here. "If it's without you, we'll never ally with you again. You'll lose us." One more pause and then he plays his ace. "And you'll lose the three dragons gathered here to fight with us."

They respond in unison, spurting flames toward the center of the room as their wings flare. Hovering around the group, every part of them poised to attack, they don't stop until I look up at Astarot. *Enough.* He dips his chin and settles on his haunches, snapping his jaws closed. Vulryn and Khirta do the same.

Troels is pissed, but his shoulders droop a bit as he stares at them. He's lost and he knows it. "It's impossible," he says at last, but his voice holds less steel.

"I've done the impossible more than once," I interject from my space along the wall. "I'll do it this time, too. I want your help, but like Joralf, I'll go without you. My dragon and I will never stand with you if you don't join us."

Frida's voice surprises me. She rises and walks over to stand in front of Troels, her hands on her hips. "Enough, Troels. We're going after Fhord and Tindera. If you're not with us, leave. We'll rescue them without you."

Troels's expression nearly draws a laugh from me. His mouth falls open as his eyes blink furiously—the only part of his body that's moving at all. After a moment, he lifts a hand as if to pull Frida toward him but then drops it. "You'd choose them? After all these years?"

"I chose them when I joined Liv to go meet Astrid and the others." She looks at the gathered rebels, her palms lifting into the air in supplication. "We've been getting nowhere," she exclaims, her tone sharp. "For years, we've been searching for information, no good idea what we're doing. We need Fhord and Sifa and we desperately need their dragons."

Heads are starting to nod, but she's just getting started. "We've all sold parts of ourselves to get closer to the bastards who run this country. We've done things that made our skin crawl—kept us from sleeping at night—because the Dróttning holds all the power in this land. We've become people we never thought we could be, just to try to wrench ourselves from her grip.

"Where's it gotten us?" she demands, her hands flinging up. "What have we accomplished in all this time? Every one of you knows the answer to that but I'll give it words. Not a gods-damned thing. We might even be worse off now than we were then."

"Because of Fhord," Troels fumes, twisting around to find me, "and that fucking elf."

"That elf is the reason these elves are here, Troels." Joralf's even angrier now than he was before. Troels may have been in charge, but he doesn't command much respect. The tables have turned.

"She and Fhord are the reason we're all here," Troels spits out. "It's not safe in Revalle anymore. The Dróttning turned everything upside-down searching for them, and she's still at it. She won't rest until the elf and those gods-damned dragons are hers."

I stare at him, stunned at his tone. A threat lurks beneath the surface. He tried to hide it but not well enough.

Before I can say anything, though, my world turns upside down. Bevin—fucking Bevin!—strides through the front door, a wicked smirk twisting his lips, and then walks over to Joralf to pull him up from the floor and into a deep hug. My heart beats a dozen times or more as I watch my former boss—the overseer who controls much of Revalle—embrace the elf who escaped from the Dróttning's prison with me and stands at the center of the rebellion. Bevin steps back, clapping Joralf on the shoulder twice, then spins and folds his arms around Fróðr.

When they turn toward us, all three of them have enormous grins on their faces. And I'm more confused about Bevin than I've ever been about any person before.

"Good to see you alive, Sifa," he says with a crooked grin before striding toward Ulfhild and drawing her up to stand with him. The courtesan's eyes sparkle as she laces their fingers together. And then he kisses her, a lover reunited after too long away.

"What the fuck?" I ask, my voice barely a whisper.

"Surprise." Ulfhild's smirk doesn't fade as she looks at every person in the room, their mouths slamming closed or legs twitching nervously as her gaze finds theirs. "I've heard all your comments about Bevin and I've taken notes. Now I have ammunition."

"But, seriously, what the fuck?" That seems like the most appropriate sentiment right now. I'll keep asking that question until one of them answers it.

"You've done well, Bevin, if none of them suspected it." Joralf's eyes sparkle nearly as much as Ulfhild's.

"I had a good teacher," Bevin responds with a respectful bow of his head toward the elf I helped rescue, who I obviously know nothing about. "I made sure everyone saw a cruel manipulator."

"So, your true self?" Ulfhild squeezes his hand with her question, one side of her lips curving up.

"My best self," Bevin amends, leaning over to kiss her cheek. "They don't know about this side of me because I've given them plenty of reasons to believe the side they saw."

"You've been working for the rebellion all along?" I'm probably a bit slow here, but seriously, what the fuck?

"I've been working for the rebellion for a very long time. Since before you showed up in Revalle and convinced one of my people to give you work."

"You've been convincing." I bow my head toward him as Joralf had done earlier. "And I'm usually very good at reading people."

"Your skills aren't slipping, Sifa. I just have a rare ability." Bevin turns in place, his gaze finding everyone in the room. He seems to be measuring them before twisting back toward me. "Magic doesn't touch me. The skills you've grown to rely on are useless on me."

"You're a sieve? Fhord said there are only two in Vanatia, and they're held in separate prisons."

"Relatives," Bevin tells me. "It's a family trait. The Dróttning doesn't and can't know." He pauses to glare at everyone, a warning in his eyes. "I'd be in prison too if she did."

"Bevin and I grew up together," Joralf explains. "I introduced him to Ulfhild many, many years ago. We realized we'd need someone in his position and convinced him of the righteousness of our cause."

He shrugs. "I want a dragon," he says. "Not just any dragon," he clarifies after a moment. "My dragon. The Dróttning bound him to a bastard who mistreats him."

"How did you bond with him? I thought the Dróttning killed anyone who threatened her hold on the dragons."

"He chose not to reveal me to his rider, and we've found a way to spend a little time together—enough to have a tenuous connection. I feel his pain and misery. It's motivated me to lend my talents and connections to this group of dissidents. And I'm far from the only one. Many dragons hide their allegiance from the Dróttning. We're only now realizing how many."

"Is something shifting within the dragons? Are they moving closer to rebellion?" I ask these questions to the room, but I'm turning to look at my dragon as I do. "You and Khirta defying the Dróttning's demands, dragons and riders forming bonds even when the dragon is ridden by another. We're getting hints about the Dróttning's control over the dragons, but if it was as simple as water, we should have realized it long ago. Why didn't we, and what's changed now?"

Bevin is the one who responds. "Do you know why I ordered you to work with Fhord to free Thyra?"

His question catches me by surprise, drawing my gaze back to him. He's doing a lot of that today. "What?"

"Why do you think I ordered you to work with Fhord?"

"I was losing your trust. You wanted me to have a partner."

"You have never lost my trust, Sifa." His eyes are calculating, intense.

"Why, then?"

"It was time for you and Fhord to finally stop fighting fate."

I nearly drop back to my ass, the shock from his words rips through me so strongly. "What did you say?"

"Fhord's a stubborn ass and he's been playing both sides too long, trying to protect everyone without doing the one thing we all need him to do."

"And what is that one thing?"

"It's time for him to defeat the Dróttning. He can do it with his mating bond in place. Your strength combined with his—and your dragons—may be enough to finally destroy her. But he needed a little push."

"And I was that push?" Puzzle pieces are starting to fit into place. My fists clench as a low growl rumbles out of Astarot. "You knew?"

"Of course, I knew. Very little escapes me."

"Nobody knew. I didn't have any idea."

"Fhord knew. Mikkael knew."

"Mikkael swore he didn't tell you." I don't manage to keep the tremble out of my voice, my surprise forcing its way into the room.

"Mikkael keeps no secrets from me. He's known for a very long time where my allegiance lies. I've made sure he always knows what he must for his work, as he does for me. He gives me every piece of information I need. And I definitely needed to know that you and Fhord are mates."

"Johan too?"

"Not Johan." Grief flickers through his eyes for a moment but disappears almost as quickly. He's been playing a role long enough to hide emotions like that. "I try to keep the circle of people who know my secrets small. Only Mikkael and Ulfhild. They were my intermediaries." He laughs, a rueful bark as his gaze flits across the room again. "Well, small until now."

"Why now? With so many people?" I wave my arm at the three dozen people who now share his secret.

"Your dragon, of course." Bevin turns to wink at Astarot, who responds with a grumble.

"Astarot defied the Dróttning." More puzzle pieces fall into place.

"We've been waiting a long time for a dragon to do that. None have lasted as long as he did. It's really remarkable."

"Was it a coincidence that Fhord arrived in Revalle and started working for you shortly before Astarot rebelled?"

"Fate, I suppose. She always makes sure dragon and rider will find each other when the time is right. And the time is right."

"But you couldn't have known Astarot and I would bond. I'll admit I'm impressed by all you did know, but not even you could be that prescient."

"I knew you *probably* belonged with Astarot. You and Fhord are mates. When Astarot and Tindera found each other, I realized you must be destined to ride Astarot. In all of Vanatia's history, dragons and riders have always been mated pairs."

"And how in all the worlds did you know Astarot and Tindera are mated?"

"That we learned from the dragons. They're little gossips. But they've kept it from the Dróttning. Only the dragons who believe in our cause get the inside dirt. They've found a way to communicate without the Dróttning eavesdropping on them."

I can only stand there, stunned. I don't even know the man standing in front of me. He's playful, smiling and winking at dragons. My head is spinning, and I really do wish I could plop on my ass and think through everything I've learned in the last ten minutes.

"Tell me, Sifa. Have you accepted your mating bond?"

I look around the room, reluctant to share such a personal fact with all these strangers, and this strange man I used to think I knew. He's intense, though, so the answer must matter to him. "I have," I confirm at last.

"Splendid. All the pieces are in place, then." Now he's smiling again, his eyes crinkled as his thumb caresses the back of Ulfhild's hand. "I've learned that the Dróttning didn't want to risk moving Fhord yet. Even restrained by the manacle, she fears he'll find a way to free himself. She's keeping him in the southern Nest until she can weaken him enough to take him north. I have contacts here, and with your mating bond, you have the information we'll need to get into the Nest and get him out alive."

He turns to face the others, his smile growing even larger. "We're going to free Fhord and Tindera, and then they'll help us liberate this land. Starting with the elves."

CHAPTER TWENTY-EIGHT

SIFA

A PREDICTABLE PLAN

WE'RE GOING WITH A predictable plan. It's familiar because it works, Bevin assures me.

Bevin will pretend to capture Astarot and me to get us inside the Nest. Once we're in, he'll set us free and work with rebels he has hidden in strategic positions to find and free Fhord and Tindera. I'm nervous—still not convinced I can trust Bevin despite the assurances of Ulfhild, Joralf, and Fróðr—but we need him. So Astarot and I have agreed to be his sacrifices. We'll kill Bevin and free Fhord and Tindera by ourselves if he betrays us.

The others will wait nearby, ready to breach the Nest when we call for them. Astarot will carry Fhord away while Bevin and I go to free Tindera. Khirta and Vulryn will be just outside the Nest, prepared to help Tindera escape if we call them.

We're reluctant to include Vulryn—she's too unpredictable—but after what they've done to Tindera's wings, we may have no choice. She won't be able to fly today. Maybe never. Astarot knows he must be fast delivering Fhord to the Ætt, in the hope he needs to return and help his draikana. If he can get back in time, we won't need Vulryn.

The timing will be tight. Everything needs to fall into place, and we're not sure if we'll be able to get the others into the Nest to help us. If we can't, we'll end up fighting our way out alone. But it's possible and that's the best we've got right now.

The biggest problem with the plan is that we have to wait two more days. Bevin's got someone in the Nest who can give us information we'll need as we clear a path to Fhord and Tindera. He'll make sure there are a limited number of soldiers on duty. He won't join us—he's too important to Bevin to risk—but his help will be critical.

More importantly, in two days, the Dróttning will be in the northern Nest and too far away to return quickly. If we follow the timeline we're setting for ourselves, we'll be gone before she can get back.

It's a gods-damned long two days. The wait kills me because my connection with Fhord goes only one way. I know how brutal the Dróttning's torture is. How much he's hurting. How desperate and hopeless he's becoming. But I can't tell him we're coming. That he needs to hold on a bit longer.

Finally, though, the day of our "capture" arrives. I'm up early, restless after a lousy night of sleep and ready to get started. My thoughts drift out occasionally, anxious for the others to wake up, and I have to fight the urge to rattle them out of their beds. I want them alert but admit to myself that the real reason I don't jostle everyone's minds is that Bevin's a sieve.

We need him and I can't reach him. If the last two days are any indication, he could sleep through a hurricane. Any noise the others make won't matter.

Instead, I sit with my dragon. Astarot's quiet, as unsettled as me. Maybe more. He's never been with Tindera, and I can feel his need for her increase, almost on a daily basis. He's assured me dragons are patient, and he can wait to fully bond with her. But it's been a long, nerve-wracking wait. I want this for him, nearly as badly as I want to free Fhord for me.

"Today's the day." Leif's voice shouldn't surprise me, but it does. He's been up as early as me the last two days. "We'll get them out."

"We will." My words hold no uncertainty. We *will* free Fhord and Tindera today.

"Fróðr and Toffer found a place for us to go after. We should be able to escape without the Dróttning discovering us—give Fhord time to heal before we go north."

I drop my head to look at the floor as tears fill my eyes. I can't let myself think about what we're going to find. I haven't been able to see him. The connection doesn't work that way. I know what he's experiencing, but for now, my imagination alone provides images. They're fucking horrific because I've spent too much time on the rack myself and I know what the Dróttning's soldiers are doing.

"I've never seen him injured like this before," I say as I lift my eyes to look at him. "How long will it take him to heal?"

"He regenerates quickly, and it'll be better with your bond. A few days, I suppose."

"I hope their spot is safe. Once we get him there, I'm not moving him. Those days will be hard enough as it is."

"It's safe," Bevin says as he comes into the room. "They showed me. It'll work."

"It better."

"It will." He turns toward the bedrooms and then looks back at me. "We'll leave in thirty minutes."

"Good. I'm ready."

"You better be." He smiles as he throws my words back at me, but I glare at him instead. Today's not the day for levity. "Thirty minutes," he repeats before striding over to the fire for food.

The trip to the Nest is quicker than I expected. I assumed we'd be vikus away, but we were hiding in plain sight, barely an hour from the entrance. We travel unchained for the first part but as soon as Astarot senses soldiers nearby, we stop to adopt our disguise. My throat constricts as I realize how vulnerable I'll be until we get inside and he frees me, but this is necessary.

We can trust Bevin.

I hope.

Within a few minutes, I hear a group of soldiers riding toward us. They're loud but have little to fear around here. The Dróttning's control is absolute.

"Well, fuck me," one of them says with a low whistle when he sees us. "If it ain't the gods-damned dragon and the female who freed him. Bevin done won himself the jackpot."

"Damn right I have. And I've come to collect." He jerks on the chain attached to Astarot, drawing an angry howl from my dragon. I have to hold back my smile. I never knew Astarot could act.

"Dróttning ain't here. Don't know when she'll be back."

"I've got time. It'll be worth waiting for her." He nods his chin at one of the soldiers. "The dragon's too gods-damned slow. Go ahead of us and tell them we're coming, to ready a cage for my prisoners."

We fought about this part of the plan. Bevin's convinced if they know we're coming, they'll be spread out more thinly, giving us a better chance to escape. I think giving them time to prepare will make it harder. But he knows this Nest and the soldiers assigned here, so we've followed his suggestion. Astarot and I don't like it.

It takes us another twenty minutes to get to the Nest with my dragon dragging his feet as Bevin had requested. My heart beats more quickly with each step, a combination of dread about willingly entering a Nest as a captive and anxiousness about our plan. About Fhord. But my fear is just an echo of what I felt when Fhord and I entered the northern Nest to free Thyra. This place doesn't inspire the same terror.

The only thing that truly scares me now is the possibility we'll fail—that Fhord and Tindera will be trapped here forever. That terrifies me, but it also centers me. It gives me the focus I need to do anything—and I mean *anything*—necessary to free them. I will sleep next to my mate tonight, and Astarot will fly with his draikana soon.

Just as we arrive, I realize Bevin's plan has a benefit we hadn't anticipated. Fhord's heard about our supposed capture. I feel his conflict as he wavers between fear we truly were caught and hope this is part of a plan to free him. I wish I could reassure him, although I don't know if I would try. I still have no idea how our new bond works and whether the Dróttning might overhear anything we say if she were close enough. We can't take any risks.

Fhord's a smart man, though, and he goes with hope. I feel his focus on his surroundings, his intention to tell me everything he can about where he is and what he's facing. He's in a room with no windows and remembers going down at least three, maybe four, flights of steps. Three soldiers are in the room, two focused on him. They're taking more skin. He shifts his thoughts away from the pain, trying to shield me from it, I think.

I can't tell anyone, not even Astarot, because I can't risk someone overhearing it. But my connection with Fhord, the knowledge he gives me, will guide our search.

A half-dozen guards meet us as we approach the gate. My stomach clenches but Bevin just smiles at them, no hint of worry or fear in his gaze. "We'll take them from here," the closest guard, a large male, tells him.

"You will not," Bevin responds, infusing each word with the authority he holds in Revalle. "These are my prisoners, and I'll deliver them to the Dróttning myself. Until then, they stay with me."

"Meistari," the male begins in a conciliatory tone, "it doesn't work that way here. We take charge of the prisoners."

Now, I see the Bevin I've come to know and fear. He rises to his full, intimidating height and glares at the male foolish enough to argue with him. "These are not your prisoners. They are mine until I personally give them to the Dróttning. You people have fucked up more than once and I will not trust *my* captives with you. You will show me to a dragon cage and give me the keys. Nothing more."

If we'd come with anyone else, the gambit wouldn't work. These guards are trained and conditioned to rule like the Dróttning—ruthless and uncompromising. This is their kingdom and only the Dróttning holds more power. But Bevin is unlike anyone else in this part of Vanatia. He wields the Dróttning's sword everywhere in the South. Everyone knows defying him can be a death sentence. The Dróttning has killed people for less.

So the soldier stands down. I have to hold in a sigh of re-lief—keep the look of frustration plastered to my face—as the large male bows to Bevin, gesturing for us to walk farther into the Nest. He strides at Bevin's side, directing him with an occasional wave of the arm, as we descend. My terror rises with each step, my thoughts waffling between fear for myself and Astarot, and agony at what Fhord and Tindera are suffering.

We're deep inside when the soldier opens an enormous cage and hands the keys to Bevin. "Your prisoners can stay here. We'll have a room for you in the western sector. Tell the guard in that area Einar sent you."

Bevin responds with a very quick dip of his chin—an ac-knowledgment but *not* a bow. A male of his reputation would not bow to a soldier, even a high-ranking one. "Restrain the dragon and then leave us," he orders as he hands over the chain attached to Astarot's collar. He turns to me, a lecherous smirk lifting the corners of his lips, and adds, "I haven't yet played with my prisoner. I think it's time."

A wave of disgust rolls through me, despite my belief he's acting. I sneer at him, straightening my back and spitting in his direction—close enough to look like a real attempt without hitting him. "Fuck you," I snarl.

"Oh, you will," he purrs. Turning to the large male, he barks out, "Now!"

The male grins as his gaze roams up and down my body. "Do it," he demands, prompting one of his soldiers to take the chain from Bevin and tug Astarot into the cage.

Astarot starts to put up a fight, but Bevin yanks me into his arms, my back to his chest, and holds a knife I didn't see him draw to my throat. "I'll enjoy her whether she's breathing or not," he growls at Astarot. "The Dróttning may want you alive, but she doesn't give a fuck about this female. You'll go into that cage, or I'll kill her."

Astarot's eyes narrow and flames trickle from his snout. But he doesn't fight as the soldier leads him toward a far wall and locks him in, his gaze on me the entire time. When he's secure, the soldier backs out, little bursts of flame chasing him as Astarot struggles to restrain himself.

He fucking hates this and I don't blame him. We're completely at Bevin's mercy and Astarot is as conflicted about that as I am. I keep pulling up the image of Joralf and Bevin hugging, reminding myself that I trust Joralf. He has a history with Bevin that I don't. This will work.

I just wish my pounding heart agreed. It's echoing in my ears, filling me with terror. I can't center myself and I *need* the soldiers to finish what they're doing and get the fuck away before I start vomiting.

And then I feel Fhord, his thoughts fluttering over me like a caress. I don't know if I'm close enough for him to sense my distress or if he just knew I'd need him. Whichever it is, it's working. He's helping me calm a heart that had been beating out of control, slow my breathing, and focus on what matters and what doesn't.

He and Tindera will be free today. Nothing else matters.

Finally, agonizing minutes after they led us here, the guards stroll away, laughter echoing down the cavern. Bevin sheathes the knife and drags me into the cage as far away from the entrance as we can go. Leaning into me, his lips at my ear, he whispers, "We'll give them a few minutes. Then we'll unchain Astarot and go."

I nod my assent and stride over to Astarot, digging my hands into his feathers. Too long after the guards leave, Bevin finally nods, almost to himself, and raises the keys toward me. "Much as I'd love to get to know your dragon, he doesn't seem to be in the mood right now. You can free him."

"Thank you," I breathe as I take them and unhook Astarot from the wall. He stands tall and shakes his feathers, flickers of light spurting from between his teeth. "I can't sense anyone nearby. Is that strange?"

"It's what I expected," Bevin assures me. "This Nest isn't as fortified as the northern Nest. They've brought carvers here for Fhord and a few extra guards, but they still hold many valuable prisoners in the North. We came early for a reason. Those who are here are scattered through the cave system. The next shift will be fortified. We have a short window."

"Lead the way." I step back, keys jangling from my raised arm. He smiles—such a strange look for Bevin—and takes them from me as he stalks forward. We're all on high alert, our senses reaching out to find any threat.

Bevin turns right as we exit and takes a flight of stairs at the end of the hall, guiding us deeper into the Nest. The rock turns into steel at the last step and Bevin starts to slow, waiting for me to catch up with him. "There should be two guards up ahead," he tells me in a low voice, "but they have weak minds. You shouldn't need much time."

I smile and let my mind stretch toward them, as the smile turns into a smirk. They're just as malleable as Bevin said. With the speed and flexibility my mating bond with Fhord gave me, I construct a memory ordering them to reinforce the guards in the upper levels, far away from anywhere we might be today. They hesitate for a moment, perhaps discussing their odd new order, then jog away as I add urgency to the command.

Twice more we have to clear our path but only one guard causes any problems. She's got a stronger mind than the others and spends a minute or more arguing with her partner. I put that time to good use, focusing on her to find the memories

I'll need to convince her. As soon as I add those new details to her orders, she starts walking and then running.

Finally, perhaps fifteen minutes after we left the cage, we're a dozen feet away from Fhord. Now I'm nervous. This is the part of the plan that could fuck us up. We can't just kill them because as soon as they see us, one will send a message to the Dróttning.

I need to trick them. But the Dróttning always chooses strong minds for this job, especially after my escape ten years ago. These people aren't easily manipulated. Bevin plans to distract them while I dig into their brains, creating a scenario convincing enough that they'll race away together.

It will involve fire and a lot of pain.

I'm looking forward to this part of the plan.

Bevin mouths a "good luck" to me, then turns to stroll into the pit—their name for the torture room in the southern Nest. He's the Bevin I recognize, all swagger and arrogance. I take a deep breath and get to work.

I'm stunned at first by the depravity of these guards. The first memories I find are of Fhord. Everything they've done to him while he's been here. All the blood he's lost. Every body part taken from him. Each scream of pain when he's fighting to hold it back.

They've reveled in it. This is what they do.

Now they're going to see what I do.

I smile when I find what I need within each of them. Dani and I talked about how she's played with phobias and fears.

She's never been strong enough to create memories, but I am. I'm going to bring their nightmares to life.

It only takes a few minutes to build a scene that manipulates all their horrors. It involves fire because I want them to feel that pain, along with the small spaces one of them fears, the spiders that terrorize another, and the birds that will send the third into a panic. I start with smoke, relief filling me when their conversation stops and I hear confusion about its source. Then I unleash the rest of it. Birds and spiders attack together as the guards huddle in a miniscule closet, trying to escape the flame that will melt the skin from their bones.

Less than a minute passes before the first wail echoes from the room. I let the illusion grow, forcing them into a corner, before Astarot and I enter. Watching the bastards for a moment—not quite ready to see what they've done to Fhord—I make sure they're trapped.

"They're yours," I murmur to Astarot before I turn to look at the man I love.

I can't hold back the sob. I knew what they'd done to his body but seeing him makes it real. He's ripped to shreds, hardly any skin visible in the midst of the blood and gore. He'll be sitting or lying on an open wound for days, in agony no matter what we do.

His gaze is fixed on me, a sad smile twisting his lips. As if he's trying to comfort me.

I force myself to smile as I hold his gaze. "Joralf was right," I mutter, a hitch in my voice and tremble in my hands. "It really does grow back bigger. I'll give the Dróttning my thanks before I take her head."

Fhord's smile tips higher for a moment but then his hint of a laugh is replaced by a grimace.

Tears drip down my face as Bevin hands me the keys to release him. Striding forward, I drop to my knees and unlock his ankles. I need to be strong for Fhord, but I can't. I am sobbing as the iron swings away to reveal bone, unable to ignore the horror that is Fhord's flayed body.

"Can't wait to test it out," he grunts as his body drops—his legs no longer holding him up, putting pressure on arms that must feel like fire is eating his shoulders. I free his right hand, and he reaches for my cheek as he drops again, nearly to the ground this time as he's suspended just by his bound left wrist. Running a thumb along my bottom lip, he groans, "Fuck, I missed the feel of your skin."

"I missed you so gods-damned much," I cry, letting my eyes tell him what my hands can't.

"Thank you for coming for me, rabbit." Taking a deep breath, he drops his hand and nods at his left wrist. "I thought I'd be wearing these for many years."

"I will always come for you, Fhord." I free his left hand and embrace him before he drops, my hands drawing a raspy inhale from him as they grasp on to open muscle and wounds. He struggles to steady himself, somehow finding strength to stand without my help.

And then I unlock the manacle, crying out my relief when I feel his mind again. "Finally," I gasp. "I felt empty without this connection between us."

He grins, his back growing straighter, as I toss it to the side. But just for a moment. The smile drops from his face as his head turns toward the door, a look of horror taking its place. "She knows," he snarls, turning toward me with flashing eyes. "And she's almost here."

CHAPTER TWENTY-NINE

FHORD

I CAN'T LEAVE HER

"WHO ARE YOU TALKING about?" Sifa's horror at the fucked-up condition of my skin has turned to fear. She knows who I mean.

"The Dróttning," I confirm. "She's been gone at least a day. Said she was going north. She shouldn't be back yet, but she is. I can feel her getting closer."

I need to get all of us the fuck out of here, but right now, I can't do anything. With the manacle gone and Sifa holding me, my power has surged. Adrenaline is flowing through me, pulling strength from her and the room around us as magic I haven't used for two weeks sparks to life.

And my girls are back in my head. Though I've wanted nothing more every single moment I've been hanging here, it's gods-damned overwhelming. Sifa's fear combines with Tindera's pain and worry, compounding the inferno that is my body, as every inch of me—inside and out—burns.

I stand motionless for a few moments, struggling to process the sensory overload. Finally, I can focus on my breaths, forcing them to slow as my mind adjusts to the onslaught. My heart finds a normal rhythm and I release clenched fists, relaxing even more as it releases a sharp pain I hadn't even noticed. Looking down at my hands, I can't hold back the laugh. They're as fucked up as everything else. Of course clenching my fists hurt. I need to stop doing that shit.

Sifa's gaze hasn't left me, her eyebrows slammed together as she experiences everything I do. When I finally get my shit together and nod at her, she spins to look at Bevin—who apparently is on our side? When the fuck did that happen?

"You said she'd be too far away to get back." Bevin's face twists in confusion at Sifa's words, or maybe just the fact the Dróttning is returning and shouldn't be.

I'm gods-damned confused too.

And then the asshole who runs the mansion at the southern training grounds adds to the shitshow that this rescue quickly is becoming. Fucking Knut strolls into the room, a smirk on his treacherous face, before turning to Sifa to answer the question Bevin couldn't. "I warned her she should come back. That her favorite captives won't be here if she waits too long."

"Why the fuck would you do that?" I rage. I'm barely holding myself upright—my power whipping through me as it searches for a release I won't give it yet—but I need to kill somebody after the fucked-up weeks I've had. It appears Knut has offered himself up. Gentleman that he is.

"You should understand, Fhord," Knut tells me with a smarmy grin. "You've been playing both sides for a long time. You've chosen a side and so have I."

Now I know who betrayed us, leading the Dróttning and her soldiers to our trail when I came back to Vanatia without Sifa. Knut sent the stable boy to that gods-damned compound, claiming he needed to get away from Aksell. It was a fucking ruse, and I'm even more pissed than before. This bastard's treachery led to the agony Tindera is suffering.

"You chose the wrong gods-damned side. You're going to die today." I take a step forward—not even reaching to Sifa for a blade because I want to feel Knut take his last breath—but he just laughs. "How much of a fool do you think I am, dragon rider? I didn't come here to fall to you."

I feel his weak power rise and reach for mine. My eager magic whips toward Sifa, asking her to join me, and her trust caresses my mind as she opens herself willingly. I can't hold back the smile as my magic strengthens even more, joined by the control my overwhelmed brain hasn't recovered yet.

"I wouldn't do that, Fhord," Knut purrs. "The Dróttning's patience is running out. The guards punishing Tindera are ordered to kill her if I don't return. Or if you escape."

"That's bullshit." I spit out these words, my fists clenching at his threat.

"Test me." Knut smiles and I realize he may be telling the truth. Because why the fuck would he come into this room if he wasn't certain he had a way to get out.

"Why are you here, Knut? Why reveal yourself now?" Sifa's voice is so soft, confusion in each word. She, Astarot, and Bevin are positioned at my back, a few feet between us.

"I'm here to slow you down," he responds, as if it's obvious, "give the Dróttning a chance to get here. And I wanted you to know it was me who stopped you." These words are to me alone, layered with years of our conflict and hatred. "I'm not hiding my allegiance to the Dróttning any longer." He straightens his back, his eyes dancing between the four of us. "None of us are leaving. We'll all stand with the Dróttning as she defeats her enemies."

"The fuck we will," I growl as I step forward—tugging Sifa with me—and throw my fist, breaking his nose. "I don't know what game you're playing here, but I don't have time for this shit."

Releasing a pulse of my magic, I will the closest wall to stretch toward Knut, yanking him in to trap him. And then I step into him, inches between his nose and mine. "I'm gonna go free my dragon. Then I'll come back and kill you. Just in case that treacherous mouth is telling the truth and I need you alive for a few minutes longer."

"Wise choice, Fhord," Knut chokes, the rock caving in his chest just enough to hurt.

"You're still dead," I remind him. "I'm just giving you a little more time. When I come back, this stone is gonna eat you alive, crushing you bit by bit until you're screaming for death. I'll be back soon," I promise as I reach out to pat his cheek. "Very soon."

I stride out the door, knowing exactly where they're holding Tindera. Sifa jogs to catch up with me, her hand lifting toward my arm as if to stop me but pausing just short of a touch. And thank fuck. Because I am on fire right now—in the worst gods-damned way possible—barely holding on to my sanity. As much as I want to feel my rabbit's hands on me, I think any contact would push me over the fucking edge.

"You're leaving with Astarot," Sifa barks out. "We'll get Tindera and follow you.

"Fuck no," I snarl. I don't want to be an asshole—they are rescuing me, after all—but there's no gods-damned way. "I'm not leaving without my dragon," I tell her. "We go together."

"Fuck, you are frustrating."

I pause, turning to hold her gaze. And take a deep breath. She doesn't deserve to see this side of me. "I will always choose Tindera over me," I whisper, begging her to understand. "Just like I will always choose you over me. Please don't try to stop me. The Dróttning is minutes away. We need to get Tindera and get the fuck out of here."

I don't see the flame that Astarot belches out, but I feel it rippling across my frayed skin. "What the fuck was that for?" I yell as I turn to stare at him, flames still spitting through his teeth.

"He's just agreeing with you, Fhord. You win. Let's get Tindera before the Dróttning gets here."

I jerk my chin forward and turn to start jogging down the hall. The motion rattles my bones, sending waves of torment up and down my entire body, but I grit my teeth and keep running. I can feel the bitch getting closer. We don't have much time.

When the Dróttning shifts, a wave of nausea rolls through me, nearly strong enough to force me to stop. She must be desperate to return if she chose to reveal her wyrm form to whoever travels with her—although she probably just killed them. Her wyrm is faster than my savage. We have less time than I thought.

Sifa feels the battalion of soldiers when I do. I hear her sharp intake of breath just as I sense a hundred people or more running toward us. "The others weren't able to get in," she mutters as she tugs on my hand. "Wait, Fhord. We had three dozen people outside, waiting until we'd freed you to come help us. Khirta told Astarot that the Dróttning's return fucked it up. They can't get in."

"Then we'll do it ourselves." A shadow creeps into her eyes, and I step into her. "We won't have another chance. Them being out there will help. They'll keep out anyone else the Dróttning might try to bring in." Letting my magic pulse into Sifa to remind her how strong we are, I dip my head, tasting her lips. "We can do this," I murmur. "We don't need them."

She dips her chin, raising it again quickly to hold my gaze. "We can do this."

"We can. If we go now. This way," I grunt as I sense an enormous group to our left and veer right. It's a less direct route but we won't have to fight our way through.

This is almost as bad, though. Dozens of guards wait for us at the end, our only route out. I lift my hand, pausing us for a second as I think about what we need to do. "We'll go this way," I say at last, "but Astarot can take the lead. He'll burn as many as he can, and we'll take the rest."

Sifa nods, unsheathing one of the swords at her back and extending it toward me. "Can you fight?"

I glance down at my palms and smirk. They're not as bad as other places but holding a blade would hurt. And I'd rather *feel* the Dróttning's soldiers as they die by my hands. "I don't want it. I'll be better off with my fists and my magic. If I have to, I'll shift. My savage would love to see you again. But that'll just be a last resort. If he controls us, he may not let go and he's too big to ride a dragon once we're in the open."

"Your savage?" Bevin asks, drawing my attention to him as he drops a mask over his head—probably hoping to hide his identity if he can.

"Nothing you need to know," I tell him. I still don't trust him and the less he knows about me, the better. He's another reason I won't shift unless I need to. "Astarot, go," I bellow at Sifa's dragon. We're wasting time we don't have standing here.

He responds with a howl and jumps over us to take the lead and start running down the cavern. He'd been holding back before, moving at our speed, but dragons are fucking fast when they want to be. We run after him, pushing ourselves as hard as we can. Within a few minutes—just as I'm wondering how much farther I can run, because my body is fucked after the last two weeks—I feel Astarot's fire.

We reach his front, searching through the flames for the Dróttning's soldiers, just in time. Three toward the back have rolled in a cart holding a massive dragon ballista. I hear them call "Retreat" and lash out with my magic, heaving up the largest boulder I can find to throw it in the arrow's path. It skims the shaft, sending it off course but not enough. The arrow grazes Astarot's shoulder, ripping a wide gash through his feathers and skin, releasing crimson rain to splash down around us.

Astarot roars, his flame aimed toward the soldiers who attacked him. But they're ready for him, abandoning the cart to throw themselves behind a nearby wall. As soon as Astarot's fire dims, they drag out another, just far enough to aim. It's soaring toward him before I can catch my breath, and I reach deep inside for the magic to haul up another rock and throw it in the arrow's path. This one aims true, stopping the arrow before it can reach Astarot.

"No more fire," Sifa yells at her dragon. "We can't risk you. Take cover until we can stop the arrows. We'll take care of the rest."

He growls out a reluctant assent—even I can hear the stubborn resistance in his response—but complies. And we fall into the fight.

I can't focus on Sifa, desperate as my savage and I are to keep our mate safe. She's stronger than me right now and I know she can protect herself. My fucking heart, though, is ripping in half. Letting her go just as she's returned to me is the worst gods-damned thing I've done in a long time.

Sucking in a deep breath, I force myself to concentrate on what I can do. Two dozen piles of ash decorate the cave, but the others must have been hidden behind walls or boulders. We have just as many to fight through before we can reach Tindera.

My magic calls to me but my savage and I need to feel someone die. Giving in to that *need*, I jog toward the closest soldier, smirking up at him as he tosses a knife—missing me entirely—and then draws a sword. My lips drop into a sneer as my arm hits his, deflecting his blow. Then I grab his wrist, breaking it with a quick flip of mine. His blade clatters to the ground and I kick out, groaning at the agony that rips through me as my leg muscles stretch to throw him to the ground.

I drop on his chest and latch on to his neck, a shiver rolling down my spine as my thumb finds his erratic heartbeat. He knows he won't survive this, and I can feel my savage soothe as it watches him die. I shudder in a deep breath, releasing some of the tension gathered in my gut. My palms and fingers are pounding, pain washing through me, but I barely notice it.

Because, *fuck*, that felt good.

I'm not usually so bloodthirsty, but I've been picturing my vengeance for too many days. We needed that.

The sword that nearly removes my head catches me by surprise. I duck just in time, watching as it decapitates the dead soldier beneath me instead. A fitting end. Barking out a laugh, I'm on my feet and then barreling into this attacker, my shoulder landing in his gut and throwing him to the ground beneath me. His sword clangs to the side and I reach for a knife at his belt.

I need this one's blood.

His hands reach up to grasp my wrist, but I've got too much fury rippling through me. I push through his weak resistance, shoving the knife into his right eye, a vicious smile creasing my cheeks when I see the moment he resigns to his death. Sucking in one more trembling gulp of air, I yank my blade out and push it into his other eye.

Pain rolls back through me as my mind focuses on it again instead of the fight for life, so I look around for another. I'm too late, though. Sifa and Bevin are finishing off the final soldiers, Astarot hovering behind his rider to attack if she gives him a chance. She doesn't. Her sword takes the male's head just as the dragon's jaws snap forward. He huffs as he watches it roll away and Sifa smiles up at him.

"That one was mine," she mutters as she slaps at his jaw. He responds with one more gust of air and then turns toward the cave where they're holding Tindera, striding and then galloping forward. "Guess he's anxious," Sifa says as she glances at me, nods when she sees I'm alive, and turns to run after her dragon.

"We all are," I murmur to myself. Releasing the knife still wedged in the soldier's eye, I rise to race down the cavern on the heels of the others.

I don't even have to cast out my thoughts to feel the Dróttning approach. She's a few vikus away at the most, throwing everything she can into her drive to get here before we can free Tindera and leave. We're close to my dragon, but she's not alone. As we reach the outer corridor, Astarot impatiently waiting for us, I sense another few dozen soldiers gathered in her cave, ready to give their lives to slow us down enough for the Dróttning.

"Go ahead of us again, Astarot," I tell him. "Take as many down as you can before we get there."

He grunts his approval and disappears down the corridor. We're close enough to hear the screams as he unleashes his first wave of fire. I just hope it's enough.

We enter a minute or more after him, my eyes straining through the flame and smoke as we hover on the edge, barely out of sight, trying to figure out what the fuck is going on and what we have to do to get out of here. I hear Sifa call my name but the chaos has my thoughts so frenzied—part of me still trapped on the rack—it doesn't register for a moment.

"Fhord," she repeats, her voice rising as she stalks toward me. "We can't get out the way we came. If we can fly out of here, we'll have a chance. Can you open a hole above us? Get us access to the air or someplace closer to the surface?" Her jaw is clenched, wrinkles creasing her brow. Lifting a hand to gently place it on my cheek, her hesitant touch drawing my gaze to her, she repeats. "Can you open a passage above us for the dragons to fly through?"

I finally drag my erratic thoughts away from the hole they were falling into. My power, buoyed by a rush of adrenaline, carried me this far, but I don't know if I have that much to give. It will take every bit of my magic to do what Sifa's asking.

"I'll check," I tell her, casting my mind out to search the stone above us, hunting for some fracture or weakness I can exploit. When I find it, I can't hold back the sigh of relief.

"Yes," I tell her as she drops her hand from my cheek. "I can do this."

Not yet, though. Tindera's trapped in the same stone but she's on the other side of the cavern. I push my mind into the rock again, searching for some fissure or fault I can use to free her at the same time. If I don't wrench the chains holding her from the cave now, we may not be able to do it at all.

This one's tougher to find. It's nothing but a sliver, running from one of Tindera's chains to the weak spot I plan to exploit. Ripping it apart without dropping half the ceiling on my dragon may be impossible. I may end up hurting her even more. But this is the only chance we'll have.

Reaching for Sifa's hand to ask for her magic, I suck in a deep breath, intermingle her power with mine, and spear our combined will toward the crack above us. It shudders when we reach it, trembling with the force pushing into its midst. Caution but speed. I need to tear this thing open and then use it to free Tindera without burying us all in the rocks and debris I'll be moving to make enough space.

But it's so fucking hard. I'm only half the male I was when the Dróttning dragged me into this cave. My flayed flesh is trembling as the effort required to move so much earth shivers through me, triggering nerves and fibers that should never be exposed to air. My mind is still a jumble of conflicting images as it struggles to make sense of thoughts I'm receiving from Sifa and Tindera and the gods-damned Dróttning.

I'm too weak to wall them off completely, but I can focus on this one task. Sucking in one more shaking breath, I push everything except the stone above us to the side of my mind. I'm widening the crack as fast as I can—sun starting to seep into this cavern, casting its light on the golden dragon being tortured at its center. My thoughts stray for a moment, searching for the Dróttning as dread about her approach filters into my concentration, but I heave them back.

Our escape route and freeing Tindera are the only things that matter. We'll deal with everything else when we have our path out.

A minute or more passes as I shove at the stone, turning a crack into a gap and then an enormous hole. Rocks and a few boulders have tumbled to the ground, but I've managed to shift away any that would threaten us or Tindera. With one more surge of energy, I thrust my magic into the tiny fracture leading to Tindera and blast away the rock holding her chains, sucking in a deep breath as I use every bit of power remaining to shield my beast from the avalanche falling toward her.

Finally, I drop to my knees, cringing as my palms fall to the ground beside them and pain radiates up my arms and legs. It's enough. The dragons can carry us away as soon as we free Tindera.

But my magic was too fucking slow.

When I see her above us, I know the Dróttning sensed what I was doing and abandoned the caverns that would have brought her here. We've lost the few moments we needed to free Tindera and escape. Her wyrm blots out the sun for a second as she hovers on the precipice, and then she attacks.

I can't hold back the shift. My savage responds instinctively to defend us from the beast who defeated us before—my gods-damned mother. Before I can move, my bones are cracking apart, turning into the wolf that hungers for her blood and aches to avenge her last attack, which brought us to these caves.

We shudder, shaking our damaged skin as Fhord collapses within us. He was too slow in giving me control last time. Our dam trapped us before we could defeat her. We will not make that mistake again.

She did not aim for us when she fell from the sky because she knows how to control us. Her tail is wrapped around our mate's ankles, tugging her forward as her teeth attack the fire dragon our mate rides. The male who brought them to these caves has disappeared. He cannot risk being seen by the wyrm.

Our mate's dragon needs to attack the soldiers. The wyrm will hurt the dragon. He will not be able to resist her commands. And the wyrm is ours.

We snarl at the fire dragon, driving it away from our dam, and attack. She's quick, though, and ready for us. Releasing our mate, she spins toward us, lashing out to capture one of our legs and drag us forward. We attack, our sharp teeth drawing her black blood, but before we can do real harm, she twists and tosses us up, throwing us toward our mate.

Pivoting to stop the fall that could kill our mate, we land on our front shoulder, half a dragon's-length away from our dam. She lashes out, stretching far enough to grab our neck and wresting us into her. Before we've regained our feet, she drags us closer and traps us in her coils.

She will not beat us again. We sink our teeth into her side, ripping out a massive chunk of skin and sinew, and she recoils for a moment, dropping us again. Leaping to our feet, we launch ourselves at her neck, but before we can jump, our side erupts in pain, as if a hundred arrows have pierced us at once. We shudder, struggling to understand as we swing our head to look at the massive bolt sticking out of our side.

"No!" Our mate's voice echoes off the walls, but we barely hear it. Collapsing on our other side, we lift our head to watch the fire dragon attack our dam, flinging her toward the side of the cave. Out of the corner of our eye, we see the emerald dragon hover at the hole we've created above us but there's nothing she can do.

Fhord throbs inside me, demanding I let him take our skin. I'm too weak to fight him. But he's too weak to take control. We can only watch as our body shifts into a mongrel, neither wolf nor male.

"Is the Dróttning alive?" Sifa demands from our side. We hear her dragon grumble a response and force our thoughts to focus on our little rabbit. She turns to us, her eyes full of grief. "The Dróttning is stunned but she's still moving. We can't take Tindera with us now. We need to get you safe before she attacks again. We'll come back for Tindera."

"She's right fucking there, Sifa! We can't leave her." In our in-between state, half wolf and half male, it's little more than a growl, but our mate comprehends the words.

"We don't have a choice." Sifa lifts her hand to our cheek, pulling our gaze toward her. "The Dróttning will kill you. She nearly did. We won't leave Tindera here for long. I promise. But we won't be able to save her if we don't save you first."

We release a sob, the first time we've shed tears since we were a pup. "We can't leave her," we rasp out. "She's already suffered so much because of us."

"She'll suffer more if you're dead."

Sifa's pleading with us now but we can barely hear her, the whimpers of our dragon drowning out everything else. We're so close. We can't leave our dragon here.

"I'm sorry, Fhord. I have to do this." Turning toward her dragon, she whispers "Come. It's time to take him."

Astarot launches himself at us, extending his wing as soon as he lands to let our mate scramble up. And then he's airborne. His claws wrap around us but we're still so large, they're barely long enough to get a good grasp. With three flaps of his powerful wings, he gathers the strength to lift us. In a few seconds, we're soaring toward the hole above us.

I look down, searching for one last glimpse of our dragon. She catches our gaze and screeches at us and her drake, urging us to go. To leave her behind.

And we do.

CHAPTER THIRTY

DANI

THE SUN BEAST

*D*OES OUR MALE REQUIRE *the sun beast?*

He's not our male. He's Sifa's. And the sun beast's name is Tindera.

Vulryn snorts derisively, shaking her snout like she does when I've frustrated her. *He has been in our head. We have killed for him and will again. He is ours. Just as the starry female is ours.*

Fine. I can't argue with her when she's like this. She's claimed Fhord and Sifa and she's going to do whatever she has in mind with or without me. *Fhord rides Tindera. The Dróttning won't let her go. We came to free Tindera along with Fhord but could only get him out.*

Vulryn lifts herself from the ground, standing taller as she swings her head back and forth. *We shall free her. Then our male will know he and the starry female are ours. And we are theirs.*

The Dróttning is dangerous. She won't let Tindera go. I pause before adding the rest. *And there's a reason Sifa and Astarot asked us to stay behind. They don't trust us.* I'm astride Vulryn, waiting for them to call for help, but they won't. After what Vulryn did in Njordheim, they can't risk it. And I get it. I'd keep Vulryn and me far away from the fighting too.

Vulryn spins her head, her eyes flinty as stone as she stares at me. *We do not fear the wyrm. Nor do we care if the starry female or fire beast trust us. We will show them how strong we are.*

I don't even try to argue the second point. It won't matter to her. The first one, though, should. *We're fools if we don't fear the wyrm. She's powerful and pissed.*

As are we. Vulryn's voice is as calm as it was before she burned the Monarch's regiment. *I will tell the fire beast what we shall do. He will deliver the male and starry female and return to help us. The sun beast cannot fly, and I cannot lift her alone.*

When?

Now. The wyrm is weak, and her humans are dead. She doesn't wait for my assent, flicking her wings out and launching into the sky. We're less than two vikus from the Nest so this trip won't take long, especially with Vulryn's speed. She's pushing herself hard.

She slows, though, when we see Astarot approaching us with Khirta close on his heels, something I don't recognize hanging from Astarot's claws. He's got a rider on his back, and I can only assume that whatever he carries is Fhord in his other form. It's unlike anything I've ever seen, a skinless monstrosity that's neither male nor beast. With hints of Fhord's face hiding beneath so much blood and gore, I can't imagine how he still lives.

Shaking my head to dispel the image of what I'll look like if they manage to capture us, I try to catch Sifa's eyes. But she's not paying any attention to me, her gaze unfocused as she talks to Astarot. Vulryn is growling and snarling beneath me, Astarot responding with a sharp screech or deep howl every few seconds. Within a minute, they're done. Astarot rips out one last yowl and turns toward our compound. He and Khirta fly even faster now than they did when they approached us.

The fire beast believes the wyrm will be able to control me, Vulryn reports as we turn our back to Astarot and the others and she drives us forward again. Her words rattle with scorn. *The wyrm holds no power over me.*

How do you know? The Dróttning's magic is strong. It's been rumored for years that her power compels Vanatian dragons to follow her commands.

I know. I can't detect a hint of doubt in my dragon.

Is he going to help us anyway?

He will return.

Why don't we wait for him? We'll have a better chance with another dragon.

The wyrm is weak, Vulryn tells me again.

You want her for yourself, don't you?

Vulryn's head spins, her lips tipping up as she watches me. *I will free the sun beast. And then they will know they are ours.*

Vulryn desperately craves connection. I've learned enough about dragons from Sifa and Fhord over the last few weeks to understand they're pack creatures. Except when a female lays eggs and nurtures her hatchlings, they need other dragons. Their lives in Njordheim are unnatural. As soon as Vulryn and I bonded, her desperation to *belong* to other dragons and their riders—and for them to belong to us—began to drive her decisions. And mine, because I can't deny her anything.

Sooner than I wanted, we're soaring toward a hole in the top of the Nest. Vulryn's quiet, the stealth she learned fighting other dragons in the North kicking in instinctively as she shifts into attack mode. I'm reminded again of her thoughts just before she attacked the Monarch's soldiers two weeks ago. How cold and calculated she can be.

She's a sociopath, but she's my sociopath. And at least she has some conscience, not that I'll see it today. She'll do whatever it takes, sacrifice anything she must—except me and the others she's claimed—to free Tindera.

Vulryn's anger when she sees Tindera ripples through me. They've chained her wings, a hundred bolts shoved through everywhere that would cause pain. I'm not positive, but I think the chains were attached to a ceiling that's been caved in. Debris lay all around her in a semi-circle, as if someone very powerful cast a net to protect her.

It's fucking impressive magic. If Fhord did this after what he's been through, he's stronger than I imagined.

Tindera isn't moving, other than shallow ripples of her chest. She's barely alive and I don't know if she'll survive being lifted out of here. She leaves now or she dies here.

Vulryn is soaring in the cavern above, her wings still as she chooses a path that won't block the sun. We've somehow entered the cavern without the Dróttning noticing and I give a quick thanks to the gods for Vulryn's years of fighting for survival in Njordheim. She knows how to sneak up on other beasts.

The wyrm is just starting to move, lifting her head to shake it. Vulryn tenses for a moment and then tucks her wings, spearing toward the still dazed Dróttning. When the wyrm's gaze jerks up, I tighten my grip.

Our fight against the dragons when we entered Vanatia will be child's play compared to what we're about to do. The Dróttning is the most powerful creature in this land and we're fucking crazy to think we can defeat her.

But I already knew we're crazy.

The wyrm is still for a moment, watching us, before something that looks like surprise fills her eyes. It's gone in an instant and the wyrm rises up to spew out a surge of fire, hotter than any I've ever felt from a dragon. Surprise flickers through Vulryn's mind as she spirals away from the flame. Snapping out her wings just before we hit the ground, she flips back toward the wyrm. Attacking from beneath the wyrm's raised jaw, Vulryn wraps her teeth around the beast's neck and clamps down.

Hold, Vulryn tells me in a calm voice as her body spins in a way that will give her claws access to the rest of the wyrm's body while protecting me from the fire she'll be spitting out soon.

Are you going to let her burn you? I demand, unable to keep the panic from my words.

I will live. Again, she's ridiculously calm, unconcerned about the damage the Dróttning can do to her.

We don't have to wait long. The wyrm spends a few seconds trying to shake us off—while I cling to Vulryn like I'll be flung back to Njordheim if I let go—and then huffs out a shrill warning. Vulryn ignores it, of course, and digs her claws deeper into the wyrm's belly.

The first burst of fire shoots down Vulryn's back just beyond where I sit, singing feathers but not yet reaching the skin. If I wasn't terrified, I'd be astounded. That flame would have turned me into a pile of ash, but it did hardly anything to Vulryn.

My dragon snorts out a laugh at the Dróttning, clamping down on her enemy's throat as her claws dig deeper. The wyrm's furious now. I can see the quiver that ripples through her as she gathers herself for another attack. This one's fierce—an extended inferno, burning so hot, even white and blue dance in the midst of the red, yellow and orange. Its heat washes over me and for a moment I wonder if my clothes might succumb.

Eventually, though, the wyrm gives up, her blaze snuffing out. Again, Vulryn's feathers protected her. She's lost some but so many remain, it's obvious nothing will penetrate her plumage. My scrappy dragon barks out another laugh, sinking her teeth and her claws deeper into the wyrm.

Hold, she tells me again, whipping out her wings as she squeezes even tighter.

But the Dróttning's done with this game. She shifts—a wyrm one second and a pissed-off female the next—dropping to the ground. Before Vulryn has a chance to respond, she shifts again. Her wyrm, now fully healed, whips up to clench Vulryn's neck, capturing my dragon in the same hold she just escaped.

Well, fuck me. That was impressive.

Vulryn doesn't respond, which terrifies me. Because she's an arrogant bitch and she's been eager to dispute and dismiss the threat the Dróttning poses. Instead, I *feel* her pain as the wyrm clutches Vulryn's throat and starts to pulse flames into her bite. The wyrm spears them out one after another, split seconds between them, and each one feels like a dagger digging into our necks and twisting.

I've never experienced such agony before. Knives and normal fire don't come close to this pain. I wonder how long a body can suffer this kind of trauma before giving up. Even my fearless beast experiences a moment of panic as she twists her body. But then a calm washes over her.

I have defeated more dangerous beasts. I will defeat this one.

Fuck yes, you will.

I hope.

Vulryn thrusts out her wings, flapping them with a strength I didn't know she possessed. The wyrm responds by flinging its body around one of them, but my dragon tucks it in too quickly for the Dróttning to trap her. Three more times the Dróttning tries, but with every effort, Vulryn evades her whipping tail.

When the wyrm pauses for a second, leveraging herself to get a better grip on Vulryn's neck, my dragon fights through the anguish to push into the wyrm, forcing her a few feet closer to the ground. And then her wings stretch out, flapping five times to lift us from the ground.

The wyrm is enormous, larger than anything Vulryn has carried before. Still, my beloved beast manages to hoist her up and out of the cavern. I blink as the sun reaches my eyes, spinning to see Astarot and Khirta racing toward Tindera. Vulryn gave them a window to rescue her and they're back in time to take it.

But my dragon hasn't won. The beast at her throat is digging her teeth in even farther, torment from the pulsing flames shattering us. We are glass, breaking anew with every flare forced through her body. Still, Vulryn is shooting toward the nearby mountain, desperate to put distance between the wyrm and her Nest. The Dróttning must be far away when she starts her race back, for the other dragons to have any hope.

The pain in Vulryn's neck, though, is crushing her. She *needs* to escape it.

The Dróttning decides for us. Vulryn doesn't push herself higher when she approaches a mountaintop, and the wyrm lets go as we fly over a lake. Glancing down at the sapphire sitting amongst a sea of emerald and agate, I watch the beast twist in the air to position herself to land in the center of the lake. She disappears for a moment as the waves part to embrace her, and then she's on the surface, flying through the water like a creature born to it.

Vulryn grunts and flings herself toward the ground to land abruptly in a field between the lake and the Nest. *Off*, she howls at me, shaking her feathers vigorously.

You're not leaving me here! I'll fight with you. Now I'm pissed at my dragon too.

I cannot fight while I carry you. I will move more freely if I do not fear dropping you. She whips her head toward me, eyes flashing. *Off*, she repeats. *Now.*

Fuck. I know she's right. And I love that she cares enough to get rid of me. I slide down her side and jump from her wing. She tucks both of them, runs three steps, and throws herself back into the air.

Be safe. I don't know what I'd do if she got hurt.

I am always safe.

The arrogant bitch I love is back.

I look around, searching for something that might give me a way to watch my dragon. She's dropped me in a field—enormous trees everywhere—and unless they're nice enough to fight right here, I won't be able to see a thing. When I find a tree taller than the others with strong branches, I run for it. It's better than nothing.

I check in with Vulryn occasionally but she's ignoring me. Which probably is good, because she needs to focus on her fight. She's not in any more pain than before—although her neck still feels like a hundred iron brands are pressed against her skin—so at least she's not getting any new injuries.

Precious moments pass as I pull myself high enough to see anything. Just as I do, Astarot and Khirta fly by, a half-viku away. Astarot carries Tindera on his back, her wings folded in as much as possible to give him room to extend his. The bolts still puncture Tindera's shredded wings, their chains clustered together in Khirta's claws. She flies a dozen feet above the others, struggling to hold up all the iron and fly even with Astarot.

They're fucking spectacular. Tindera's enormous, but I think they're going to make it.

When Khirta's head snaps toward the lake and she pauses in the air, I can almost see the anger that ripples through her. She tenses, as if something shocked her, but Astarot spits out a command. She needs to keep up with him or Tindera will fall. Shaking her head, she snarls a response, focusing again on helping carry Tindera to safety.

When I look in the direction of Khirta's gaze, I find Vulryn. And what I see terrifies me. Vulryn is fighting the wyrm—giving Astarot and the females time to get far enough away to not risk being tracked—but a massive blue dragon is soaring toward her. He's there in a few seconds and I can only watch as Vulryn attacks the Dróttning while trying to shield herself from the other beast's assault.

He's vicious, claws and teeth ripping through Vulryn's wings as he tries to keep her away from his liege. Every slice and pierce of my dragon's wings burns along my back, explosions of agony to compound the open, throbbing wounds on the neck. Occasionally, the dragons' tumultuous dance gives the blue beast access to Vulryn's belly or tail, and I feel the attack there. But those are rare. He knows Vulryn's wings are her weak spot, and his assault focuses on them.

She's even more vicious. Like the other dragons she's fought, the blue dragon has no idea how to defeat one of his kind. Somebody told the Vanatian dragons and their riders to target the wings, but they haven't yet figured out the efficient, ruthless fighting style Vulryn uses. She's lucky in that. Soon, these dragons will fight as well as her.

I can only cling to the tree, gritting my teeth through the agony of each wound, praying to gods who abandoned me long ago that my dragon will survive. Finally, a minute or five after Astarot and Khirta carried Tindera away, Vulryn abandons her attack on the wyrm. Focusing on the blue dragon, she positions herself and strikes him just like she did Bob in the field.

She doesn't break his neck, though. And I can't figure out why the fuck not. I feel a wave of confusion ripple through her, followed by acceptance and then resolve. Only a few seconds have passed, but something changed. She grips him for a few more beats of my heart and then lets go, rising into the air to squawk at him. I almost laugh at her imperious tone.

I glance down for a moment, shuddering as the wyrm races back to the Nest, a trail of black blood blotting the field in her wake. When I look up, Vulryn and the blue dragon are hovering in front of each other, barks and growls echoing around us. He breaks their contact, barking one more time before flinging himself toward the Dróttning to follow her home.

Vulryn turns to land nearby as she screams her victory. I climb down to the ground, then jog over to her waiting wing and pull myself up, careful of the gashes and wounds scattered across it. We're both anxious to get back to the others and confirm Fhord and Tindera still live.

But my mind keeps replaying Vulryn's odd behavior with the blue dragon. *Why did you release him?* I ask as she launches into the air and pivots toward the compound.

He is ours, Vulryn tells me, a satisfied note in her voice that I haven't heard since she incinerated the Monarch's soldiers. *We will give him a chance to prove himself worthy. If he cannot, then we will kill him.*

I'm surprised and more than a little scared. I don't want Vulryn connected to a beast devoted to the Dróttning. This is going to make things very fucking confusing.

I shrug to myself, though, because what else can I do? I can respect her decision.

I'm giving mine a chance, but I'll probably need to kill him too.

Astarot

It Is Worth It

MY DAYS ARE FEW.

My rider and my drakaina do not know how weak I've become. How little this body has left to give.

I have been away from the Nest too long. Separated from the waters the Dróttning controls and the food that keeps us alive. I will carry my rider north, soar with my drakaina when she can fly again, and then I will let go.

They will grieve me, but I cannot regret my choices. It is worth it. My drakaina is free. She and my rider will live. Their mate will care for them. In time, they will do what they must. Fate is in charge now and they cannot fight what she has planned for them.

I have done my part.

I am tired.

I will rest soon.

The End,

For Now ...

Sifa, Fhord, Dani, and their dragons
are waiting for you in *Divine Dilemma,*
Book III of *Tales of the Vanir.*
Get your copy here.

Thank You

Thank you for reading *Frenzied Fate!*
I hope you enjoyed this chapter in Sifa and Fhord's story, and
I would appreciate it so much if you could take the time to
leave a review on Amazon, Goodreads, or wherever you review
books!

Author's Note

I'M SO LUCKY TO be able to do what I love, supported by family and friends. Thanks to my hubby Al, our boys Albert and Stephen, and the amazing friends who have been cheering me along.

Thanks also to everyone who read *Frenzied Fate* and shared their thoughts with me, starting with my alpha reader Cynthia, who's read all my books and given me great feedback.

With this series, I relied heavily on beta feedback.
Many thanks to Cindy Ray Hale and Keele Publishing,
Kaitlin Slowik, and Keeya Marquez
for all of their comments and suggestions.

And last but definitely not least, thanks to everyone who gave this series a try. I fell in love with this world and hope you do too. As an indie author, your support means everything. I'm grateful to everyone who talks about my books, through a review or on social media, and just as grateful to everyone who reads them. Thank you!

Also by Rochelle Wilcox

The Road to Ragnarök
(mostly closed-door portal romantic fantasy;
Heavy Heart has one spicy scene)

Fickle Fate
(the spicy prequel, available to subscribers
to my newsletter at RochelleWilcox.com)
Lost Long
Enemies Eternal
Alive Again
Heavy Heart

About the Author

Rochelle Wilcox is happily retired from practicing law, focused on writing what she loves to read. You can find Rochelle at rochellewilcox.com and at any of the social media sites below:

amazon.com/stores/Rochelle-Wilcox/author/B007PEWME6

goodreads.com/author/show/6951175.Rochelle_Wilcox

bookbub.com/authors/rochelle-l-wilcox

facebook.com/TheRoadToRagnarok

instagram.com/rochellewilcoxauthor/

tiktok.com/@rochellewilcoxauthor